The Inspirational Classic

MASTERS AT MY TABLE.

Guidance from the Sages.

DOUG MCPHILLIPS

2

Also by Doug McPhillips:

Other Visionary Stories

NOVELS

From Darkness to Light.
The Sword of Discernment.
Santiago Traveller.
 I, Prophet.
Awake to my Gutted Dream.
We is Me Upside Down.

ALBUMS.

Country Camino.
Santiago Traveller.

Doug McPhillips 2020.

ISBN 978-163752039-0

National Library of Australia Catalogue-in-publication data:
Autobiography-Walking the Camino, Alcoholics Anonymous,
Authors references throughout this book.
Google research on myth, legends and folklore-unknown authors.
References:Van Loon's Lives, Hendrik Van Loon. Harrap & Co.Ltd. Londo
1943.Think and Grow Rich, Napoleon Hill. Ballantine Books 1937 addition.

FORWARD.

For The Benefit of all Concerned.

Much of what has been researched and written here may strike the reader as old fashioned, quaint and retrograde or even out of touch with reality. I make no apology for what I am given to express within the pages of this little work, for it comes from the lives of people who have been dead and buried for decades and in some cases centuries. From such men I have been guided to play my own tune, sing my own songs, develop business success over decades and in turn write stories, like the one that follows herein. Whilst I am now retired and have the time to take it easy, I cannot rest on my laurels for I am inspired to write even more poems, sing more of my songs and write more stories that seem to materialise unexpectedly, causing me to work hard once again and travel far and wide on adventurers for my cause. In reality and that of my imagination I would never have continued my dream of doing such things in my former life before being granted the gifts of Masters that now serve me. My journey, like so many others who may have dared to tread this path has given me insights into the use of our sixth sense in communion with those who once walked the earth and through their wisdom and guidance help improve my lot and that of others who have the most need. Once the Masters at My Table grant me a lotus flower of creative ideas, I find I have cause to act upon such ideas with faith and confidence believing in the outcomes inspired by their guidance essential to the natural benefit of all concerned.

Such men in their lifetime, the Masters of the stories embedded in this book, had a genius far beyond the level of the common man. Even today the willing may still tap into their world beyond the curtain achieving greatness beyond their wildest dreams. The forces of their masterful spirit and energy in the here and now may spur even the greatest sceptic into a belief in a Higher Power and inherit gifts from those great leaders, inventors, poets, writers and thinkers of days long gone. These Masters are still willing to serve you and me from beyond the grave to use our talents to the full. This may seem rather odd to you dear reader, but I urge you to read on and try not to be sceptical, as the riches that may be bestowed upon you within these pages are beyond bounds. Great riches may be gained if you but act using the gifts on offer for the common good and not for evil purpose. This is my only warning, for these same powerful gifts may be used also for the wrong reasons resulting equally in great evil as opposed to great deeds for the greater good.

Long ago and far away I happened upon a magical formula for success that was directly inspired by the coaching of Andrew Carnegie, the great Steel Merchant and one of the wealthiest businessmen of the 19th century. By 1889 he owned Carnegie Steel Corporation, the largest of its kind in the world. In 1901 he sold his business and dedicated his time to expanding his philanthropic work, including the establishment of Carnegie Mellon University. Carnegie demonstrated the soundness of his magic formula when coaching brought fortunes to those young men to whom he had disclosed his secret. Andrew Carnegie has been dead for just over one hundred years now but his secret and the application of it still lives on. It was passed on by Carnegie to Napoleon Hill who passed it on to me.

I happened upon the teaching of this simple basis secret after reading Hill's 'Think and Grow Rich' which I applied to the letter. It was from that book the distilled wisdom of distinguished men of greatness and achievements appeared to me and I rose from the ranks of failure and mediocrity to business success and later wealth of family, multiple gifts and material reward. The secret worked perfectly well whilst I applied it from the spirits of the past that influenced me. However a day came where I no longer utilised the teaching and the lessons learnt from them and I began to fall into the dragon's mouth of heart break, loneliness and despair. For I had lost my all, my confidence in the God of my own understanding and those men of greatness from the other side whom I had once relied upon for wisdom. It was on another adventure, walking the highways and by-ways of Spain, Portugal and Germany in this 21st century that I recalled my life changing experience of near five decades ago, when I began to apply the secret formula that has been passed down for generations from the spirits of the past. On my acceptance of the wisdom whispered to me then, the simple formula applied as if by magic changed the direction of my then life.

So, with the lessons that I had applied to get me to the top of the ladder of life I found myself once more back on the first rung. With the wisdom of hindsight I returned to the location of where I first made a commitment to apply the secret. I received that same further boost from another Master in the application of the Carnegie secret formula for success, that of one Hendrick Willem van Loon, who died the year I was born. He gifted me with a copy of his works and I confess to have utilised his historical references of the Masters at my Table to add credence to my stories. So now my dear reader, please read on for you will discover within the majestic mystery of these pages a new way of life for you and yours if you apply the influences within these words. It is the secret truth that I have to pass on here in the spirit of my imagination, in the words from the Masters at my table, in the lessons I have learnt of love, life and recipes for living with acceptance of health, wealth and happiness that has been bestowed upon me.

This book is dedicated to my grand children

ISLA and KADI

May you gain insights into the elixir that pours within
the essence of these pages, so you may march
ever onward to the sound of a different drummer,
the one that beats to the rhythm of your precious hearts.

AN UNSUSPECTED INNER RESOURCE.

With few exceptions our members find that they have tapped an unsuspected inner resource which they presently identify with their own conception of a Power greater than themselves.

Alcoholics Anonymous. Pp.567.568

CONTENT.

Only one who devotes himself to a cause
with his whole strength and soul
can be a true master.
For this reason,
mastery demands all of a person.
- Albert Einstein
www.DreamThisDay.com

CHAPTER 1.

THE CAPTAIN OF MY FATE

It has been five decades since I last strolled through the busy streets of Cologne as a lone backpacker. Back then the Cologne Cathedral stood tall above a city of lesser structure, a monument to God that was a timely reminder of a building of solidity that had suffered fourteen direct hits by aerial bombs during WW11. It did not collapse in an otherwise flattened city. Cologne is a 2,000 year old city spread along the Rhine River. This the western region of Germany's cultural hub boasts this Gothic architectural masterpiece housing gilded medieval reliquary mixed with a sweet meditative overview of the river that winds below from the rear, and looks down on other museums showcasing 20th Century masterpieces along with new structures of commercial significance still in their infancy.

This time I arrive in style, dressed casually just like any other tourist might, with my iPhone camera constantly clicking anything and everything that my eyes are drawn too. Vain glory that I felt may have some future purpose or that I could put up on social media to keep the masses informed of my comings and goings. Things all tourists seem to do these days when they are in a free mood but still needing to cling to something. I wound my way along the Hohenzollern towards the bridge of the same name, intent on making my way to the water's edge, to sit in the Rheingarten Park. Once again to view across the Rhine river, watch the ferry boats making their way up and down stream, taking in the warm spring sunlight and viewing the city from the back of the park. The moving shadows form from otherwise sunshine and cast a spell of interruption against the twin towers of the cathedral structure that still marks the ultimate heart of the city. It was Saturday morning and the streets were full of locals shopping for their weekly groceries, buying up bargains and sweet treats to eat with their coffee at sidewalk cafes. Tourists were coming and going with their eyes intent on building architecture as much as photographing a vision of a day in the life. It seemed to me that I was the most conservative person on the street. The masses coloured in greys, pinks, purple and green, as well as sparkling grey, browns and blond. I speak of their hair only for I had never seen such fashion of hair colouring and strange hair cuts in all my life. It was not just the hair, it was the coat of many colours and unfashionable fashion of dress. Everyone seemed to be oddly dressed and the noise of the crowd was maddening. Whatever had happened to that old conservative dress of the German people of the 70s. Then, it was us young travellers that were the odd ones out, in our made-for-the-road dress of corduroy jackets, short sleeve T shirts and flared blue jeans and desert boots. My mind flashed back to strolling this same street back in the 1970s. It was much quieter with people walking slowly and the dress sense, save for us young back packers of the road, was typical German conservative and well tailored.

My thoughts were broken by the screech of a tram, as people hurried to board one or left another. I just wanted to escape maddening crowds. I quickly made my way to the Cathedral, to once more gaze upon its Gothic majesty and appreciate many statutes of saints and gargoyles that protrude from ever facade. I took a quick tour of the inner sanctuary to bath in the freedom from the disturbance that had come over me in that cool darkness had broken only by the light that penetrated from the stain glass window on the sunny side.

The last time I took the winding metal stairs to the top of the towers I was fascinated with the view of a city rebuilt on ruins. The tower stairs had not changed, save for a safety rail to stop one from falling into what seemed an abyss below. As I climbed my thoughts drifted to the multitude of towers I had climbed in my lifetime. Ancient structures of European Cathedrals to God, T.V towers for mass communication in my former work life, modern day commercial buildings with observation decks and even a ship's mast at sea in a cyclone blind drunk at the time.

 I stopped before I reached the top of the tower, preferring to remember the last time I took in the view. It was when the city was still being rebuilt after the war and he Cathedral had a dark soot stained appearance which stood out as now, but the surrounding buildings back then were light greys and whites with modern architecture. Cityscapes are always evolving, the old being torn down to replace the new, but not on the scale that Cologne had experienced after the Allied bombings of 1944. I had viewed it all just two decades after the bombings and it was then a young, fresh and progressive city. Now it appeared older, somewhat worn out before its time and invaded by aliens. It reminded me of my own need to a renew my zest for living , to dispense with the alien self and hand over to fate. I had my fill of towers and for that matter passion for cathedrals, museums and lust for living the ways of old. I needed to escape the maddening crowd, do what others wish they could do. I had my mind's eye on the secret to it all, the way for me and the opportunity to know the secret inspiration for achieving real spiritual goals, not only for myself but for others too.

 It was time to plant my two feet on solid ground and set a new vision for the future, as I had visualised and done all those many years ago in Rheingarten Park, here in Cologne. I had set a new vision to embrace the now of me with the gifts I had been given once and squandered. Those Masters from the past who allowed me to use to the full my then passion for leadership, power, money and all the material things the world had to offer. I once thought in using the secret the way I did that it was my God given right, but now I had come to believe I had my vision all wrong. For though it rewarded me the fulfilment of my dreams of abundance, I had set out to achieve in the material world, it ultimate left me with nothing but heartache and sorrow. However, this was the wisdom I could not have achieved if I had not travelled the path I chose. For now I had a clear vision to fulfil a new destiny and the methods I used back then to achieve my past goals, I would recall and review but I would embrace this day, utilising the methods in a different way, a more in-tune way with the Masters of my fate than I could have imagined. I now believed it to be a matter of meditating with the help of universal law and the guides that I would select for my assistant from the other side to achieve my aims.

I sat by the flowing Rhine once again in the park, captured by the image of the glitter of diamonds on the water reflected by the morning sun. I was lost in my head, thinking of my own life experience and the means of selecting the intangible forces of the world about me. This was a forceful influence I failed to utilise in my past life for the benefit of all concerned when I called those past Masters to my imaginary table. The intangible forces that are wrapped up in the soil of the earth embraced me, provided every morsel of the food I atet, the clothing I wore, and every bit of currency that I carry on my iPhone wallet.

The influences of the forces of nature in the now, of wind, rain, thunder and lightning, of the sounds in the storm and the waves of the sea as they crash to the shores. My subconscious mind was once more sending signals from my brain, vibrations through my creative imagination, opening up to the energy to forces beyond. I was now in deep mediation and every bit of the nature around me seemed to stand still for just an instant. In that moment I pictured and old man laying half upright with his back against the base of a tall Poplar tree. He was of solid build but not tall, dressed in fine clothing with a serious but kindly look on his face. The most notable feature on his round full face was his piercing dark eyes and the tartan cap with a peak that he pulled down slightly to give him some shade from the morning sunlight. I recognised him immediately from a photo I had seen of him in his mid-life, it was Andrew Carnegie himself the great steel merchant, the man who had taught Napoleon Hill as a small boy, the formula for personal achievement. The canny old Scotsman lay back against the tree like he was sitting in a chair, displaying a twinkle in his eye and watched to see if I had brain enough to grasp what he was about to state. He began to speak in an unmistakable Scottish brogue: "You sat here three decades ago and tapped into the essence of what I had taught that young Napoleon Hill when he was but a boy more than a century ago now. I had asked him if he was willing to spend the next twenty years or so, preparing himself to take my message to the world. I told him my secret and he grasp it and mastered the techniques I planted in his brain back then. He did keep his promise and spent the next thirty years taking it to the world. The lessons I taught him you yourself gleaned from his book 'Think and grow Rich.' The secrets contained in that book, my secrets, have been practically tested by thousands of people in almost every walk of life ever since.

It was my magic formula which gave him stupendous fortune, that I suggested to be placed within the reach of people who do not have time to investigate how men make money, achieve fame or indeed live a way of life suitable to their natural talents. Young Napoleon, true to his word, tested and demonstrated the soundness of the formula to the letter." He paused then took a deep breath, looked steely eyed at me and continued: "You tested that formula and applied it from the content of Napoleon's book. Here in this park, back three decades ago, you set in motion your mission statement from the guidance of my secret for a time." He made a pregnant pause to empathise the point "But you made two mistakes; you sought leadership for selfish reasons and it brought you power, fame, fortune and the family you desired, but you lost it all though pride, vain glory and your compulsive nature. You had the tenacity to achieve your goals and you did with sheer determination, but you had your ladder up against the wrong wall all along and you've paid the price of pain of loss for your folly and your lack of love. I glean that you have the wisdom to apply the formula again, not for your benefit though, for the suffering souls who are going through what you have overcome and now need the wisdom of your experience and knowledge for their betterment. Your actions will be rewarded as a gift of love." The old man vanished from view and I came out of my trance-like experience. I checked the time and I had been in that zone for just a few minutes but it seemed like hours. The old Scot had certainly left me with food for thought and truth that I knew in my heart of hearts to be so. The dilemma now was how and what to do to bring his message to life for the benefit of all concerned. It could not be done for selfish motives.

Mr. Carnegie had already wised me up on that and my own past lifestyle had proof therein. I could see no reason for rewriting what had already been written, tried and proven by Napoleon Hill's book. For that matter, such principles have been and still are copied, tried and tested and plagiarised by many a past author and current day entrepreneur. The words of each are extracts from the same hymn sheet, that of the secret of that grand old Scot. No, if I need to pass on the wisdom of thought, desire, faith, autosuggestion, specialised knowledge, organisation, planning, persistence and power, I need look no further than the inspiration of Napoleon Hill's book. I did not need to rewrite the lessons to be learnt therein, but maybe suggest to the listener, the book as a worthy starting point for change. So what was it in the secret that I could foretell? How could I apply it for the continuance of the Master's plan who tapped into it in the first place?

I put the thought out of my head for a time and commenced to walk down to the wharf to catch a boat downstream for a leisurely trip on the Rhine. Seated out in the open on the upper deck my relaxed state embodied the typical foreign tourist and the give away was my smart casual dress and the continual action of photographing everything that attracted my eye on the shoreline. The ferry's motor hummed along against the tide at a slow pace. I had already made up my mind with a plan to go ashore at Linz Am Rhein, take the old-timer train slog up the steep hills through the forest to Kalenborn and walk the bush track down the hill via the Brewery at Kasbach and back into Linz for a quick lunch and tour of the shops before catching the next available ferry back to Cologne. I figured the round trip would take about three hours in all, allowing for delay or some other change in the order of the Universe.

The Coxswain had the task of keeping a straight course mid-river and the ferry behaved accordingly, leaving no doubt to mind that he had travelled this way before. I ordered a soft drink from the waitress doing the round of the deck, noticing her well built curvy figure, a blond of Polish appearance. She had a pretty face, blue eyes, high cheek bones and a devilish smile. My attention once more distracted from her and the monotonous dialogue of the Coxswain pointing out notable landmarks along the river's edge, with sudden disruption to his voice, the sound of piping of jolly German drum beat music through old speakers on the deck. I watched as the waitress returned with my drink carefully manoeuvring between the passengers chairs, holding my cold drink in a tall glass on a tray in one hand and using the other to keep her balance. I had the presence of mind to take her into my arms swiftly, dancing as I did between the amused passengers with the Polish blond blushing as we danced and crying aloud: "I could take you home," to which a tubby middle aged man seated near the bar room door responded ,"take him." Whilst all the deck passengers laughed aloud, my dancing partner showed the first sign of complaint and with a high pitched voice shouted, "He always stops me having some fun, I do all the work and he just sits on his fat acre and gives orders." She turned on her heels and retreated to the bar again. I took my cool cocktail like soft drink and sat down next to the tubby middle aged German who had winked at me when he made his statement. It so happened that he was the owner of the Ferry, the Polish woman husband and was a true entrepreneur. He had but one other staff member, the engineer keeping the motor running whilst in motion up river with ferryman duties tying the rope on mooring of half piers when passengers boarded or alighted. He was an interesting chap and I figured, despite his Polish wife opinion to the contrary, was not lazy at all. On that journey he spoke too many a passenger in friendly conversation in many languages including his native German. I also noticed the ferry was clean, freshly painted and ran like clockwork despite its age.

One should never judge a book by its cover, the German ferry master had a Coxswain who doubled as a tour guide, an engineer who doubled as a ferryman and a dancing waitress who happened to be his wife. Our conversation was interrupted by the crackle of the speakers again , as the Coxswain pointed out Angela Merkel's, the Germany Chancellors weekend home on the nearby shoreline. It was a palace of a place with large grounds that reminded me of our own Government House on the waters edge of Sydney Harbour, our Australian Prime Minister's weekender.

 I said farewell to the German Ferry Master as I alighted at Linz Am Rhein. I wished I could have had more time with him to pick his business brain a little more, as he had only just explained that he owned a fleet of these ferries that ran up and down the Rhein river from near its source in the Swiss Alps to the North Sea, some 1320 km to the Netherlands. This clever Ferry Master had captured the bulk of the trade of humanity across all European countries that used the Rhine for transportation. They all paid cash for their tickets and the money had been rolling in for most of his adult life. He didn't need an inventory of cargo nor a manifestos of goods he was carrying. The whole record of his cargo was the butt of a ticket from the fare paying passengers linked to a ticket machine at each port of call. I was tempted to ask him if he had ever heard of Andrew Carnegie but time did not permit me. I waved goodbye to the good natured man and his pretty wife as I made my way to the old-timer train station for my excursion. I had proof now that one has to be sure of career choice before leaning one's ladder against the wall and climbing it to be sure of remaining successful.

I enjoyed the climb up the hill through the forest on the old train. I tasted the brewed non alcoholic beer at the brewery and slowly walked through the forest and back down to the village of Linz Am Rhein. I wandered through the Medieval village looking into shops and purchased a small wooden sovereign as a memento of my visit. The place had a multitude of restaurants and cafes with every conceivable food type of Central Europe. I settled for what appeared tp be a more Spanish lunch at a small cafe inlet, ordering salami sausage, a mediterranean salad and ice cold water. The cook in the kitchen was singing a Spanish marching song as he prepared my order. He appeared smiling from the kitchen and served me at my table like I was royalty. I ate my fill and decided I would walk it off on my way back to the wharf to catch the ferry back to Cologne. The Ferry Master and his polish wife were not on this one and the trip back ran smoothly. The jolly German owner was not only a clever businessman. He knew how to save a few Euro on all return trips by just cutting the motor and letting the fast flow of the river dictate the speed. I was being lulled to sleep in the afternoon sun with a full belly and contented to listen to this Coxswain explain the topography of the opposite shoreline. A fresh pitch to his voice startled me as we approached Cologne. The Coxswain shouted with some excitement from his usual monotonous tone: "Look, there is our local beach. Families take their children there on hot days like this." I glanced towards the shoreline to see what all the fuss was about. There on the opposite bank was a park with a small strip of white sand to the waters edge. It was not much longer than a cricket pitch and no wider, but it was enough to excite this riverboat man. I couldn't help but muse to myself that no more than 30 minutes as the crow flies from my home in Sydney there spread 1000 kilometres of surf-able beach as far North as the eye could see and equally when looking South it was equally so. Cologne had its ancient beauty but it was living in its past in spite of it all. I reckoned the Ferryman would have given his right testicle to the highest bidder if he had the opportunity to experience the beauty of the Australian coastline and untamed wildness of nearby National parks. I thanked God then and there for the gift of being a native Australian.

The streets were almost void of people when I retraced my steps back through the centre of the city. It was mid-summer, an unusually humid afternoon for Cologne and by the empty surrounds and great discomfort to the majority made plain of local Germans and visiting tourists. There were some faces appearing from the shadows of buildings, taking the opportunity in the remaining few minute to shop before sundown. I made my way down a side street of restaurants and cafes away from the heat of the afternoon sun. My mind was distracted by a signpost at the entrance to an alley. An arrow pointed the way, the sign said simply, 'Beach Bar.' The reminder of the so called local beach on the rivers edge was enough to make me realise not to expect much, but a cool drink seemed like a good idea. The sign led to an almost derelict building where an internal lift had another sign a stated simply " beach bar on the roof.' The lift creaked its well worn way to the roof top of a six story building and I alighted to what was a man-made marvel.

Everywhere there was white sand with bikini clad women laying on deck chairs, well oiled and sun baking, surrounded by young and old men alike, dressed in beach wear. The bar was at the edge of the roof top; a mobile arrangement with a van like open window dispensing drinks to waitresses taking drink orders. The place was alive with beach boy music and the drone of voices in personal conversation. I ordered a drink admiring the curves of the waitress who took my order, gave her a knowing smile and made my way to a spare deck chair on the beach front. I adjusted my sun glasses and lay back with my thoughts. My only distraction was on the adjoining building, the biggest Coca Cola sign I had ever seen in my life. Perhaps subliminally I had picked up on that sign when I ordered a Coke to drink. The only other landmark skyward, apart from the wisp of clouds in sunny sky, were the Cathedral spires.

My mind drifted back to my purpose now and how to achieve what I wished to set out to do using the intangible forces that lay within the Universe. I reconsidered those masterful characters of the past whom I had chosen as guides from the other side to assist me in my then quest for leadership, power, fame, financial reward and what I perceived back then a successful and rewarding life. I had succumbed to the influence of bringing to mind past Masters of achievement to help me in my own goals. Yes it was true, my subconscious mind, creative imagination and energy resulting from the autosuggestions I fed my mind in the past ensured I achieved those aims. In hindsight, prior to ever considering the forces of the Universe, I had figured that I was destined to be a leader. In fact, from an early age I felt I was for to it, demanded it to be so without fear of failure or favour. As far back as I can remember I was influenced by the stories of Great explorers, frontier adventures, comic book heroes, Saints of the Church and sporting personalities. I did not just perceive of the lifestyle and adventures of these childhood imaginary mentors I took on their persona and lived it when and wherever I had the mindset to do so.

My first greatest achievement was as a leader in sport. The Mid North Coast of NSW had an annual Junior Rugby League competition. I was selected for my Primary school side and when it came to determine who should be Captain , the coach enquired. I shouted:" Me Coach." Being the smallest kid in the team he smiled and replied:"And why should you be Captain Doug?" I quickly lied: "Because, if we win the competition, my father is going to donate a trophy to the school." He could not argue with that logic and so I was duly appointed Captain. It was my task then to convince my Dad that the school wanted him to denote the trophy for the winning team. Dad, being a mathematician, quickly calculated the odds of that happening, considering every town on the Coast had a crack team that we would be playing against. He agreed to buy a trophy and when we won , Dad true to his word donated the trophy.

I was not only a winner but hero in my own eyes and those of fellow team mates because I took the lead, played my little heart out in all matches and with sheer grit and a team effort of determination, we won. Later, as a teenager, I coached and led as Coxswain three GPS school annual rowing events. The school rewarded me with an honour blazer for my efforts. Later, with nothing better to do, I joined Australia's leading bank and made my way up the banking ladder for a time. I always marvelled at this as math was my weakest subject at school and yet I made it in the field of everyday banking. The career path that followed led me to sales and financial planning but I wanted so much to find my feet in a leadership role. It was some years later that I had sat by the edge of the Rhein river in the Rheingarden Park, behind the Cologne Cathedral and devised a plan to become a Manager of the largest Insurance Company of its time in in Australia, using the principles of Andrew Carnegie. It was there I selected the leaders of past history to be my guiding influences to help me reach my objective.

I set to work preparing a brief of my work, social and sporting achievements, highlighting my talents as a leader of men. Often I enlisted the help of my heavenly guides through the power of the imagination to give me the right words to write and express when I got my interview to be appointed to a management role. Hill's inspiration book, its guideline and the influences of the Masters at my table helped me climb that ladder of success. Yes, I had imaginary guides at my table when called upon to participate, as I sought their circle of influence. I did get the foreseen Management role and was the youngest Manager ever to be appointed at that time. It took but a few short years to be rewarded with the honour of recruiting, training and motivating the largest number of commission representatives for the company, being rewarded with achievement certificates, generous bonuses sand the opportunity to increase my salary accordingly.

After a number of years I moved on, forgot about the influences of the book and it appeared from a casual observer's prospect I had the Midas touch and achieved much success as a entrepreneur and reached a level of financial independence,. However, at the height of my achievements a series of personal tragic events saw me fall into the dragon's mouth of depression, anguish and despair. Like all the workings of the Almighty, recovery was slow but I did recover to change my pathway in life, set out on many a new adventure, writing novels and songs inspired by handing over to my creative imagination, often in times of the greatest of difficulties. The essence of my creativity was that I now believe I was inspired, not by logical linear conscious means but by the fire of creative imagination. All it took was a handing over to put my boat of personality upon the waters of life, trim the sail and allow the spiritual waters to flow. I now concluded that all it had taken was a simple tap of the rudder every now and again to remain on course. Yes, I had fallen in the past down into the dragon's mouth only to find that what lay within was the seed of a new wave of creative ideas. For a time I was fired with enthusiasm completing one project after another, driven by my desire to succeed before I once again crashed into an exhausted mental, physical and unfilled void of the spirit. I had lost roots of my character for a time, turned to my undisciplined ways and my defects rather than a Supreme Master, ignoring the call of the energy of those guiding angels of the past who left the world with changes for the betterment of mankind; the Masters of my table. Perhaps it was not so much that I had forgotten how to use those forces for my betterment and the good of all concerned, but rather that I had selected the wrong guides from the other side in the first place. I needed to think about that, re-evaluate those guides I had chosen, look for the reasoning in my selection, to consider who I should now select and my purpose in doing so for the good of all concerned. Perhaps I had not only taken on those past Master's individual skills and talents to help me at the time, but possibly too I had taken on their defects of character in my enthusiasm to achieve the success in my progressive realisation of what it was I was seeking.

So as I lay back on my deckchair looking skyward, I began to think about those Masters of the past whom I had enlisted to help me. Then I began more clearly to look at each Master I had selected and the reasons for my selection. Had I not had a burning desire with a definiteness of purpose back then, in achieving my aims? Yes, I had but I squandered my talents for a pocket full of gold, succumbed to the negative forces of alcoholism and the pleasures of the flesh, which ultimately caused me much hardship. In my pride to achieve, my covertness, my competitiveness to gain the upper hand and not so diligent research of the character of The Masters chosen, I had enlisted not only the gifts of their talents but equally their defects of character in my endeavour to success. I had been right in being guided by the unseen. However, those I selected of past masters had left me with vexation of the spirit in the long. So, all those years ago , as I sat by the nearby Rhein, I had honed the sub-conscious mind to bring to my guidance those Masters of what I had perceived would guide my destiny. I had concluded that the Supreme Infinite Intelligence should be my future guiding light as my mentor from the beyond. Though bitter experience and a lifetime of learning, I came to believe in an ultimate Infinite Intelligence, a Higher Power to be the essence of my soul's guiding light.

However, in due consideration to the spirits from the past, I felt I may learn from a selecting of new Masters and life experience worthwhile guidance to motivate my spiritual nature. It had taken a life time of living to understand, assimilate, and apply the principles of Hill's ' Think and grow Rich.' in my past understanding of his book. Whist I did not endorse Hill's notion of mentors in many undertaking on the physical plain, I had them none the less as spiritual advocates. I did for a time attempt to reshape my character by emulating the thoughts, feelings and actions of those Masters, acting out accordingly. There was nothing wrong with hero worship I surmised, but I had ultimately over time let go of such methods of thought and action. In the end it was not heroes, nor the Carnegie principles as outlined by Hill's book I adhered to in finding new ground, it was the Steps of Alcoholic Anonymous that proved to help me beat my defects. It was the way forward that led me away from the grip of the grape and taught me to let go of the grip on ego. I had to admit that I was powerless over alcohol, and brought me to believe in the power of the Almighty in a mature fashion and the most difficult of all, hand over completely to that power.

Here I was now returning to the sixth sense of Carnage's principle, mindful of who really runs the Universe; my guide the Almighty. Through his power, his servants would be my guides as Masters to dine at my dinner table. Those from the curtain beyond death who during their lives working here on earth, who endured and overcome much hardship during their lifetime I need to call upon to consider their principles that seemed beyond the workings of the common man. I myself had suffered the slings and arrows of outrageous fortune, due to circumstance beyond my control, as equally as I had succumbed to my defects of my-character to bring me down., I could now depend upon my Master's team of guides in my own quest now to complete a new vision for life, for the benefit of all concerned and not just my own desire.

It was the law of the natural Universe that I was contemplating, as I made my way back to the river's edge. There was just enough hours of daylight to visit the birthplace of a Master for further inspiration. I paid my way on the ferry for my excursion to Bonn, the birthplace of Beethoven. He was himself a Master with the affliction of deafness who achieved, despite his disability, creation of the greatest musical masterpieces know to mankind. He had been inspired by nature and so was I for a brief moment. I recalled the success of the jolly German boat owner and his Polish wife on my morning ferry to Linz Am Rhein. Maybe it was fate that had turned me in my thinking to Masters of influence and creative inspiration, and just maybe it was the Ferry master or my own relaxed mood at the time.

Had I been inspired in my impulse to dance with his Polish wife on the deck or it may well have been my return to the location of the Rheingarden Park that determined my past direction in life using the Carnegie principle as laid down by Napoleon Hill. Then again, maybe it was the fact that I was now turning back the clock to my youthful inclinations to listen to Beethoven's symphonies. Nature had instilled in me the joys of listening to Beethoven, but equally it was in the outdoors of nature that the great tones come to me.

My ability to play piano was limited to a regimented schooling. I had made it to intermediate stand and the ability to write theory. I have with regret long since lost the skill for both. I can still develop a melody or a lyric, but have no skill in picking a guitar or belting out notes on a piano key-board. Beethoven himself was grounded in some mysterious law of nature, despite his affliction to deafness. He was tuned to the vibrations of the earth, the sea, the air; encumbered with a disharmony of ill tempered personal nature and harmony with the lofty heights of his genius. He brought to me in my youthful days of rock n'roll a diversion into my own poetic nature, succumbing to a vision of future happenings and freedom of thought. There was never a musical genius before Beethoven who displayed such an ability. I now had a humble conviction that by the means of my sixth sense I could vividly reawaken the vibrations from the man in the great beyond. Yes, Beethoven, I had already set the seeds in motion to my request for him to be one of my first guests as a Master at my table, it was just a hunch I now had.

The streets of the old city of Bonn and the house where Ludwig van Beethoven was born in 1770 now stands in the city centre. It has been turned into a museum and cultural institute celebrating the life and work of the composer and pianist. The place was crowded with obvious music lovers from far afield, visiting to conduct research, listen to his compositions in an adjacent chamber and exchange ideas. Beethovens legacy is celebrated throughout Bonn, but after my being caught up in a crowd, I needed to seek seclusion, be alone with my thoughts. I chose a park bench on a hilltop overlooking the city on one side and the river on the other, to regather my thoughts on Beethovens life and consider how I might entice his spirit to join me as a guest of my table of Masters. Whilst I was mindful and considerate of the good in my character, I did wish to rid myself of the cardinal vices of my defects and to no longer eat the forbidden fruit of the world. For I was not just seeking a cause to complete goals for the good of all concerned, but wanting to improve my own mental wellbeing, physical health and spiritual harmony in the process. I needed to reshape my character by following the habits of past Masters as my centres of influence to trying to imitate the life and works of those who most impressed me. I had done this in the past and it worked to my temporal betterment.

However in hindsight, had I had done this to increase my former material benefit now, I would seek to rebuild my character so that it would reach a composite of my imaginary counsellors, focusing on the spirit of my ancestors, I wondered who of my ancestors would now ancestors help me to select other Masters at my table. It was up to me , for this his time I would be even more selective in my choices than before, for I had a vision proven from previous activity that I needed to improve my gift of speech, as well as the words I would be destined to write in the future. It was true the recording of my songs had moderate success. This was true also of the novels I had written and the speeches made in business presentations. I knew now I needed to enlist assistance from the beyond for me to create what I now envisaged my destiny. To hone in on my new Masters and their abilities to achieve my aims.

 I had previously enlisted writers of renown in reviewing their character and they all lacked some defect of character that resulted in proud outcomes. The success of each of those I had admired from the past had resulted, in most cases, in their early demise having suffered from the ravages of excess in the things of the flesh. The majority of those I had once admired had ultimately committed suicide, died of some malady of the flesh or ended up in hopeless poverty. I had long since dispelled with them as the best course of communion to improve the lot of others in life by my creative pursuits. I felt that I at least deserved for my future efforts some feeling of acceptance among the Masters in tapping into the source of their muses. It dawned on me then that I had to give something in return for their efforts; some token of my appreciation. So how was I to do this I wondered as I caught the final ferry back to Cologne for the night. Not far out of the city, I began feeling hunger pains and realised that apart from the drink I had at the rooftop beach, I had not eaten anything since that early lunch at Linz Am Rhein. I thought about the friendliness of the cook who served me and then thought that perhaps I could enlist the help of my centres of influence from the great beyond by inviting my chosen few to a meal. It had to be the best in preparation and I could perhaps kill two birds with one stone by learning a thing or two about cooking and choose the right delicacy to suit the taste of the Masters. It had to be my reckoning to determine if I was making the right choices in not only the selection of food for the occasion, but the guides to elect to attend my kitchen feast. I also came to realise that if I was to do just that, I would have to wait until I returned home to Australia, to utilise local meats, seafood, vegetables, fruits and deserts and wines to achieve the best of food for each occasion.

 It didn't take long to realise that I could have no more than two Masters at a time at my dining room table. This was due in no small part to the fact that my cooking experience for a large number of guests was limited and my kitchen was small.So too was my ability to prepare the food and serving skills. I figured that I could not do it all alone and would need to involve local vendors in selecting all I required for my ghostly diners. I put any negative thoughts out of my head and began to make a list of experienced food connoisseurs I could depend upon to guide me. I also determined who of my friends I could ask for help, those who would not scoff at the idea of an evening shared with imaginary Masters. I reckoned on focusing on two of the Masters to invite in the hope that over dinner conversation I would maybe hear of their immense talent to guide and influence me in my endeavour and gain their input into the wisdom of my ideas.

I needed their suggestions on how to channel my creative energy and spiritual talents to help me reach my goal in serving others of greater need I had to select my prospects suitable to my purposes and reject those who were not suited to my current aims. I needed to figure out which Masters were suited to my purpose and not to offend those I had rejected.I needed the right team, so to speak, for the tasks at hand. For I may well wish at some future date to avail myself of the services of those Masters I was to reject as first dinner guests. When I arrived back at my Cologne accomodation, I quickly showered, changed into clean clothing and headed out to a nearby restaurant. I was not only hungry to fill my belly with food, but keen eyed on the work ethic and services of the staff. I began to take notes for and against the staff service or lack of, the meal itself and its presentation; the quickness of delivery of food and drink to my table. I had already concluded I was alive with my new objective and the idea of tracking and evaluating the ability of the restaurant staff to provide the best of food and drink, would not only serve to work in in my favour when I came to serve my first meal to my invisible guests, but I would learn through taking copious note in the coming month to hone my skills for the Masters who would dine with me.

CHAPTER 2.

DINING WITH BEETHOVEN AND NAPOLEON.

On fire with the desire to get my project underway I returned to my room and began making a list of likely Master guests to my table, writing down the names of all those that immediately come to mind without initially qualifying them as to their overall suitability. I knew the right candidates would materialise after I had made sufficient enough list to began the process of elimination and determine the best two as my first guests. I was first seeking one Master of great leadership in past earthly endeavours and the other with complementary skills in the use of creative imagination, applying their particular skills in the way best for the good of humanity. It was in no particular priority that I did my choosing, I just preferred to run in alphabetic order to select the names of those to whom I thought best qualified. The winning candidate to sit at that first dinner as my guest may be of a pleasing personality but then again it was not an essential, as it did not so much matter if his mood be sympathetic to my cause and understanding in earthly endeavours. Then again he had to be be a master of detail with the backbone to assume full responsibility for decision making irrespective of outcome of the decision.

He needed to be of the people for the people and it did not particularly matter in my formulation of my decision whether the chosen one be a leader by consent, had or had not the sympathy of his followers or leed by brute force. Such was the nature of my choosing for the one of leadership. Likewise the Master of creative talent had to be one who had a natural link to nature, commitment to his art irrespective of personal misfortune, health or defect. This master must be honest, reliable and unwavering in commitment to leave the world with something for the betterment of mankind. Equally in my choosing I set a standard that despite defects of character, I would overlook those in preference to the cause. However, if I could find the Masters who displayed a strong discipline over their lower nature, then those candidates would be given priority as my choice as first dinner guests. It did not take long to start my process of elimination using a SWOT test as my mythology in process of elimination. By using the tried and prove method of personality strengths, weaknesses, opportunities and threats to my best Master candidates, two soon emerged above the rest as my ideal first guests. I had already evaluated their characters to a great degree and my decision was now engraved in my mind.

I had mediated on each of the Masters selected, using something I knew of their personal profile to arrive at my decision. Napoleon Bonaparte was my final choice as a Master leader of men and Beethoven was chosen for Master of the arts. So it is without any further ado that I embarked on my mission to bring these two Great Masters, despite their once love and respect for each other that deteriorated into loathing, together as my dinner guests. It was their inspired moody dispositions that added an extra dimension to my challenge, their troubled health in the midst of earthly brilliance was another part of my reasoning. They had once blazed a trail unequal to their ultimate journey to the other side of the curtain. In my critique of the best of the masters to invite first , I had visitations from many a Master seeking to be first choice on my list. Napoleon had been in the crowd of Masters seeking to be first chosen but had sat back pout mouthed, like a spoilt child, insisting that he should be first chosen. As it happened I did choose him, but with the reasoning he may well have thought. That was my own little secret that I would spring on Napoleon the leader of men and my Master of his Art Beethoven, over our dinner conversation.

 My approach to both of my first chosen ones took some complex intent on my part. It was done on a meditative plane and they had come to me quickly. However, now chosen, Beethoven seemed to be playing hard to get and his image to my minds eye drifted into the shadow somewhat, but he was still there attempting to listen.. I assured them both as I meditated upon it, that apart from those on this earthly plane I would need to serve them at my table, I would be very discreet in my actions. No other one outside of my earthly realm of the providers of food and wine, and a good friend whom I would call upon to help me in my choice of recipe, would need to know of our meeting at the time chosen , nor indeed the conversation at the table. I did seek their approval, promising that I would write off my experience with them long after they had returned to their spiritual realm in the heavens. that the whole world once more would be reminded of the greatness of Napoleon and the music genius of Beethoven. They both had warmed to the fact of the importance of this once, but further empathised it had to be long long after they had supped at my table. I had not told them of my mission to tap into the source of their character to improve my own. I was seeking an insight into the realm of the spirit and I knew that my choice of my first two dinner guest would set my thinking on the right path.
 My flight from Germany to Paris seem to be over before it began. The pilot interrupted my train of thought with his announcement in a thick Irish accent as the small aircraft landed: "This has been another Ryan Air flight, arriving on time as always." I had limited luggage with me as I made my way to the Metro train to the city. My destination was to my usual little hotel on the Rue de Seine, the "Welcome' Hotel. It was my habit to leave a suitcase with clothing for the street, some fancy boots, toilet bag and a spare set off sun glasses in the storeroom at the hotel. On the crowded morning city bound train I tallied up the number of times I had accomodation at my little hotel over the past decade. It was twelve times in all, in my comings and goings throughout Europe. The last time I stayed at the little hotel was as a stop over, before catching the train to St.Jean- Pied-de-Port, on the French side of the Spanish border, at the base of the Pyrenees.

 It was just over a year ago I recalled, on my third walk of the Camino de Santiago. The first Camino I had walked to let go much of my suffering. The second was in search of love, a quest to find it in the arms of another lover instead of the realm of God in the spirit. The third walk was to lick my wounds, to overcome my yearnings for more for more's sake. It had proved a difficult time mentally, physically and spiritually. for it rained the whole time I walked. I was very ill with an influenza I could not shake, my body was in stress as was my mind and spirit, but I tramped on doggedly anyway. My wake up call came after I had completed the Camino again, tramped over hill and dale on the Wicklow mountains in Ireland, walked and peddled a push bike around the Aran islands and tramped on through the wild winds on the Burrow Way. I returned to Australia worn out and exhausted after a near 1200 kilometres of tramping with a heavy backpack on my shoulders. I was near seventy four at the time. As I made my way from the Metro underground at Orion station along the busy promenade of the boulevard St. Germain, I vowed I would not return again to walk another Camino, although my heart cried out for it in the streets of Paris. What more could I add to my lot in life by returning to walk The Way again? Age and a little bit of timely wisdom quickly dispelled any further desire on that course. Besides, I was here to meet up with my Australian friend Martin as he was returning to London via Paris to visit relatives there, before returning home to Australia. Martin like me was of the older vintage and he was just returning from his third Camino when I phoned him to meet in Paris.

I had enough time to shower and change into clean clothing after my flight before my prearranged rendezvous with my friend. Martin was already seated outside the Brasserie on the corner of the Rue de Seine and Rue de Buei, near the Latin Quarter which he had chosen for his overnight stay. We talked of the short walk down to the Stein river and decided after our coffee and chat that we would take a stroll along the rivers edge to discuss the idea that I had planted in his mind when I had phoned him earlier for our meeting. We dispensed with formalities, gave each other a bear hug and with some degree of enthusiasm I, for a change, gave Martin the opportunity to talk about his latest adventure on the Camino Way. Martin recounted the trails and tribulations of the wear and tear on his body, the torments that beset him in his recall and the loneliness he encountered on this last adventure. He too was worn out and weary like me, but likewise more spiritually attuned to the guided groups that influence our lives. We were both raw in our encounters on our Camino journeys and it just dawned on me then that Martin's experiences on his Camino Way almost duplicated my own experiences and encounters. It could well have been a recording of my last Camino, as I listened with intent to my friend's journey.
Two old men, sitting at a sidewalk cafe in the heart of Paris, still attempting to be adventurers. Warriors of a bygone age who had not yet found the will to completely let go. I could hear in my head the words of Carl Jung: "A man who has not passed through the inferno of his passions has never overcome them. As far as we can discern, the sole purpose of human existence is to kindle a light in the darkness of mere being. Everything that irritates us about others can lead us to an understanding of ourselves." I was about to denounce Jung for such an utterance as I felt no such irritation that I could detect with my friend Martin. Jung once more interjected: "We should not live the afternoon of our lives as we lived the morning of our lives." Maybe I was getting it at long last, this challenge to let go, hand over to one's higher self spirit, for as I gazed at my old friend Martin, I saw clearly a reflection of my self image, my own folly in pursuit of uncovering the layers beneath the surface of my personality instead of just accepting whatever comes up. I felt Martin and I were now as

ready as we could ever be in endeavouring to tap into the source of The Masters whom I sort to dine with me as my guests.

 Once we finish our coffees, we walked the Rue de Seine arriving at a bench seat where we sat gazing at the restorations of the Notre Dame Cathedral on the opposite shoreline. The fire of April 2019 had destroyed the iconic spires and the roof had collapsed in the process. It was not known the extent of the damage of artwork and relics housed inside the Cathedral but it was by the grace of the Almighty that the building still stands and old drawings had been kept for centuries that were a reference point in the restorations taking place. I remarked to Martin that we had our inner temples damaged by the fires of our own former folly but were being restored by the forces of the Almighty even as we spoke. He nodded in silent agreement and we began to walk across the nearest bridge on our way towards the Bois de Vincennes, the largest green space park in the city sprawling with trails and a zoo. Louis V11 first built a a hunting lodge there in the 12th century and later PhilipV1 in 1336 began construction of the Chateau de Vincennes. Martin and I were discussing this as the place where Napoleon returned with many artefacts and animals from the countries he had conquered after the French revolution.

 I turned to hear the sound of hoofbeats on cobblestone and saw an image of the little General astride a black stallion. He was closely followed by many hundreds of marching troops with heads held high as they marched. The images faded as Martin broke my spell of imagination. He remarked: "Did you hear the sound of marching feet just then my friend?" I nodded but said naught, preferring to let sleeping ghosts lay for the present, for I was keen to involve Martin in my own ghost quest, to wine and dine my Master guests on return to Australia and I needed no other distractions to waver me from my quest. Martin warmed to my idea and I was glad of it as he had in his younger days been a chef, trainer of chefs and had even been the chief cook and bottle washer for the United Nations. Martin was interested to see why I was so keen to have Napoleon as a first guest."There were so many other leaders of good character who could fulfil your requirements as a dinner guest that would be more deserving, so tell me please for I am curious, why you picked Napoleon?" I paused for a moment to gather the words for my response: "Most of us, when we bid farewell to this earth, are quite satisfied that our time has come. What with all the years of trials and tribulations we have seen, the unquestionable cruelty, the endless stupidities and disappointment, we are more than ready to go. For most of us I feel are more than satisfied when God's angel of death touches us to be prepared to follow him. However even now and then someone is born who can never have enough, who is insatiable, who has reached out for everything and yet still wants more. Such a man was in his lifetime and still is Napoleon Bonaparte."

I paused before continuing my reasoning to encourage Martin to help me in my quest, as I would need his input into the meal to be prepared for Napoleon as my first guest. "You must remember, he was the Emperor of the French, and at one moment in time it appears he come close to ruling the whole world." Martin was taken in now. "Well, I don't like him but there are others like you

that do. " I could not in good conscience give a definitive answer to my friend as to my opinion of Napoleon but added " Well, he got things done." Martin was on a roll now: "What sort of things, remember he caused more people in his time to be killed the anyone else." I responded : "It's not for that I have admiration, it's because he got things done." And as an additional carrot to get Martin's participation in my plan .I added: "But now you come to mention it, perhaps we should ask him his opinion." Martin was a little incensed : " What, as to why he murdered so many people? " I reminded Martin of the history books and record of his efforts to win at all cost: " It may be difficult to sit in the same room as him over a meal, but I am keen to do just that because he seemed to cast such a spell over everyone he came in contact with,"
A pause in the conversation and I added: ' I had a dream the other night and one of his victims appeared to me. He told me that he still had admiration for the man despite him being killed by him. My ghostly soldier added that his own health deteriorated as a result of exposure to the elements on his return from the battle of Waterloo. He had also lost his property and the two of his own sons in battle and three toes as well." Did he say anything else, this untimely ghost of your dream?" I look Martin in the eyes, " Yes, he worshipped the ground Napoleon walked upon despite all his personal suffering and material loss." I reckoned the ghost of my dream was a simple Grenadier Guard I had been reading about a day or two earlier. He had volunteered for that ill-fated expedition against Russia in 1812 and as an afterthought I mentioned to Martin that I should like to invite him to be at the dinner. Not as a guest mind you, but as an additional hand to help with the meal. He would no doubt get some joy out of attending to his old general and may well help with any lull in the conversation. For as I explained to Martin, our other guest had also fallen for a time under the little Corsican General's spell but had recovered and forever cast him out of his life.

I referred to the Master of Music, Ludwig van Beethoven. With this last connection, I had Martin in to the fullest. "I hate that dreadful little Italian" he said. "I loathe the very name of him. But I should like to meet him, just twitch old Ludwig go after him! I just hope on the night of the meal Beethoven is in one of his ferocious moods. That would be magnificent to behold." Martin was right into it now. "We may have a problem with the food. Napoleon never wasted time with his meal, setting a limit of 15 minutes to be precise." I was keen to have both my guests stay for at least two hours remembering something a philosopher once said: 'I can never stay with parties of pleasure for more than two hours, the frivolity makes me bored.' I knew that like a military exercise, between Martin, the help of the Grenadier Guard and myself we would hatch a plan to ensure the hours ticked by. The way to a man's heart is through his stomach came to mind. So with Martin's help we would devise a menu fit for the Masters at my Table. In the excitement of the day, Martin and I retreated to a sidewalk cafe in the Latin Quarter to enjoy some French cuisine and a couple of alcohol free beers before saying our goodbyes. He was due to catch a flight to London the next morning and I would be winging my way back home to Australia. We both agreed to pick up were we left off on our return home and put time aside time to work out our menu selection before the chosen date.

I considered it was now not the meal that was my major issue, but my ability to meditate over the coming weeks on attracting my guest from their heavenly realm to come to my place for a dinner at a future specified date. I watched Martin as he walked down a cobblestoned street on his way back to his refuge for the evening. He was whistling a happy tune and had a renewed spring in his stride. Martin was obviously excited about our common goal on his return to Australia too. I returned to the "Welcome" Hotel room in the attic, and like an artist creating a masterpiece on canvas, I began to write down the names of providers of fine food and wine. Those who could be relied upon to keep my secret and who would assist in the selection of fine cuisine for my dining room table.

 A month had passed since Martin and I had strolled the Rue de Seine and sat in the Bois de Vincennes Park hatching a plan for a pending invitation for the Masters at my Table, with Napoleon and Beethoven as dinner guests. We sat talking over coffees at the Bonjour Patisserie, a cosy little local French style bakery and coffee lounge. It reminded me of my favourite Paul's cafe in Paris; just as busy with customers ordering coffee and croissant for breakfast with one exception, it was void of anyone speaking French. I was needing so much input from Martin on the dinner menu for our guests. " The food is a problem mate, the Emperor has a monotonous taste for chicken. My other guide sources tell me, he always eats a cold leg of chicken for breakfast, the same for lunch and roast chicken for dinner. Anything outside of that was apt to be sent back to the kitchen," Martin chimed in: " You know how I hate that dreadful little Italian."
He thought for a moment: " If you want to prepare a chicken soup, I'll go along with that but I know he hated fish so that's what I will prepare." Also, Martin added: "Let us serve champagne at our meal, for Napoleon liked Claret but I would like to see his reaction to the main meal and drink not being to his liking." I noted Martin had taken ownership in his comment, addressing the subject matter in the singular and not in the plural. So it was no longer my dinner guests but his too. I didn't have an issue with Martin's proposal, as I had in my mind a vegetable soup with roasted chicken wings as a bonus.This would keep Bonaparte content to begin with and I reasoned that Beethoven would love the fish and would not mind either way, being a careless eater without discipline for the hour of the day or of what food or drink he took.

 Beethoven it seemed was always too busy composing, communicating with his Great Tone Master to bother with what food to eat or what he drank. It was perhaps a little undignified of Martin to use his culinary skills to get even with the little Corsican, but Martin's mind was set on making Napoleon suffer a little for his murderous transgressions during his time on earth. There had to be vegetables I was thinking; fried potatoes in olive oil with a lot of finely cut parsley and a decent quantity of cooked Sauerkraut for the inner health of our guests. That settled in my mind. we had a good cross-section of foods in entrée and main to keep the guest satisfied. "I reckoned Napoleon would have had his fair share of potatoes on St Helena, Martin. What do you think?" Martin went along with my suggestion, considering the hell of Napoleon' banishment to the little isolated lonely island of St. Helena after his defeat at Waterloo, he had some compassion for him under those circumstances. "Six years of being buried alive on that island after twenty six years into which he packed more activity and more glory than has ever come to any other man."

Martin spoke of his British ancestors then: " What else could the British Government have done, as they wanted to rid the world of a human being who was a volcano, who had more energy than a hundred million ordinary human beings, who had fewer scruples than the lowest type of highwayman, who commanded more power over his fellowman than anybody else on record had survived, who could do more work in a short space of time than two dozen statesman, and whose ego was so great that he needed an entire planet as a background for his ambitions and his vanity?" I thought of Hitler who would have be considered of equal standing in all aspect of volatility, power , influence and vanity as Napoleon , but I let Martin win the day with his viewpoint.

I felt, based on Martin's summation of the Emperor, that I had to come clean as to my purpose in having Napoleon as my dinner guest and embracing Beethoven in the plot. I reinforced my desire to uncover more from Napoleon himself as to his extraordinary energy and how he used the forces of nature to do his bidding. I emphasised that I wished only to tap into his energy for my purposes in passing on my findings to help others who were suffering misfortune and to improve my own energy levels too. As Martin like me had walked the Camino de Santiago three times t's Camino Way has on body and mind on that journey of the spirit. I for one had gained some insight into a miracle of change which has since propelled me along the path of writing books, recording my own songs and building online presence to benefit fellow Pilgrims on their journeys. It has come at a price, resulting in long periods of exhaustive recovery and even rehabilitation in hospital to get my being back into shape and balance.

So Martin understood when I explained that I had no real admiration for Napoleon's conquest, ruthlessness, foul temper or indeed his murderous ways. It was the fact that he was still admired and even idolised by those that suffered and died in following him on his missions and managed to keep up such a strong presence of mind, physical drive and attitude of winning at all cost. He had a presence second to none and the energy of God that fascinated me. Due to my own burnout when I too attempted to do more than I could control, I wanted to learn more from this demagogue, to learn to harness such energy should I be in need on some future long and winding road. Besides, now being in my mid seventies, it was imperative to tap into those forces known only to the few that Napoleon had in spades. I had to admit it wasn't the energy he harnessed from food for he lived on chicken. Martin nodded his approval and his mission to cook for the dinner seem to take on a new light when I had explained my purpose.

I therefore needed to take stock and be precise in my intention and to do that I needed to look into Napoleon and take a brief of the man and his bloodline- the Napoleonic style. I reread the literary works of Hendrik van Loon, to gather a brief of the main characters to come to my table as dinner guests. History has shown Napoleon was born in 1769, the year after his native island of Corsica had been incorporated into the kingdom of France. He was not really a Frenchman but a violent Corsican patriot from his youth he was a rebel with a dream of liberation and independence for the Corsican nation. He was an ideal-ist who maybe dreamed of being one-day 'His Majesty Napoleon 1." These patriotic sentiments he inherited from his parents, but mostly from his mother. For his father was just another shiftless scion of an old Italian family who prid-ed itself in Tuscan origin, and had two centuries before moved from the main-land back to this rude backward island belonging to the Republic of Genoa.

Since moving to the capital city of Ajaccio, the family had never done well. Neither had they entirely slipped out of their own class. Carlo Bonaparte was a lawyer a small scale landowner and a local prominent patriot. He was far dif-ferent to the mother! She belonged to a tribe of the Romanies, and her first name was Letizia. It was she who was in the shadows of every move her son made throughout his history. A deeply pious women who preferred to remain in the background, but to the end of his day, remained a tower of strength. She was the only person on earth that Napoleon was afraid of. For she had a tongue as sharp as a razor and he continued to hear, despite repeated victories gaining mastery over another country, her voice repeating: "If only it lasts!" Most of what Napoleon instructed came from his heart and voice, for he never learnt to write French without grammatical errors. I paused for a moment to admit to myself I had the same issue with my writings. Maybe I had to learn to be like Napoleon, a bit of an orator to get my message across. Carlo Bonaparte re-alise not long after picking up the family pieces in Ajaccio, at the time of Napoleon's birth, that Corsican freedom from France was a lost cause. So he soon set his cause in getting on with his new masters. He had a large family and too many mouths to feed, so made himself useful to the French Governor. He believed his sons could make their own way but the daughters had to be provided for.

In 1779 the Governor felt the need to send a trusted emissary to Versailles to consult the home Government and so chose his son Carlo for the mission. He had asked to take his second son Napoleon with him and as a goodwill gesture, left his 10 year old dangerously rebellious boy with the French. His namesake son had proved to be a very apt weapon overtime, for the son was cut with the cloth of a Corsican patriot and that was the beginning of Napoleon's career as a Frenchman.

To the French he was not a particularly attractive child, for he was as white as a sheet, thin as a whipping stick and terribly awkward, he wore ill fitting clothes and everything he said or did proclaimed that he was a provincial. It was however another feature that got everyone in; a pair of eyes no one ever forgot. Alas, he also had terrible attacks of temper which occasionally led to outburst of fury and made people suspect he suffered from epileptic fits. It was not so, for many leaders of renown had emotional outburst of sorts. Bismarck was renowned for breaking forth in uncontrollable weeping whenever he was angry, but was never accused of being epileptic. Likewise, other famous leaders throughout history, like Caesar, St.Paul and Mohammed showed signs of uncontrollable temper. Christ himself had displayed such anger when he took to merchants trading at the temple gate, beating them with a chord rope for their transgression in using the house of God as a den of thieves. *

Father Carlo died when Napoleon was sixteen and he become the serious provider and protector of the family. His brother Joseph never amounted to much, so it was Napoleon who took it upon himself to provide for his mother and sisters. In this respect he became the perfect Italian, heaping favour upon his family when he could bestow some abundance. They were never satisfied and showed little in gratitude to him. However, when he fell on difficult financial times himself, they found ways themselves to make ends meet. It was only his Mother Letizia, who remained faithful to him, even when she proved to him that she was right, whatever he achieved it could not last. Napoleon studied the elements of his future trade in the military school of Brienne and did a year of post graduate work at the Ecole Militaire in Paris. He therefor received the best of old French kingdom military training and in 1785 received the military title of sous-lieuxtant, or under lieutenant. Then came the Revolution and Napoleon found his "second father" that sired the future Emperor of the French.

For the people of France were on their way and Lieutenant Bonaparte was ready to begin his career. The world was setting a stage on which he would be able to play his role to the best of his unlimited abilities. An underling officer in a revolution was strutting his stuff around Paris, living from military barracks to barracks, from time to time returning to his native island attempting to support his mother and sister when he found the funds to do so. At one point in the revolution when at his lowest financial ebb he could not even afford to pay for his washing bill of one shirt and was dabbling in local politics with certain literary plans too. He did his best to make a living marketing books from door to door in Paris. It was in the most difficult days of a revolution. He pawned his watch after selling the last of his books. He no longer had his daily coffee at the cafe de la Regency and was noticeably absent from daily games of chess there. Fate was to play a part, when in the depth of a brewing revolution of the people he met Amschel Mayer, a Jew who was a foundation member of an embryonic formation of a secret society of Jewish One World Order, were he rose from poverty street to found and flourish under the emblem of his red flag, which in German spells 'Rothschild.' (*footnote) Amschel liked the fiery little Corsican who had the savage eyes and a motto of kill or be killed for the greater good, or so it seemed and it was Amschel who, with his political connections, caused Napoleon to be introduced to Citizen Barras, an alias for Comte Paul Francois Nocolas de Barras. Seeing the way the wind was blowing he had joined the revolution from its beginning but somehow kept his head where so many others had theirs cut off. Nobody liked him except for the fact

*Footnote: Hendrik van Loon -Van loon's lives- George G harper & Co- 1943

that he had an inherited ability to bark orders, which steered the direction of the revolutionary winds for a time. He proposed that Bonaparte be entrusted with the command of troops loyal to the Convention ruling Paris at the time. Nothing could suit Bonaparte better than that.

 Napoleon hastily accepted, for he was a man of law and order and hated to see Paris being run by the rabble, whether it be the rabble of the left or the right. The morning of October 5th 1795 the mob was set to find out who was the real master and who would run the capital and the nation. The revolution had been a haphazard coup de'tat in the first place and leadership was the rule of mob and the guillotine was the rule of law. The bellowing voice of Citizen Barras could be heard above the crowd at the Convention of so-called politicians running the show. Early in the morning the crowds began to move down on the Convention to be met by a young man in charge telling them to go back. They laughed at the young Italian leading a small garrison of troops and bade him shoot. That he did without hesitation and many were killed or wounded in the scuffle that followed. The rest ran as fast as they can from the scene and that evening the French revolution was over.

Four years of Directory government was passe and the rule of a new guard defeated, destroyed and annihilated the subject of the the old dynasty. At least from the outside looking in France trumped on every front. Napoleon went on to defeat Austria, who lost Belgium in the scuffle, turn to Italy and when the shooting was over he had for France the border west of the Rhine, and a number of newly founded republics inspired to self government. To the outside world France had triumphed, but not on its domestic front. It is an old axiom that states : 'When a democracy has achieved victory, it runs the greatest risk of defeating itself' So, I wonder if God is on the side of this now little General. For this leader seemed more than a man. He was as complicated as some of the mountain ranges I have traversed in my wonderings. It seems to me that before he could reach the highest peaks he was mindful of the endless valleys to be traversed and the four dozen minor peaks to be conquered.

 It is the year 1799, General Bonaparte has knocked the rest of the challenges of Europe out of the ring so to speak. Since he has now proved to be the ablest of man in France and not the least the whole world, he takes pride in the fact that he should rule. Why should he not be given the chance to rule the whole of France as the rest of the Continent has been forced to submit it to him? An able thinker once stated " Every philosopher is a king an every king a philosopher." Such a view might look alright on paper but in reality should not be taken too seriously in a practical life for it is more important to function effectively than to philosophise.

 Let me talk now of the renowned Josephine, a Creole, women, the former widow of the Noble Vicome de Beauharnais who died on the scaffold. She has had many lovers and now Napoleon is bewitched and must have her. She knows that her beauty is driving him crazy and she is not at all in love with him, is much older and makes the little Corsican go through the paces like an organ grinders monkey. He marries her in one night of bliss and rushes off to

Italy, another war, writing off his account of incredible victories, and tells her how he loves her, adores her, wants her, needs her, and lives for nothing else but news from her. Josephine knows it would be folly to throw away the opportunity to become rich and provide for her children from her deceased nobleman. She does not love her bewitched General. Besides he bores her to tears with his talk of empire, army divisions, of the hundreds of millions of francs of loot that can be taken out off Italy to improve roads in France, build a harbour and a navy fleet for France, for there is but one Power that can defy his plans, that of England.

Josephine is soon on the loose again in Napoleon's absence, often on the arm of some well-dressed good looking young hussar, instead of being the goodly wife of a man who is always dressed like a hurricane putting his clothing on. She takes her lovers to the silk sheets from Milan sent to her from Napoleon. All the while the spiteful whore of a women is feeding facts and fiction back to the Elite group behind the throne who are using the information to help bend the will of the little General. In time Napoleon gets wind of Josephine's not so wifely ways, her excessive spending, her lovers and her trickery. He dispenses with her and finds another lover, but it is not so much this act, but the fact that those who finance the wars and the objectives that have planned for Napoleon are now at a loss to control him. To digress back a year to 1798, Napoleon is obsessed to rule not only Europe but the world. The General loves maps and traces the route he proposes to take England which by far has the most continental control of the world at large. First he traces how he proposed to fulfil his mission. France south to Egypt, then by way of Asia to the Indus River, and a sudden plunge into the heart of India itself. In that way the British Government will be deprived of its wealth, it will no longer be able to support its European Power base. He surmises that soon after the continent would collapse , England would be on her knees, suing for peace and begging for mercy.

In the May of 1798 the general, accompanied by thirty five thousand men, disappears in a cloud of ocean spray and news reaches Paris that he has taken Malta. On July 1 he disembarks in Alexandria and in three weeks destroys the arm of the Sultan in a battle at the foot of the Pyramids. The road to the East lay open, so from then on fantastic stories drift back to France of his defeat by Nelson at the mouth of the Nile.The world now seems to be a great deal bigger than his maps had indicated to him. The Turks, reinforced by the British put up a much better fight than expected, so the little General is forced to put his wounded out of their misery in the mercy of what they would have faced at the hands of the Muslim Infidel. For those heathens could not forget the murderous twelve hundred prisoners Napoleon had killed when he had promised to spare them.

Meanwhile back in France one disaster followed another, the diplomatic representatives of the people had been violated and the decree to a peace conference had been hacked to pieces by a squad of Hungarian hussars. Then in October of 1799 startling news came. "He has come back and will be in Paris within five days." Josephine doomed to face the temper of a volcano, packed her bags, dispensed with her lovers, left unpaid creditors and fled. In less time than anyone expected the great man is back in Paris. There is a mysterious midnight meeting as the Elite that ran the show in his absence are doomed. They are divided amid themselves and unable to act within any degree of safety. Soon the soldiers of Bonaparte surround the Government Directory at Saint-Cloud. Angry words are exchanged like before when Robespierre was deprived of his power, but this time the bayonets of Napoleon quickly settle the argument.The Directory ceases to exist.There is a council of three members elected as a Consulate to take its place and a first Consul is elected for ten years and his name is Napoleon Bonaparte. Other members elected are soon forgotten as if they never existed and history indicates that perhaps they never did.

So that is all there is to this story. For a more accurate picture I refer back to Plato to summarise it in his eternal circle theory: "First of all we have a king with much power, who abuses it, and is pushed from his throne by the common people, who thereupon get much power and abuse it until other classes in society combine against them in fear of what may happen to their own heads. Then the whole performance is repeated , and we find a nation dominated by one man on horseback who gets much power, abuses it, and is removed from office by the discontented masses who get much power, who abuse their power until in turn — and so forth, world with end, Amen.

The first thing the French needed after Napoleon had become First Consul was peace abroad and order at home. Napoleon gave them both and even made a peace treaty with England. Then he paid his respects to God by concluding a peace treaty with the Pope and the Catholic Church and most of its former rights and privileges he reinstated. Next, a new universal code of law in France which still prevails to this day. So in August 1802 Napoleon becomes Consul for life. Two years later, he drops all pretence and crowned himself Emperor of France, with Pope Pius V11 standing by unable to play the life role that his predecessor had enacted in the year 800, when he coronated the Great General Charlemagne.This time the Emperor had taken the crown and placed it firmly on his own brow, to the insult of a predominately Catholic France. The rest of the story is known to every school boy.This salesman of enlightened ideas and revolutionary ideals suddenly went from the sale of goods and services to only sell himself. For now he had grasped the greatest of all curses, delusions of grandeur. He divorced the woman who had made of fool of him, married an Austrian Princess who was to bestow upon his dynasty a slight touch of respectability and legitimacy. That was the beginning of the end, for gradually the Emperor lost all touch with reality and came to believe in the role he was playing as if ordained by God instead of the result of a happy combination of genius and good luck.

CHAPTER 3.

THE GASTRONOMY

Not to belittle his talents for any sensible historian can not deny his superhuman abilities, but a perspective of some two hundred odd years allows us to see that half of Napoleon's success was a matter of good timing. Good luck will only play its part just for just so long. Napoleon in his conceit ceased to play the role which made him truly great, so as a prophet and apostle of revolutionary ideas and so he was doomed. From then on, timing and even nature itself turned against him. The financial backers slowly reduced their finance for his Russian war effort and plotted his defeat at Waterloo. It was not the fighting, but the retreat in the dead of winter where many of his troops froze to death whilst others starved. For the Russians did what Fabius did to Hannibal's army; they burnt crops and cut Napoleons' food supply. He tried to come back, but he delayed too long at Waterloo due to irritable bowel and haemorrhoid issues. This allowed Blucher, the Prussian Field Marshall to appear upon the scene just as Wellington's centre line was beginning to crumble. The battle should have been a French victory, but the might of the new contingent of Prussian soldiers with Wellington on another front, drove the French into retreat and both nature and providence took its toll. A tired and broken man was fleeing for his life, followed by a few thousand stragglers and the curse of millions of mothers of dead sons. He tried to come back for one hundred days of takeover and many rallied to his cause, but he was captured and once more banished. The man who once new all the names of his subordinate officers, who at any moment had been able to recite the numbers of horses and caissons attached to each regiment, had been a walking dictionary of detail, had overlooked one item which, after years of ghastly suffering carried him to his untimely end at the age of fifty two. He had never paid any attention to his meals and gastric ulcers was the ultimate consequence. Hence, the stomach issue and haemorrhoids that had made him unable to sit in his saddle at Waterloo, forced him to delay the battle and was the prime cause of the end of his leadership. It is not nice to be so clinical, but stomach ache, headaches and sluggish bowels played a greater role in the history of Napoleon at his end than most people realise. If Napoleon have eaten less chicken, consumed fine vegetables and some other main meal like fish and taken more time over his meals to aid his digestion, history may have told a different story of this once great Emperor.

But for now I must turn to my other dinner guest., another victim of his own genius and irregular habits, but what a difference in the two men. For Beethoven wasted and exhausted himself trying to bestow upon the world the most extreme beauty that which had never been heard before. And whilst Napoleon had dominated his time on earth to the first person singular, Beethoven was centred on the second person plural. It was the 'I ' against the 'You' and the 'You' won. Beethoven has over the past two hundred years been a secular saint in the tones we receive from his muses, whilst Napoleon's name survives in a rich and unwholesome sort of pastry . The milling of the God's grind slowly, but they grind exceedingly fine. I had dispensed with Napoleon for the time being, although he keep interrupting my dreams anxiously awaiting the day, date and time of the proposed dinner. My focus now was Beethoven and to refresh my friend Martin to the history of this Master as our other dinner guest. I left Martin contemplating the menu and called on Pontus, the baker at Bon Jour Patisserie. He was in the kitchen preparing dough for the next morning supply of bread and pastries. I let him in on our secret proposed dinner guests from the other side. He warmed to the idea the first invites and promised to bake a special loaf of bread for the occasion. I thanked him for his support left him starry eyed and advised I would let him know when I needed the bread.

Beethoven's father was an often slightly drunk tenor of the archbishop - the elector of Cologne. His mother Maria had worked for the same dignitary as a kitchen hand washing the dishes. The family live in Bonn where Beethoven spent most of his time. They were of Dutch-Flemish origin and had little German in their bloodline. A detail which would no doubt fill the old Master's heart with great satisfaction. For the Dutch and Flemish at the time were quite radical and the master himself was a firm believer in human rights, especially when pressed on issue of social inequality. How Beethoven survived the old ways of the Habsburg dynasty of central Europe shall forever remain a closely guarded secret. A the age of five Beethoven began his musical career, not because he felt the urge to spend hours and hours playing his little fiddle, but because the family were in need of money to pay his father's drink bills and had somehow heard of the fortune Leopold Mozart had made out of exploiting his children's talents. He reckoned on the fact that what Leopold could do Beethoven could do, but Ludwig was no Wolfgang. He was an ugly unattractive child, headstrong and obstinate, whereas Wolfgang had adored his dear father; Ludwig mostly detested his drunken male parent. To add salt to the wound, Leopold Mozart had been quite a personage and an excellent impresario with a fine feeling for the setting of the stage upon which his two darling children were to perform. One can only guess what would have happened if old man Beethoven had undertaken such a role for his son. The plan of the topsy alcoholic father came to naught, but as he himself had some musical talent, he spent a larger than he could afford sum of money on his sons musical training.

He had logically considered that perhaps little Ludwig may one day be a singer in a choir like himself or even become a musician in the Court of royalty. He also considered that as music was on the same employment level as a painter, he may well find work in the field of the arts as a music teacher in either Bonn or Cologne. It was also a given that a child who showed exceptional talent, irrespective of his bloodline would be sought out to perform in the homes of local nobleman to entertain dinner guest in their homes. So the father had a mission his young son and encouraged him to be educated in his musical skills, so that when he reached an acceptable age he could step out on his own with the ability to make a living. Young Ludwig was an ungracious receiver of the gifts of his talent and would have failed every enthusiastic driven objective of the Dale Carnegie. However, in his time, the good city of Bonn was kind to this boy despite his rude outbursts of uncontrollable anger, particularly in the presence of women and his insistence that his genius be recognised. So without all the airs and graces of the Mozarts, the young son of a tipsy court singer scraped through to get his music education. He was given the privilege of presenting before a King and was advised to lift this hat to the King before he performed. Beethoven replied with inverted snobbery: "Let the young King lift his hat to Beethoven first, for am I not the Jupiter of music?" Despite his gruff manner and untidy dress, he polished up sufficiently enough in those early years in Bonn to hold his own in almost any kind of society. And when he fell from grace, as the extreme talented often have a tendency to do, the mighty ones of this earth and friends were sufficiently impressed with his extreme abilities as conductor, musician and writer of fine theory to overlook these very painful outbreaks of bad behaviour. It was also perceived by those in the know that he would do well in Vienna as there was no other talent at the time who could write sonatas, symphonies and concertos like this one. So the Gods smiled on this Master from Bonn and the music lovers of the times concluded that their interest lay in his music and despite his lack of social graces he was accepted and somewhat forgiven for his abnormalities.

As one who has been afflicted with maladies of great grievance and grief in my latter years, as have so many others I might add who have lived as long as I, a biblical reference to the trials of Job is not out of the question when it comes to adversity. If there is indeed another candidate for the honour of the extremes of adversity, then Beethoven wins hands down. I am not thinking of the thirty years of hell he experienced at the hand of his relatives. Nor the worthless nephew upon whom Beethoven centred all his affection, as a common slug who had no notion of his uncle's genius's except to extract favours from the poor man. Nor am I referring to Beethoven's outburst of passion for at least a half a dozen women who at different intervals in his life tore his heart to pieces and from one of whom he may well have contracted a tertiary sexual disease which later played a major part in his deafness for the remainder of his days. I have no proof of that, but it has been considered in the history of medical records of the gifted and famous. Such unhappy encounters with lovers has happened to many throughout history, but unlike most, Beethoven never encountered any satisfaction. No, it was not his clingers on, unsatisfactory relationships, his ungrateful family and in particular his blood sucking nephew. No it was the unhappy circumstance of a genius composer who suffered the extremities of growing deafness.

It was in his twenty eighth year in 1789 that he discovered the first symptom of his affliction. He wondered if it was the aftermath of a common cold, for he often forgot to even light his stove in winter to keep warm and was known to walk for miles into the forest irrespective of climatic conditions. In his days in Vienna, he suffered the discomfort of badly ventilated and draft ridden living quarters, because he could not afford better, and as the weeks and months passed by he suffered increasing deafness. Panic stricken he visited all the known hearing specialists of his day and when he found no relief he turned to quackery. Nothing worked and as his writings show, he had a suspicion of the cause of which sexually transmitted disease was one opinion, a form of TB another, and general ill health of which he had cause to write down in his so called 'will.'

It was not that he considered himself a bad person, nor indeed had cause to do an inventory of his defects of character, he just wanted to do his best to write down his woes for his own examination, the understanding of his kin, the examination of science and for the love of God, his Great Tone Master. Beethoven was in fact a deeply pious man and had an interest in the noble principles of the French Revolution, as laid down in the Rights of Man. Beethoven was profoundly interested in everything that effected the human race, which almost all sensitive spiritual persons do to this very day. Beethoven had 'his hero of the hour' Napoleon to whom he devoted his Third Symphony ,but who turned out to be the biggest despot of all. In his deafness, his life lacked companionship and the outside world was cut off. So he honed his listening skills, his isolation and will to the vibrations of nature, his own and the Universe. In 1824 he tried for the last time to conduct a concert, but gave up in mid- performance, as he had no idea what the musicians were doing. After that he could only communicate with the outside world by means of little slips off paper which he scribbled his questions when he met a friend at a regular coffee house. These have been preserved and reveal the most pathetic but subtle manifestations of human courage. For a moment in time, whilst contemplating this most uncommon of common man, I visualised him seated at that coffee house with understanding friends doing their best to divert him from his morose state of mind with idol gossip or the occasional joke on some well known character of the age. The puzzlement and frustration on their faces as they realised all their efforts were to no avail.The reality was a morose poor creature who lived inside himself as he had done for the majority of his life, save for the times he struck the chords of vibrations from his muse, The Great tone Master, his God. He would return back to his lonely quarters and disorderly room full of pianos, one of which he had cut off its legs so that he could lay on his tummy with his head next to the key board to feel the vibrations as he composed. The kitchen always stacked with dirty dishes, the floor strung with crushed paper from failed attempts to write yet another masterpiece, sheet music everywhere. an excess of chairs everywhere with clothing slung across for ease of selection should he venture out. The washbowl remained full for the quick splash upon his face and arms for days. His bed almost permanently unmade. It is there that he died on 26th March 1827, six years after his former hero Napoleon voiced his last words on that lonely little island on the other side of the world.'Tete d' armee -head of the Army.'

I was reminded of Beethoven's death when a thunderstorm accompanied a hurricane, for a short period as he passed across the curtain. It is said at the death of Christ, the sun darkened, the earth trembled and the dead arose and appeared to many. I can relate to this, as in my youth I was inflected for a time with a kind of deafness, constant inner ear infections rending me with gloomy moods like the Master and Christ the Father. Likewise I ventured out in stormy weather to sit upon rocks at the edge of the ocean, in thunderstorms and lightning, I was inspired to hear the 5th Symphony in my head, for I was once taken to listening to classical music, particularly Beethoven. I wrote many a poem in that sullen state and even the Master's prose I took to reading. For like him I was alone and lacking a sense of direction. I took to painting in oils and worked a portrait of Beethoven, which a young German backpacker was fascinated. So, like all the material possessions I had then, I did not hesitate in giving her my 'Masterpiece,' perhaps in the vain hope she would come to bed with me. With such passion, I now firmly desire to invite to my table Beethoven after all these years. Even on this two hundredth anniversary of the Master, I am reminded of his carriage to the grave. He had every good reason to feel proud. Both sides of the streets were lined with soldiers and even the House of Habsburg payed homage to this strange man, who in his own inimitable way was a great icon and perhaps a more dangerous rebel than any other subject o a double-headed eagle.

And so to the dinner. It took some doing to get Beethoven to accept the dinner engagement, whilst Napoleon keep driving me mad in my dreams until the appointed hour of the meal. Beethoven was coming out of sufferance as he still detested the little Corsican. I reminded him of his piety and will to forgive and he finally accepted the invitation reluctantly. I remarked to Martin that the Master Beethoven's view was similar to his own, when it came to Napoleon. Martin had arrived early with pre-cleaned and prepared fish, chopped pickled cabbage and a quantity of small potatoes already sprinkled with olive oil garlic and herbs to bake in the oven. I meditated for a time and the old Granada Guard appeared to be of service to join us at the table. My entree was ready to put on the boil, the wine flask full of red claret, champagne on ice and table setting complete, with a large white candle set in the middle of the table; to be lit on the arrival of the main guests. It was to be a strange combination-Emperor Napoleon, Ludwig van Beethoven, and a humble link in the chain of the old guard of Freed soldiers, one Honore Clauzel. My two guest of honour arrived punctually. Napoleon as we would expect took pride of place on the Carver chair, at what he considered to be the head of the table. However it was a round table of Mahogany wood with the remaining chairs being identical to the carver except for the fact they had no arm rests. The old Honore sat directly opposite his former Emperor and immediately fell into his old role as a soldier at arms, as did Napoleon: "What is your name brave one?" Honore gave his name. " What regiment?" Napoleon enquired. Honore gave his regiment "Battalion?" Honore stood up and saluted and named his battalion. "Aaw, then you must have been at Borodino!" Napoleon retorted. " Yes, Your Majesty?" "So you would have been on the right flank? "said Napoleon. Honore sounding now like a tape recording on replay."Yes Your Majesty." Napoleon sized this old survive of Waterloo with a non characteristic concern: "Did you get wounded?" " Yes" responded Honore."I got shot in the left arm, but it was nothing. I also lost three fingers on my left hand caused by the freezing temperatures and two toes during our untimely retreat." Napoleon held his hand and inspected it and with a soft voice said : " This is the hand of a brave man."

Honore was taken aback and responded : "Thank you your Majesty, I would do it all again because I am ready to fight with you if you so desire."

The old man forgot for a moment that Napoleon was only a figment of the imagination inspired by myself and Martin to serve our guests and give some cause for conversation. I did not have the heart to remind him of this, he was too busy staring in admiration at his Emperor. I served my chicken soup comprising grated carrot, onion, tomato, and Vegeta, brought to the boil with chicken wings. I had drained off the broth at the top and served the wings separately. I felt that if Napoleon did eat the fish Martin was preparing, at least the soup would be to his liking and his digestion. Meanwhile Beethoven just sat at the other end of the table lost in some other place, content to attempt to listen. During the rest of the evening Napoleon treated the old soldier as a comrade in arms, addressing him as 'Mon Corporal,' and even drank to his health. Honore, now caught up in he moment raised his glass and toasted Napoleon: "To the day of our revenge, your Majesty." It came as somewhat of a shock to see such devotion in a person who had been dead for two centuries. It gave me great cause to think of the power of the Little Emperor, for it upset many of the former ideas I had for the evening. As the hours ticked by and Martin served his fish, vegetables and potatoes for our guest, we toasted with wine and a little of Porous's bread, Napoleon kept up his patter. I learnt more about the philosophy of world history of the time than I had ever done in all my time on this earth in former studies. The thought came to me that time I had spent buried in books seemed now to be a waste.

 I turned my thoughts to Beethoven, starting with his 3rd Symphony on my music system to bring the conversion around to why he had changing the name 'Emperor' in honour of Napoleon to the 'Eroica' (heroic). I was hoping to get some exchange of emotional recall between my two guests, but Napoleon was too caught up in his own importance to hear the music and Beethoven could not hear a note anyway. So I signalled Martin to open more wine and then turned off the music after he had served each guest with another glass. "To your health Gentleman." We clicked our champagne glasses together before tasting instead another wine. I of course could not enjoy the alcoholic beverages because of my alcoholism, but settled for a sparkling water. As we settled back for coffee and cake, I tried to engage Beethoven by talking to him as if he wasn't deaf, but this soon proved hopeless. So I resorted to written communication and made myself popular with poor Ludwig by painting a picture in words for him, so that we could communicate despite his deafness. Beethoven seems to enjoy that but remained still little aloof.

Meanwhile Napoleon ate heartily, busy recalling his past battle encounters with Honore to notice the amount of effort both Martin and I had gone to preparing his meal. In particular the chocolate cake Martin had prepared for desert. As he presented Napoleon with a slender piece with whipped cream and a red liqueur running from the top over the cream, he remarked with some sarcasm: "I call this 'The Prince of the desert' in honour of the young royal nobleman you murdered, it seems without cause." Martin was doing his best to disturb the Emperor for his transgression in killing a young prince. The effort was worth it as Napoleon responded with a direct glare at Martin " Oh, poor soul , I should not have shot him." Then he paused, took a bite from the chocolate cake, considering the red liquor as symbolic of the blood of many and not as Martin had intended, the blood of one Prince. "People tend to forget the thousands of men killed in my campaigns, yet they always seem to recall the death of a lowly Prince." Napoleon continued: " Oh, I guess the world will never forgive me, but I had to do it at the time. He, like so many others now plotting against me, so many exiled royalists. I had to make an example of him as a message to others of royal blood who hated me and my cause for France." He waived his hand in dismissal of the thought: "That is past history and nothing can be done about it now." He seemed to have no shame or guilt about his killing of an innocent young man, for I was now leaning more to Martin's opinion of the little Emperor as he spoke these words. For a time Napoleon hesitated, waiving his spoon up and down, took a sip of his coffee and continued again: "I was the Emperor of the people that extended across the known world, have they all forgotten who I was?" I was a little incensed at his arrogance and narcissism, but held back my emotions. "But you inflicted much damage to the commerce of the world in your cause to control it." He quickly responded : "It is not as simple as that, let me show you." He began to rearrange the table setting, putting the Claret flask, the empty plates , the remaining desert and potatoes in various locations, so that it now resembled a map of Europe and great Britain . He reached over and took Beethoven's pencil from his hand using it as a pointer. Master Ludwig was incensed, but like me he kept his cool. Napoleon was on a roll now.

"This is France" he said, as he moved the lighted candle a little and this is England." He pointed to the claret flask as he moved it further away towards the edge of the table. "and those potatoes spread around, they are the countries of Europe, for these I had organised to do my bidding." He continued: "I caused, what you might call a blockade, so England could not trade with Europe without coming to me." It worked except for the bankers. Those who funded England out of its financial difficulties as a result of my blockade of their commerce." He further hesitation with a new frown on the forehead:
"It was a golden opportunity to destroy the strangle hold England held over the financial world at the time. If only those mongrel bankers had warmed to my ideals, the world would hav been a better place because of what I set in motion." he lied. Martin, Beethoven and I sat very quiet as Napoleon continued his monologue on his war efforts. The dialogue was broken occasionally by the now tipsy Honore commenting " How true it is." The table began to look like a battle field as Napoleon use knives, forks and spoons and ever empty dish as countries and food that was still edible, including the remaining bread as opposing armies. At an appropriate interval in the conversation I began to clear the table.Napoleon seems nor to notice and went on and on. My purpose having Napoleon as guest seemed to have been a mistake, that is until the hour of his departure. As he left and faded into the mist of the night, a wild storm broke out across the Universe and my windows rattled, lightning flashed across the sky, and ten thousand emotional soldiers in the afterlife appeared for a brief moment to welcome him back. Somehow it was the passion of the man that

was left behind with us. That passion left behind here on this plane, my own burning desire to do the very best with what talents I possessed for the remainder of my days. It was worth it just to have him here for such a brief time, despite his boastful claims, wild imaginings and grandiose idealism. For he was a guiding light in having Faith in what one believes, be it true or false. I would not call him for his services from the other side of the curtain again, I had touched the source of his passion and I had my own now to contend with. Beethoven, on the other hand had written on a slip of paper: " I am so glad to see him go." The Master Musician was now in a highly creative frame of mind, as the storm, the role of thunder and the lightning had effect the vibrations of the earth and for the moment Beethoven was already formulating wild notes on sheets of paper in the process of what may well be the makings of a 10th symphony. I had not noticed until then, the table was now full of sheets of disused paper he had dispensed with and other flat sheets of musical notes he no doubt intended to keep . Beethoven had taken over Napoleon's war game mapping with musical theory on sheets written in haste. He may deep down have felt the magnetic force of the personality of Napoleon but because he had no longer any respect for the man I didn't press him on this thought of mine. It was at this point that Beethoven took a sheet of manuscript from an old leather folder he had by the side of the table. He asked if he could have his pencil back and proceeded to write a full page of words. Beethoven gathered together the other remaining musical creations and tucked them into the old leather case then placing it under his left arm, picked up the pencil again and was using it like a conductors baton. He had been rather quiet all the evening but voiced: " I need to get some fresh air," and explained:"I shall step out in the garden for a moment." Old Honore Clauzel wiped his teary eyes and walked out with him to enquire why he had not left the 3rd Symphony as a tribute to the Emperor. Beethoven was heard to say: "He is not deserving of the title Emperor because he crowned himself, but my brave man, I did not entirely disregard his genius. I changed that symphony entitled Bonaparte to Eroica, which as you know means heroic. In that sense of leadership and devotion to his cause I named it, because he was."

 Martin and I began to clean up the aftermath of our meal and encounter with our former dinner guests, the two Masters at our table. I stepped out to invite them both in for a final night cap, but they were nowhere to be seen. As I cleared the scrunched up pieces of paper from the table, I noticed a sheet nearby on the floor, the last thing Beethoven had on before he took his fresh air stroll in my garden. It was one of a final page amendment to his Heiligenstadt Testament which he had no doubt dropped by accident.

 So I sat down with Martin over a coffee, and began to read it aloud. it was halfway through a sentence the page began: "... *and yet I found it impossible to say to others: speak louder: shout! for I am deaf! Alas! how could I proclaim that deficiency, a sense which ought to have been more perfect with me than with other men, - a sense which I once possessed in the highest perfection, to an extent, indeed, that few of my profession ever enjoyed! Alas, I cannot do this. Forgive me therefore when you see me withdraw from whom I would so gladly mingle. My misfortune is doubly severe from causing me to be misunderstood. No longer can i enjoy recreation in social intercourse, ...*" Martin and I concluded that maybe the Master did not mistakenly leave a sheet of his final Testament behind, but rather it was his way of excusing himself for his lack of communication on the night. I remarked to Martin, I believe that we all suffer for our art or lack of compassion. If we need to make any progress we have to go through our own fires of hell before relearning to trust in the slow work of God. Before we learn to put our boat of personality upon the waters of life, set the sail and go with the flow, then all it takes is just a slight touch of the rudder to stay on course.

Martin was in agreement and as for myself, I knew that if I needed my own muses to create a song or two in the future, all I had to do was tune in to my Great Tone Master, failing that, there is always Beethoven. On the back of the sheet of paper were some musical notes he had been working on silently while we ate our meal. He had taken a line from his opening title of the 3rd Symphony which read in German and Italian : "Composed to celebrate the memory of a great man," Then we noticed under the notes a further notation in pencil:" I see no reason to revise the name of the Symphony, he was not really a great man, but he was a hero to some." So there it was, he had spoken of it to Honore Clauzel as he stepped outside with the old soldier and now we had it in on paper. The hour was getting late as I ushered Martin out the front door with gratitude for all his efforts in cooking the meal and providing the desert. I returned to blow out the candle on the table and took up the pencil and wrote on the back of Beethoven's sheet of paper personal benefits I had gained from the night. 1. Have **faith** in my goals 2. I am commit with **a burning desire** to achieve them.3. **Listen to the tones of your Go**d **given nature**.

I was now satisfied that I was on the right path and the night had really worked out to my satisfaction. I blew out the candle and went to bed, lying on my back, consulting the spirit of my ancestors and discussing the nights activity with them. Old Honore Clauzel appeared in the midst of the spirits of my ancestors, smiled and waved a last goodbye. I had no notion of what Master would be at my table for the next Saturday night dinner and I decided to hand it over to the one who rules all. I was almost asleep when I had an afterthought. I got out of bed and made my way back to to the table. The moon was now shining brightly through the window and I made a further note on Beethoven's sheet of paper. I had written down my three points of reference for my goals, but I had not addressed a note to either Master, so I wrote a 'Thank you for coming to dinner' and added how I appreciated their input in guidance to my future objectives in life. I had a strange feeling the two old Masters might now come back long enough to let go the past and become friends in the heavenly realm thereafter. It was unlikely, as neither Master bothered to acknowledge one another throughout the dinner.

I left the note on the table with the hope that this may happen, reopened the balcony door just in case they revisited. I had the hope that Beethoven may return to collect the paper he left behind. maybe he had left it for Martin and my benefit. Either way it was in the Higher Power's hand and not mine for either or both Masters to revisit. I closed my eyes and soon fell into the lap of the Gods and as I drifted other Masters in the shadows came to me in my dreams.One was my old physician who stared :'One of the many assumed causes of Beethoven's deafness was metal poisoning from a medication he had been taking to help with his on-going malady. Among other evidence, the finding of shrunken cochlear nerves at his autopsy, consistent with axonal degeneration due to heavy metals such as lead. Chronic low level of lead exposure causes a slowly progressive hearing loss with sensory and autonomic findings, rather than the classic wrist drop due to motor neuropathy from sub-acute poisoning. Beethoven's physicians thought that he had alcohol dependence, as he did particularly like wine that happened to be tainted with lead as a preservative at the time. It may therefore have been Beethoven's chronic consumption of wine tainted with lead being a better explanation of his hearing loss than other causes, like that of a sexually transmitted disease.'

CHAPTER 4.

A VISION FROM ST. FRANCIS AND EMERSON

Nature itself can be both cruel and kind. A walk on the wild side of any bush or forest will bring the traveller into the presence of God as equally as that of the devil himself. It is a Garden of Eden of checks and balances. In the natural order of things, the bush possibly has no equal. It is for me the best I can offer to illustrate the workings of the mind of God. By way of a simple illustration, one tree may stand tall, spreading its strong branches of healthy growth, reaching out and ever upward to the sky, gaining strength from the sun and giving birdlife a place to build a home, feeding upon its seeds and singing for joy. It offers a canopy of protection for the flora living in its shadow or smaller plant life that grow from its seeds around its trunk, or indeed the animals feeding from the trees seeding offspring. All the while it's spreading its tentacle root system into the soil below the surface, absorbs nourishment from inorganic and organic matter and nourishing waters from former rain. That tree continuing the miracle of strengthening its root system, spreading its tentacles to stabilise its trunk, and continuing in the cycle of life. Just as equally another tree may be barely surviving, it's life being choked out of it by a clinging vine that appears to have more chance of survival than the source of its being. While yet another, in a time of drought, fire or flooding rains will perform yet another miracle. For one may clearly refuse to drop seeds to the surface floor for future growth of its offspring until it has been forged by fire. In Australia this is evident more often than not in summer months when fires are most frequent. Yet another tree conscious of this almost annual event has over a lifetime built up a thick trunk with a dark bark to save its skin from the damaging fire. One can also discover, after such apparent disasters, small saplings growing after renewing rainfall, replacing former parents turned to ashes by bushfire. Others trees in times of drought remain evergreen despite lack of rainfall, having retained excess waters from former rains in its trunk and root system to sustain life. Some trees are gnarled and twisted due to the environment they live in, while others cling to life in some awkward way having fallen on rocky ground where they hold onto life around rocks at their base penetrating deep into an earth surface nearby.

One may feel touched by the beauty of wildflowers, feel the pain of a stinging nettle, the soothing relief of a plant sap, bathe in the sound of cicadas, be amazed by the noise of chattering birds or awakened by the shadow of an eagle soaring in the heavens above. One may appreciate the wisdom of studying a single tree leaf vein or be saddened by the death of another fallen one. Be cautious of poisonous snakes lingering nearby in the grass, take care not to tread on a bull ants nest for fear of angering them or eat sparingly of bush bees nectar, wild berries or native fruits, keeping the balance of nature in check. Nature's bush has it all, the beautiful and the ugly, the cruel and the kind, the weak and the strong, in the balance of the cycle of life, all in the lessons of the God of nature for humanity.

It was one man from the township of Assisi, in Umbria Central Italy, that attuned himself to the fact of nature more than any other, and from the spirit of this nature he devoted himself by way of example how to live life to the fullest in service of his fellowman. That man was known as Francis of Assisi. He took from the nature of a tree and the life cycle of all that came within its universe, a way to live Christlike. Francis saw within the tree the words of Christ 's example, when he stated: "I am the vine, you are the branches," Francis added a further dimension: "For some of us are branches, some of us are leaves, some falling leaves, some fallen leaves, and we all come under the power of the sun, and like the Universal Father, Son and Spirit, we are all one." Like Christ, he did not need in-depth philosophical teaching to explain how it all works, he led by parable and he led by example. So it was that it came to me that he should be my next guest Master at my table. I had much to learn in my quest for cleansing and renewing the spirit of my own nature.

I was a little perplexed for a time as to who the other guest should be. For both Masters would not only need to be of benefit to me, but to each other, as after the lack of communication between Napoleon and Beethoven at the last dinner, I did not wish to make the same mistake twice. I would need to invite someone like St. Francis who had learnt to live in the moment in everyday life and did so with simplicity and humility. So it was that I entered the local bush near my home, lay my body back against the butt of a tree, like Andrew Carnegie had done when he visited me in that Park at the edge of the Rhine River in Cologne. Now in deep meditation, it did not take long for the appropriate guest to appear. For in the spirit world he had it on good authority that I had St.Francis in mind to come to the table as my guest. So it was that I decided, knowing something of his daily comings and goings, that I was convinced too choose Ralph Waldo Emerson to be my other guest at my table. He too was a humble man and one who lived an upright life with a philosophy of servitude for others. He, like Will Rogers, could so easily state:'I never met a man I didn't like," but I wanted to learn more than that from him. He, like in the teaching of Dale Carnegie, though not related to Andrew Carnegie, had a simple way of staying calm, cool and connected-he 'lived his life in day-tight compartments.' So it was that I considered the way of life of two great men of simplicity, one from the mid 13th century and the other from the 20th century. I believed by inviting both these Masters to my dining table, the philosophies of each would rub off on me and you dear reader. I had a mission to obtain a philosophy for a more simple way of living in what is a complicated fast paced 21st century world. So it is that I return now to give you but a brief look into the lives of these saintly noble gentleman before their appearance as Masters at my table. Enter one Francesco Bernardone, born 1182 to his father, Pieto, and Lady Pica of France. Pietos was a moderately wealthy family and well respected clothing merchants of Assisi, a small township in the Umbrian hilly district north of Rome and east of Florence.

The low rolling Umbria hills seem to have an excellent influence upon the poetic streak of human nature and someday I may well list the world's slender output of geniuses and tabulate according to their geographic background, for I have come to believe that highlands are the ideal breeding ground for people of poetic tendency. Little Francesco, let us call him Francis, for which he come to be known, had a natural poetic streak and was often heard singing in French but more often than not the native Italian tongue of the locals.

Francis was not a particularly scholarly youth although he studied Latin and French, he preferred to escape into the world of the troubadour, those lyric poets of southern France, Northern Spain and Italy. Writing in the languedoc Provence; troubadours flourished from the late 11th to the late 13th century, Their influence was unprecedented in the history of medieval poetry. Favoured in the courts, they had great influence on freedom of speech, occasionally intervening into the political arena, wooing women into men's quarters with elaborate love lyrics, expanding into ballads, tales of knights of the realm, a way of conversation in matters of the heart, religion and metaphysical satire. A troubadour therefore was one who invented new poems, elaborate love lyrics, stories and musical rhyme that has lasted to this very day.

Francis, it may be said, was more fond of worldly pleasures than reading and writing, and in that regard he was no different than any youth of today. He was probably expected to learn his Dad's lucrative trade as a local tailor, succeeding him in the business. It may have proved so, if it were not for a provincial war between Assisi and the neighbouring township of Perugia in 1202. Francis had only just recovered from a serious illness when he set out with the local youth to fight. Assisi lost-the battle and Francis was imprisoned for a year. On his release from prison and return to Assisi there was big celebration, for the war had ended. Francis was urged to come to the celebrations by his companions to help him forget his recent imprisonment, but he slipped away into distant hills, for the old Francis Bernardone no longer existed. It is not easy to glean from his history what Francis was about. Perhaps the thought filled statements of Thoreau on man may give a hint: "Most men lead lives of quiet desperation." I think Francis quelled his desperation by following his heart in lieu of his head. For the other memorable statement of Thoreau : "Every man's heart beats to the tune of a different drummer; let him follow the sound of the drummer that he hears." Francis did that and his prayers centred around God and nature, confirm, a way of life uniquely lived. For other than his mentor Jesus, who of course it is reported died on a cross for mankind to be released from their defects of character. Francis took his place among the poorest of the poor, died in a paupers grave, body worn out long before his appointed time by a life of labour and want, his sound faith living on, as it does in all who believe. He was our divine comedy of laughable wisdom, which may yet prove to be the better course of spiritual food than that of a doctorate in theology. We have not had another like him in a long time as it would take an almost superhuman effort to accomplish or indeed play the role of Francis in these times. Perhaps Mother Theresa of Calcutta of the 20th century did live in a Francis conscious way and of course many a poet, artist and writer of note, has by necessity and not choice lived a paragraph of St.Francis story in private poverty for the sake of their art. Francis was not a social worker, nor a modern day evangelistic activist, in the vein of a Martin Luther King, even though he preached to larger multitudes than any other man before or after him. He was not interested in religious doctrine or written philosophy to live by, even though he was the author of more spiritual prayers, poetic quotes and songs than almost any other man.

The man who was later to be canonised a saint was not out to form a new cult or religious school of thought. So many people followed his way of life at the time and ultimately his teachings and followers had no choice but to form a defined organisation in their gatherings of prayer, communal living and working tirelessly for the poor. It was not Francis' style, he was not fitted for being a head of an organisation. He had no choice but to leave such things to others of greater ambition to perform executive orders.

Francis was not diplomatic in his approach to any given situation that irked him and on more than one occasion did what no-one else had done then or since. The first impulsive act was during an attendance at Easter Sunday Mass, when all the local wealthy middle class displayed their finery in dress, jewellery and apparel in proof of their importance. When even the priest was dressed in garments of opulent splendour and the altar itself was adorned with the finest of golden candle holders and chalices of gold, Francis jumped to his feet in the midst of the ceremony and uttered at full voice something in the vein of any critic: No! No! No! this is not the way of God, no it should not be the way of the church." Well, it wasn't exactly those words but something similar enough to embarrass his Father and Mother seated there in their finery. Francis abruptly left the proceedings, returning to his father's business and took a quantity of the best materials off the shelves, gathered his horse from the stable and headed out to the nearest township. Therein he sold all the material and his horse and made his way to the local Dominican friar who refused his offering. Francis, insulted by the priest's refusal to accept his gift, threw the loot out into the street to be gathered by passing rich and poor alike. On return home his angered Father had him locked away for a time and then hauled him before a local magistrate to admit his sorrow and repay his dues for the goods taken. In truth Francis in his own mind probably only took what he considered his share for fair labour to the business. He refused to yield before the Magistrate so his father took him off to the Bishop but Francis refused to acknowledge his authority. Then and there he stripped himself naked in the presence of Bishop and father announcing: "Until now I considered you Father on earth, but no more shall that be. For I have but one Father now, and He is my heavenly one. Only for him will I pay homage and work for until my dying day."

On another occasion, Francis set himself as a newly appointed brother of Christ, dressed in sack cloth with a rope cord to hold his now poor man's tunic in place, went to the Holy land to inform the Pope of his intention in following Christ in a natural way, living as a poor man, feeding the poor with bread for their stomach and spiritual harmony for their soul and encourage others join him in a similar lifestyle. Its was to everyones great surprise then the Francis baptised the Pope on the spot into the Christian faith of a new brotherhood. Imagine anyone doing that to a Muslim leader of our times or indeed to Adolf Hitler at the height of his program of Jewish annihilation, recommending that he embrace Jewish doctrine. Nor indeed convincing Vladimir Putin to turn from Orthodox Christian to Catholic! For that matter blessing an instrument of death and forgiving it the for the torture it may cause. Francis in his latter days did this on many an occasion. Indeed, he had not found a cult nor a way of forced dogma. God forbid there are so many of those fanatics in our day. Nor did he promise to cure the world of virus by some kind of spiritual means. For Francis would have dispensed with them all like Mohammad marching on Mecca to voice without bloodshed a new way of belief. For Francis, inspirer of the meek was an expert psychologist, for he understood his fellow man, he knew how to dig deep into the soul and ignite a light that in most men had all but been extinguished.

Conversely he seemed more popular amongst Protestant sect than Catholics. Those of that persuasion seem to at least understand him a little better as a typical representative of a medieval mentality, overlooking unreasonable and unusual acceptance of disease and other afflictions of poor hygiene that he had advocated could be eradicated with a bar of soup and a cup of soup. Francis himself ate moulding bread from the bins of Assisi whilst feeding the poor of the city on the best of dough given as charity by kindly folk. Who can foresee but a man who visualised Assisi upside down, the poor being on the top and the rich on the bottom. He spent his nights in prayer, fasting into hallucinations, suffering stigmata on both hands and feet. This was after his visit to Mount Alverno where he may well have penetrated his wrist and feet in an imitation of Christ during a trance like state, not realising in reality what he had done. To examine further serves no purpose, but followers at the time looked upon it as a miracle.

There are the simple people of this world who are devoid of inner complications. Those perform simple tasks in honest, sober, willingness to serve. They too gain the respect and possible affection of the mass of mankind, because they excel in stewardship as they so rightfully see as their duty. Then there are those like St. Francis, who seem so simple because they are so hopelessly complicated and that is at best the only hope we have of explaining them. They are the ones who are most likely to move the world out of its hum- drum common existence and do so with far more infinitely far reaching beneficial results than the greatest of conquering heroes.. Then there are the masses of men who muddle their way through life, devoid of its meaning and its spiritual significance. St. Francis, like my other intended guest, Ralph Waldo Emerson were not so far apart in their methods of leading by example, forsaking the materialism of their time with a focus on the reality in the here and now.

I had already set in motion St. Francis to arrive for the dinner on the next Saturday evening, and now Emerson was waiting my call to introduce him to you the reader before his acceptance of my request for him to join us for dinner. It would be extremely unfair of me not to give you the reader a brief of Emerson the man, for though he be the lesser of the two Masters at my table, he relates

to my personal quest of spiritual understanding. He never the less is to play an important part as his views on belief were not unlike St. Francis in that the order of things centred on nature. For now I shall tell you of that kindly loveable Ralph Waldo Emerson, who for his time in the decades of the first half of the 19th century, there was no other of equal standing in the Americas. Emerson saw the first light of day in Boston, Massachusetts on May 25th 1803. He inherited seven dynasties of family members who were all ministers.
He was the last in line of a family of ministers who through the ages were as devoted to their religious occupation as Amschel Meyer, the founder of Rothschild and his descendants were devoted to being financiers. He was schooled in the John Harvard education principles at the University founded by the educator and graded with his name too. After graduation in 1821 he tried his hand at school teaching but finding it not to his liking returned to Cambridge to study theology, qualifying as a minister of religion in 1826. The old time religion of his fathers and forefathers was being progressively liberalised with new ideas. So the traditional ways of the trinity of Father, Son and Holy Ghost in certain sects to become God the Father only and the Trinity went out with the baby and the bath water were tossed out.

The desire of such new ways of religious practice for many followed the way of Christ to the letter and were considered unworthy to be called a part of Christianity because of their radical views. Others followed the guidelines of Unitarians believing the Bible to be the only source of fact but they demanded to interpret Holy scripture as they pleased and as one might draw an analogy of the doctrine of the declaration of Independence, courageously but with some interpolation, championed human freedom. They evolved from a sect whose foundation goes back centuries in European history but with no record of when, nor where the ideas of the religious philosophy had its initial foundation. The Unitarians of Emersons era evolved to reject Calvinistic and Lutheran doctrine of salvation, inherent guilt and eternal punishment, for they used further reference material outside the Bible, suggesting that the divinity of the human soul be found in such works and even more correctly interpreted the stories in the Bible. Emerson, who was on the fringes of these movements got himself married at the age of twenty six and a year later becomes a widower. It was around this time that the young preacher turned away from the teachers according to his ancestors and ever so politely got himself into disagreement with his flock.

In his utter truthful expression of his opinion, Emerson stated that he was willing to only celebrate the Communion of the Faithful as an 'act of spiritual remembrance.' In that sense he was aligning his belief with that of Catholicism; i.e. that the announcement of Christ at his last supper in serving bread and wine to his Apostles reportedly stated: "When you eat this bread and drink this cup, do this in commemoration of me. For unless you do so, you shall not have life in you. Those who eat the flesh of the son of man and drink his blood have life everlasting." It has been a bone of contention through the ages of Christendom, especially among non spiritualists, that Christ was advocating to take Communion as an example of doing his work here on earth as an offering to

God by such action. Spiritualists to the contrary believe that by eating the bread and drinking the wine Christian's partake of the spirit of Christ and exemplify his sacrifice by his death on the cross, the aftermath of which is the third person of the Trinity whom God has imposed for all mankind to benefit from in the here and now. It is both a simple and equally complicated explanation. Suffice to say that the traditionalists follow the human action of Christ in eating the host like a prayer of remembrance. Spiritualist on the other hand are caught up with the benefits of the belief in the third person of the Trinity being present at the time of partaking of Communion. They believe it to be a gift imposed on all by God for mankind's salvation as a result of Christ's sacrificial death on the cross. In Emerson's case the congregation complained and as he could not see it their way, he resigned.

So it was that he could no longer be a parish minister, but rather a lay preacher of the world at large. So without any further ado, he took to the sea and headed out for England. He soon become friends with Thomas Carlyle, an acrimonious Scot who lost his faith, became a British historian, satirical writer, translator, philosopher, mathematician and teacher. He suffered much with stomach issues from a bad diet and was often a grouch of the worst order. Carlyle remained friends with his American preacher, who but for a bout of TB as a child was blessed with good health and equally good diet. Carlyle unlike Emerson, devoted his spare time to belief in Deism; the philosophical position that rejects revelation as a source of religious knowledge and asserts reason and observation of the natural world as sufficient to establish the existence of a Supreme being or Creator.

Emerson, who himself become a renowned essayist, poet and popular philosopher achieved world fame as a lecturer and author of such essays as " Self-Reliance," The essay " History," and "The Over- Soul," and " Fate" The two men complement each other and remained firm friends and corresponded till the end of their days. They had one common bond, which must have given them both satisfaction. They both believed that the progress of the human race depended upon good leadership. In their ties and those since, mankind has taken the collective view of leadership through Church and State and in particular has come through past wars where leadership of despots was the norm for a time,. We, the modern man have become sceptical of dictatorship or any individual form that smacks of power. Carlyle and Emerson, in their time knew the history of our world and held their viewpoints with the courage of their conviction in spite of individual moral doubt. So, in that sense I looked forward to hearing further his viewpoints during our planned dinner engagement. On his return to America, Emerson moved into the family manse with his mother in Concord. So in order to provide for his simple needs he hit the lecture circuit. Two years later he married for the second time, built himself a house near the old family homestead, and became Concord's most distinguished citizen.

Lecturing was still a very uncomplicated affair. During the next half century, Emerson as a lay preacher lectured as he travelled throughout the land, spreading the gospel pf physical and spiritual independence; urging all listeners to try all things and due to that experience, do what proved to be best. Occasionally he spoke a little more plainly, pointing out the defects of historical Christianity and begged his listeners to cast conformity aside and get in direct touch with the Deity. The word of his so called heresy got back to the Deacons and Supervisors in charge of New England Churches and the theological seminaries. Emerson was asked to explain himself, but with the wisdom of foresight, he declined. He explained that he was entitled to a judgement only by a jury of his peers and maintained that his detractors hardly qualified as such. Like all dogs of pray do when cornered, they reacted with much bark but little bite. There were attempts to isolate him from the religious community, but Emerson who preferred his own company and that of a few friend in common did not react, as he had nothing in common with them anyway. Whilst he did not actually love his fellowman, he did have a great respect for individual opinion. Whilst he never gave them praise for their actions, he did try to show them a better, happier and more reasonable way of living and thinking. He, as a man of the cloth wandered alone in his cause and as such was truely a representative of the people.

Emerson lived until almost eighty. He continued to work steadily and regularly at his literary labour, baking in his own melancholy meditations. His output was large but nothing to the extent of a Voltaire, or other notables, but his efforts of influence in the difficult business of making people think for themselves was a credit to the man. It was his commitment to the cause, his tenacity that enlightened all with a living proof of practicing what he preached. Emerson will always be remembered as a man who wrote with his heart rather than his brain. So it is that I look forward to next Saturday where I will have as Masters at my table the man with a simplistic view of nature being the source to an encumbering God and the other a prophet of the heart. For now I had best not tarry, run along to the store to collect the groceries I needed to prepare the meal for my guests. The task of preparing the food, a well planned simple menu, that is easy to prepare . Oh! and then an afterthought, I jotted on my grocery list to get two sticks of crusty bread for St. Francis to enjoy, instead of his usual diet from some nearby garbage bin. Also, not to overlook the culinary delights of Emerson, I added red wine to the list and considered perhaps I may find a pouch of snuff, for I understood it was his only vice.

An interruption in my meditation just prior to the arrival of my guests annoyed me. It was from some sailor of misfortune at sea who appeared from the other side. "It seems your old fellow guest has landed himself in New Zealand. He is on a boat now which should arrive in Sydney Harbour at this appointed hour. So I suggest you concentrate your powers to the docks and keep an eye out for his boat." I thanked the sailor for bringing the delay of Emerson to my attention. I had in reality landed by ship on that very same birthing place a year ago to the day, so it wasn't hard for me to visualise the scene there. Sure enough the old Emerson obviously suffering from his rheumatism, stiffly made his way down the ships ramp to arrivals. I suggested he take his time and not to worry as I would arrange for a friend to come and guide him to my home for our appointed dinner engagement. " I got a bit lost." he remarked. " I get rather vague at times these days, but invariably there is always someone to help me find my way to my preconceived destination."

The old man was in his eightieth year as I remember. He did not see the next New Year in before the angel of death made his call. He didn't apologise, but rather turned his mishap into a positive. I noted that throughout his life, his attitude was always looking at it all as a glass half full not half empty. I explained that I had to get back to the reality of my kitchen before my other guest arrive. Emerson understood, and before coming out of my meditative state I telepathically contacted my friend Tony the Uber driver, who said he would pick up Emerson up at the dock within the hour. I explained "He has no money from the heavens, so I will pay you the fee for services rendered when next we meet." Tony was in agreement, so I left my trance-like state to get on with the meal preparation.

It seems like that in no time I had the meal prepared. I returned to my meditative state just as my guests simultaneously arrived at my door. St Francis was garbed in his brown sack robe with rope around his waist to give the appearance of a belt. The only purpose was to tighten the robe a little on the waistline, to hold the make shift wooden cross like a knife at his side. The only additional items of interest, his hand-made sandals of leather and twine. It seemed to me that Francis liked simplicity in dress as in his nature and did not much care for fashion. Emerson had obviously changed his garb from that of his attire on-board ship, he had dressed in a white shirt with high collar and a small scarf tucked behind a black vest and coat to match his well pressed trousers and clean black shoes. I reckoned this attire had been worn many time on his lecture tours. It was old but could still pass as being in fashion in any company. Both men sensed that I was checking out their attire and as Emerson took his place at the table, he looked knowingly at St. Francis in his garb, which might even today for anyone interested in living a spiritual life be considered a brand statement. Emerson was first to speak: "For, the advantages which fashion values, are plants which thrive in very confined localities, in a few streets, namely. Out of this precinct, they go for nothing; are of no use with the farm, nor in a forest, in the market, in war, in nuptial society, in the literary or scientific circle, at sea, in friendship, in heavenly thought or virtue." Then as a bridge to justify his barb being a little more in tune with the day, and so as to not bring St. Francis down he added: "There is only one reason for dressing well, namely that dogs respect it, and will not attack you in good clothing." St.Francis was in agreement as he had affinity with all animals and had even calmed wolves in the wild.

The subject matter turned to food and both men got into deep conversation about giving instead of receiving, using food as the basis for their discussion. I poured both a red wine and left some bread for their communion like consumption, while I hurried to the stove to pour each a bowl of vegetable soup. I had done nothing more than boil a variety of mixed vegetables, added vinegar and a little salt to reduce any bitterness, pureed it all through sieve, returned it to simmer in the saved boiled water, adding a spoonful of gourmet dried vegetables powered with a dash of turmeric to enhance flavour and colour. My two Masters continued in deep discussion as I returned with the soup. The two men complemented each other with such clear natures as they sipped away on their soup and continued their discussion. The discussion led to how St, Francis first became aware of his natural affinity with the Universe. "It all started with sister bird." he said. "I was but a young man recovering from a fever and when the fever broke I lay by the window in my room and a little sparrow come through the window and landed on my shoulder. I knew then that my destiny was to change," He paused: "It didn't happen right away though as I was destined for war and prison before the change in my life really began to come into effect." He began to explain how he had heard Christ speak to him from the crucifix, telling him that his destiny was not that of the common man.

He carefully took the makeshift crucifix from his rope belt and studied it symbolic significance to the statement he had just made. Then he added "All things under the heavens are my brothers and sister, brother sun, sister moon, the pain in this ass of a body is my brother, as are all things of nature," Just then a great commotion could be heard from outside in the garden. The large red gum that overshadowed the garden from the summer heat was full of birds of every kind. The birds were making such a noise of cross chatter it left all other sound barely inaudible. St. Francis having run into the garden, looked up at the tree and remarked: "I know why. They do that sometimes when I am around. they merely want me to say a few words to them and then they will go away."

 Francis spoke so gently: "My little brothers and sisters, you know how much I love you. Tonight this kindly man is having me as a dinner guest with another gentleman of supreme knowledge too. So you can see that it would not be polite of me to talk for too long as the food he has cooked would be spoilt. So, now would you all please go back to your nests and rest.It is time for you to go to sleep anyway. Good night my little brothers and sisters, I love you so very dearly, but that must be all for this evening,"

 At that point the birds took to wing with coloured feathers like a rainbow cloud in the sky." One old pelican who was slower off the mark waited to be fed something, I called out to the kindly saint: "Would some bread do?" Francis took a tiny piece, then knelt by the birds side and fed him: "And now my fine feathered friend, that is enough; now off to bed with you." The Pelican in complete obedience took to wing heading for the coast. Francis returned to the dining table as I served up the main of barbecued fish, Mediterranean salad, dashed with balsamic vinegar, a dash of lemon juice and fried potatoes as an additive. Emerson had the larger appetite of the two Masters, but neither over ate,; one being used to eating a lot of food throughout his lifetime and the other a careful small quantity due to lack of need for his age. Francis did not need any further example of his affinity with nature as the appearance of the birds expressed his feelings and his philosophy of life. Emerson as he had so often done in his lifetime retreated into himself. As I poured his coffee and watched him partake of a little of the snuff I had provided, I took the opportunity to request of him a little example of living life in daylight compartments.

I had previously informed the guest of my long standing wound in my heart for the loss of my second eldest son who died by his own hand near two decades ago. I was not so much struggling with his being in the spirit world now, but of the loss of ever seeing him again in this lifetime or the next , due to the circumstances of his tragic end. For some strange reason he, unlike my Masters would not come to my Table. It was my belief that he suffered much on the other side for his action, but I took surety in the fact that I handed him over to the spirits of my ancestors of the past on frequent occasions before I fell into slumber. The hour was getting late so I pressed Emerson for an answer on his living in daylight compartments. The answer come in a roundabout way." Do you have a photocopier?" he said. I answered in the affirmative. So with that the old nobleman took a rather large notebook from his coat pocket."This is my daily diary." he said."You will find the answers herein for your purposes." He then insisted that I photocopy the entries for January 27th and 28th., 1842. I did so and returned the diary to him. He said no more, but added just one piece of advice: " Trust in the slow work of God."

 As a final gesture St. Francis asked if he could say grace after our meal and on my acknowledge began: "We give thee thanks O' Almighty God , for all thy bounty…" Then he hesitated and went into a trance like state, thus began that well known prayer of his that has captured many a humble person on their pilgrimage to sainthood. "Lord, make me an instrument of your peace, where there is hatred, let me sow love, where there is injury, pardon, where there is doubt, faith, where there is despair, hope, where there is darkness, light , where there is sadness, joy. God grant not so much that I be consoled, as to console, to be understood as to understand, to be loved as to love, for it is in giving that we receive, it is in pardoning that we ourselves are pardoned and it is in dying that we are born to eternal life." It was just after midnight and the candle in the middle of my table began to flicker. It was a time of departure, and as quickly as they had arrived, my two guests disappeared,. I returned to the kitchen, cleared the remaining dishes of the table, loaded my dishwasher and returned to the table to recap on the lessons learnt from the evening.

The copies for Emerson diary entries for the given dates were there in front of me, so I began to read by the light flowing into my dining room from sister moon. It was clearly in Emerson's hand writing on 27th January 1842.

:My son Waldo died today. He was nearly 5 years old. My wife and I called him "Willie' so as that w he would not be confused when my name was called by wife . friend or neighbour. It was only a week ago that we three sat by the fire side ,as he hammered away on a piece of wood .I remarked to my wife at the time. that I considered he may well be a carpenter when he grows up. as he is always nailing something together or bang-

ing away with timber with some imagination ve construction. We are so sad this day and will surely miss him."

The very next day, January 28th he wrote in his diary; *The neighbour called this morning, he was having trouble assisting a cow who was giving birth at the time. I held/ed him with the delivery, it was hard work for the cow, calf and for that matter us, but it was worth it. God in nature personified. A joy to behold.*

So the lessons were clear to me now as shared by the Masters at my table this evening. Pay attention to the lessons God teaches through nature and the universe, be charitable in my undertakings and trust in his slow work in setting me on the course he has mapped out for me. And of course the diary entries, I gleaned the message : 'sufficient to the day is the trouble that is in it.' So, let go the yesterdays and live in the present, one day at a time. It was lights out for me then and so I relived the day, felt happy and contented that all went according to plan. I gave thanks to the God of my own understanding, to the nature of my Masters who come to my bidding at the evening meal and the lessons therein learnt.

CHAPTER 5.

ENTER BILL WISLON AND DR. BOB SMITH

A new Saturday dawned with my mood being somewhat sombre. I had not slept very well and was suffering the after-effect of consuming too much sugary desert the evening before. I awoke with a sugar hit hang-over The effect of consumption of sugary desert is always a pleasantly heightened delight for me but it always has a downside later. My chemical imbalance that rendered me an alcoholic was not just the fact that I could not stop my drinking once I started, but that the ethyl alcohol as a result of the fermentation process in the making wine, spirit or even beer rendered me an addict. The medical profession call alcoholism a disease but I have a sneaking suspicion its sugar addiction that' heightens my addiction to alcohol. The consumption always gave me a high when I drank which after over indulgence left me feeling hopelessly down in a dark hole. This morning was the aftermath of eating far too much chocolate the evening before but was relieved that it was not an over indulgence in alcohol. Sobriety came after much regret and I could not afford to repeat my old life-style.

 Alcohol for a time was my only friend, but I had long since burnt all bridges that caused my falling to the bottom of the heap. It was before the realisation that I was alcoholic and had to do something about my addiction. Tragic circumstances had ended all that I thought life was about. Now my past life, and the material things of my old world had faded to nothingness. The fear of what would become of me could only be quelled for a time with even more drinking, turning to other lovers instead letting God of my own understanding guide me. The final straw came when I crossed that thin red line and found myself a screaming mess in my first rehab. It would not be my last before I had the realisation that I had lost my way, that I was powerless over not only alcohol but everything that my former life had given me as good cause for living .

The road back to sobriety was slow. Providence dictated that I was moved into a hospital bed next to a recovering alcoholic who happened to be a well known psychiatrist. He had obviously had another bust on the booze and had to restart his recovery programme all over again. He did not seem to be too fazed about this and instilled in me that recovery comes a day at a time and the answer was not to take the first drink. He said "It's the first drink that does all the damage." I could relate to that as one drink was too many and a thousand not enough for me. I just couldn't stop once I started. Of course I didn't recognise that I was an alcoholic at the time, but he soon wised me up to that fact. Every night my alcoholic friend would ask me to sit by his side and take notes.The wisdom that flowed from the man astounded me. I did not know it at the time but he was quoting directly from the Big Book of Alcoholics Anonymous; a veritable bible for AA fellows of like minded addicts. It was on my last night in rehab that he called me aside to suggest I attend an AA meeting and just let it flow over me. He stated with conviction: "You are a dyed in the wool alcoholic Doug. How do I know this? Because when you walked in here for the first time, I saw myself in the mirror at your age." I had no place to go when I left the hospital so I took my lonely self off to the next AA meeting and from that day forward, my life changed for the better.

I showered, shaved and sat down to meditate on my next two dinner guests, I had been milling over the excesses of my drinking life and the consequences of my actions back then. An awakening thought occurred that my next two guests should be none other than the founders of the AA programme. I knew so much now about these two founders of Alcoholics Anonymous. Bill Wilson, the stockbroker and his co- founder Dr Bob Smith. Both once hopeless drunkards found a way to sobriety and pasted it on to the likes of me and millions of other former drinkers. I ascertained that I would need some assistance during the evening meal and decided to call on a friend and fellow Alcoholic. His real name I dare not utter as it would break an AA tradition of maintaining personal anonymity. As for my own, I have long since accepted that many of my friends outside AA know that I am Alcoholic and as I am retired I have no fear of business or clientele being drawn into my fellowship to adversely effect the principles of AA's spiritual foundations, its workings, its service to others or indeed its tradition of not seeking financial benefit nor other benefit by media promotion. I conclude that It is not that I seek personally rewards or gifts from breaking my own anonymity, it is more to the fact that I find I am more often than not in the company of people who do drink. I find it much easier to let them know upfront that I am an alcoholic and thus gain their respect by not offering me any drink that may contain alcohol. For if I were to partake even socially in the drinking habit, it would not be too long before I would once more be in the the grip of the grape. As for my AA fellows, I with ardent vigour continue to maintain their anonymity, for I do adhere to protecting their rights and that of our programme.

So for the sake of my helping hand in preparing the meal and joining with these Masters at my table in a fine social discourse, in order to protect his anonymity, he will be known as "my friend." On my inviting him to join in the dinner he felt it more an honour to be of service than a chore. Like me he so wished to meet these two gentlemen who indirectly saved our lives by founding the programme, coming up with twelve suggestions for maintaining sobriety and helping others to do the same. It is equally these twelve traditions that has AA operating since its first meeting of the founders in Akron, Ohio in 1935.
And so it came to pass on that Saturday event that my AA friend and I, prepared the meal for our guests. As Americans we figured that they would enjoy a variety of popular local foods. So we hit upon the idea of a veritable smorgasbord of food variety for their choosing as their dinner. We would start with small hamburgers of both meat and cheese followed by traditional gourmet fast foods of bacon sliders, green chilli, all as an entree. As for

the mains, a poke bowl, of saucy tuna fish, sticky brown rice, carrots and cucumber with lots of avocados topped with spicy mayo. I was for Kentucky fried chicken as an added extra and was persuaded by my friend, who is more health conscious than yours truly, only to purchase, in his words 'a small quantity of those greasy fried chicken wings at our local KFC.

In my absence my friend decided to cook a traditional apple pie served with whipped cream for desert. I helped him as much as my limited cooking ability would let me. However, I soon realised his cooking expertise rendered me more a hinderance than a help, so I politely left him with the preparation of the remaining meals and quietly withdrew to the dining room to set the table for the evening event. Once I was satisfied that all was in order and could smell the apple pie baking in the oven, I knew we were ready to serve our guests. So sitting in the lotus position I began to meditate.

It has always been a common practice in writing an essay, manuscript for study purposes or indeed a novel, to begin with a forward, followed by an introduction of the characters, before getting into the body of the subject matter. In my considered opinion I believe I have covered the forward with respect to AA but not quite the detailing, apart from a little of my own story, of the introduction of those founders who are to be our guests, Masters at my table. To this end I believe you the reader will be interested in a formidable opinion of a medical professional as convincing testimony of the tormented suffering of an alcoholic and a witness to the recovery of one by a member of the medical establishment who considered his method of recovery somewhat unique and later wrote a brief introduction to the first of what is commonly called 'The Big Book of Alcoholics Anonymous.' So it was that I consulted the good medical doctor in his heavenly realm to introduce the workings of the book, which in turn he used to introduce Bill Wilson, the co- founding father of our fellowship, the first of my evening guests. Dr Silkworth advised me to read the letter from the 'Big Book' word for word, referring me to its inclusion as his opinion. I reread the forward in Alcoholics Anonymous and came to the Doctors Opinion:

"To Whom it May Concern: I have specialised in the treatment of alcoholism for many years. In late 1934 I attended a patient who, though he had been a competent businessman of good earning capacity, was an alcoholic of a type I had come to regard as hopeless. In the course of his third treatment he acquired certain ideas concerning a possible means of recovery. As part of the rehabilitation he commenced to present his conceptions to other alcoholics, impressing upon them that they must do likewise with his method. This has become the basis of a rapidly growing fellowship of those men and their families. This man and over one hundred thousand others appear to have recovered. I personally know scores of cases who were of a type with whom other methods had failed completely. These facts appear to be of extreme medical importance; because of the extraordinary possibilities of rapid growth inherent in this group they may mark a new epoch in the annals of alcoholism. These men may well have a remedy for thousands of such situations. You may well rely on anything they say about themselves. very truly yours. Dr William D Silkworth, MD "

The good doctor later gave further opinion of Bill Wilson: "His alcoholic problem was so complex, and his depression so great, that we felt his only hope would be through what we then called 'moral psychology,' and we doubted if even that would have any effect. However, he become sold on the idea of he and his co founder Dr Bob Smith. Together they developed simple steps of the AA programme, helping suffering alcoholics like themselves. He has not had a drink for many years. I see him now and then and he is as fine a specimen of manhood as one could wish to meet."

 My mind was set now on recalling the lives of Bill and Bob, the founders of Alcoholics Anonymous. To be fair I really needed them to go back to the beginning of their programme for Alcoholics. I reckoned it to be paramount in my thinking as to the spiritual benefits to be gained in my quest. Bill Wilson's story seemed to be as good a place as any to get the ball rolling. For he was first cab of the rank so to speak in discovering this way of staying sober and writing a programme of recovery for the still suffering alcoholic. In my meditative state I asked Bill to give us a brief of his life. A typical alcoholic way of sharing is to begin with what happened, what changed and what it's like now. In this vain Bill Wilson began to tell his story. My mind was open to the muse of Bill and whilst he didn't speak aloud I heard it all in my head.

"We were new enlisted young officer graduates from Plattsburgh when the world war fever ran high. The first citizens in the New England town to which we were assigned took us into their homes and made us feel heroic. Here was love, applause, war: moments sublime with intervals hilarious. I felt part of life at last and in the midst of it all I discovered liquor. In time we sailed for England, I was lonely and again turned to liquor. At twenty two I returned home a veteran of foreign wars. I fancied myself a leader of men, head of vast enterprises which I would manage with utmost assurance. I studied law and was employed as an investigator for a surety company for a time. My job took me to Wall Street and there I become interested in the market. I ascertained that many people lost money but some became very rich. So why not I? I studied economics and business as well as law, and nearly failed my final exams because I was too drunk to think or write. Though my drinking was not yet continuous it disturbed my wife." By the time I completed my law degree I knew that not to be my direction in life." So with delusions of grander and my leadership aspirations I headed for Wall Street and began trading in what was known then as penny dreadfuls. They were cheap, rather unpopular stocks but I reasoned that one day they would rise and make me rich."

 Bill broke off his train of thought to explain that most people lost money in stocks through ignorance of the market. How he gave up his position with a stockbroker and convinced his wife Lois to give up her job too. So together they roared off on a motor cycle together with tent, blankets, a change of clothing and three large volumes of financial reference material. "I funded the trip with monies I had won on speculation." he continued: "We covered the whole eastern United States in a year. At the end of it my reports to Wall Street procured me a position there with a huge expense account." I let Bill's voice rest for a time in my head, recalling that for a few years the Midas touch threw money and applause his way.

 The boom of the roaring twenties was in full swing, people like Bill spent in thousands and bled in millions. He made a host of fair weather friends as his excessive drinking continued. The Stock Market and Golf fever went hand in hand. Moving to an affluent area in the country he was often seen well tanned at golf club bars of the well to do. The local banker watched him with amused skepticism as Bill whirled fat checks in and out of the bankers till.

 The money ran out when all hell broke loose in the 1929 stock market crash. The job went and Bill found another but the excess of drinking soon put pay to that. Lois kept her part time work with enough money to put food on the table. Gradually things got worse and her parents saved the house by paying the mortgage. Bill promised to stop drinking but soon liquor ceased to be a luxury, it became a necessity. A tumbler full of gin followed by half dozen beers would be required before he could eat any breakfast. Stock markets were at an all time low point by 1932 and somehow Bill formed a buyers group. He was to share in the profit but another prodigious bender and the chance vanished. He had made a lot of sweet promised to Lois and finally a wake up call. Lois happily observed that he meant business, and he did. Even before he got home from seeking work, he was drunk again. He tried and failed so many times, it was to no avail. All-night benders, withering nerves, stealing from his wife's slender purse to once more go on an all-night bender. the process continued.

The body endured this punishment for two more years. The stock market would recover but he would not. The hidden bottles of gin found and drunk and the cycle repeated, Bill just could mot stop drinking. A doctor came and gave him some sedatives to help him sleep. He took the sedatives and washed them down with liquor. People feared for his sanity. He could eat nothing without first drinking. He was grossly underweight from the damage to his system. A family physician placed him in a known hospital for mental and physical rehabilitation for alcoholics. Under the so called belladonna treatment his brain cleared. Hydrotherapy and mild exercise helped. He had been seriously ill bodily and mentally but through it all he recovered. Doctors had explained his position, at least from a medical viewpoint. He felt he understood himself then and went forward with hope and confidence that he would drink no more. It became Bill's routine to go to town regularly to trade and he made a little money. He believed at the time self knowledge was the answer and for four months it seemed to be but it was not. The curve of his decent into a hell again was like he fell over a cliff. The excessive drinking and foggy head landed him back in hospital again. "This was to be the finish of me." Lois was informed by the doctors that it would all end in heart failure during delirium tremors or he would develop a wet brain. She would soon have to hand him over to an asylum or an undertaker. Bill had prided himself on his ability to beat all odds, win at any cost, as in his mind he had a capacity to surmount any obstacles but now he was plunged into darkness. How could he ever stop drinking? Would he ever be able to make amends to his wife for the troubles he caused her?

It was all over and in his despair found that bitter morass of self pity. He was spent, a physical and mental wreck, quicksand surrounded him in all directions. He had met his match and alcohol was his master. Friends and past clients resigned themselves to the certainty that he would have to be shut up somewhere or he would stumble along to a miserable end. How dark its was before the dawning.

At this point in Bill's conversation and my recall of his life as a drinker, I ceased my connection with this Master and his story to ultimate sobriety. I figured I best set the table for the appointed hour was near. My friend of AA persuasion had everything on the ready for the meal. The candle lit and places set, I added a jug of ice water and some glasses on the dining table for my non alcohol drinking guests. Knowing Bill's habit of excessive verbosity a little hydrate fluid may well save his throat from becoming dry and besides it was a humid night and water with the meal could be a necessary additive for all present. A refreshing glass of cold water did the trick for me, clearing my head of in-depth thinking. A final check that all was ready for our guests; my fellow non drinking friend and I sat down for a joint meditation session to call our founders, Bill Wilson and Dr Bob Smith from the other side of the curtain to our dinner table.

Both old friends arrived simultaneously, laughing and talking as they entered my dining room. Bill was first to hold out his hand. and I shook it warmly. "Hullo, I'm Bill and I am an Alcoholic." It was the traditional greeting for all AA members since the two men founded the fellowship. " Me too." responded Dr Bob, a man of fewer words when compared to Bill Wilson. He shook hands too and we all sat down together with Bill at one end of the table and Dr Bob at the other. My friend and I had planned it that way, so that we in turn, sitting opposite each other in the middle seats could direct our questions equally face to face. "Shall I say Grace?" enquired Bill. I acknowledged with a nod. He began: "Bless us O Lord in these thy gifts, which of thy bounty we are about to receive…." He trailed off and then added a caveat to the prayer: : "Lord grant me the serenity to accept the things I cannot change, courage to change the things I can and the wisdom to know the difference." It was the exact introductory prayer recited at the start and end of every AA meeting. I also had it typed on paper and glued to my motor vehicle dash board. A timely reminder to slowdown when driving as in the past I lost my licence for a time as a result of speeding infringements. The serenity prayer it is known has been of great comfort in times of trouble and one worth repeating from time to time. I wished to get to the point of his miraculous recovery as quickly as possible after many years of sobriety and to find how he came to form AA with out fellow guest Dr Bob Smith. So I opened the evening with question to Bill: "What happened to cause you to stop drinking and come up with a plan to encourage other alcoholics to do the same? Bill sat back for a moment recalling how he was catapulted into what he liked to call his fourth dimension of existence. He was thinking about the happiness, peace and usefulness of his life that became even incredibly more wonderful as time passed. He paused a little bit longer contemplating at what point to start his reply: "It was a bleak November evening as I sat drinking in my kitchen. It was with a certain satisfaction I reflected there was enough gin concealed about the house to carry me through the night and the next day. Lois, my wife was at work. I wondered whether I dared hide a full bottle of gin near the head of my bed, for I would need it before daybreak. My musing was interrupted by a phone call from an old school friend and drinking pal, asking if he might come over. It was years since I remembered him coming to New York in a sober condition. Rumour had it that he had been committed for alcoholic insanity and I wondered how he had escaped. His coming to meet me was an oasis in the dreary desert of my existence. I thought only of recapturing the spirit of our former drinking days together.

The door opened and he stood there stone cold sober. There was something about his fresh skin and glowing sparkle in his eyes that was inexplicably different. I pushed a drink across the table after we had exchanged pleasantries, I wondered what had happen to him, he wasn't the Ebby I once knew. I asked him what it was he was all about now? He looks me straight in the eyes and replied 'I got religion.' So I was thinking , last summer an alcoholic crackpot and now cracked about religion. I didn't; believe in any religious stuff and as he seemed to be on fire, I decided to let him rave on, but he didn't. In a matter of fact way he told me how two men had appeared in court, persuading the judge to suspend his commitment. They had told of a simple religious idea and a practical programme for action. That was two months ago, and as you can see the rest is evident, I don't drink any more. It worked.! He had come to pass his experience on and asked if I cared to listen. I was shocked but interested, I had no choice, as I was in such a state of hopelessness anyway."

Bill's voice drifted as I lacked the concentration to listen to what I already knew. Ebby had talked on for hours about his own childhood, the sound of the church bells and the preachers voice on Sunday, the temperance pledge he never signed, grandfather's good natured contempt of some church folk and their double standards, his denial of the preacher right to tell him how he must listen, be and do. Ebby's recollection of the past that was not unlike Bill's upbringing nor of mine for that matter. We both had to swallow hard the bitter pill of our former belief that I was now again being reminded of. Since my childhood, I like Bill, had through the influences of the world and hard knocks in life graduated to a state of being a doubting Thomas. Sure my intellectual heroes of astronomy, science and evolution had long since swayed my thinking into a simple belief in a spirit of the Universe who neither knew time nor limitation. Life had taught me through bitter experience that the preachers of the world's religions had their own agenda, as did their Churches. The new wave of money grabbing evangelist teachers of the message of Christ preaching the attainment of the grace of God through cash donations from believers who had, like their spiritual mentors sorted worldly pleasure and treasures, whilst three quarters of the world starved. They had one hand in God's pocket and the other in the devils. The religious who talked of God as personal to me, who was love, had superhuman powers giving strength and direction; such theories to my mind I had long switched off.

 Christ had entered my being from childhood indoctrination and I recognised his prophetic greatness and the excellence of his moral teachings. Again like Bill I had adopted the parts that suited me and disregarded the rest. In the decades of my lifetime I had been educated to the perils of wars, religious disputes, freedom of some people one week and the killing of them in the next. On balance, the power of God in the world had always looked grim when it came to human affairs and I honesty wondered if religion had ever done any real good for man. Bill's voice came back into focus: Despite my agnostic views Ebby seemed to declare that God had done for him what he could not do for himself. His human will had failed, doctors had pronounced him incurable, society was about to lock him up. He like me had admitted complete defeat. Yet, here he was announcing that he had in effect been raised from the dead. Suddenly taken from the garbage dump of life and raised to a level of life he had ever known before."

Bill paused, drank half a glass of water and continued "Had Ebby Thatcher any more power in him than I had in me? Obviously he had not. Yet he seemed to have something and I had nothing at all. That floored me. It began to look like those preachers had been right all along. Here was living proof that something in the human heart had done the impossible. Despite my scepticism about miracles happening, here was living proof of one right before me now. He shouted tidings of great joy, he was on a different footing and the very roots of his being grasped a new soil." Bill paused again, took another sip of water and continued for he was on a roll now."despite the living example of my friend before me, there remained in me the vestige of old prejudices. Words of God and preachers raise apathy, but when the thought that there might be a God personal to me presenting itself, my apathy intensified. I could go for the conceptions of a creative intelligence, a universal mind or the Spirit of nature but I resisted that there might well be an 'Emperor in the heavens' who ruled everything. However loving he might be, it was not my way. Then Ebby floored me with a question; 'Why don't you choose your own concept of God?' It melted the ice on my intellectual mountain and the whole shadows I had lived through all my drinking days. It was only a matter of believing in a Power greater than myself. Nothing more was required of me to make my beginning. I saw that growth could start from this point. On a foundation of complete willingness I might build what I saw in my friend. At long last I felt, I believed. The scales of pride and prejudice fell from my eyes and a new world was coming into view." With that Bill broke off and suggested we might eat something.

So after we ate and I listened to these good old friends chat away freely, I could see a great deal of respect that each had for one another, their mutual agreed opinion as well as views to the contrary in everything from the importance of daily reflection on prayer, the steps and traditions of AA and the methodology in promotion of the AA to the still suffering alcoholic. It posed further questions in my mind to ask both gentlemen, but the one question that was foremost in my mind was how Bill came to believe in a Power Greater than himself. It was a tall order but I put just that to Bill initially. "Well, at first, after that evening with Ebby, I had a humble willingness just to have God with me. However so soon the world clamoured for my attention and the necessity of finding work to precedence over my contact with God. I went back to the booze for a while. Ultimately I did stop which led me back into hospital, as I was then suffering delirium tremens. I am not clear if it was hallucinations from the sudden withdrawal from alcohol or the medication I was administered to overcome the shivering, shaking, racing heart and sweating that I was experiencing, but a miracle-of a sort did take place for me. I awoke one morning in the privacy of the room in which Dr Silkworth, my medical practitioner had arranged for me, for peace and quietness. It was there that a white lightning experience came over me and I found a sense of victory and peace the likes of which I had never yet experienced in my life before. The Father of Light presided over me and I fully accepted him. I felt lifted up with utter confidence, as though a great clean wind off a mountain top blew through and through. God comes to most men gradually, but his impact on me was sudden and profound." The silence at the dinner table in the slight flicker of the candle light on the image of Bill's face and Dr. Bob's enquiring one, left me feeling that God was about to repeat the miracle. I knew it wasn't so for me, for I had entered AA at the suggestion of that old psychiatrist in the bed next to mine. My recovery was slow and I lost the desire for alcohol after often repeated utterance of the Serenity pray in a dawning light of day after six months of sobriety. To this day I am mindful of the risk of falling down the pit of darkness into an alcoholic mess again. It is a recognised "a day at a time" sobriety for me, and the words that I so often acknowledge in my head are: "Trust in the slow work of God."

Bill interrupted my train off thought again, for he had not completed his story of enlightenment: " I recalled that my friend Ebby had promised that I would enter upon a new relationship with my Creator, that I would have the elements of a way of living which would answer all my problems. It was that the belief in God's power, plus enough willingness, honesty and humility to establish and maintain a new order of things were my essential requirements. It was simple enough but I had to pay a price for making this changes. For a moment I was alarmed, as was my doctor, to reflect on my sanity. He listened with great wonder as I talked and he stated. "something has happened to you I do not understand, but you had better hang on to it for anything is better than the way you were." Bill then related how, as he lay there in that hospital, he was reminded of the thousands of hopeless alcoholics who might be glad to have what he had just so freely been given. Perhaps, he thought he could help some of them and they in turn might help others. He remembered St. James statement recorded in the Bible: "Faith without works is dead." Bill knew these words to be true for himself and he felt sure that he, and for that matter any still suffering alcoholics had to perfect and enlarge his spiritual work and self-sacrifice to survive the certain trials and low spots in his life ahead. He recognised with some fear and trepidation that if he did not work at it, he would surely drink again, and if he drank he would die. So it was that Bill become a member of the Oxford Group were Ebby had learnt and put into practice the principles to sobriety and helping other still suffering alcoholics to sobriety. Ebby had passed the message to Bill on that fate filled evening he called and announced he had "found religion." Lois, joined Bill in his enthusiastic quest to help other alcoholics become sober and arranged regular meetings as a member of the Oxford Group, using their principle in their efforts to help others. Bill's message was simple; first he told his story of what happened in his drinking, what changed for him as a result of his so called conversion and how he now lived in the spirit of a God of his own understand using principles laid down by the Oxford Group. That as alcoholics, they were powerless over alcohol, that they would come to believe in a Higher power, that by handing over to a God of their own understanding they would recover. It was then he asked others to tell their own story and be guided back to sobriety.

 Bill had very little work for the next year and a friend who knew Bill well remained sceptical of his zeal to make this sobriety thing work. Bill himself in his sobriety sometimes felt in complete despair, plagued by doubt and resentments, returning often to his old hospital for help from his doctor.

Nothing else seemed to work for him save for turning to talk to another man about alcoholism. It always seemed to revive him and lift him up when he attempted to help another alcoholic. He and Lois had upwards of 200 people at their home meetings on a regular basis, So many unloved, desperate, lost, comic and tragic alcoholics. One poor chap even committed suicide in their home. It nearly broke Bill but he didn't go back to the bottle. Others he did help and he held on to his belief. The biggest test came when after a long absence he met Ebby and the message of Bill's sobriety was sorely tested. Ebby was back on the booze again and Bill's heart went out to his friend and he was tempted to drink but he didn't. Something inside him held strong and instead he focused on helping Ebby as best he could. It was to be a lifetime of pain and suffering for his friend until the day of his death. I hadn't known it then but an unexpected surprise was to await my dinner guest in the case of Ebby before this night was over. My attention was drawn to my other guest for Dr Bob Smith had been sitting there all night without utter a word about his story. So I engaged him in the conversation.

"Dr Bob, how did you become sober and co-found the AA fellowship with Bill here?" It was Bill's turn to sit back and enjoy the fellowship and reacquaint their joint journey in founding AA and bringing millions throughout the world to practice its twelve step programme to this very day. Dr Bob took a sip of water and thus began his story: "I come from a small New England village of some seven thousand souls. It was a dry town, no liquor was sold in our neighbourhood, except for the State Liquor agency where perhaps you could convince the agent that you really needed it. Without a script the expectant purchaser would leave empty-handed. Later I came to believe that liquor was the panacea of all ills. The town had ample churches and schools in which to pursue any education of one's own choosing, but liquor was not on that list. My parents were professional business people with above average intelligence and I their only child, spoilt and selfish. A perfect start for a budding alcoholic. Churchgoing was a daily activity throughout high school. I declared that I would never darken a church door as soon as I was free from parental domination. I kept that up for the next forty years. After high school I had four years of the best college education and drinking was a major part of my extra -curricular activity. I kept that up more and more and had the fun without much grief. Never once in my life did I suffer a hangover which make me later believe I was an alcoholic from birth. My whole life seemed to be centred around doing what I wanted without regard for the rights, privileges or the wishes of anyone else. I graduated 'summa cum lasde' in the eyes of the drinking fraternity but not the Dean of the College. The next three years I was employed by a large manufacturing company selling railway supplies, gas engines and the like; moving between Boston, Chicago and Montreal. I drank as much as my pay would allow but with a penalty, I always had morning jitters at the time.

Next I set about to study medicine and took the business of drinking a step higher. In examinations, my hands would shake and my head go blank from excessive drinking. I had enormous capacity for beer. I was elected to membership of the drinking societies and soon became one of the leading spirits. Things went from bad to worse in my Sophomore year. After a prolonged period of drinking, I quit the course, packed my bag and headed South to spend a month on a farm to dry out. I returned to study and convince the faculty to let me complete the course. I passed with credits and migrated to another leading university and I ended as a Junior in the fall. My drinking escalated to the point that fellow students contacted my father, who arrived to straighten me out. His words had little effect as I increased my drinking and graduated to spirits.. I sat exams but due to delirium tremors put in many a blank paper at examination time. The upshot was I was given an ultimatum, dry out if I wished to graduate. I proved myself to the faculty, graduated and got a coveted internship in a western city where I spent the next two years. There I was kept very busy, I hardly left the hospital at all, so I stayed out of trouble. When the two years were up I set up my own practice. I had money, all the time in the world and considerable stomach trouble from former excessive boozing. I soon found that drinking a little relieved my stomach trouble for a while, but I was soon drinking to excess again.

In time I was beginning to pay physically and in the hope of relief voluntarily incarcerated myself at least a dozen times in local sanitariums. I was between a rock and a hard place, if I drank I would die and if not my stomach issues would torture me. I even had friends smuggle me a quart of spirits whilst in hospital or I would raid the dispensary for a drink. Consequently I got rapidly worse and my father took me home, were I was confined to bed for two months to recover. When well enough I returned to my practice, with the passing of the Prohibition Act I felt safe. I could buy a few cases of beer or spirits as the law permitted but no more.

However, as a doctor I found out I could have unlimited supply and so I was back on my downward spiral again. Over the next two years I developed two phobias. One was fear of not sleeping and the other fear of running out of liquor. As I wasn't a man of means, I resolve that I would not take a morning drink so I could see patients and do my hospital rounds. The plus in my life was I got married but my wife and I were more our less ostracised by our friends because of my antisocial behaviour whilst drunk. My phobia for sleep-lessness demanded I get drunk every night. This went on for the next seventeen years. It was a horrible nightmare of a cycle of earning money, getting drunk, morning jitters, taking large doses of sedatives to make it possible for me to earn more money and so on "ad nauseam." I used to promise my wife, my friends and my children that I would not drink, but seldom ever did I keep promises, even though I was sincere about it when I made them. In time I was thrown in with a crowd of people who attracted me at the time because they seemed to be poised, healthy and happy. They spoke with great freedom from embarrassment, which I could never do. For me I was ill at ease most of the time, my health was at breaking point I was totally miserable. I sensed they had something I didn't have and it turned out to be something of a spiritual nature. I gave the matter much time and study over the next couple of years, but I still keep getting drunk every night. I read everything I could about this group. My wife became deeply interested too as they seemed to be doing good works for others without seeking personal reward. I never knew that it would be an an-swer to my liquor problem.   June 10, 1935, that was my last drink."   Bob paused after such a long spell of talking at length, and he withdrew with; " I'll let Bill take up the story from here.

So being a verbose man Bill took great delight in continuing: 'Yes the day Bob stopped drinking was the day we founded AA. But I need to digress back a year or so for I had been lately attending the Rescue Mission meetings that Ebby had told me about. It was where he had his religious conversion from Rowland Hazard's teaching about the Oxford Group's life changing program, as well as the prescription of Carl Jung for conversion. Ebby got his conver-sion to cease drinking from attending those meeting but it didn't last for him. I got mine as I said before in hospital as a patient." Bill paused long enough to down a glass of water before continuing again: "Bob's conversation come from practicing the Oxford Group steps with me but it was initially a call I made at his home to talk about sobriety that made the difference." A purposeful pause in the conversation and then he continued. "I was in Akron, Ohio on a business trip and staying at an up town city hotel. It was a couple of years into my sobriety and I had taken the trip to Akron in the hope of gaining clientele for a new business venture. I decided to take a walk around the block before retiring to bed for the night. As I walked through the hotel lobby I heard music and laughter coming from the bar room lounge nearby. The old urge to drink returned and I found myself in a desperate situation. Giving into temptation, I made my way to the bar thinking a nightcap would do no harm. Sanity prevailed as I reached into my pocket for money to pay for a drink. Instead of ordering the liquor, I had the presence of mind to ask for change for the pay phone located in the lobby. Somehow the repetition from the Rescue Mission meetings came to my rescue. I figured if I could talk to another still suffering alcoholic on sobriety, the urge to drink would pass. I took up the phone book and commenced to call local Churches to see if any of their flock was having difficulty to remain sober. A local priest referred me to Dr. Bob here and indicated that he was always in his cups and could not control his drinking. I quickly jotted down Bob's phone number and dialled him. Bob's wife answered and I explained my reason for meeting him. She was keen for me to come to their home the next evening." Bill added:. " I'll let Bob tell the story from here."

 Dr Bob with some enthusiasm picked up the story: "Bill was the first living human with whom I had ever talked who knew from personal experience what he was talking about in regard to alcoholism. He talked for some time about how difficult it was to stay sober when craving for a drink. He related how long he had been sober and how the Rescue Mission Group had held. I in turn related my own experience in trying to beat the grip of the grape. I told Bill that he could not help me stop drinking. It was then Bill dropped the bombshell that was the starting point of our AA movement. ' Oh, I didn't call here for you Doctor Bob, I am here for me.' he said he realised that only by calling on another alcoholic and seeking spiritual guidance could he relieve his craving and come away feeling uplifted. It was a lightbulb moment for he was a man who had experienced many dreadful years of frightful drinking, cursed by the very means I had been trying to employ, that is to say a spiritual approach. We both agreed we would put a plan into action to call and visit a patient of mine who was in the horrors and the depth of uncontrollable anguish from his alcoholism. This poor soul asked that we tie him to the bed for fear that he would kill himself if we let him loose. So it was that we two now highly motivated souls went about to do God's work and our efforts saved this fellow and so AA was born."

So, Dr. Bob with some enthusiasm picked up the story:. Bill returned to New York where he with others continued their work encouraging Alcoholics to follow the six steps of Alcoholics Anonymous taken from the guidance of the Rescue Mission who got them from the Oxford Group all those years ago. Any Alcoholic who was at the depth of hopelessness, Bill and his fellows, including the partner of the Alcoholic, transported the poor devil to Akron hospital under the care of Dr Bob Smith. Bill went on to write the Big Book of AA, adding six more steps for good measure, the suggestions to stay sober. Like Bob he suffered much personally in a sober mind, but neither men returned to the drink. Bill went on to write many books of guidance and prayed to help Alcoholics maintain a spiritual path by helping others remain sober and in this way it held themselves also..

 The night was drawing to a close, then a breath of fresh air entered the room , it was Ebby T right three with them, Both Bill and Bob were delighted to see their old comrade in arms. Ebby spoke: "Just to refresh the memories my fellows." For he was directing his words at me and my friend of AA in the now, as much as Bill and Bob, he continued: " I battled my whole life as a hopeless alcoholic, and whilst I introduced Bill to sobriety… " He looked lovingly towards his old school chum and continued: " I could not stay sober myself. Many of the fellowship tried and failed. I slowed down for a short while but continued to drink in a restrained way but spend the rest of my waisted life either on health farms to dry out but more often than not in mental institutions." Bill interrupted. "One of the sadnest days of my life was when Ebby got drunk after two years of sobriety." Ebby returned to his story: " Although I went to Oxford meetings regularly in those early days, I could not stay sober. I had a most erratic career mixed with periods of sobriety and long periods of drunkenness."

As Ebby continued his tail of woe, I recall how he had been arrested three time, spent time in jail, sobered up for a time but went down the drain again. Ebby's final years were spent in a pleasant small Alcoholic treatment centre- McPike's Farm, near Saratoga, New York He arrived there on May 30, 1964 and died two years later .21.03. 1966. The McPike's had cared for him and rightly saw him as a troubled man. Ebby piped up then to my dinner guests and announced: " I live in another house in our Fathe's Kingdom my friends, so that is why I don't see you. However, you will be pleased to know that I died sober. " That part was true, for he was too sick to even take a drink or take drugs, that he had also been suspected of being addicted too. The night ended with the serenity prayer, that we had begun the meal with. Dr Bob, Bill and Ebby faded into the mist of the night and I and my good friend sat in silence for a time. I recalled that Dr. Bob had saved over five thousands Alcoholics in his time at Akron Hospital. He had but three suggestions that he passed on to them.1.Trust God 2. Clean House .3. Help someone. I too had no excuse but remain sober a day at a time, attend meetings and practice the 12 Steps of Alcoholics Anonymous. which Bill had intruded to nth fellowship of a group go drunks all those years ago.

CHAPTER 6.

THE ILLUMINATION OF JESUS AND MOHAMMED

Andrew Carnegie, the great steel merchant was asked to solve a problem for the Government of the day at the time. He reportedly met the Elite group of gentleman in a boardroom at a convenient government location in Washington DC. He listened intently to each of the delegates to ascertain the nature of what they wished his opinion on and sat for a moment or two in contemplating. At last he spoke: "How many of you can empty your minds completely and think about nothing after a moment of contemplation. They all agreed that they could do it, as it was not the problem. Carnegie then ask them all to meet his challenge to think about nothing for a mere thirty seconds. They all said it was dead easy to do that. It must be remembered that Carnegie was an Avatar, at least in a business sense. He had the ability to achieve the embodiment of an idea using the forces of the Masters of guidance from the heavenly realm. The delegates all sat in total silence for the thirty seconds and then Carnegie looked at the far delegate and stated - "You lasted only five seconds before you had a thought." He then pointed to each delegate in turn and knowingly stated: "None of you were without thought for the allotted time, you have not practiced to free your mind of thought." Looked around the room at each delegate once more; "until you can do that" he said', " I can't help you." With that the he got to his feet and quietly left the room.

Sitting on my balcony overlooking the bush land and garden that surround my property, I began the task of determining who next to invite as Masters to my dinner table. I was thinking about Avatars. The old oak tree directly in front of me on my verandah reminded me of that biblical lesson of not eating of the fruit of the forbidden tree of knowledge.. Avatars had visited me previously in my writings, in my minds eye and my imaginary interpretation of the meaning of life. Three distinct Avatars of enlightenment came to mind in determining my next Masters to invite to dinner.. For I was keen to learn more of those Higher beings who once walked this earth. So I decided to choose the most relevant to this age, for their varied beliefs were being practice religiously by millions on this earth today, yet the old world was still in spiritual darkness.

In a seemingly meditative state of mind the three Master names come to light. alone. I wrote the name on three individual pieces of paper. intent on delving a little into the lives of the three whilst on earth, to determine which two would be the best choices for my cause. I headed the first piece of paper with The Buddha, for he roamed the earth six centuries before Christianity, making his religious philosophy one of the oldest still being practiced today. Next I headed the second page up with Christ and the Christianity that followed his death and resurrection, being a religious force over two thousand years and and still practiced today by the majority of humanity who follow religious teachings. Mohammad The last prophet was the next on my list for Islam started on the insights of Mohammad some 7 centuries after Christ died nailed to that cross.

So taking pen to paper I began to write a little synopsis of the teaching of each of the individual Avatars lives to help determine my choice of the two Masters I would meditate upon and invite to my table. The first of my choices being "The Buddha," I began to write about., the Siddhartha Gautama, the founder of Buddhism, was born around 580 BC as a Prince of Sakya, a kingdom in the fertile plains at the foothills. He was born into luxury and had every world pleasures at his disposal. During his youth he lived in three different palaces - one for the winter, one for the summer and one for the rainy season. His father kept him entertained with beautiful dancing girls and musicians so that he would not be tempted to venture out into the world. Siddhartha enjoyed good health and was proficient at many sports particularly archery. He lived that life of luxury and didn't leave his sumptuous palaces until age 29. He was always known to be very compassionate, even from childhood. He had never known the realities of the world outside the walls of his confinement. When Siddhartha did finally venture out to see the world with his charioteer, he came upon firstly, a diseased man, then a senile old one, a corpse and a funeral ceremony with grieving relatives and finally a wandering holy man. On the fourth trip out , he met with the wandering holy man whose asceticism inspired him to follow a similar path in search of freedom from the suffering that caused the endless cycle of birth, death, and rebirth. Upon witnessing the cycle of life for the first time, Siddhartha reportedly exclaimed : "This is the end which has been fixed for all, and yet the world forgets, it fears and takes no heed. Turn back the chariots, there is no time or place for pleasure excursions. How could an intelligent person pay no heed at a time of disaster, who knows of his impending destruction."

 It is said from there, the Gods sent forth a religious mendicant who told Siddhartha that it was his mission to deliver mankind from suffering. "O, Bull among men." The mendicant said: "I am a recluse who, terrified by birth and death, have adopted a homeless life to win salvation! Since I ask this way to live , my extinction is doomed, salvation from the world is what I wish and so I search for that most blessed state in which extinction is unknown." Reportedly, the mendicant then rose to the sky like a bird and vanished. It was upon this vision that Siddhartha intuitively perceived and made plans to leave the palace for a homeless life. He renounced his rich upbringing and decided to become a monk. He left his wife of 13 years in which he was instructed to marry when he was but 16 and their young son and embarked upon a journey to seek the meaning of life. Wandering he searched for Enlightenment, studied and tried Hinduism and the Jain faith. The teachers were reported to have psychic powers, but the teaching did not satisfy him. He abandoned the teachings because the practice of the times followed sacrifices and rituals beyond the common man, so this is when he became an ascetic. The Buddha looked inward to seek knowledge, then sought the advise of a holy man and for the next six years he became an ascetic, attempting to conquer the innate appetite of food, sex and comforts by engaging in various yoga disciplines. Self punishment become a diet of pleasure in reverse, a kind of addiction, so he moved on. He soon realised that he was near death from fasting, so he accepted a bowl of rice from a young girl. After eating some more he regained some strength and realised physical austerity's was not the way to spiritual liberation. "This is not the Dharma (cosmic law) leading to dispassion, to enlightenment, to emancipation. Inward calm could not be maintained unless physical strength is constantly and intelligently replenishment. It was how he gained the spiritual strength to win enlightenment. His journey gave him the vision to see the bridge to cross to the other side to fulfil his enlightenment. In and earthly sense he pointed the way to Enlightenment, but did not cross that bridge. Perhaps he would have if he had not had taken the poison food that ended his earth life.

I in turn to having a story to tell of The Buddha's path to enlightenment towards the end of his life. For the last six months of his life he suffered greatly. Then in the agony of his being he saw the way to his heavenly realm. Whilst he suffered much in the physical sense, his soul and his spirit was in grace. He saw in the spirit of his life, the afterlife after so many inner journeys. The vision of being fed his last meal at the home of a poor man was a great honour to the poor man.   Lord Buddha would be his guest, but he had nothing to feed him except mushrooms. This man was a farmer who grew mushrooms in wood in dirty places on rainy days. Due to the passing of a snake at that location the mushrooms become poisonous but the poor farmer didn't know of this at the time. The snakes had died in the very location of the newly acquired food, so that snake poison entered the mushrooms.

 The poor man unknowingly made a poisonous vegetable soup for his dinner guest. When the Buddha ate he could taste the bitter poison, but so as not to offend his host ate the soup all the same. It was not until after he left the mans' home that he became gravely ill. The man himself tasted the soup and realised his error in feeding his Godly Master the soup and was greatly troubled. The Buddha realising he was dying told a follower to explain to the poor man that the Buddha believed he was lucky to eat the soup and not to be troubled by it. The Buddha only smiled and reportedly said "This thunderbolt was bound to fall. What difference does it make which way I enter the kingdom. As far as I am concerned, no lightning has fallen on me because I have known him who is the nectar. There is no death. Another will follow in many centuries to come who will be the light within the light, look to him for comfort in your sadness, in your days is the way, the truth and the light in your journey inward.

The piece of paper with the Buddha story was full now , so I turned to the next sheet head up Jesus Christ and began to write again. " In historic terms Jesus was born in Roman ruled Palestine under a puppet Jewish regime, at the end of the first century AD. He grew top in Nazareth and become an itinerant preacher in Northern Palestine for three years, during this time he gathered many followers who were attracted by misinterpretation of Jewish law and the miracles ascribed to him. His criticism of Jewish religious leaders and warnings of imminence of God' rule replacing human rule provoked opposition from the Jewish and Roman establishment leading to his crucifixion on a cross. The Gospels of Matthew, Mark,Luke and John portray Jesus as living a life without material security or family support, often mixing with the poor and society' outcasts, and constantly teaching that he would be rejected by the authorities, persecuted, suffer and die to fulfil God's purpose. It is claimed at the death of Christ, the sun darkened , the earth trembled and the daed arose and appeared too many. It is also claimed that after three days he rose again, visited his Disciples and ascended body and soul into heaven. This was to fulfil Jesus claims that he was the Messiah, that be the Son of God. Historically Jesus is viewed among non Christians as being a moral reformer, a political revolutionary, Palestinian peasant and charismatic Rabbi. To Christians he might well be considered thus but above all else he is thought of as a Prophet with a unique relationship with God, with evidence of a   divine birth, death and resurrection for the delivered salvation of mankind.   The Christian movement that swept the world spread throughout the Mediterranean and was savagely suppressed in the first century AD by Roman Emperors Claudius and Nero. By the end of the first century Jewish authorities in Palestine had adopted policies aimed at sharply differentiating Christian from Jews. However, a world religion had been born, one that would underpin the development of Western Society and culture.

I was thinking of the way of Christ's teachings. Regardless of what one may think about him, Jesus of Nazareth has been the dominant figure in history for almost twenty centuries. Jesus did many things well. If every theme about Jesus were written down, the whole world would not have room for the books that would be written. Even if the Gospels don't offer a complete unabridged biography of Christ's earthly life, they do give the world enough information to keep pouring over this story. Jesus knew, from the moment the angel announced to Mary the Mother that he was highly favoured. It was announced in the heavens that he would be called the son of the Most High. The Lord God would give him the throne of his father David and he would reign over Jacob's descendants forever and his kingdom would never end. He was sighted as a child sitting among the teachers in the Temple, asking them questions and they were amazed at his answers. Then follows a gap in his story, for it is thought that he wandered far and wide and was further enlightened in the deserts of Egypt. He was thirty three when he began his ministry. He worked many miracles, changing water into wine, healing disease and raising a loved one from the dead, chased out demons and in his ministry when questioned showed much practical wisdom. He spent much time in solitude and prayer and simplified his teaching for simple people by teaching in parables. He fast in the desert for forty days and forty nights and was tempted to takeover the earthly kingdoms but cast out this temptation to evil in preference to focus his preaching and love on the kingdom of heaven. He taught of the work of God alone. It was the custom of the Jewish priest to offer a lamb as sacrifice to God sending the smoke filled essence of the burnt sacrifices to the heavens as a grace filled act, then eat the flesh of the lamb in homage to God. Jesus ultimately sacrificed himself as the Lamb of God, suffering as an offering for the forgiveness of the defects of character of humanity. He asked of his followers to eat the flesh and drink of the blood as a communion of the people. As a result of Jesus' supreme sacrifice, it meant that each and everyone could call on the third person of the Trinity, the Holy Spirit of God as a key to enter the doorway to the kingdom of heaven. Of the forty reported miracles of Christ, the feeding of the 5000 with only five crusts of bread and three fishes leaves one speechless. It is significant in that he asked us to do likewise, feed those in need and eat his bread and drink of his wine, his body and blood. To call on the Trinity message in times of great spiritual need. Christian followers to this present day are still confused by his request and are still not listening. I resolved to leave it at that, as I still had one more Avatar Prophet to write a synopsis of life on the final sheet of paper.

 So, it was that I set to work doing a brief of the Prophet Mohammed on the other sheet of paper. He was born in 570 , in Mecca, western Arabia. Orphaned at a young age, he was raised by his grandfather and uncle.. Mohammed reported, at the age of 40 that he had a vision of the Angel Gabriel who transmitted to him the first of many divine revelations. Although classifying himself as the Prophet of God, he never performed a miracle.He had no formal education, no religious training to speak of when he announced he was the messenger of God, bringing word of the true religion. He was ridiculed and labeled a lunatic and banished from his native Mecca. He had nothing to show for his preaching in the first ten years of his new found one man religion. Yet before another decade passed he was Dictator of all Arabia, ruler of Mecca and head of the new world religion which swept the Danube to the Pyrenees like a wave of spiritual power and might. The mighty force was not a Trinity, did not have a three fold force; being of the power of the word, the intent of prayer and kinship with God.

 Nothing about Mohammed made sense, born to an impoverished leading family of Mecca, the city of the magic stone, great city of trade and trade routes of the time, it was an unhealthy place to live. Its suburbs were unsanitary and thus its children were sent into the desert to be raised by the desert tribes. So Mohammad was thus nurtured, drawing strength and health from the milk of the Nomads of which his grandfather and uncle belonged. At age 25 he was hired out and married to a rich widow, tendered sheep and became the leader of her caravans. After his vision at age 40 he travelled to all parts of the Eastern Word talking with many men of diverse beliefs and observed the decline of Christianity into warring sects. Mohammad developed into a rich and shred trader and one day he took to wandering the desert for a time, returning with the Koran the revealed the word of God. He did not have the gift of speech like Jesus, neither did he have a gift of the written word nor poetry. Yet he did receive the gift of words, the Koran and recited them to the faithful. The Koran verses were better than the professional poets of the tribes of his time. This was the miracle, for the gift of words of a poet were considered all-powerful. The Koran stated that all men were created equal before God and that the world should be a democratic state of Islam. This was considered political heresy and particularly the fact that he wanted to destroy all idols in the courtyard of The Caaba; for this he was banished from the City. It was the sacred stone and the idols that brought the desert tribes to Mecca and that in turn meant trade.So with the capitalist businessmen setting upon him, he retreated to the desert and there he demanded sovereignty over all the world. So the rise of Islam began like a flame that could not be extinguished, backed by a fanatical army fighting as one prepared to die without winching. Mohammad took the opportunity to invite Jews and Christians to join him for in his mind he was forming one religion. He was calling on all mankind to join him who believe in one God, to be of one faith. Not one would accept Mohammad's innovation of humane warfare. When the army of the Prophet entered Jerusalem not a single person was killed because of his faith. When the Crusaders entered the city a century later, not a Moslem man, women or child was spared. However, the Christians did accept one Moslem idea, the place of learning, the university.

It was late on Friday evening when I finally put down my pen, arranging the brief of the three Avatars on my table, the Buddha, Jesus and then Mohammad. At this point in time I had not selected what to prepare for Saturday evening meal nor who the chosen ones would be. I could not see any difficulty in feeding Jesus, nor Mohammad, as I had knowledge of the foods of their day. The Buddha would prove a little more difficult but I had considered that in choosing him there would definitely not be any mushroom on the menu. I also considered that he was the less likely of my chosen ones to be selected. Despite the fact that he was a Holy man, and kind hearted, he was not exactly one for conversation and didn't seem to have much sense of humour. In his favour though, he was very human and extremely decent. I decided to forget about my selection of my candidate until the next morning. So leaving the briefs I set to bed in the hope that a good night sleep would make the next days selection of the two chosen ones a little easier. As fate would have it the universe in that regard was working in my favour. I awoke to the sound of the buzzer of the front door. So quickly I arose and opened the door to a courier with a small parcel for me. I opened it in some haste to find an arrangement of flowers and fruit and a picture of the Buddha in a reclining position. On the back was a note in Sanskrit, which I had only recently learnt. It read: "The Buddha is deeply grateful to you for your kind and courteous consideration in arranging for Masters to dine at your table this evening. Unfortunately, he left fifty seven years ago for a century of meditation and therefore will be unable to attend." It was signed by one of his ardent devotees. So my task in selection of my dinner guests was to be made easy. All I had to do was to select the menu for the evening with Jesus and Mohammad. So I set to work looking for a simple meal arrangement for two of the greatest Avatars that ever walked this planet.

Based on the Bible and historic records I ascertained a Mediterranean diet of kale, pine nuts, dates, olives, lentils and soup would be suitable. Baked fish would also be suitable for protein and I had no issue in preparing all of these dishes.   So then I set to work on what food to present Muhammad. I considered that camel or goat meat for that era of desert tribesman was popular. I had no way of finding such meat, so I settled for lamb chops and rump steak, for I had read that both cow and lamb were popular meat at the time and I had no issue with supply locally this day. Surprisingly mushrooms was used in many diets and considered   the best source of vitamins, minerals and fibre. Mohammed had once reportedly stated : "The truffle is one of Allah's favourites and it's waters cures the eye." So it was that I set to work preparing the meals for both my Master influences. I had just enough time ready to pour them both a wine to wet their whistle so to speak whilst I prepared the meal.

I recalled that Jesus had, at his mother's request, performed his first miracle by turning water into wine at the marriage feast of Cana. He also advocated the health benefit of drinking wine in a biblical statement: "a little wine for thy stomach's sake." Further, it was wine that Jesus consumed and demonstrated the making of a self sacrifice in memory of him. " He broke the bread and with the wine gave it to his Apostles and said : "Take this wine and drink this cup for this is my blood , the blood of the new and eternal covenant...." Then breaking the bread. 'Take ye and eat this bread for this is my body, do this in remembrance of me." I realised by statements that he had made that Mohammad had taken of wine early in his mission but later advised his followers to refrain from drinking : " Intoxicants are from these two trees," whilst pointing to the grape vines and date palm. In a verse in the Quran, alcohol derived from grapes, dates or raisins is forbidden for Muslims. It was first given as a general warning (Quran 4:43) to forbid Muslims from attending parties in a drunken state. Then in a later verse the Prophet Muhammad said that whilst alcohol had some medicinal benefits, the negative effect of it outweighed the good (Quran 2: 219). There are other references I recalled as a warning to people to abstain. The Prophet Mohammed also instructed " if it intoxicates in a large amount, it is forbidden, even in a small amount" for this reason, most observant Muslims avoid alcohol in any form, even small amounts that are sometimes used in cooking. Considering all this I resolved to partly fill two small cups with wine and serve them both a small quantity of bread too. It was not for me to determine if they drank or ate, for they being Avatar Masters, I left it to their own discretion. I felt it would be rude of me not to make an offering so without any judgement I placed the cups at their disposal and left the small loaves of bread to eat as a appetiser.   Once I had served them the meal and they each in turn blessed the food and offered it up to God before beginning to eat, I broached my first question, directing it to Jesus. " Some of my colleagues are Christian fundamentalists who believe in a direct contact with you and not on your Mother Mary to be prayed to, so what do you say to that?" Jesus answered as I expected he would:

" You have been thinking about my first miracle turning water into wine at the marriage feast. Who requested that I do that?" He paused before answering his own question. " It was my Mother who made a simple statement, Son they have no wine." Another pause: " My Mother didn't ask me, she simply made a statement, an indirect indication you might call it, for I made the decision to turn the water to wine based on her concern." He continued: " In my Father's house there are many rooms, as Mohammad will support. My Father and I are one in all things and there are many duties, miracles and matters in the spirit of the heavens and upon this earth that I respond to. They are prioritised according to their urgency.When one prays through my Mother, not to her, I am obliged as the utmost respect of son to Mother to consider her request often as a priority over another request. So you may respond to your fundamental Christian friends, that one does not pray 'to' Mother Mary but 'through' her, asking for her intersession to me for help in times of great need."

Jesus then turn to Mohammad asking his opinion as to my question. The Prophet answered: "You, the Prophet of the people who came before me on earth sacrificed yourself for the glory of God to save your followers and those of other faiths, by dying as you did in great agony on that cross. It united in many a passion and zeal to live a spiritual life by embracing in their hearts the spirit of God which true believers understand and live by. It was by no mean act of coincidence that I came across another in my time in the desert centuries after you passed this earthy realm. It was the Angel Gabriel who handed me a scroll of instruction in Sanskrit, of consecrated Hindu, Buddha and Jain teachings of a holy man. Being not off my language and myself at the time not being able to read nor write, I consulted a master of language who taught me how to read and interpret in my own Arabic tongue. This Koran was the words of Allah as revealed to me seven centuries after you Jesus ascended into the heavens."

 Mohammad paused, closed his eyes for a moment in acknowledgement of the Power of God within Jesus and then continued. "The world was in war at the time, various sects fighting one another, all the believers of one faith or another or no faith at all fighting for supremacy. Initially like all men of faith, I and the followers of the prophecy by the Messenger from God, turned towards Jerusalem to pray. Among the revelations of God's instructions as dictated to me was one concerning the new direction which I and my followers were to pray. It was not towards Jerusalem it was towards Medina, the ancient city where Jews, Nazarenes and Christians also worshipped. It was in those troubled times that we fled there and I was drawn to and some what troubled to turn to the Ka'aba, the cube, that ancient shrine of worship. It had historically been a place of idols and that is what troubled me. It is the site of the modern day pilgrimage to what is known as Mecca. I was reminded by Angel Gabriel that it was historically the house of the prophets Abraham and Ishmael, rebuilt centuries before but at that time was a new house of idols. I was thus instructed to destroy the idols and I in the lineage of prophets from Moses to Jesus was to be the seal of the Prophets.' So like the prophets before me, Abraham represented a supreme example of godly humility because he submitted to the word of God in offering to sacrifice his son to Him. Islam itself means ' submission to the will of God.' So in answer, or in summary, I was instructed to turn my face to heaven, turn then to a prayer direction, turning towards the sacred Mosque and whenever I turn towards it the will of god prevailed, and those who have been given the scriptures most surely know that it is the truth from their Lord, and Allah is not at all heedless in what they do." and then he added:" and everyone has a direction to which he should turn, therefore hasten to do good works, wherever you are, Allah (God) will bring you together, surely Allah has power over all things." He broke off and recommenced to eat.

Jesus, looked at him as loving as any brother might to a younger sibling, smiled and recommenced eating.

CHAPTER 7.

MOHANDAS.K. GANDHI AND RASPUTIN

I was left contemplating my own lack of disclipine to pray, mindful that I believed in a Power Greater than self but often wondered in search of new answers to what was a given. It seemed that both the Masters at my table had the same ultimate message, submit to the will of God. Mohammad without any further ado turned to the East fell to his knees, and prayed : "God is one and Mohammad is his Prophet." The evening meal complete, I was keen to consider what Jesus had to say of prayer, after Mohammad's demonstration of turning towards Mecca to pray. Jesus simply referred to the Beatitudes as Matthew had written (Verses 3-11). "Blessed are the poor in spirit, for theirs is the kingdom of heaven. Blessed are they that mourn, for they shall be comforted. Blessed are the meek, for they shall inherit the earth. Blessed are they that hunger and thirst after righteousness, for they shall be filled. Blessed are the merciful; for they shall obtain mercy. Blessed are the pure in heart, for they shall see God. Blessed are the peacemakers: for they shall be called the children of God. Blessed are they which are persecuted for righteousness sake: for theirs is the kingdom of heaven. Blessed are you when men shall revile you, and persecute you, and shall say all manner of evil against you falsely, for my sake. Then Jesus quietly said, remember to pray the Lord's prayer and faded in the highest heavens with Mohammad tagging along by his side.

New horizons seemed to be dawning for me with the rising sun on this Saturday morning. In a trance like state I had caught the attention of Mohandas Gandhi and Rasputin approaching in a mist of my mind. A rapid knock on my door broke the connection, but I was aware that the two men of mystic right and spiritualism were still there in the shadows. " Who is there?" I cried out. " It's your neighbour, I've come to borrow a cup of sugar." I was disgruntled by the interruption." Go away, you must not disturb a man of contemplation, when the mood for spiritual pursuit comes on." I replied. "Come back another time." Had I X-ray vision I would have witnessed an angelic looking young women, still dressed in her see through nightie, exposing all the vital part that would normally drive this man wild. Thanks to the limitations of my ability I do not possess X-ray vision and so was blissfully unaware pf the reality of the 'angel of temptation' at my door. If I had opened the door, the sight for sore eyes would have absorbed me. I no doubt would have been distracted enough to give her a cup of sugar and some just desserts just for the asking.

It was a good thing that such temptation had not befallen me, otherwise I would have not returned to my meditation, being absorbed in sexual desire as a consequence and may well have had some regret later to contend with. Besides my desires were more of the nature of drawing Masters to my table and this took priority over any sexual fantasy, physical desire or acting out such a fantasy. The switching of the mind from physical expression to thoughts of some other nature is discipline that only time, sufferance and regular practice make it possible to do. While being driven by sexual desire also brings with it a keen   imagination, courage, will-power persistence and creative ability is heightened, it also has the downside risk of over indulgence, sometimes the loss of reputation and often grief to those involved. Equally and more attuned to one's Higher self, when the sexual desire is harnessed and redirected into imagination and the courage of will power, the desire for sexual content can be channelled into creative expression. So it was that I returned to my meditation with the will to let go all earthy desires including those of a sexual nature and return to getting in touch with Masters Gandhi and Rasputin in the shadows. They were still awaiting my imaginative former state before the knock on my door had interrupted my spiritual equilibrium. It was Gandhi I wanted for his spiritual awareness which drove him and for his stubborn determination to achieve his goal for India,. In truth for the non violent demonstrations in the face of British rule and for his love, compassion and altruism. I knew by conversing with him that I could learn a thing or two in my own personal pursuit for living a better life of service for the good of all concerned.

As for that peasant Russian mystic and self proclaimed holy man Rasputin, who gained so much influence over Nicholas 1. he had such a powerful presence over the last Emperor of Russia, his wife and children and his ultimate political influence in the latter days of Imperial Russia that there was much to be gained and subsequently lost by understanding his mystical power and influences. It was not long before I had both highly spirited Masters in agreement to dine with me. I decided to involve them in what was to be our menu for the evening meal. For I knew that Gandhi had written keys to health, diet and health reforms and concluded that raw vegetables, fruits, unpolished rice, seeds, ground cake and boiled vegetables were essentials to his disciplined, well being. He had learnt through trial and error to offset his protein intake with goat milk and although cow or buffalo milk was against religious practice, Gandhi new that small quantitities of consumption sustained life so he would partake of such protein necessity when his protein deficiency required him to do so. He disciplined himself over his lifetime to only take a small intake of food, but had a sweet tooth as the saying goes and was partial on rare occasions to overindulgence in the eating of mango. It was a lifetime of disciplined search and research on food that led to this choice and which influenced his protest based philosophy of life and his latter day activism.

 Rasputin on the other hand stuck to his more traditional peasant diet, for he liked 'ukha'- fish soup- and dark bread, radishes, onions, plain vegetables and the like. He never delved into fad diets like Gandhi but rather was content to eat the food that was placed in front of him. Growing up in a peasant family, food was not in great supply but fish attainable from the nearby ocean and local vegetation from the Siberian village of his birth. Although he had a constitution that could eat fatty food too and had a liking of tea, plain cake and the fortified wine from the island of Madeira, he never become fat or portly. His body seem to remain trim for his whole life. So it wasn't hard for me to lay out before my guests dietary foods to suit the palates of both. Being careful of course not to provide any large quantities of any one food stuff so as not to offend the strict food intake discipline of Gandhi and the natural simplicity of Rasputin's tastes. I provided a large pot of black Russian tea, plain damper rye bread in lieu of dark bread following my grandmother's methodology of baking. As for fish soup, I settled for New Zealand Hoki, the closest seafood I could find to Russian 'ukha'a and as an added bonus sardines fried in oil of garlic and onion. I also presented a large variety raw and boiled vegetables to stay within the requirements of both their tastes. Warm goat milk was also on the menu for Gandhi and I knew that Rasputin that would not partake of the milk but would be more than content with the Russian tea I had managed to source especially for this occasion.

It surprised me somewhat, considering his lifetime diet of raw foods and simply tastes, to find that Mohandas Karamchand Gandhi was born, not of peasant stock like Rasputin, but of a wealthy political family in the princely state of Porbandar, Gujarat, West India. At the time of his birth in 1869, his father, Karamchand was Chief Minister for the area and had taught Gandhi from childhood political astuteness that would serve him well in life. Gandhi's lifetime pursuit of the perfect mental, physical and spiritual diet for his being was from the indoctrination of his devout mother, an adherent of the Jain religion. She taught him the tenets of her faith: sanctity of life, vegetarianism, abstinence from alcohol, fasting for self purification, and mutual tolerance across creeds and sects. These principles were the framework to help guide his adult political life. At the age of nineteen he was sent to University College in London were he studied law and graduated in 1891 and trained as a barrister of the Inner Temple. He failed to find a job in India as a barrister, so he took a post in 1893 for a one year appointment in Natal in South Africa but he remain there for the next twenty years championing the legal rights of the Indian community and there he adopted his strategy of non cooperation.

An incident in the early 1890s one day in South Africa was revealing.. As was expected in those days two Indians walking along a pavement were expected to walk in the gutter when approached by white folk. On this occasion, as they passed Gandhi reportedly remarked to his Indian companion: " It has always been a mystery to me' he stated without anger: " how men can feel themselves honoured by the humiliation of their fellow beings." He was twenty two at the time and such audacity in the face of any white South African was a sign of things to come, when he would shake the world with his advocacy and belief in 'Satyagraha,' the name he later gave to non-passive resistance to British rule in India.

Gandhi returned to India in 1914, at the beginning of World War 1. He joined the Indian National Congress, campaigning for civil rights and Indian self Government. It was in that first year that he initiated protests against social injustice, which continued for the rest of his life. Soon appointed leader of the Congress, he introduced non violent boycotts of British Institutions. He was tried for sedition and imprisoned until 1924. On release, he withdrew from politics to travel around India for the next three years promoting his crafts and the plight of the 'Untouchables' (Dalits), the lowest rank of India's caste system. He married and continued on his passive aggressive campaign cumulating in his 1930's ' Salt March.,' where he called thousands of followers to march to the ocean to make salt, to campaign against the tax on salt that the British had imposed on India. To those followers who feared being jailed by the British for this unlawful march he simply stated : "There are only 40,000 British in India and we are over 400,000,000 at this time. They can't jail us all." He did ultimately land himself back in jail but not over the " Salt March.' It was his resolve not to support British India's wartime role, when he launched in 1939 a "Quit India" Campaign against British domination. He was jailed in 1942 with other Congress leaders after negotiations for Independence failed. When Independence final came, he was opposed to the Mountbatten plan of dividing the country on religious grounds , thus forming two states, one of India and the other Pakistan. This of course suited British political influences after World War, as they sought to checkmate Stalin's Russia from in taking over oil rich areas surrounding India and Pakistan which the west ultimately controlled. Gandhi's lifestyle and beliefs ultimately was the cause of his assassination by an extremist Hindu in 1948. It was this brief of Gandhi's life I was going over in my mind as I prepared the food for these Master holy men. Both Masters sat quietly at my table discussing their house in the heavenly Father's kingdom in which they dwelt. Neither seemed to be jealous or concerned at the spiritual height they existed, but it seemed to me that the were both above the seventh heavenly status. I had already served warm goat milk and the damper rye bread for Gandhi and a goodly pot of Russian tea and some small portions of cake for Rasputin. It was like I didn't exist, as they sat speaking quietly eating sparingly and drinking their respective hot beverage.I took the opportunity to slip back into my state of mind to examine the brief of Rasputin's life. Thus, I would be well armed to pry them both with questions whilst I served the main meal.

So in brief I now recall the life and tales told of Rasputin He was born of peasant stock in the village of Pokrovskoye, along the Tura River in the Tobolsk Governate, Siberia on 21st January 1869. The day after his birth was the feast day of Orthodox Saint Gregory (Grigori) of Nysa, he was thus named Grigori Yefimovich Rasputin. Yefim, his father juggled a peasant farm and duties as a church elder, government courier and ferryman of goods and people across the Tura River. All of Rasputin's seven siblings died in infancy or early childhood except for a ninth child Feodosiya whom Rasputin was very close to and was Godfather to her children. Historians agree that he was not formally educated and remained illiterate well into his adulthood. There are archival records suggesting that he was a somewhat unruly youth-which possibly involved heavy drinking, small episodes of theft and showed total disrespect for the local authorities. There is no evidence to prove truth of his horse stealing, blasphemy and bearing false witness, of which he was accused. In 1886 as a young man he made his way, probably on foot to Tyumen, some 250 km to the east by north east, then headed due east for another 2,800 km to Moscow. There he met Praskovya Dubrovina, a peasant girl. After a brief courtship he married her in 1887 and returned to his native village. Praskovya remained there for the rest of her life, raising three children, one boy born Dmitri (1895) and two girls. Maria (1898) and Varvara (1900). Rasputin continued his wanderings and from time to time returned to the village to be with his devoted wife Praskovya and their family. In 1897 Rasputin left his pregnant wife on the family farm and went on a pilgrimage as he had developed a renewed interest in religion.

 It is suggested but not proven that he had a vision of the Virgin Mary and set out on a spiritual quest. But it has also been suggested that he left the village to escape charges for his role in a horse theft. It was after this time of his initial pilgrimage that a theological student Melty Zaborosky may have influenced him. Whatever the reasons for Rasputin continuing pilgrimages, he cast off his old life at the ripe old age of twenty eight and despite having been married ten years, left his wife with an infant son and another on the way. It was apparent that he was occasioned some sort of emotional conflict or spiritual crisis in his life. On shorter pilgrimages he had stayed at the Holy Znamensky Monastery and also on another at the Tobolsky's Cathedral. It was the visit to the St. Nicholas Cathedral in 1897 that he was transformed. There he met and was profoundly humbled by an elder known as Makary. He apparently spent several months there and learnt to read and write. He later complained of some monks being engaged in homosexual acts and criticised the monastic life as being to coercive. Returning to the farm and his wife, looking disheveled and behaving differently, he became a vegetarian, swore of alcohol, and was often seen praying and singing out much more reverently than he had ever done in the past.

He would leave his wife and family often on pilgrimages for months and even years at a time, wandering the country and visiting holy sites. It is believed he wandered as far as Mount Athos, the centre of Eastern Orthodox monastic life in 1900 and where the gifts of the the Magi, wise men are still housed. The three gifts to the infant Jesus at his birth; gifts of spiritual meaning: gold as a symbol of kinship on earth, frankincense a symbol of deity, and myrrh, an embalming oil as symbol of death,. Like all Prophet's seem to do, by the early 1900s he had developed a small circle of followers, primarily family members and other local peasants, who prayed with him on Sundays and on holy days. He returned to his home and village church from time to time and eventually built a small chapel in g his fathers root cellar where his family household group and followers met in secret from the local villagers and the priest who considered his activities with some suspicion and hostility. It was rumoured that female followers were ceremoniously washing him before each meeting, that the group sang strange songs and that Rasputin had joined a religious sect whose ecstatic rituals were rumoured to include self flagellation and sexual orgies. However, repeated investigations failed to establish that Rasputin was ever a member of a sect, and rumours of self flagellation and sexual orgies have been unfounded.

Word of Rasputin's spirituality and charisma spread through Siberia in the early 1900s. At some point in 1905 he travelled to the city of Kazan, where he was admired as a holy man who could help people resolve their spiritual crisis and anxieties. Despite rumours that Rasputin was having sex with female followers, he made a favourable impression on the Father Superior of the Seven Lakes Ministry outside Kazan as well as the local church officials. They recommended to Bishop Sergei, the rector of St. Petersburg Theological Seminary at Alexander Nevsky Monastery, for Rasputin to travel to St.Petersburg. Sergei had introduced Archimandrite Theofan, inspector of the theological seminary, who was well connected in St. Petersburg society and later served as confessor to the Tzar and his wife. Theofan was so impressed with Rasputin he invited him to stay at his house and introduced him to influential friends in St. Petersburg, thus   gaining him entry into salons and aristocratic gatherings for religious discussions. It was through these meetings that Rasputin attracted some of his early influential followers though many would ultimately turn away from him.

Alternative religious, spiritual and theosophy movements were popularised among city aristocracy, so Rasputin's ideas and strange behaviours made him the subject of intense curiosity. His appeal may have been enhanced by the fact that he was a native Russian unlike other self described 'holy men' before him.He formed friendships with several members of the aristocracy, including the " Black Princesses," Militsa and Anastasia of Montenegro, who married the Tsar's cousin, Grand Duke Peter Nikolaevich and Prince George Maximilianovich Romanowsky, and were instrumental in introducing Rasputin to the Tsar and his family. They met at Peter's Palace on 1st November 1905 and the Tsar wrote in his diary: "...made an acquaintance of a man of God- Grigori , from Tobosky Province." Rasputin returned home after that meeting and after six months returned to St Petersburg sending Nicholas a telegram asking to be presented to the Tsar. He met the royal family again in July 1906 and in November was introduced to their children. At some point the Royal family become convinced that Rasputin possessed miraculous power to heal the son's affliction. Due to the fact Alexei hereditary condition causing painful internal bleeding, Rasputin was initially asked to pray for the child. Much of Rasputin's influence over the Royal family and others was the fact that on several occasions the pain eased and the bleeding stopped. Princess Alexandra had a "passionate attachment" to Rasputin, believing he could cure her son's affliction. The fact that son Alexia's bleeding condition ceased immediately after Rasputin prayed for him in the spring of 1907, Rasputin was then hailed as 'an indispensable member of the Royal entourage.' The Tsarina's good-friend, Anna Vyrubova became convinced as a faithful follower of Rasputin, that he had miraculous powers. She became his most convinced and devoted influential advocates. It is thought that Rasputin controlled the bleeding of Alexi's by disallowing the administering of Aspirin and other psychic abilities.

During the summer of 1912 Alexei developed a haemorrhage in his thigh and groin after a jolting in a carriage he was riding at the royal hunting grounds at Spara. He was in severe pain and delirious with fever and appeared close to death. Alexandra asked Anna her friend, to send Rasputin a telegram in Siberia were he was staying, asking him to pray. Rasputin quickly replied: "God has seen your tears and heard our prayers. Do not grieve. The little One will not die, Do not allow the doctors to bother him too much." The next morning Alexei's condition had not changed, but Alexandra was encouraged by the message and regained some hope that her child would not die. Alexei's bleeding stopped the next day. The attending Dr. Fedrov later admitted: "the recovery was wholly inexplicable from a medical viewpoint." He understood how the press had faith in Rasputin as a miracle man. "On another occasion, when Alexie's bleeding occurred, Rasputin would come, walk up to the patient, look at him and spit. The bleeding would stop in no time. How could the Empress not trust Rasputin after that?" History has it recorded that Rasputin stopped the bleeding by calming both mother and child, by hypnosis. Of course his healing powers gained him considerable status and power at the court, The tsar appointed him ' lamplighter,' charging him with keeping the lamps lit before religious icons in the palace, and gained him regular access to the paace and the royal family. He become close enough to ask a special favour of the Tsar, to a change his name to Rasputin- Noviy (New). Rasputin used his influence to gain sexual favours from admirers and worked diligently to expand his influence.

Rasputin become a controversial figure. He was accused by his enemies of religious heresy and rape, was suspected of exerting undue political influence on the Tsar, and was rumoured to be having an affair wit the Tsarina. Opposition to Rasputin's influence grew in the church and he was soon denounced as a heretic; the local Bishop accusing him of spreading false doctrines. In St.Petersburg, Rasputin faced opposition by prominent critics, including the Prime Minister Peter Stolypin and the Tsar's secret police force. Stolypin on ordering an investigation about Rasputin's activities, approached the Tsar with his report. However he did not succeed in reigning in Rasputin influence nor exiling him from St.Petersburg. One of his former followers, a Kehioniya Berlatskaya accused him of rape. Rumours multiplied that Rasputin had assaulted female followers and behave inappropriately on visits to the royal family. Particularly with the teenage daughters Olga and Tatyana, which was reported widely in the press of 1910. Whilst World war 1, the dissolution of feudalism, and a meddling government bureaucracy all contributed to Russia's economic decline, many laid the blame on Alexandra and her evil advisor Rasputin. In November 2016, an outspoken member of the Duma Vladmir Purishkevick, stated that the Tsar's ministers had "been turned into marionettes slating him as 'the evil genius of Russia and the Tsarina'- who has remained a German on the Russian throne and alien to the country and its people." The die had been cast and it was not long before the Royals would be exiled in a revolution and Rasputin would be brought to death.

In July 2014 Rasputin had survived an assassination attempt by a peasant women back in his home at Pokrovskoye. He had been seriously wounded but somehow survived after a long recovery in hospital Another earlier attempt on his life in 1911 was by Guseva, who was a follower of Iliodor, one of a group of established figures who attempted to drive a wedge between the Royal family and Rasputin and failed. Iliodorr was banished from St.Petersburg and ultimately defrocked. Guseva the former priest who had supported Rasputin before denouncing his sexual escapades and self aggrandisement, claimed to have acted alone having read in the newspapers and believing "the false prophet was an Antichrist." Both the Police and Rasputin believed that Iliodor had instigated the attempt on Rasputin's life....he thus fled the country before he could be questioned and Guseva was not found to be responsible for reasons of insanity.

 Rasputin was murdered in a plot organised by a group of noted leaders led by Prince Felix Yusupov, Grand Duke, and right wing politician Vladimir Purishkevich, who decided that Rasputin's influence over the Tsarina and the whole Royal family threatened the empire. They concocted a plan to kill him in December 1916, by inviting him to a dinner engagement on 30th December 1916 at the home of Felix Yusupov. On arrival Rasputin was usurped into the basement dining area, was offered tea and cakes laced with cyanide. However after eating his fill of cake and drinking the tea he appeared unaffected by the poison. Rasputin then asked for Madeira wine which was also laced with poison.

 He drank three full glasses but still showed no sign of distress. At around 2.30 am Yusupov excused himself to go upstairs where his fellow conspirators were waiting. He took a revolver from Dmitry Pavlovich and returned to the basement, pointed the gun at Rasputin and declared: "You better look at the crucifix on the wall and say a prayer, then shot him in the chest. The conspirator then took Rasputin's coat and in disguise drove to Rasputin's apartment in an attempt to make it look like he had returned home. They then returned to the the the Monika Palace, wherein Yusupov returned to the basement to ensure Rasputin was dead. Suddenly Rasputin leapt up and attacked Yusupov, grabbing him by the throat. Yusupov freed himself with great effort and raced upstairs. Rasputin followed and made it to the Palace's courtyard before being shot at point blank range by Purishkevich in the forehead. The conspirators then wrapped his body in cloth, tied him in chains and weighing down his body with rocks, then drove to the Petrovsky Bridge and dropped his body in ice cold waters of the Malaya Nevka River. It was later reported by the two workman who noticed blood on the bridge and Rasputins boot on the ice, that his body had been found 200 meters downstream from the bridge. Once retrieved, it appeared Rasputin had broken the chains and crawled along the bottom of the river before his death.

 Dr. Dmitry Kosorotov, the city's senior autopsy surgeon, reported that Rasputin's body had shown signs of severe trauma, including three gunshot wounds, one at close range to the forehead, a slice wound on his left side, many of which he felt he had sustained post-mortem. He found no water in Rasputins lungs. He found only one bullet in Rasputin' s body but found it too difficult to identify the type to be traced. Rasputin's funeral and burial on January 2nd 1917 was attended by the the Royal family and a few friends and he was buried in the grounds of the Royal palace. Rasputin's wife, mistress and children weren't invited, His body was exhumed and burned by a detachment of soldiers shortly after the Tsar abdicated the throne in March 1917, so that the grave would not become a rallying point for supporters of the old regime. The royal family were ultimately captured by revolutionary forces, denied asylum to Britain, and then brutally shot at Ekaterinburg on the 16th July 1918.

There is a theory that the British Secret Intelligence service were involved in Rasputin's assassination, as the British agents were concerned that Rasputin would urge the Tsar to make peace with Germany, which would allow Germany to concentrate its military efforts on the Western front. The planned assassination being carried out under the command of Samuel Hoare and Oswald Rayner, who had attended Oxford University with Yusopov. Another theory exposed that Rayner had personally shot Rasputin. The British Intelligence archives state: "There is no convincing evidence that places any British agents at the murder scene. If British agents had been involved we would have expected to find some trace of that." The British archives on Rasputin are well buried now as is the smoking gun, reportedly a British revolver that fired a Webley 455 inch bullet found in the courtyard were Rasputin fell. British agent Rayner's chauffeur later wrote: "it is a little known fact that Rasputin was shot, not by a Russian but an Englishman,'" and implied that his former boss was centrally involved. On his return to England, Oswald Rayner not only confided to his cousin that he had been present at Rasputin's murder, but also showed family members a bullet which he claimed he had acquired at the murder scene. Sadly, Rayner burnt all his papers before he died in 1961.

It is thus difficult to conclude whether Rasputin's death was indeed the result of the machinations of the British government or the plot of a group of conservative aristocrats and Romanov relatives. No one was ever charged for the assassination of Rasputin. The mystic and holy man died as he had lived with a powerful fight and much passion to live until his untimely death. I broke free from my recalling of Rasputin's life to the voice of Gandhi. "This is indeed a nourishing and exceedingly health selection of food for us men of heavenly realm." he stated. Rasputin, turns to me with those dark piercing eye, raised his glass of red wine to me and acknowledged in agreement. "Indeed." he responded.

It was time now, having recalled the nature of both men and their revenant pursuit of the spiritual, mystic and holy works, to ply them with questions to satisfy my curiosity on their relevant mission and to fulfil the yearning that I have to know more. It was almost as if Gandhi had read my thoughts. He began: " To achieve anything of notability in life you not only have to have persistence, you need to be stubborn." He paused for a brief moment, adjusting his glasses and continued: " In my lifetime, I spoke of many things, I always had an inner voice guiding me. The spiritual force emphasised truth, non-violence, love, compassion and selfless concern for the wellbeing of others. It was the-way I chose to live, the way of action by example." I quickly piped up: " But what about the violence caused to you and others in your promotion of non violence in all things?" Gandhi replied: " From my youth and my Mother's Jainism religion I took the principles of doing no harm and developed the principle of ' truth force' on life. I hoped to win the people over by changing their hearts and minds, and advocating non-violence in all things. I read many books on religions, but I always remained a committed Hindu as I saw so much hypocrisy in organised religions."

So in all your readings," I asked, "what spiritual leadership did you gain the most from?" Gandhi replied: "Jesus' Sermon on the Mount and Leo Tolstoy." "Huh, Tolstoy, on the same spiritual plain as Jesus?" Grandi pricked up his ears, smiled and in a quiet voice responded. "it was the philosophies he wrote of, relating to his time, and I with my spiritual voice as a guide, adapted and applied those by way of example to myself as much as to others." I pressed him for more: "Pray tell." I asked. "Well" Gandhi said: "in the words of Tolstoy, everyone thinks of changing the world, but no one thinks of changing himself.' If you look for perfection you will never be content. We can know that we know nothing, and that is the highest degree of human wisdom."

I recalled how his time in South Africa as a young man, Gandhi had been disgusted with the treatment of Indians by the white settlers there. He exhorted his countrymen to observe truthfulness in business and reminded them that their responsibility was the greatest since their conduct would be seen as a reflection of their country. He asked them to forget about religious and cast differences, to give up unsanitary habits, to demonstrate suitability for citizenship by showing they deserved it. He spent the next twenty years there and finally gained Indian citizenship rights. On his return to India, his immediate problem was to settle his relatives and associates in an ashram- "a group life lived in a religious spirit." I reminded Gandhi of Tolstoy's happiness philosophy: "A quiet secluded life in the country, with the possibility of being useful to people to whom it is easy to be good, and to who are not accustomed to have good done to them; then work which I hope may be of some use; then rest, nature, books, music, love for one's neighbour- such is my idea of happiness."

Gandhi responded: "My Ashram was a small model of a whole moral and religious ideal. The community did not enforce on its inmates any theology or ritual, but only a few simple rules of personal conduct.It was more like a large fan mill than a monastery, it was filled with children and senior citizens ,the uneducated and American and European scholars, devout followers and thinly disguised sceptics- a melting pot of different and sometimes opposing ideas, living peacefully and usefully with each other. I was considered the moral Father of the Ashram, and would fast as penance when a wrong was committed within its walls. Everyone was bound to me only by love and a fear of hurting me. It was there I learnt to take responsibility over every method that instilled a truth force that I called 'Satyagraha.' Now days you would call it a force that is inherent to truth of non-violent action."

When he failed to convince authorities over various inequalities that was Indians but were subject to under British rule, he would go on hunger strike as a protest which drew media attention to his cause. He was dismayed over the British refusal to grant Indian independence which resulted in a violent turn out of events, copious correspondence with the Government and civil unrest during and after WW11. It was only after he inspired love in both Hindu and Muslim for him, that he was enabled to control the violence when he was treading too fast until death to get Indian independence. I suggested to Gandhi: "It seemed you used eating sparingly and fasting as the main means of convincing the British authorities to reduce taxes, change the status quo with regard to class and ultimately gain independence? "I hoped to win people over to change their hearts and minds, advocating non violence in all things, by making self sacrifice in all bodily discipline, in food intake especially the type of food eaten which so often links with the spiritual and religious culture of the times. Occasional severe fasting to draw attention to a particular matter had the best result in effecting change."He added:' I never did get the diet thing right for myself though and tried many times what you might call today ' fad diets.' I even wrote a book on that subject. "

I drew Gandhi's attention to British law by reminding him of his march to the sea to make salt and his prospects of being arrested for breaking the law. " The march tp the sea with followers to protest the British Salt Tax was the most controversial act of mass civil disobedience that the world at large had awakened to, don't you agree?" He responded: " My task was done to win or perish." he added. " Then it was up to the Working Committee of Congress to show the way and then it was up to each Indian to follow the lead." He added. " You remember in my speech on the way to jabalpur to make salt?, let nothing be done in conversation to the authority voted in me by Congress.' No -one who believes in non-violence, as creed, need, therefore, sit still. "

My compact with the Congress ends as soon as I am arrested. In that case... Wherever possible, civil disobedience of salt laws should be started. These laws can be violated in three different ways ; by manufacture, by possession of contraband salt, or by the carrying away of natural salt deposits on the seashores, all are likewise a violation of the law. In short you may choose any one or all of these devices to break the salt monopoly." Gandhi had not finished to make his point: "We can refuse to pay taxes if we have the requisite strength. We are not content with this alone.....other similar measures may be adopted. I stress one condition, the pledge of truth, as the only means for attainment of home rule must be faithfully kept." he went on to say : " Much can be done in many other ways besides these. The Liquor and foreign clothing shops be picketed." Gandhi himself led by example weaving his own cloth and making his own clothing and he did not drink alcohol. "lawyers can give up practice.

The public servants can resign their posts... do not despair. The number of government servants in this country does not exceed a few hundred thousand. What about the rest? A Public Service collector will not be able to afford the number of servants he has got today, he will be his own servant. Our starving millions have no means to afford the enormous Public service expenditure. If, therefore, we are sensible enough, let us bid good-bye to government employment, no matter if it is the post of judge or police. Let all who are cooperative with government, in one way or another...withdraw their co-operation and support in as many ways as possible." He went on with his means of rejecting payment of taxes, withdrawing children from Government schools, etc etc." "I have faith in the righteousness of our cause and the purity of our weapons."

The civil disobedience marches and Gandhi's mobilisation of peaceful non-aggression continued for the reminder of his days, until the day of Indian Independence. It was the way the British had it's say in control by way of the Mountbatten plan that disturbed Gandhi. Whilst he was pleased to see progress, be it not perfection, he took to his sleeping mat in protest whilst the Congress argued about the process of breaking up India and Pakistan into two countries. He strongly opposed the partition of India at independence in 1947 and he refused to eat for some time. In 1947 he was assassinated by a Hindu extremist, who saw him as too accommodating of India's Muslims.

Rasputin had listened with intent to Gandhi's words. He himself knew of the power of words, of the political influence he swayed over Russia and the Royal family, of his own powers to heal. He believed in the power of prayer of speaking in tongues and the influence his own natural had been granted to him by God from his birth. It seemed like the man already knew what I wished to question him about, so before I had an opportunity to even frame a question in mind, he commenced with his own correctly assumed summation: "You want to know about my healing powers and my ability in particular to heal the young Prince Alexei of his pain and haemophilia. Well it was no trick, for i just knew a little more than the doctors of the day through my vast experience in the natural world as well as my belief in prayer, the use of extreme concentration of my energy, hypnotic spell and the power of mind over matter in the use of a natural placebo."

It told me everything and nothing. So, I was about to probe a little more deeply into the mind of this so called ' faith healer.' I could see by the intensity of his eyes, he was trying to cast some sort of spell over what he perceived as a lesser mind. He was reluctant to expand on his formula,. However, I knew that I had somewhat more power over him then and there and he knew it. I was alive and he wasn't, and he knew that I could just as easily switch off and cast him out of my mind without the slightest emotion. He just smiled calmly with a more intense look, but I achieved my effective desire and he began to explain:

"One of the best things to do when a person is in sickness or in extreme pain is to keep them as calm as possible. Thus it was my advice to the doctors treating little Alexei, not to disturb him, let him rest thus aiding his recovery. It also helped to keep his mother Alexandria away from him, for her tension and anguish at seeing him in so much pain was transmitted to the child too. I also knew that Aspirin thins the blood which was the last thing the child, whose blood would not clot because of the condition, needed to ease the pain. Of course, Doctors today know this but it seemed back then that I was the only person who bothered to do the research. So by calming the child and the mother I reduced much emotional stress on Alexei, dispensed with the aspirin and used hypnosis on both, and used a natural placebo." He thought he was done with me, but I persisted: " What natural placebo did you use?' Rasputin smiled and demonstrated. He spat on his hands whilst staring deeply into my eyes and applied the spit on my chest and said: " Therein lay the placebo. You see my friend, much of the talk of my magic, miracle works, healing powers are all in nature of man and the planet, and of course God played a very impor-tant part too, as the power of prayer always works over the power of man."

 On that note both Masters and Holy men of the heavenly realm began to leave my table and disappear into the shadows of the night. As the two Masters and old friends walked and talked together, I heard Gandhi asking Rasputin: "I had for the better part of my days on earth kept a strict diet and disciplined myself by fasting frequently, I then always remained thin. In your case, you ate and drank what you liked, lived to excess in most instances, particularly food. How then did you remain so thin yet physically and mentally healthy and strong? ' I was not privy to all of what Rasputin's responses were, but I did manage to hear before this voice faded "It had a lot to do with my partiality to Ukha fish soup, the black bread and raw vegetables of my native province as a child and of course the Madeira wine. My gut health was always adequate for any food presented to me as a holy man."

Being a little at a loss as to who would be my next dinner guests as Masters at my table, I decided to stroll to the park near my apartment. I just wanted to clear my head of thought, get a little fresh air and unwind after the previous absorbing interrelation with the spirits of the Masters, Gandhi and Rasputin. I had been inspired to call those 'holy men' to my table but confessed I was a little perplexed at the answers they might give me to the questions I had planned to asked that were whirling around in my head at the time. When questioning my motivation now reason escaped me, but I had to admit I had learnt a great deal in my research on both men and gained insight into not just their spirituality but in matters pertaining to their health, diet, and way of life. I know felt assured that I could apply some of their teachings fro my own wellbeing.

It was the Saturday after New Year and public access to a park near my home was still approved, despite interstate border closures and some local suburbs being in lockdown. Fear of a new pandemic was being broadcasted on the air-wave, both the previous Covid and new strain of the virus had been detected in two capital cities. Authorities panicked and closed their boarders once more until further notice. I believed that if the case numbers for people who were testing positive didn't start reducing soon then visits to the park would not be available for much longer. So I enjoyed the freedom of of the vista of flowers, trees and grassy areas, watched as children played and dogs keep their owners in control with ball games and stick retrieval. I sat on a park bench, mindful of social distancing rules and drank a take away coffee with a friend, chewing the fat over the state of the nation and the world at large. Everyone seemed to be wearing a face masks again, so I prayed the dark cloud of the evil bug would soon vanish and we all could get back to some semblance of personal con-tentment and economic order.

Casting away thoughts of the pandemic, I wandered back to my apartment intent on determining who my next dinner guests would be for the Saturday evening. I was sure I had locked up but could hear a great deal of bumping and thumping and unearthly shrieks from within. To my surprise the place had been turned upside down, food crumbs scattered on the floor with my biscuit tin on the kitchen bench lying on its side. My writing desk draw appeared to have been pried opened, as if some knowing party was searching for something of importance. There seemed to be no sign of human presence, but to my surprise I discovered a spiritual visitor of another kind. Sitting squat on top of a dining room chair was a possum eating a biscuit held in one paw and a sheet of half chewed up paper in the other. I did my best to encourage the little fellow to leave via an open door but he seemed determined to stay put. After chasing my nocturnal visitor around the lounge room for what seemed an eternity I finally coaxed this potential squatter out the front door and locked it up to ensure no further interruption for the night. I returned to clean up the crumbs in the kitchen, put the biscuit tin with lid on tight and back on the shelf were it belonged. I then turned to my office desk to tidy up the papers where the curious critter had scattered them. I just flattened out the paper he had in paw earlier this evening and had a snack before retiring for the night, to check in with the spirits of my ancestors, content that I had done the best that I could have done with my dinner guests that evening.

****

CHAPTER 8

INTERMISSION: A STRANGE TWIST OF FATE

I awoke in the dead of night to the noise of the vent roof opening and closing in my ensuite. It was the return of the possum. I heard the little creature running about in the shower and as I had had enough exercise earlier in the night chasing him around the lounge room, so I made sure the window in my bedroom was open, pulling back the curtain to let in the light. I left the door of the ensuite slightly ajar too, so my visitor could leave at first light without bothering me any further. Once done I drifted back into a deep sleep and awoke again just before dawn. Turning on the light to head to the bathroom for nature called, I was confronted by a ball of fur on my adjoining pillow and two bright eyes staring back at me. I took fright which in turned scared the poor creature and it quickly dashed behind a brief case I had left near the window and stayed there. I went back to bed and pretended to fall back to sleep. The little possum seemed to assume he was welcome to stay this time and sat there until dawning light and then quietly slipped out the window and was gone.

My broken night's sleep resulted in my rising late, quickly doing bathroom duties and heading to the kitchen for a late breakfast. Seated on my verandah watching the world pass by, I began to contemplate the previous night's visit from my furry friend. Most nights before I go to sleep I handover myself to the protection of my guardian angel and ask the spirits of my ancestors to look after my son Peter, who died by his own hand. Whilst I no longer feel the pain of his loss, he is oft in my thoughts, as he was the previous night. It dawned on me that it was possibly Peter in the spirit of the Possum who had come to visit. It was most like him to raid the biscuit tin or check out some form or other in my office activities out of curiosity. We had given him a nickname as a child "Possum Pete," so it was quite reasonable to my mind to consider he was return ing to make contact again. Peter initially followed me as a Cockatoo from the day of his burial, it became his habit to greet me every morning perched on the verandah rail. Peter was much like that bird, naturally affectionate, resting his head upon my shoulder, cuddling up to me and sometimes sticking out his beak for a kiss, or doing annoying things like screeching, chatting, bobbing up and down; in fact anything to gain my attention. When the seasons change to autumn and winter, he would vanish for a time only to return again in springtime and start his attention getting regime all over again through to summer end . As I grew to accept Peter's passing, the cockatoo returned less frequently and ultimately stopped coming all-together.

This I learnt to accept as a sign of emotional progress on my part and that of the Peter, the Cockatoo. However, the Possum turning up and its antics in the kitchen and my office desk had me assuming that Peter had returned in a new form. He may have thought it more appropriate given regard to my present circumstance to appear thus, or perhaps the fact that he had died of his own hand, he may have felt he could not take on human form at this point in time from his place in the heavens. Particularly now that I had grown the habit of spending so much of my time contemplation Masters for the heavenly realms to come dine with me on most Saturday evenings and that I was not taken to thinking so much about him of later. Returning to my office desk, I considered the note the Possum had extracted from my desk drawer, it was in Gandhi's hand written scrawl. An extract from his lifetime search for a prefect diet included the balanced nutrition of salt. British taxes had banded the making of salt by Indians, imposed heavy taxes making it impossible for the starving millions of poor to get salt in their limited nutrition.

 I took to trying to understand why the possum had drawn my attention once more to Gandhi's methodologies for non violent protest. It would be the sort of thing my son Peter would have done now that I had come to think about it in retrospect. I recalled events in his life were he had done just that - disagreed with authority; government and private enterprise in their lack of care for the common man in matters pertaining to health. He deplored their pseudo intellectual pomp and ceremonious display of knowledge and would sometimes cry out in despair. "They know 'jack shite,' about the difficulties of the common man." It had certainly been the thing that my next two guests certainly did to their own perilous end.

 I returned to the kitchen and prepared some crackers with cheese and tomato topping, heading then to my verandah armed with my plate of snacks, salt and pepper shakers and a pot of tea. My objective was to contemplate my navel for a time before partaking of my mid morning nutritional break. After some time of meditation I salt and peppered up the toppings on the biscuit crackers and ate heartily. The tea had cooled a little to much for my liking so I returned to the kitchen to boil another brew. On my return to the verandah who should be perched next to the remaining crackers? None other than my long lost visitor, the cockatoo. He was busily picking away at some salt spilt upon the table. I responded: "Well this is not Gandhi's time and besides we have no British Salt Law that stops us making or buying salt." The cockatoo took a curious glance at me as if he got the picture, gave a final squark and headed skyward. I sat there watching his flight path and wondered if our paths would cross again in this lifetime.

****

CHAPTER 9.

LESSONS FORM CIVIL RIGHTS LEADERS

It was Thanksgiving day 2020, and my mind drifted back to a past Thanksgiving. I recalled my being seating in the lotus position doing a healing meditation under the instruction of a guru teacher. Still in the depths of a psychological recovery from depression and no longer drinking alcohol, the need for stillness of body, mind and spirit was paramount to my wellbeing as it is now. I was recalling that the American celebrate of harvest and other blessing of the past year with a national Thanksgiving holiday. The traditional celebration is believed to be modelled on the 1621 harvest feast of the English colonist, the Pilgrims of Plymouth at the end of their first year in the new world, celebrated with the local Wampanoag Indian tribe. Its the story deeply rooted in America's curriculum- the one that arguably inspires the most important and tradition-filled holiday in American culture. The history books tell us that in 1620 the Pilgrims fled the harsh religious suppression in Britain, sailed the Atlantic, and in December 1620 stepped ashore at Plymouth Rock, in what is now Massachusetts. With little food and no shelter, the colonist struggled to survive a brutal winter until a friendly Wampanoag Indian, Squanto, came along and showed them how to cultivate a crop. The first harvest resulted in a feast, as the Pilgrims gave thanks to the kind Indians for helping them to bring the colony to life. This version of the story is pleasant but isn't terribly accurate. We pay homage to the Pilgrims and the story but the Indians part is a forgotten role, as if their history doesn't matter.

About four years before the Pilgrims landed, British fishermen had already started making their way through the New England area , storming through Indian villages kidnapping native people for profit and selling them into slavery. The British and Europeans settlers who arrived there, not only took slaves but they bought epidemic illness resulting in large numbers of native death as a consequence. The Pilgrims already believed they were a part of God's plan and that initial explosion of death saw empty village which they had no consideration in taking ownership from the nomadic natives. The Wampanoag were no exception loosing entire villages with the onslaught of disease. Only a fraction of their nation survived. When the Pilgrims arrive in 1690 the surviving Wampanoag nomadic tribe had suggested a mutual benefit relationship, exchanging weaponry for food and then teaching the new settlers how to grow crops for a bountiful harvest. It was from these natives that the Pilgrims learnt to give thanks for their bountiful harvest and thus was born the annual harvest Thanksgiving feast each year in October. The story did not end there, as these white folk not only took the Indians into slavery, created segregated land title for them, but returned from Africa with more immigrant slaves to work the cotton, oats and wheat fields to harvest crops of every variety.

Thus was born nation of peoples who grew rich in trade and diverse business. It was not long before the British were defeated in the War of Independence that America gained its freedom. A Civil War broke the backbone of the slave trade that had flourished through the south. The Declaration of Independence was born boasting a truth that 'all men are created equal.' After the death of generations, surviving Indians whose lands had been stolen were forced on to small land allotments known as 'Indian reservations." Today there are some one million Indians living on those government allotments;, the majority having assimilated into the mass of all races that populate America. The last census quotes a population of 328 million throughout the land. It is the land of opportunity according to the marketing brochure. Negro American ancestors taken into slavery from their native African homeland would not agree, as do a large majority of races of all colour and creed today. The history that American equality of race has proved by a bloody past not to be true, as the Bill of rights has been proven be a Bill of wrongs. The Negro cries out today " Black lives matter" as the masses cry out for a better standard of living, as equally as other races and the growing mass of unemployed cry out for food, clothing, shelter and work of any kind. Presidents and men of the Pulpit, men of position and power and civil right workers of all race colour and creed still fight for the rights of freedom, challenge the laws of the land, the religions of faith and prejudice alike. Over my seven score years and six on this planet, I have seen and heard of the death of many a charismatic leader fighting for the rights of the oppressed, seen the poor and the indigenous man on the troubled streets of America continue with in its quake of authority over the oppressed.

So it was on this 2020 Thanksgiving morning that I began to contemplate the meaning of the Thanksgiving harvest and men who lived by the courage of their convictions, those who spoke out, fought and died for the freedom of the American people. So many of those men of good character who championed the way to that freedom under the flag have died by the assassin's bullet. Men of courage and determination speaking out in a cause for everyday common man. America still flows with the blood of those who have stood up for human rights in the land of the free, still suffering for lack of freedom, even on this day of Thanksgiving. For this year has not so much been a bountiful harvest, but a harvest of death and distrust of an economy in the midst of millions of deaths in a pandemic of a different kind of evil. It was with such thoughts clearing from my mind that I heard in my head a line from a lyric of Bob Dylan: "Well, now time passed and now it seems, everybody's having them dreams, everybody sees themselves walking around as some one else. Half the people can be part right all of the time, some of the people can be all right part fo the time, but all the people can't be all right all of the time, I think Abraham Lincoln said that." The thought of Abe Lincoln's words: "Most folk are as happy as they make up their mind to be," rang in my header. I was determined now to attempt to think of nothing in my attempt to meditate on the hope that my inspiration would attract the next Masters at my table. A desire to be fulfilled, to live in the now in a spiritual and peaceful way despite external circumstance. A way of life of well-being to be used to pass on to others reflecting the influence of the Masters.

As I drifted into the meditative state, so many Masters appeared as the ones to be chosen. I initially had a vision of the inside of the Liberty Bell inscription: "Proclaim Liberty through all the land and unto all inhabitants." I heard it once more ring as in President Washington's birthday; saw those attempts to justice and freedom when the crack in the Bell was repaired. Heard the sound of the Bell ringing symbolic again as the sign of the anti-slavery movement, on the public announcement of the Declaration of Independence. It rang, with the patch in the crack on that signing of the constitution into law as it did on the death of the founding fathers, Benjamin Franklin, George Washington, Alexander Hamilton and Thomas Jefferson. Visions of these Masters of progress and goodwill were followed by a vision of Lincoln, Garfield and John F Kennedy who were all assassinated in their battle for the freedom of all Americans. Then the ones that come forward most clearly in my vision were the assassinated civil rights leaders, Martin Luther King Jr. and Medgar Evers; they were walking arm in arm with Bobby Kennedy. As my meditation deepened I realise that it was those three that I had to do my choosing from as my dinner guests. For they were the most recent on this planet who fought for freedom under the American flag, under the symbolism of the Statue of Liberty and as I began to come out of my meditative state, I heard a dull ringing once more of the Liberty Bell. Being Thanksgiving day I knew it was not appropriate to prepare a meal for my pending guests for this occasion, for my proposed dinner engagements with the Masters at my Table was as I had always arranged, to be on the Saturday evening. Still I figured that as both my guests were American they would appreciate a good old turkey dinner with vegetables and a traditional apple pie for desert, I would need to enlist the help of my good friend Mirjana to cook the turkey. As another friend John would insist: "Nobody can cook a turkey they way Mirjana can." I had to agree, for John had once enlisted her services to cook a turkey dinner and I, being invited along as a guest on that occasion, enjoyed the meal immensely. Mirjana being of Croatian decent used the recipe handed down by her grandmother, so not being of American style, it would never-the -less be a superb meal for my guest. So with the meal menu already taken care of in my mind, I turned to a brief of my pending guests. It being my habit to help with my selection of dinner for two who would be my two allotted finalist.

I first set to work on the final hours of Robert Kennedy: I began with the 5th April 1968, the day after the assassination of Martin Luther King, when United States Attorney-General Robert Kennedy delivered a speech in Cleveland Ohio. It was a short but sharp critical attack on hatred and prejudice. "What has violence accomplished? " he asked. "What has it ever created? No martyr's cause has ever ben stilled by an assassins bullet…No one, no matter where he lives or what he does, can be certain whom will suffer from a senseless act of bloodshed."It was a month to that day that Bobby Kennedy fell victim to an assassin's bullet. It seemed like no political leader was safe in America. It seemed like he was ordained to be the next President. In March 1968 Johnson had announced he would not stand for re-election, bowing out for his vice president Hubert Humphrey to run. Kennedy had already established a clear lead over Eugene McCarthy in the early primaries, with his youthful enthusiasm of reformist ideas, compared with his democratic rivals old and unvaried approach.

 Nixon had narrowly lost to his brother John Kennedy in the 1960 election and Bob's rise to Attorney General, the route to be President would follow after his brother's term in office would seemed to have him next in line. The exhilarating expectations was ultimately dashed by the assassination of President Kennedy in 1963. His former political adversary Lyndon Johnson was automatically sworn in as Vice President. Now in 1968 it was Bobby;'s time to run for President and he felt confident that he would win this election, thus carrying the Kennedy banner forward for the betterment of his country as his brother John had done before him. Robert was born on 20th November 1925, the seventh child of the ambitious Joseph Kennedy and his long suffering wife Rose. The family was destined to suffer many tragedies not the least of which was the death of eldest brother Joe in the war and the assassination of both brothers John and Robert in their political stance to improve the lot of Americans. Nine months after his brother's assassination Robert left government.

 Bobby then turned to running for a seat in the Senate election representing New York and won it by a landslide. He used the following years in his path to the Presidency to launch a campaign against poverty, desegregated buses, increase voter registration, enforced human rights and most controversially stopped the escalation of the war in Vietnam. Initially he had decided not to run in1968 but Johnson's narrow win over the little known McCarthy convince him his hour had arrived. On 16th March 1968 he declared: "I do not run for presidency merely to oppose any man, but to propose new policies. I run because I am convinced this country is on a perilous course and because I have such strong feelings about what must be done and I feel that I am obliged to do all I can." Kennedy's victory in the California primary effectively knocked McCarthy out of the race. The same day, his victory over Humphrey in his latter day home state of South Dakota suggested Humphrey would be no obstacle. All seemed set for the party's nomination at the August National Democratic Convention in Chicago, which he hope would win his peaceful coronation as Johnson's heir apparent. Bobby left the stage after midnight 4/5 June after addressing his euphoric supporters at the Los Angeles' Ambassador Hotel. He kept talking to reporters after his victory speech and took a short cut through the hotel kitchen. He was shot in the head at close range by his assassin. Kennedy was not the only one who died that night; for thousands of Americans, hope in a brighter, kinder, more peaceful future died too. Many still ponder what might have happened if the 'best candidate for American ever' had gone on to be President.

Robert Kennedy appeared in my next meditation but he declined to be my guest, as he thought the civil rights Martin Luther King and Medgar Evers would be more likely dinner guest for my cause.. Before I had a chance to ask who he was behind his killing he answered: "Some may think it was my Brother John's killers, others the Mafia, and still others think it was done under the Instruction of Hoover who detested my investigation into organised crime, others think the CIA in the shadows. I know, but it is best to let it go, as these men in the shadows are paying their own price for their folly now." Then without any further ado, he vanished from my sight. So I then focused my two best choices as civil rights activists and began to write down a brief of each, starting with Martin Luther King and then Medgar Evers. I recalled how King came into prominence as an outspoken leader of boycotting in civil rights activism.

The segregation of black Americans from the whites came to a head on a bus in the township of Montgomery, Alabama, when a young black seamstress took a seat in the bus reserved only for white folk. When the driver asked Rosa Parks to move to the back she refused. The State's segregation laws resulted in her arrest which propelled African Americans to boycott Montgomery's buses. This in turn produced an historic US Supreme Court decision outlawing racial segregation on public transport. The leader in that boycott was a young Baptist Minister with a Ph. D in theology under his belt, Dr. Martin Luther King .Jr.

He had been born 15th January 1929 as Michael King in Atlanta, Georgia but his father in honour of the reformation theologian Martin Luther change his name. He had obtained his theology degree at Boston University and took up as resident minister of the local baptist Church in Montgomery when the bus boycott took place. It spurred him on to co-found a civil rights organisation, the Southern Christian Leadership Conference in 1957. He survived a stabbing at a book launch in 1958 and moved back to Atlanta where he became a pastor in a baptist church in his old neighbourhood in 1960. In 1963 his Christian Conference under his leadership marched on Washington for jobs and freedom. President Kennedy was initially opposed to it, as he was concerned it would retard the passage of civil rights legislation being enacted.

King eventually won the right to the March with a less stringent tone. The campaign demanded an end to racial segregation in schools, meaningful civil rights legislation including a law prohibiting racial discrimination in employment, protection of civil rights workers from brutality, a \$2 minimum wage for workers and self government for the largely black district of Columbia. The march proved a resounding success with a turnout of 250,000 people. This was his finest hour and where he delivered his " I have a dream" speech, electrifying the crowd. It is considered one of the finest speeches in American oratory. Using the rector skills as a Minister and his biblical knowledge, he took the old European metaphors of the New World for whites as a promised land for the poor and oppressed and applied them to Black Americans. By 1968 he could have rested on his laurels had he desired to. He had won the hearts of the masses five years before with his speech to that large audience, had seen the passing of the Civil Right Act in 1964 and won the Noble Peace Prize. But in

March 1968 he embarked on a new campaign to beat poverty and was in Memphis Tennessee, supporting striking African Americans when he was assassinated. Five weeks after his death, demonstrators began to show up in Washington D.C. for his so called 'Poor Peoples Campaign.' It had been Kings' final catch cry, without his leadership and inspirational rallying ability only 7,000 turned up- a far cry from his 1961 rally. It was to be in the economic Bill of Rights that the poor people would have full considerations but the campaign demand was never enacted. The night before he died, 3rd April 1968, he gave a personal, poignant and eerily prophetic speech to striking garbage collectors for whom he was rallying.Reflecting on his recovery from the stab wounds he received in 1958 and his own mortality: 'Longevity has its place. But I'm not concerned about that now... I'm happy, tonight. I'm not worried about anything. I'm not fearing any man.' The very next day he was killed by a bullet from the assassins gun, as he stood on the balcony of the Lorraine Motel were he had been staying.

Many murders and violent acts were committed at the high of the civil rights unrest in America's deep south in the 1950s and 1960s. Like John and Bobby Kennedy and Martin Luther King Jr. another that resonated high on the list that fired public reaction was the assassination of African American Medgar Evers. It took thirty years after the tragedy and two subsequent trials, with failed attempts to reach a verdict before police arrested Byron de la Beckwith - a former fertiliser salesman and member of the Ku Klux Klan and charged him with the murder. The body of Medgar Evers had to be exhumed for an autopsy and it was found to be surprisingly in an excellent state of preservation perhaps because of the embalming technique applied back then, or maybe it was because he was such a good man in his lifetime, the spirits of the God of his own understanding saw to it that the body remained in good order so that the culprit responsible for shooting him was found out. Following the retrial, Evers body was reburied in a second funeral, enabling his grown up children to say goodbye properly.

Evers was born in Decatur, Mississippi in 1925, and lived there until being drafted into the army, aged 18, in 1943. He fought courageously in Normandy and was discharged in 1945 with an impressive war record. However, after the war he soon found that the colour of his skin had not only stopped him getting a job but precluded him and his negro friends from voting in the local Mississippi elections. They were forced away from polling booths at gun point. He applied to go to University and graduated with a degree in business administration from the Alcorn University. Medgar was a model student, a star of football, track and field, a keen debater and singer, and served as president of his junior classes. After graduation he married Merle Beasley on Christmas Eve 1951, joined Magnolia Mutual Life as a salesman and perhaps more importantly joined the RCNI, the Regional Council of Negro Leadership, a Mississippi civil rights organisation. He helped organise a boycott of service stations that denied African Americans use of their restrooms. The group produced bumper stickers that read:" Don't buy gas where you can't use the restroom."

Evers then applied to the segregated University of Mississippi Law School in February 1954. When his application was rejected, he became the focus of the National Association for the Advancement of Coloured People (NAACP) campaign to discredit the university, using the US Supreme Court's recent rule that segregation was unconstitutional. The NAACP founded in 1909 had as its mission: 'To promote equal rights, to eradicate caste or race prejudice among the citizens of the United States, to advance the interest of coloured citizens; to secure for them impartial suffrage; and to increase their opportunity or securing justice in courts, education for the children, employment according to their ability and complete equal right before law.' In December 1954, Evers became the NAACP first field officer in Mississippi. Desegregation was finally won at the University of Mississippi in 1962 and in the years that followed Evers profile rose, and he was coming to the attention of a number of hostile constituencies. He pursued vocally a highly publicised investigations into two events: the murder of Emmett Till and the maltreatment of Clyde Kennard. As a result of these two cases and his outspoken protests, Evers began to receive death threats. On 28th May 1963 a Molotov cocktail was thrown into the carport of his home .Five days before his death, he was nearly run down by a car on leaving the Jackson NAACP office. The situation only got worse after he gave a pro Civil Rights speech to a local TV station. On 12th June 1963, Evers pulled into his driveway after returning from a meeting with NAACP lawyers, emerging from the car he was shot in the back. He staggered thirty feet towards the front door of his home before collapsing. He died at the local hospital fifty minutes later. A speech by President Kennedy rang true to this tragic event. "Race has no place in American life or law." Evers in death, became a national figure. Around 5000 people paraded in procession through the streets of Jackson to pay homage to Evers, including Martin Luther King Jr. Medgar Evers, like John F Kennedy and his brother Bobby, was buried in Arlington National Cemetery, receiving military honours in front of an estimated crowd of 2000 people. The former chairman fo the American Veterans Committee agreed to speak at a subsequent service, declaring that 'No soldier in this field has fought more courageously, more heroically than Medgar Evers.' Evers name still lives on.

In 1970 Medgar Evers College was established in Brooklyn, New York, as part of the City University of New York. Evers' wife, Meyrie, became a noted activist in her own right, eventually serving as chair of the NAACP. Ever's brother Charles also worked energetically for the cause of Civil Rights in Mississippi after his brother's death. Whilst he too was a college graduate, and implacable foe of segregation and violent racism, the brothers were quite unalike. Medgar was gentle, kind, diplomatic and altruistic, whilst Charles was blunt, aggressive, and ambitious. He became a businessman, small time criminal running numbers, prostitution and bootlegging whiskey in Mississippi and in Chicago. But nearly a decade after he had been run out of Mississippi, he galvanised civil rights after the assassination of his brother and returned a change man. He succeeded Medgar as a Mississippi civil right leader in 1963, became the first black Mayor in the state and a candidate for Governor and the United

States Senate. He died aged 97 at his daughter's home in Brandon, Mississippi June 2020.

So it was that I convinced these two champions of civil rights, justice and freedom to come to my table for the Saturday evening meal. Despite the fact that Thanksgiving Day had passed, I felt the roast turkey and vegetables a choice that both the Masters at my table would enjoy. It would be in no small part for Mirjana's secret recipe for cooking the turkey. Her technique, apart from applying the appropriate amount of lard to cook it in, was the fact that she insisted on pre-cooking it in her own gas oven. Apparently her technique of keeping the gas at a very low flame rate meant the turkey took twice as long to cook and made it twice as delicious to eat. Mirjana insisted on this method of cooking after including the stuffing, sweet potatoes, cornbread, mashed potatoes and gravy preparation in the oven too.I noticed she had a container with cranberry sauce and in another container home made apple pie for desert. Everything was going to plan and I was so glad I had enlisted her help to prepare the meal. It was my duty to select the wines, so I settled for a light and crispy Sauvignon Blanc and just in case either Master preferred something with a sweet fruity flavour, I selected a local Riesling. It had been a long time since I had partaken of alcoholic beverage, butI felt sure I knew my selection would be acceptable under the circumstance. At any rate the meal, knowing Mirjana's skill in the kitchen, particularly with a traditional turkey dinner would be something to die for irrespective of wine selection.

Medgar Evers arrived first and without any pomp or ceremony, just introduced himself and humbly asked: "Where do you wish that I should sit?" I pulled back a chair at one end of the table, offered him a drink but he chose water initially whilst we waited for Dr King. A sudden gust of wind through the window of the lounge room and so entered Martin Luther Kind Jr. He was known for his slightly late arrival at functions, rallies and dinner engagements, but it was never known nor asked if it he did it to gain attention, as a point to show the importance of the occasion, or the business of his schedule in protest marches and preparing a speech for the occasion at hand. He was always forgiven but he never made any apology. Instead he quickly took his place at the opposite end to Medgar after he shook my hand. Well at least that is how it appeared to my eyes.

Mirjana broke my concentration and asked if I would come and help her take the hot food to the dinner table. I had already set up the best of my plates, knifes, forks and spoons and crystal wine glasses for the occasion. Mirjana suggested I get started to serve the dinner to my guest. It was her wish not to be involved in the evening discussion and felt it was my thing and nothing to do with her, but welcomed the opportunity to prepare the meal. I thanked her profusely and made a mental note to reciprocate with gratitude in the future. For the effort she went too, it was a feast worthy of any Thanksgiving dinner.

The satisfaction of having partaken of Mirjana's turkey and baked vegetables followed by apple pie and cream left the Masters and me relaxed over our drinks exhausted in idle chat. It was a perfect time to ask my prying questions on their respective causes whilst living here on earth. I was keen to get their opinion of the worth of it all, seeing that they were both assassinated in the pursuit of an ideal.

So I turned to Dr King to get the conversation on more serious matters. "The common man it seems to me, in your time here and my own, is to be caught up in the everyday circumstance of his life, providing for himself and his family, chasing wants as much as needs. He doesn't seem to have the time for just causes anymore." Dr. King responded, acutely aware of my intent: "Rarely do we find men willingly engaged in hard, solid thinking.There is an almost universal quest for easy answers and half baked solutions. Nothing pains some people more than having to think." I was quick to pick up on this and come back with a question: "So how do you change distractions of life and lack of thought to do constructive things for the benefit of not only your self but others?" Dr King, without hesitation responded: " Every man must decide whether he will walk in the light of creative altruism or in the darkness of destructive selfishness." I persisted "But what of the duty of mankind on an everyday level?" I asked. "He has his duty to look after his family, to work for his daily bread, to feed them, to educate his children, to pay his home mortgage and put enough aside for a rainy day." Martin sat forward to emphasis his next point. "That is all fine if he first has a well paid employment, is not being victimised because of the colour of his skin or is segregated against so that he can't get an education or a job in the first instance." Then before I had a chance to respond he added: "There is nothing more tragic than to find an individual bogged down in length of life, devoid of breath."

Martin seemed to be bypassing my questioning, and so I added:: "So you think that very same man should change his priorities, put his family second for the greater good?" Martin was intense now. "An individual cannot start living until he can rise above the narrow confines of his individualistic concerns to the broader concerns of humanity." I had no argument against that, but still I persisted. " I am not advocating that the individual should only be concerned for his individual circumstance but work for the greater good of all concerned, but there has to be a balance." Dr King responded in kind. "All labor that uplift humanity has dignity and importance and should be undertaken with painstaking excellence." He was thinking he wanted me to see that critical thinking and urgent action was needed for any undertaking and must be time based to be effective. "We must use time creatively, in the knowledge that time is always ripe to do right." In an attempt to be more enquiring I stated "You and Medgar Evers fought for the Civil Rights of the African American, for the underprivileged, for freedom that has still not materialised. Ultimately, nothing much has change despite your best efforts. There are still to this very day riots, hatred of races, prejudice against the underdog, coloured people being downtrodden.

Despite all your best civil rights effort, amendments to the segregation laws, despite changes to the laws of the land and Bill of Rights, progress has been limited." I was now on a roll too but decided to cease my prying and asked a simple question."What is the point of anything you have done when you look at the outcomes, they got you both assassinated." Before Dr King had a chance to answer, Medgar Evers quickly chimed in with one telling statement. "You can kill a man but you can't kill an idea." I saw then, it was progress not perfection that they were ultimately about. It was then my guests faded into mist.

Thinking over how well the dinner went down with my guests and the excellent cooking of Mirjana, I returned to the next task in my choice of both masters and choice of food for the table. The desire to improve my diet and exercise programme had me researching Masters of creative achievement. It proved to be a three fold purpose in doing so, as I had taken the lead from Gandhi's strict diet to determine were I might gain some further insight into not only improving my overall health but in considering the next two Masters to bring two my table. It gave me the opportunity to determine the appropriate meals to prepare for the selected guests also. I was to note in my research that genius and food had a lot in common. So in scanning histories of creative minds, I found that certain foods or drink inspired some while same food selection repulsed others. Some had very peculiar dining habits. Thomas Edison had used soup as an interviewing tool. He had prospective job applicants taste soup whilst he observed them carefully. Those who seasoned the soup with pepper for instance before tasting it were immediately rejected. In his mind it meant they had too many assumptions. The French writer, Honore de Balzac took his liquid intake to another level. He would work through the night, consuming forty cups of high- octane caffeine espresso. He wrote of the benefits of his coffee consumption: " Ideas begin to move like battalions of the Grand Army of the battlefield and the battle takes place." Balzac lost the battle at age 51, the verdict was caffeine poisoning.

 Another genius who died as an indirect result of a food dislike was the Greek mathematician Pythagorus who hated beans. He apparently forbade his followers from eating them. According to legend, when attackers ambushed him, he died because he refused to escape through a bean field. It is written that de Vinci, Gandhi, George Bernard Shaw, Norbert Wiener, Issac Newton and Albert Einstein were all vegetarians. There is an ambiguous report that none of them were completely and strictly vegetarian. Food and drinks it seems had always played a part in the creative efforts of the Masters.

 Nikola Tesla was clearly one of the most creative and productive minds of the 20th century and was strictly vegetarian. He described all food other than vegetables as toxic to the body, did not smoke, drink coffee or tea, saying all three would no longer be consumed by the year 2035. Tesla consumed a moderate quantity of slivovitz (plum brand) daily and when he could not get his Serbian native drink he reverted to a quality whisky, believing it to be a necessity to healthy living. He also walked up to 16 km per day as a part of renewing energy levels to the body. Tesla slept only three hours per day for most of his life. He stated he occasionally slept five hours and admitted that it gave him a little extra energy when he did so, but confirmed that all his ancestors were bad sleepers who similarly slept about three hours per day and they all died over 100 years of age. Nikola Tesla himself died at 89 from physical complications after he had been run down by a motor vehicle two months prior to his demise. At least that is how the story goes in the history books. At age 77 he stated in an interview: "The condition of body and mind in old age is merely a certificate of how we spend our youth.

The secret of my own strength and vitality today is that in my youth I led what you might call a virtuous life." Then as an afterthought he stated : "I ate a lot of potatoes all my life because of the vitamins and minerals. It is full of potassium and vitamin C, in the skin and foliate and Vitamin B6 is in the body of the potato."

 Eating and drinking habits of other renowned geniuses seem rather odd to the rest of us. The late Steve Jobs had some funny ideas. The Apple computer and Pixel film whizz kid subsisted mainly on dates and almonds and lots of carrots. Walter Isaacson's in his biography of Jobs states: "friends remember him, at times, having a sunset -orange hue.: Jobs' sometimes embarked on week long fasts, going about it he stated " in my usual nuts ways.' He told Isaacson:: "After a week you start to feel fantastic.You get a ton of vitality from not having to digest all this food." He was not alone there, Aristophanes, the ancient Greek satirist, attributed the keen Athenian intellect to low calorie diet. Michelangelo was known to only eat an evening meal after he finished his creative work. Charles Darwin was a member of the Glutton Club, who met once a week to consume ' strange flesh' like owl, hawk and bison. Later abroad the Beagle bound for Australia he sampled armadillos, iguanas and giant tortoise.
It may not be just food and drink that fosters creativity, but the quality of conversation with friend over food and wine and the intellectual cross fertilisation that the meal engenders. In ancient Athens the 'genius cluster' was a centre piece of city life in drinking together. Participants spend hours downing diluted wine and discussing philosophy, poetry or the latest gossip. In 18th century Edinburgh, centre of Scottish Enlightenment, it waa an Oyster Club which served as the intellectual blender.   Founders, economist Adam Smith and philosopher David Hume consumed   bushels of oysters and cases of claret, while all male members conversed about every day goings on. It waa perhaps y the humble Viennese coffeehouse during that cities 1900s golden age that the coffee house was the founding sort of Democratic club, and anyone could join in for a price of a cup of coffee. The admission price for the member was the comfort of a warm room to sit in during bite winter days, for the home back then had limited heating. It also served to be the place of trivial and useful information. The Coffee houses supplied for free the days-newspaper carefully mounted on long wooden poles. This was for locals and tourists and their way of finding out what was going on in neighbourhood and half way around the world.

So armed with all the genius of age, I set about to choose my best candidates to invite to be Masters at my table, giving more than my usual consideration to not only their individual genius but their diet, fasting and personal and exercise programme. I had as my final selection two men of inventive genius, Thomas Edison and his one time employee but ultimate rival Nikola Tesla. These were my best choice as they covered the gambit of what I wish to share with you my readers. For I have in all my Masters at my table a goal as you may recall. lessons to be learnt for myself and for the ultimate good of all concerned who care to read my dialogue herein.

It was essential to get further input on my choice of food and drink as well as other persons knowledge on my intended Masters at my dining table for the next Saturday night dinner. I was keen to find out a little more facts regarding the early life of Inventor, Nikola Tesla, who it is reported, was born in 1856 to a Serbian family in the then Austrian Empire which is modern day Croatia. Serbian friend Dannie was most keen to share his knowledge on my enquiry and was emphatic in his belief Tesla's parents were both Serbian and that he was born in Serbia. It turned out Dannie's knowledge on Tesla was past on to him by his now deceased father when Dannie was a young boy. Not wishing to doubt my friend who had great admiration for the inventive nature of Tesla and the fact that he seem to be, in Dannie's opinion , an enlightened spirit who was on a different dimensional plain even when he was here in this world. Dannie had already canonised him a Saint, so I needed to dig a little deeper in another direction to get another view point. Turning to Mirjana over a coffee the very next day, I broached the subject having already explained Dannie's viewpoint about the "Serbian" genius. Mirjana arrived with written facts and a menu for consideration for the next Saturday night festivities. Mirjana was able to confirm that Nikola Tesla was definitely of Serbian parentage, but was born in the mountainous area of the Balkan Peninsula, which is in modern day Croatia.

CHAPTER 10.

TWO INVENTORS COME TO DINNER

During Tesla's early childhood the Empire was governed by the Austrian monarchy. It was later governed as a dual monarchy in 1856 between Austria and Hungary, the Austro-Hungarian Empire. Of course these historical facts meant little to a young boy in the mountain terrain of Balkan Peninsula back then. To all intention purposes, Nikola didn't inherit his far sighted genius from his parents. Tesla's father was a stern but loving Orthodox priest who was a gifted writer and poet. Tesla's mother managed the family farm and was a loving happy home body. A tragic accident, when his brother Daniel was killed in a riding accident shocked an unsettled the 7 year old Nikola. He escaped into study and went on to graduate in math and physics his early 20s from the Technical University of Graz and then philosophy at Prague. It was in 1882, while on a walk, he came up with the idea of a brushless AC motor, making a sketch of rotating electromagnets in the sand on his path. later that year he moved to Paris working on DC current with Continental Edison. Two years later he immigrated to the United States and was hired as an engineer for Thomas Edison's Manhattan headquarters. He worked there for a year, impressing Edison with his diligence and ingenuity. At one point Edison told Tesla he would pay him $50,000 for an improved design for his DC dynamos. After much experimentation Tesla presented Edison with a solution and asked for his money. Edison was reluctant to pay and responded: "Tesla, you don't understand American humour." It was not long after that encounter that Tesla quit.

Dannie's father would have experienced the economic and social atrocities that existed after WW1 and WW11. The father had escaped to Australia for work and a better lifestyle like so many Europeans, hanging on to traditional cultures of food and work ethic that had once existed in the old country. It was natural that he would have indoctrinated his son with many Serbian stories of his youth including such heroes as the inventor Tesla whom he lifted in Dannie's mind to sainthood. Mirjana broke my concentration to remind me that in her own childhood the old Empire had been broken up after WW11 and then become a Monarch dictatorship know as Yugoslavia, with a federation six republic borders drawn up on ethnic and historic lines. Mirjana lived off a farm girl life-style under the Socialist Federal Republic of Yugoslavia. She saw good reason to immigrate to Australia in the early 1970s. Tesla may not have meant much to her then, nor now for that matter, but coming from a neighbouring state were Tesla grew up she certainly knew the food. So it was that I convinced her to prepare a receipt for my planned Saturday night feast with the Tesla and Edison, Masters at my table. I had a majority of facts on Tesla, but needed to dwell a little more deeply on Edison before I encouraged both men to come to my table. Edison was one one of my earlier members of my table when I first encountered the genius that was then on my imaginative horizons having read Napoleon Hill's ' Think and grow Rich.' I had encouraged him to come to the table back then because he epitomised what I believed to be the sacred cow I was meant to be striving for.

 He was in his lifetime a typical entrepreneurial American of stature. Born in 1847 as the youngest of seven children to Samuel and Nancy Edison. His father was an exiled political activist from Canada who helped support his large family in Milan, Ohio by working as a shopkeeper and sometimes shingle maker. Wife Nancy a school teacher home schooled Thomas as he proved not a particularly bright student. He was however very enterprising, selling vegetables, candy and newspapers on trains. His family moved to Port Huron, Michigan where Thomas spent much of his childhood. He secured work at the height of the stock market rally as a ticker tape reader. The ticker tape machine was called a stock ticker which printed abbreviated company names as alphabetic symbols followed by numeric stock transactions, prices and volume information. The term 'ticker' came from the sound made by the machine as it printed. Since there were hundreds of companies being traded and prices updated every minute, it meant the whole stream of information was being held up, so the company names were reverted to symbols.

 Edison could read the continual flow of tape at lightning speed and report his findings to his employer, while fellow staff members were still trying to keep up with the market. He was often seen with his feet up on a desk drinking his coffee and staring at his fellow employees with amusement at the pace they read the machine reports. He spent much of his spare time coming up with patentable ideas, be they his own or what he could get for nothing from other people's brainwaves.
In his lifetime he patented 1,093 ideas and become the driving force behind the innovation of the photograph, the incandescent light bulb and the motion picture camera. He also created the world's first industrial research laboratory, setting it up on an unsuccessful real estate development site called Menlo Park. It was within a community location within Edison's township of Middlesex County, New Jersey. He cunningly set it up as a unincorporated community business model which faired well for him tax wise and he encouraged many inventories and men with smart ideas to come and work for him. He had no moral compulsion in patenting their ideas in his own named and justified it all as they were in his employ at the time. Edisons was a performer of conjuring tricks that earnt him the title; " The wizard of Menlo Park." He rose to great heights of fame and wealth as electricity spread around the world. Edison's various electric companies continued to grow until in 1889 they were brought together to form Edison General Electric, which we simply know by its brand " GE."

Like so many workable inventions the masses usually end up with the rough end of the pineapple and electricity in that regard was no exception. Edison in fact stole Tesla's ideas and when Edison was challenged with a far superior alternative current (AC) by Tesla, which in fact was better and more efficient, he marketed and sold his direct current, as he was more adept to the market place than Tesla. It went to court and the so called " Battle of the Currents" resulted in a win for Edison who convinced the jury that Tesla's AC was dangerous. In his polyphase AC motor, Tesla scored a victory over Edison. The public took to the methodology of direct current on wires as the preferred method of providing cheap electricity. Edison had put it out there that micro technology for proving electricity had great risks, as he had done in court. He was a born marketeer and raconteur, as with all his inventions, be they originating from him or taken from another, he was prepared to do anything possible to win. Edison, on the back of creating a way to charge money for electricity, controlled energy resources. Although a philanthropist, he only gave money in areas that would benefit him in the long run. Nikola Tesla, invented and created renewable energy and cared more for people than making money. Edison died with $12,000 in his bank account while Tesla died penniless. Both men certainly changed the face of the modern world with their inventions. While Edison had some 1093 patents at the time of his death., Tesla was responsible for over 700 patents of which 278 patented inventions are in use today. There is some speculation that Tesla patents that continue to come to light long after his death, were before their time. The likes of the mobile phone, and basic discoveries like radio, robotics and computer science are all credited to the man. He was known as the man who caused lightning to strike by harnessing energy from a basic triangle and demonstrated this happening.

It was after the bombing of Pearl Harbour that Tesla contacted the US Military advising he had invented a 'death ray," that could melt the engine in an approaching aircraft some 40 miles away with microwaves. He reportedly died that night and military personnel turned up to take away a chest full of patentable ideas which are slowly being released to the public as the authorities see fit to do so. Tesla was probably murdered for his creations to ensure they would not fall into the wrong hands and could then be under military control or as we know, some big business of the day hold some.

We will never know for certain but more and more Tesla inventions are surprising us in our modern world now. Possibly his electromagnetic field dynamo alternative current grid which has now been adopted to use in such every day uses as washing machines, electricity generators and modern motor cars to name but a few is best known. He also came up with the best known fuel based solutions to world energy and spoke as a green environmentalist on the best method to clean up the needless use of fossil fuels over a century ago. It was not until after his death in his hotel room in 1943 that the Supreme Court voided four of Marconi's key patents, accrediting Tesla's innovation on radio transmission. The AC system however that he championed and improved remains the global standard for power transmission even today. The TV towers and cell links for mobiles was another of his patents that were realised for manufacture long after his death. He also invented electric oscillators, meters and improved light and high quality transformers with his Tesla coil. He had demonstrated his invention of the X ray, gave short demonstrations of his radio communication two years before Marconi came on the scene. Together with Westinghouse he lit the 1891 World Columbian Exposition in Chicago and partnered up with his old rival , Edison's GE to install AC generators at Niagara Falls creating the world's first modern power station.

Saturday rolls around and Mirjana turns up with a real meal plan: Stuffed Cabbage 'Sinj' style. It was so named after a township on the Split- Dalmatian country in Croatia, near were Tesla was born. I was so taken by the fact that she had gone to the trouble to prepare this ancient delicious meal that I think it only fair to share it with you dear reader, being the method of perpetration. Mirjana began by rinsing cabbage leaves in warm water and then let them drain well. She mixed together beef, pork, onions, garlic, nutmeg, cinnamon, vegetal and pepper. Place it all on top of each leaf, rolled it up, tucked the ends inside and closed them tight with toothpicks. Then she took a large pan, lined the bottom and sides of the pot with remaining cabbage leaves and sprinkled with bacon, adding bay leaves, cloves, rind and oil; covered it with water mixed with a light beef stock and brought it to the boil. Mirjana then reduced the heat to low, covered and cooked it all for two and a half hours, occasionally taking the pot and once cooled a little, shaking it. She then served the meal with mashed potatoes and 'Polenta' cornmeal baked into a bread. I watched until the meal was almost a half an hour to being ready to serve, then retreated to the lounge room to meditate, bringing my Master guests to the table.

Tesla was first to arrive, not requiring as much sleep as Edison and being full of energy, he was taken by the smell wafting from my kitchen. Mirjana was on her way, and served the meal on the table and then left quickly before she got involved in the onversation. Being a farm girl at heart, she saw it as 'men's business' when we gathered around for the meal. I had also prepared a vegetable soup for Edison and ensured I did not add any pepper leaveing it to his own taste as to the addition of the spice. I had not gone to much trouble for this man's meal, as I did not like his morals in stealing other inventors work during his lifetime, making himself rich on the proceeds. I had to conceive however that he was, despite this , a great inventor. Both men had greeted each other cordially, but with more of a careful dignity by Tesla, whilet Edison retained that look of superiority that he always maintained as his modest but artificial mask. They soon got to chatting however, and it was clear that they had great respect for each other in their appointed place in the heavens. Perhaps they did not meet much there and so this was an ideal opportunity to catch up as to the effectiveness of their inventions in this lifetime. Once they had partaken of the food, of which Edison not only consumed all the soup, but I noted he added a great deal of pepper to it. Once consumed he turned to eating at least half of the cabbage. meat and vegetable meal effectively prepared more for his fellow inventor. Tesla didn't seem to mind at all as he being a disciplined eater, hthe rest and took to a glass of whiskey that I had set aside for him, leaving Edison with apple cider. It was then I began to ask my questions, directing them firstly to the Serbian:

" Mr. Tesla, futurist have said in your time on earth that the 20th and 21st century was born in your head. They apparently celebrate conversely the magnetic field and sing hymns to your induction engine. They marvel at the way you caught the light in your net from the depth of the earth and created fire in the heavens. There you also created a weapon that causes the earthquakes vibrations. There you discovered cosmic rays. It has followed that races of people will continue singing your praises in the temple of the future, because of your great secret that Empedocles elements can be watered with life forces from ether. What do you say to that? Tesla did not make much of it and just responded: "Yes, these are some of my most important discoveries. I'm a defeated man. I have accomplished the greatest thing I could." I enquired then "What is it then Mr. Tesla?" He was more accomodating with his personal dream: "I wanted to illuminate the whole earth. There is enough electricity here to become a second sun. Light would then appear around the equator, like the rings around Saturn."

He continued : "Mankind is still not ready for the great and good. In Colorado Springs I soaked the earth by electricity. Also we can water the earth by other energies, such as positive mental energy. They are already in the music of Bach or Mozart and you heard it in the fiery music of my deaf friend Beethoven and you have heard it in the verses of the poets. In the earth's interior there are energies of joy, peace and love. They express themselves in flowers that grow on the earth, in the food we partake of and everything that makes man's homeland. I've spent years looking for the way that energy could influence people. The beauty and the secret of roses are as medicine and the rays of the sun are food .

Life has an infinite number of forms, and the duty of Science is to find in every form the matter. Three things are essential in this. And all man has to do is search for them. I know I didn't find them but don't you give up, let no man give up on them. I knew that gravity is proven if one needs to fly but it was not my intention to make flying devices for transport nor weapons of war, but to teach individuals to regain consciousness on his own wings." He began to trail of a little and as if talking to himself : " I am trying still to awake the energy contained in the air. That may be the main source of energy. What you consider as empty space is a manifestation of matter that is not yet awakened. There is no empty space on earth, nor in the Universe in black holes, what astronomers talk about are the most powerful sources of powerful energy and life."

I thought it was time to move on and to pry Edison with a few questions, but Tesla seemed to be on a role, so I chanced one more question: " What are these energy things?" I asked. "One issue is food. We need a stellar of terrestrial energy to feed the hungry on earth. With wine in limited intake we can cheer the hearts and understand that there is the God of the universe and other Gods beneath that power too. The power of evil is man's greatest destroyer and suffering continues as man's life passes. These evil outcomes from God are of a different order in space. It is an evil that man sometimes taps into to create great epidemics, one of which you are experiencing world wide now. In this century the disease has spread from the Earth now throughout the whole Universe. The other is that there is excess light in the Universe - I discovered a star that by all astronomic and mathematical laws could disappear and nothing would seem to be modified. This star is in this galaxy. Its light can occur in such density that it fits into a sphere smaller than an apple, and is heavier than our Solar System. Religions and philosophers teach that man can become the Christ, Buddha and Zoroaster. What I'm eluding to is trying to improve something wilder and almost unattainable. This is what to do in the Universe now, so that every being is born as Christ, Buddha or Zoroaster." It was far beyond my imagination what Tesla was proposing, but I get the power of manifestation in allowing ones Higher Power (self) to live according to the divine will and not ones own. It gave me pause for thought to attempt more often to hand over my earthly needs and desires to the will of the Almighty, but I knew that my free-will got in the way making it almost impossible for me and by all accounts my friend the Inventor. I made a mental note of the three elements Tesla eluded to. 1- The issue of food. 2- The issue of good over evil and 3- The harnessing of the excess light in the Universe.

I could now see that rather than discuss Mr Edison's inventions, it was entirely possible now to keep focus on the theme set by Tesla. For it had dawned on me that we have all the benefits now of the inventions of both men and that what we need now is guidance to take our duty on earth to the next level. A spiritual invention if you will. I could see that Tesla had tapped my thought and was keen to see what his friend would say. He made it a little easier by stating: "An inventor's endeavour is essentially life saving. Whether he harnesses forces, improves devices or provides new comforts and conveniences, he is adding to the safety of existence.

It mattered little to me if my creations were stolen as long as they proved beneficial to man, and that the ones who stole didn't give up on their own ideas." Well that made it easier for Edison now and he drew on his ability to get things done. "Well," he replied: "To quote my wise friend here as iI did on a past occasion." He was already taking past words of Tesla. " The first requirement is the awareness of our mission, the second condition to adapt to is determination to continue, that one might finish the task." Then he turned to me and paraphrased my thoughts : "This is guidance from all vital and spiritual energy in labor. Man will gain not lose in this undertaking," I had plenty to think about and before I knew it, as every Master who ever dined at my table had done, they returned to the ether.

I remembered Tesla once talked about the maintenance of the assembly. It dawned on me then and there that he was talking about the human body being a perfect machine. Knowing the circuitry of the body and what is good for it, he had pointed out that most people eat foods that are harmful to the body and those who cook should touch his hand before proceeding. "Adjust to your physical circuit, in addition food, dreaming is important even when you're wide awake." He had trained himself to live sometimes on one hour sleep per day which required superhuman effort to achieve his daily creative goals. He had indicated he gained that ability to fall asleep and wake up at a designated time to return to his tasks at hand. "If into something I do not understand I force myself in my dreams to thus find a solution."

Cover-19 had created an atmosphere where mankind spent greater periods at home instead of going to a work location. It was a safeguard by the Governments of the day to avoid individuals catching and spreading the virus. It was obvious to me that we would have more than one lockdown in the unforeseen future unless a manufactured cure could be discovered. It was a condition of adjustment for Tesla, and for that matter Edison, to adjust their memory to required creative tasks during difficult times. Perhaps Covid-19 was a blessing in disguise, as away from the brain keeping of knowledge about the world and what has been gained from life, time had slowed during the pandemic. I was now seeing the Master's point that the brain can be engaged in more important things than remembering past events or present difficulties. It seems now a far better idea to remember in the moment only. Tesla had indicated that light particles of energy are all around us and if we meditate upon this phenomena and consume it in the now, then what we see, hear, read and learn allows us to accomplish geniuses from these particles of light ,that are obedient and faithful too our bidding. I had been very mindful of the art of visualisation in my mind's eye as I created and wrote books, poems and songs. The events that I visualise being real in front of my eyes, visualising as each occurrence manifested. I understood now how Tesla and Edison harnessed the power to use their exceptional gifts and talent. They nurtured it, guarded the gifts, made corrections to their visualisation on most of their inventions and finished them all with some complex mathematical equations. Their abilities were beyond me but I could see now in my own small way that to make my creative effort more effective I needed to call on the efforts of other humans in my limitations. For my vision and writing I reconfirmed to myself that it was all for my betterment and the greater good of all concerned. I was beginning to feel the need for bodily nourishment, so I returned to the kitchen to pick away the leftover from our enjoyable meal. On the table next to the stove the details of the ingredient for Mirjana's dish were, and so after eating my fill I returned to my study to write it all down.

It had been a delight to have both Edison and Tesla to dinner and to gain so much beneficial insight for the future from the lips of both men. I expressed my gratitude to Dannie for his input over coffee about the Serbian St.Nikola Tesla and for Mirjana's uncovering the cabbage recipe from the region of his birth and for preparing it for the dinner with my two genius Inventors. As for Edison, well the meal was obviously to his liking, as was the soup, but I had made a preemptive judgement on his character, and so didn't not give him as much attention as Tesla. Perhaps on reflection they exposed more defects of my own character in taking his inventory than the 'sins' of such a prominent and inventive genius. So much of what I take for granted in my everyday living was provided by those men of genius. Why even the light I was working under came from the brain of Edison and the computer I now type on and communicate with via the world wide web was initially the brain child of Tesla. As early as 1900 he began to build a global communication network centred on a giant tower at Wardencliffe, on Long Island. If J.P. Morgan, the great finance broker had not balked at Tesla's grandiose scheme for a worldwide communication network, we may well have had the benefit of his radio, television and computer technology much soon.

Tesla lived his last decades in a New York hotel, working on new inventions even as his energy and mental health faded. His obsession with the number three and its multiplication and algorithmic combinations and his fastidious 'washing' of electric current were dismissed as the eccentricities of a genius. In his final years he claimed communication with the city's pigeons. Tesla died in his room on January 7th, 1943. It was later that year that the U.S.Supreme Court voided four of Marconi's patents, belatedly acknowledging Tesla's innovations in radio. The AC system he championed and improved remains the global standard for power transmission.

Thomas Edison is considered one of history's greatest inventors. He is credited with developing the light bulb, the phonograph and the motion picture camera, among many others. He is credited with a world record of 1093 patents which he held both singly and jointly. On the 50th anniversary of Edison's electric light in 1929, Henry Ford reconstructed Edison's invention factory as a museum at Greenfield Village, Michigan, which he opened . The main celebration of Light's Golden Jubilee, co-hosted by Henry Ford and General Electric, took place in Dearborn along with a huge celebratory dinner in Edison's honour attended by notables such as President Hoover, John, D, Rockefeller, Jr., George Eastman, Marie Curie, and Orville Wright. Edison's health however had declined to the point that he could not stay for the entire ceremony. For the last two years of his life, a series of ailments caused a decline in his health even more until he collapsed into a coma; he died on October 18th, 1931. The attendance of those two men at my table last Saturday evening caused me to delight in the cabbage meal Mirjana had prepared. So as promised here is the ingredient recipe of Stuffed Cabbage 'Sinj' style. Cooking details page 96.

700g. Lean Beef, Diced

200g. Lean Pork, Diced

100g. Pancetta, Finely Chopped

150g. Smoked bacon, Coarsely Chopped
1 Onion, Finely Chopped.

5 Cloves Garlic, Finally Chopped

1/2 Teaspoon Nutmeg

1/2 Teaspoon Cinnamon

4 Soup Spoons Oil

1kg. Pickled Cabbage Leaves,
lemon Rind
2 Bay leaves

Freshly Ground Pepper

1 Soup Spoon Vegeta

CHAPTER 11.

MASTERS OF THE SPIRITUAL WAY

There is a metonymic adage "The Pen is mightier than the sword" first penned by English author Edward Bulwe-Lytton in his 1839 historical play "Cardinal Richelieu." The goodly Cardinal chief minister to King Louis X111, discovered a plot to kill him, but as a priest is unable to take up arms against the enemies. He reverted to the written word and in his administrative powers used independent press, effectively used as the best tool to disarm violence as the weapon to bring the parties to a satisfactory outcome. This proving the quotation as being a real answer to the issues at hand. It could also be said in simple terms: "when in doubt for an answer that is not independently forthcoming, negotiate by any means possible, and in particular use the written word as more powerful than confrontation. In my own case, the many tragedies that beset me in the first five years of this new century we're somewhat answered by the written word more so than by verbal communication. It took until 2013 before I took my first Pilgrimage on the Camino de Santiago and wrote a plethora of poems of the dark side of my life and the light of a new spiritual journey inward, before I got the awakening call to write my first novel. Interestingly, I entitled it "The Sword of Discernment" and much of what I wrote proved the benefit of Edward Bulwe-Lytton's quotation. It didn't end there, as I returned to the Camino for two more journeys between 2015 and 2017. These journey set me on a path of writing three novels, an autobiography and recording two albums of songs and I doubt I would have gained spiritual lessons in every sense of my being had I not walked 'The Way,' as it is known. As you can see, this book is but one more extension of my uncovering the way of spiritual pilgrimages. It is a way towards manifesting in me a spiritual path for my benefit and for those for whom it may concern in the future. The previous books being but but a step towards this book.

My friend David was indoctrinated into Orthodox Christianity as a child as I was in the Roman Catholic faith. We both gained in a religious sense the essences of living a moral life which was paramount to winging our way into the Heavenly Kingdom. The black and white and no shade of grey existence of our mutual moral religious experiences, whilst of good intent and biblical teaching was based on linear logic methodology; it proved a worthwhile step to consciousness in doing the right thing in a world of good verses evil. However, at least in a modern day sense, it did not teach of the heart and in fact may well prove a hinderance to me spiritually because the scaffold of that teaching is embedded in my soul-search of the truth i.e. Spirituality is a way of life in this world but not of it, whilst my former religious teaching was the battle between the devil and the deep blue sea of faith. Well, that is my interpretation, however limited you may find it here to be. So it was the reason why I met up with David, the theologian, psychologist and great spiritual friend and over a cup of coffee we recommenced our usual weekly 'spiritual get together.' Whilst he is not an alcoholic he openly admits that the AA steps and the fellowship itself is spiritually a pathway for any human, alcoholic or not.

We were discussing the workings of Professor Henry James, an American theologian and adherent of Swedenborgianism, also known as the father of philosophy. Not to be confused with his son the novelist Henry James Jr. nor writings of his daughter Alice James. Professor James had in his younger years prepared an edition of Robert Sandeman's 'Letters on Theron and Aspasio,' which has been called the principal literary document of a Scottish sect that opposed the Presbyterian Church. In Sandeman's work, he called it "a far more faithful exhibition of Gospel truth than any other work."

What specifically interested James was its radically egalitarian message. For Sandman wrote."In fact, the whole New Testament speaks aloud, that as to the matter of acceptance with God, there is no difference between one man and another; - no difference   between the best accomplished gentleman, and the most infamous scoundrel; no difference between the most virtuous lady and the vilest of prostitutes…" In his work of investigating the spiritual he befriended Ralph Waldo Emerson but found little satisfaction in his spiritual philosophy. Likewise, the atheist viewpoints of Thomas Carlyle to whom he was introduced to via Emerson. It was in Emanuel Swedenborg, the Swedish scientist, religious visionary and teacher that Henry James found his spiritual home. He held most of the leading writers of his time in low regard with the possible exception of Walt Whitman and maybe Henry David Thoreau. I myself had used Whitman's comment on pilgrimage in a power point presentation on 'What is a Pilgrimage and why do it?' Walt in his comments of Pilgrims in a world of seekers quotes " Not I…or anyone else, can travel that road for you. You must travel it yourself," I also related to Thoreau's two famous quotes: " The masses of men lead lives of quite desperation" and later, as I have previously alluded to in this book, but I find is worthy of repeating: "Every man's heart beats to the tune of a different drummer, let him follow the drummer that he hears." But I am digressing from the path of James in working through his own spiritual crisis by following in stages the words of Swedenborg. He had his own way of expressing it : "The curse of mankind, that which keeps our manhood so little and so depraved, is the sense of selfhood, and the absurd abominable opinion of ego it engenders." He remained attached to Swedenborg's works for the rest of his life and travelled extensively devoted to lecturing on the doctrine and writing copious volumes on the subject matter. He wrote a 400 page compendium 'A variety of Religious experiences.' It is interesting to note that Bill Wilson of AA fame, in his research of the Oxford Group and his mission into the spiritual conscience, discovered this 400 page work of James and condensed it down to just three steps on the path to spirituality. Bill stated that Man firstly experiences some sort of a calamity in life from which there is no turning back. Next follows a mental and or spiritual collapse that there seems no way out of and finally there is a cry out for a Higher power to help, usually via prayer. This in truth is what happened to me, which I will speak more of when summing up this little work of a book.

So it was that David and I discussed over coffee my writings herein and he commented "So who will you invite next to dinner from the other side Doug?" I had no answer and he prompted my thoughts with: "May I make a suggestion, but I do not want to influence your thoughts, but how would it be if you varied your diet a little and invited a few of the world's great spiritualists ? Why not invite these men who influenced the world with their pens, writing books on spirituality and philosophy?"

I thought his idea most welcomed but considered that I had had enough of the Saturday night dinner engagements for a while and considered that perhaps the next meeting should take place in a back room of a local cafe. I was thinking of the Swiss cafe meeting rooms of the great thinkers of the late 19th century. A place, that for the price of a cup of coffee, participants could join in intelligent conversation on matters of the world, local issues or the latest gossip. It also served to be the place where the newspaper of the day was available to read free of charge. It usually hung like washing overhanging on a long pole where these Atlas eaters with a jaw for news could catch up on the events of interest to them. I reckoned on the fact that we could buy our coffee and sit quietly away from the crowd and enjoy the company of a writer or two in conversation on spiritual matters or world events that pertained to the subject matter at hand- Spirituality. So it was that we discussed Henry James which in turn led to his Swedenborg philosophical belief which subsequently lead to Carl Jung. David was right, it made sense to have these two great minds together for a coffee and discussion.

I again felt it prudent to prepare a brief of each before beginning to meditate upon them and invite them both into a discussion. David was most enthused to participate in this exercise and with his deep knowledge of the relevant subject matter we began to write out the briefs, beginning with Swedenborg himself.

Emanuel Swedenborg was born in Stockholm, Sweden on 29th January, 1688. During the course of his life , Swedenborg would become a scientist, cosmologist, geologist, chemist, palaeontologist, philosopher and finally, a theologian and religious reformer. He was born to Sara Nee Behm and Father Jesper Swedberg, who was a Lutheran Bishop of Skara, Sweden and after the family was ennobled by the Queen of Sweden, took the name 'Swedenborg. 'At age eleven he began his studies at the University of Uppsala in Sweden were all classes were taught in Latin. He later did scientific studies and anticipated much of the modern science, philosophy and psychology of today and wrote extensively on these subjects. Initially, as a young man, he concentrated his studies on pure mathematics and astronomy, then began his travels at age 22 and for the next ten years engaged in scientific journalism and became an assessor at the Royal College of Mines for a period of 5 years until 1716. For the next 30 years his main work was utilising his mining engineering skills and gaining a wide reputation for his abilities. While still practicing engineering he kept up his studies and wrote algebraic formula and produced voluminous works on the geometric character of physics and chemistry. He wrote three volumes on the nature of physics, conceived of the atom as a particle vortex; this theory being of the electron-nucleus framework of the atom in modern physics. He conceived of pure motion as a tendency to create any subsequent holding of creation becoming a complex of pure motion. After the publication of his work on Physics, Swedenborg studied and focused on man as a physiological and pallid whole self hidden in a relationship with God. His new studies led to the creation of two new publications of physiological discoveries of importance. He discovered the nature of cerebrospinal fluid, identified corresponding particles between body parts and other regions of the the verbal cortex. His studies of the psychology of the blood brain, lung and heart led him to characterise correctly the relationship between organs. He also attempted to describe the physiological basis for human perception and thus find a way to define and describe the soul. After all these studies Swedenborg devoted his energies to the philosophy of theology.

Although not a theologian in the strictest sense, he proved to be a fantastic theological speculator. Swedenborg combined Christian truths with scientific basis, creating a philosophical theory of God, of man, and of divine revelation and redemption. On the basis of these theories a New Jerusalem Church was founded in 1784. Swedenborg didn't himself found the church sect although his revelations sparked the basis of this movement. The basis of his speculations was his rejection of Christian teaching on the Trinity. He viewed all things as created by divine love and according to divine wisdom. Each material thing corresponding to a 'spiritual form.'. Thus he achieved a modified Neoplatonism, or mystical connection in nature; believing and preaching that all effects in the material world having spiritual causes and therefore divine purpose. He analysed the Bible from Genesis and Exodus, and Revelations of which some of his work was published posthumously. On the face of examination of Christian belief he rejected any notion that Jesus Christ was himself divine, but held the view that the inner—most soul of Jesus was divine and his divine soul had taken on human form from Mary, and the human nature of Jesus has been glorified by his exemplary life. By resisting all powers of temptation and ills of the power of darkness, Jesus had opened a way of divine life to flow into mankind. Man had thus become free to know truth, to be able to obey its dictates. Human salvation lay in this knowledge and obedience.

He justified this by defending his speculation, by claiming it as a divine call, he was maintaining that Jesus had received a special light from God. He also claimed that all of his text and speculative theories and philosophical treatise constituted a new revelation from God. Mankind must live according to this revelation in order to enter into a new age of reason and truth. Swedenborg died in London March 29,172. In 1908 the Swedish Government exhumed his remains, transferring them to Uppsala Cathedral were they still remain. There seemed much to contemplate and I was pleased that I had the time now to meditate upon meeting him together with my friend David in the quiet of a back room of my local cafe. Our purpose then to dig a little deeper into his divine theories before joining in a meditation on Swedenborg, before his pending appearance from the other side of the curtain. It was also time to prepare a brief on the other Master of divine revelation, Carl Jung.

Carl was born June 25, 1875 in Kesswil, Switzerland and was the founder of analytic psychology, in some aspects as a response to Sigmund Freud's psychoanalysis. He had a lonely childhood, like Swedenborg was the son of a Pastor. Carl was born with a vivid imagination, and from an early age he observed the behaviour of his parents and teachers, and tried to resolve their individual issues. Considering his father's Pastoral duties he was concerned by his father's failing belief in religion and tried to communicate to him his own experiences with God. In many ways the older Jung was a kind and tolerant man, but neither he nor his son succeeded in understanding one another. In his teens he discovered philosophy and read widely, and this, together with the disappointments of his boyhood, led him to forsake the strong family religious traditions, graduating in psychology at the University of Basel (1900) and Zurick, as an MD in 1902.

It was fortuitous that he joined the staff of the Burgholozli Asylum of the Universityof Zurich under the tutelage of Eugen Bleuler, whose psychological interests are now considered classic studies of mental illness. At the asylum Jung began, with outstanding success, to apply association tests initiated by earlier research. He studied patients peculiar behaviour and illogical responses to word stimulus and found that they caused an emotional charged cluster of associations withheld from the consciousness because of their disagreeable nature, immoral to the patient, and with frequent sexual content. He used the now famous term 'complex' to describe such conditions. His findings establish him as a psychiatrist of international repute, led him to understand Freud's investigations; his findings confirming Freud's ideas and for five years he waa a close collaborator. He held an important position in the psychoanalytic movement and was widely thought of as the most likely successor to the founders of psychoanalysis. However it was not to be, as there were some part temperamental reasons and also had different viewpoints towards Freud's sexual basis of neurosis, and so the collaboration ended. A serious disagreement came in 1912 after Jung's 'Wandlungen' was published and again in 1916 when the 'Psychology of the Unconscious' was released, for it was counter to Freud's ideas. Although Jung had been elected to the International Psychoanalytic Society in 1911, he resigned in 1914.

Jung wrote much on the psychology and confrontation of the unconscious incorporating accounts of his own imaginations, fantasies and induced hallucinations. He produced many a written study on transformation theory and analytical psychology, alchemy and dementia. His particular essays on modern man and the search of the soul, dreams and religion interest me in my search herein for spiritual direction. In his latter years he become Professor of Psychology at the Federal Polytechnic University of Zurich and Professor of Medicine Psychology at the University of Basel. His personal experience, his continual psychotherapeutic practice and wide knowledge of history placed him in a unique position to comment on a multiple of current events of the mind, including collective unconscious concepts combined with theory of archetypes in the study of religion; instinctive patterns, having universal character, expressed in behaviour and images. He devoted his remaining years to developing ideas especially on relations between psychology and religion. In order to shed more light on his subject matter, he thought that psychotherapists, in-order to practice their art more successfully should become more familiar with writings of the old Masters. In particular he gave fresh importance to the life of a hermit; those who live within but not without. The soul like existence of the likes of monks in a monastery is one of his examples. He differentiated between personality types of the extravert and introvert, differentiating the four functions of the mind: thinking, feeling, sensation and intuition. He was well qualified by nature for as he had striking dreams and powerful fantasies. After his break with Freud, he deliberately allowed this aspect of himself to function again and gave the irrational side of his nature free expression. At the same time he studied scientifically by keeping detailed notes of his strange experiences from what he chose to become. During his lifetime Jung's work influenced the fields of psychology, anthropology, archaeology, literature, philosophy and religious studies. He died on 6th June 1961 in London.

After David and I had completed our brief on the two Masters, we began our meditation to bring our guests to the table for discussion over coffee. I had already arranged a large pot of hot espresso coffee, milk and sugar to be at hand to ensure we wasted no time in the miracle of the moments that we would be granted to spend with our distinguished guests.

Both great minds appeared simultaneously, as so many of the Masters of the past seem to do. I deduced that it was not that they were unhappy in their heavenly realm, but would have preferred not just to be spirit and would gladly hand over all their knowledge just for a morsel of life again on this earthly realm. Both Masters were so highly qualified in such a diverse number of subject matter, but I wanted to hone down to my own spiritual journey and how others could benefit from my experiences too. As Swedenborg seemed to be elsewhere in my min's eye, perhaps working on some mathematical theory or astronomical new thought of the cosmos. I asked my question through David, as he was now channelling Carl Jung. " Much thought has been given to the light and the shadow of mankind. I was wondering how do I identify the shadow self?" David seemed to take on the appearance of Jung and the reply came in one of Jung's favourite subjects: " One of the best ways to identify your shadow is to pay attention to your emotional reactions toward other people. Sure your colleagues might be aggressive, arrogant, inconsiderate, or impatient, but if you don't have those same qualities within you, you won't have a strong reaction to their behaviour." I followed with a teaser: "So, if I don't want to have a strong reaction anyway, how do I switch the shadow- self off?" Jung, via David's expression, just smiled: "If you kill off the shadow-self, your real world version of your experience with others will disappear as a mental shut down and may cause physical illness often as a consequence." I was intrigued then, for in my own worldly business days , particularly dealing with subordinates, I had to shut down this side of me, becoming very autocratic in order to demonstrate power in giving tasks to those soldiers of my misfortune. I would under normal circumstances be more thought provoking and amiable, consider that I could catch more flies with honey than lemon, but sometimes I found it necessary to be an asshole. I explained this to David, as in his own practice we had discussed just this issue. He again answered from Jung: " Acceptance is the key. By accepting your shadow-self, it is the only path to self love. You can't live the parts of yourself that you find suitable and discard the ones that you wouldn't want to be associated with. Realise that you have to accept every little detail about your personality and appearance."

 My journey through the depths of alcoholic behaviour ultimately landed me at the doorway into the fellowship of Alcoholics Anonymous. The steps to sobriety in the programme ultimately progressed to my doing an inventory step of myself. Initially it proved to be unsatisfactory, as it was my spiritual alibi to be unrealistic about my defects of character. I used to champion the value of unrealistic self appraisal. I wanted only to examine that part of me that seemed to greatly exaggerate the virtues I supposed that I had attained and then I would give myself a pat on the back for the grand job I was doing. This by its very nature generated a hankering for even more accomplishment and even more approval of others. I was falling back into the pattern of my drinking days even though I was on the surface of it all sober. Here it came back to those same old goals of power, fame, prestige and the thirst for more applause. The fact that I did not have a spiritual objective made this utterly empty seeking seem perfectly normal. Without any prompting from Swedenborg, who was sitting observing David and myself, Jung spoke again through David: "All of us have the dark side. This dark side that includes 'qualities' we don't dare reveal to others….But embracing the negative qualities actually opens the door to happiness, fulfilment and 'true enlightenment.'

The dark personality traces of Narcissism, Psychopathic and being Machiavellian can be toxic and damaging to us personally and to the workplace at large." I was both enquiring and objective: "But can this shadow work of uncovering the defects of character be dangerous psychologically?" Jung replied: " Unless you make the unconscious conscious, to direct your life." he tendered. "A shadow can lead to limited beliefs, which snowball into all manner of undesirable outcomes: self-sabotage, destructive behaviour, ruined relationships. So, it is important to dig deep, avoid residual parachutes of artificial distractions, allow yourself to free-fall into expression. Fall into to the dragons mouth as it were." My thoughts drifted back to the wise old patient in the next bed to me in rehabilitation, there for my alcoholism and depression. He had stated: "Allow yourself to free fall into the dragon's mouth. There you will find a lotus flower of creative ideas." In essence he was saying to me what I was now gathering from Jung. "There you will find love." I realise I was on my spiritual journey now and the work was still ahead. It took suffering and change to get to where I am now I was thinking, but I took some solace from that wise old mans thinking: he could have well been channelling Carl Jung at the time, for he had once met the man himself: "Put your boat of personality upon the river of life, trim the sail and allow the boat self to flow freely. All it takes, from time to time is just a slight touch of the rudder to stay on course." I had to be mindful that I needed to wear my personality garment lightly, not to get sucked into the skill of reading emotions, mine and others for a sense of empathy and caring, for the shadow-self always lingers in the background to effectively manipulate certain situations, individually for one's own motives or indeed their own It was a complicated subject matter, so I decided to turn the table to love once more.

I turned my attention back to Swedenborg, as I was interested to delve a little more into the" God is love and the divinity." It was partly to further examine the shackles of scaffolding around my spiritual temple and partly to dispense once and for all with the linear, logical conscious thinking of my former indoctrination into my childhood teaching of faith and morals. As I was conditioned to believe in the Trinity of God as paramount to my salvation, I wanted to hear a little more of Swedenborg's views on Trinity which prompted the New Jerusalem Church movement. I asked: "What is the doctrine of the New Jerusalem as to the meaning of the Holy Spirit?" The Third person of the Trinity, known mostly as the Holy Spirit, is considered by most fundamental Christians as the gift or pathway from God for man's salvation as a result of Christ's sacrificial crucifixion, of being the only way one may tap into the divine nature of God in a three way link to spirituality through The Father, the Son and the divine connection of the Holy Spirit.

David poured us all another cup of coffee and my European Masters sipped away on their Espressos in quiet contemplation. Swedenborg eventually spoke. "It has been shown that the Divine called ' The Father' and the Divine called 'The Son,'and it is now shown that ' The Holy Spirit' is the same as the Lord." This explained nothing new to me in my former teaching. " But how is your doctrine different to other Trinity belief?" I asked. Swedenborg continued: " There is a Trinity in the Lord illustrated by a comparison with an angel who has a soul and a body, and is divine before proceeding from the Lord." I answered: "It sounds complicated." Swedenborg, a little frustrated by my interruption, continued: "This is a matter of deep investigation. I have been permitted to learn many things about the proceeding, but this is not the time nor place to present them. "

He hesitated, then added: "After death the first thing the angels teach everyman who looks to God is that the Holy Spirit is not any other than the Lord; and that 'to go forth' or 'proceed' is nothing else than to enlighten and teach in the presence, which is according to the reception of the Lord. The result is that after death very many people put away the idea that they had formed in this world about the Holy Spirit, and receive the idea that it is the Lord's presence with man through the angels and spirits, by and according to which man is enlightened and taught. Moreover, it is usual in the Word to name two Divines and sometimes three Divines, which are yet known as one or more faiths or beliefs as their way of the link to the father." This was to me like simply saying there is more than one way to believe in God, but I held my thought and my tongue. Swedenborg seemed to have cottoned on in his spiritual presence in my head and continued: " To explain in relation to your former belief, it is referenced in Matthew 28:19, expressed as .. 'it is the Lord only who is meant by the Father, Son and Holy Spirit.' In the preceding verse the Lord says: 'All power is given unto Me in heaven and on earth.' and in the following verse he says' Lo, I am with you all the days, even to the consummation of the age.' So you see he speaks of himself in that manner, about the Father, Son and Holy Spirit to make his disciples aware of the Trinity within himself to give to understand that spiritual divinity is other than his earthly self. To give humanity understanding that there is a Trinity in heaven which is divine, which in mankind varies according to his own spiriting connection of life on earth of man. It is the life of one who is regenerated, which is called the spiritual life." The Master continued with the theme that Christ on earth was not himself divine but at that point he was in the heavens as two linked with the father. He had come to earth to bear witness to his message of his being as one with the father, that by his sacrifice on the cross his divine self would give rise to our spiritual link with him as a Third person becoming the Trinity in the heavens.

 Our dense being of body self here on earth (has) the power to tap this Source as a Higher Power for our spiritual well being and ultimately our own heavenly place in the kingdom of The Father. So Swedenborg, with all his religious evaluations and years of research on this subject matter did not really believe in the bodily Christ being here on earth as divine. He seemed to be saying Christ had a presence of his divinity still in the heavens whilst he walked the earth and he tapped it for us so that we too had that link. I recalled the written word saying: " And greater things will you do also," coming from the lips of the Saviour of all the world. Swedenborg made some sense of it all to the linear logic of belief in Divinity. However, his explanation needed a little more research to my mind, considering it is recorded that Christ rose ' Body and Soul' into heaven. As Swedenborg had said "It's complicated," and "now is not the time." So I dispensed with this aspect of his belief and turned to the aspect of love, that we had formally been discussing with Carl Jung. The subject matter of love seemed more easy for me to understand for my own spiritual wellbeing and for the benefit of all concerned, than the subject matter of the Trinity; for each man has his own pathway to the heavens and it is for me to preach my beliefs and disbeliefs.

"Master Emanuel" I hastened to ask: "What is love?" He looked at me with some amusement, for he knew my heart. " Love is desiring to give what is our own to another and feeling delighted as our own." I promptly responded , perhaps a little hastily. " But is that just a spiritual act, for even the most debased of humanity are capable of that act." Swedenborg continued to labour his point "Kindness is an inner desire that makes us want to do good things even if we don't to get anything in return. It is the joy of our life to give. When we do from this inner desire, there is a kindness in everything we think, say and do." I did my bit to trap him: "So man 's base nature and paganism is ok if you are a giver?" He cunningly replied " The sky is enormous man. Love comes through being in useful service to others.'" He would not be drawn into my shadow self cynicism. "The nature of heaven is to provide a place there for all who lead good lives, no matter what their religion may be." I touched on the subject of this afterlife that he has so busily researched and believed in and the response came: "This I can declare, things that are in heaven are more real than things that are of this world." I returned his attention to his 'Secrets of heaven,' thoughts of angels, God, heavens and spiritual inspiration. "Everything good or true that the angels inspire in us is God's, so God is constantly talking to us. He talks very differently though, to one person than to another. Man, before he is regenerated to the Spiritual, does not even knew that any internal man exists, much less is acquainted with its nature and quality." We spoke briefly of the Golden rule of doing unto others as we would have them do unto us. and of the dangers of following the folly of life for a lifetime without becoming a spiritual worker here on earth. He summed it all up very quickly and stated, "We do need to realise that it is the quality of love that determines the quality of life." It was not the last utterance of Master Swedenborg. "We have the heaven with us, and people who have heaven within come into heaven. The heaven within us is our acknowledgement of the Divine and our being had by the divine. Everyone in the spirit world is and effigy of his own love here on earth, not only as to the face and the body, but also as to speech and to the action." Then he seemed to be giving me more than I had bargained for: "man, when he is reborn, passes through the ages as he is born; and the preceding stage is always as an egg in respect to the subsequent one, thus he is continually conceived and born; and this is not only when he lives in this world, but also when he comes into another life to eternity; and still when he cannot be further perfect, then to be as an egg to those things which remain to be manifested, which are indefinite." He had me in now and I was even more curious than before, on the subject of the shadow -self that Carl Jung had studied so much on and led troubled humanity on a path back to mental health. "So, on this pathway through the heavenly realm and the wonders of the spirt therein, what about those that believe this earthly realm as evil as the works of evil that they performed here?"

He was sadly solemn as he announced: "People who have intended and loved what is evil in the world, intended and loved what is evil in the other life too, and then they no longer allow themselves to be led away from it. This is why people who are absorbed in evil are connected to a 'hell' and are actually in that place in spirit; and after the death they crave above all to be where their evil is. So after death, it is we, not the Lord, who casts ourselves into hell."He then said:" let me sum it all up for you. A life of faith without love is like sunlight without warmth- the type of light that occurs in winter, when nothing grows and everything droops and dies. Faith rising out of love, on the contrary, is like light from the sun in spring, when everything grows and flourishes. Warmth from the sun is the fertility agent. The same is true in spiritual and heavenly affairs. What are typical represents in the World by object found in nature and human culture." He added: "with regard to your former Catholic concepts of belief: Don't be too hard on your upbringing. All the ancient churches were representative of spiritual things, rituals, rites, symbols and statues, according to how their worship was established, consisting of pure spiritual correspondence. It is recognised that non-Christian lives are just as moral as those of Christians, and many of them live more, moral lives. A moral life may be lived to satisfy the divine or to satisfy people in the world. A moral life to satisfy the divine is a spiritual life.

The two look alike in outward form, but inwardly they are totally different. One saves us, the other does not. This is because if we live a moral life to satisfy the divine we are being led by the divine, while regarding the moral life to satisfy people in this world, we are being led by ourselves. A spiritual inner man first becomes a Church, a temple of the Holy Spirit within, therein he is on the right path to the hereafter." It seemed to me now that, having written a book on One World Order in 2019 and detailed it all back then from much researched on the subject, the swiftly coming of it now seemed fortuitous : The One World Elite so cunningly used the UN, The WHO and their own Elite members as a catalyst in the presence of our current world dilemma, especially in relation to this current Coronavirus pandemic.* It being a part of the agenda to further their cause, for it seems now that the death of love is being manipulated by the Hand in the Dark and his foot soldiers in our present day. It troubled me that I had written something as a warning of sorts, that is proving to be coming to pass. It also troubled me that I was just as vulnerable of that human path of old that leads to destruction as I am to take the way of spiritual enlightenment. Swedenborg, spoke to my linear logic brain and felt my disease. "There are are two loves that have been deeply rooted in the human race for a long time now: love for dominating everyone, and love for possessing everyones wealth. If the reins are let out on the first type of love, it rushes on until it wants to be the God of heaven. If the reigns are let out on the second type of love, it rushes on until it wants to be the God of the whole world. All other forms of love for evil are ranked below these two and serve their army." I could see more clearly now that both these loves were well advanced in the ways of this world. I watched as old Swedenborg vanished into the ether. I had but one thing left to do and that was to work on my own defects of character and pray. If I would but allow, then maybe the Divine love for the God of my own understanding would come. As David and I said our farewell to Master Carl Jung he had the last word: " I am not what happened to me, I am what I chose to become."

Once the two great Spiritualist had returned once more to their place in the heavens, David and I sat silently ingesting the spiritual food of which we had just partaken. David interrupted my contemplation,"So, whose is next?" he asked. " You have covered the gambit, slaughtered the savage beast with all your previous guest and made use of your writings, so isn't it time to consider a Master of the words of entertainment, or perhaps a dreamer or a skeptic of most notable causes?" I had to agree, I had been bogged down with those I thought that I could manipulate and gain the most from in my spiritual question and steering their answers in my head for the common good of all concerned and of course my own. Yes, I needed to used the Great Masters of the spoken and written word for my course. For thou there are many writers of renowned over the centuries that I could drawn upon, I had only to cast my mind back to consider my youth and education, to those writers that gave me the most pleasure and insightfulness in reading their work. For those who in my latter age of misery and discontent did I gain the most solace. And now in my dotage, the tellers of tales who fill my heart with the hunger for adventure once more; to go forth like a knight of old and champion the cause for future adventurers?

 David gave me a little more of his precious time and we spent most of Sunday afternoon considering a variety of diets as we browse through a list of candidates. Ultimately, I agreed that I would call on in mediation but three who fit the template of the lessons I had learnt from their writings and my own misguided misfortunes in my former life. Apart from their profound influence on the people of the history of their days, the chosen ones were to me a figure of amusement. I copied their names on a piece of paper intent on a later brief of each as I was accustomed to do, intended Master-guests at my table that next Saturday.

 We had concluded that as the playwright guest was English, as was the sceptic writer of famous stories and the johnny come lately, a dreamer and novelist, a Spaniard of the noble order, our meal would be rather a simple one. I knew that the playwright, Shakespeare, the Bard reportedly had bad teeth and would not welcome anything tough to chew. So a good soup of the vegetable kind would do, with some soft bread I surmised. David was in agreement and added that the Spaniard Cervantes could be a difficult one but as he had spent many years of his life in a Barbary prison he would practically eating whatever was served up to him. David, also confined the English novelist Dickens, my other writer of note, had also taken up residence in prison in his youth, thou more as an unpaid guest, as his parents having no where else to live for a time were grossly in debt, so took up residence there. So cabbage soup with smashed boiled potatoes was the main dish, with a filtered John Dory, infused with lemon, garlic and parsley to add to its taste. I hasten to add a note to include a fair amount of onion to absorb the effect of the garlic taste somewhat. Soft and easy food digest was the game plan and the intended meal would suit all palates. Should the guest then find the need for a salad, it would be no issue to put one together quickly before serving the meal. Mirjana I contacted once more and enlisted her services to cook a duck aa a back-up meal, knowing that my guests may have room for more tucker, a duck would do the deed. I knew it to be just the ticket for me later, for I always enjoyed the leftovers and Mirjana's 'Duck dish' was always a treat to as was the left over Turkey last time she cooked.

So, once David had said his goodbye I set down once more to write my brief on the next Masters at my table .I had been reading a letter of the Spaniard, Don Miguel de Cervantes; of his being carted off to prison and how he had fallen on bad times and was broke, as poor as a church mouse so to speak. I reckoned he could do with a good feed and I figured he would welcome the visit to eat drink and talk with the other Masters at a table devoted to him and his fellow writers.

CHAPTER 12.

MASTERS OF THE WRITTEN WORD

The Don sounded rather elegant and the self proclaimed title must have meant something to the Spaniard. It meant little to me as every one of historic characters that had chosen to be cited, like Count, Earl, General, Emperor, Monsieur, Herr or Your Royal Majesty and so on and so fourth had proved to be in most cases granted to the rascals of the worst order. The entitlement of title was to my way of thinking an impediment of status that took away the humility from what we all should aspire to, that of being of the simple common man or women. To my mind title is unnecessary, except maybe as a mark of respect for the position held but not the heart of the person of common nature. Of course, having said that and knowing the nature of this dreamers imagination, the title 'Don Miguel' sticks with me in a more personal and comical way. In my early twenties I was forever dreaming up new schemes and madly attempting to complete them.

I recalled good friend Kevin, a school teacher by profession, who came to town from Brisbane. He was in Sydney for treatment for a kidney disease and need dialyse on what was the first machine of its kind in Australia. Kevin was ultimately a recipient of a kidney transplant and whilst undergoing recovery in hospital he bashed out a bronze statue of Don Quixote on horseback with his Squire, Sancho Ponca pointing at a windmill and presented it to me. It was fixed to a board frame of Spanish style dark mahogany wood. Kevin had grand imagery, was insightful in a creative depiction of me as 'The Don,'and himself as his trusted servant and Squire. The comical rendition of this sculpture rang true, much like the relationship between Don Quixote and Sancho Panza in de Cervantes novel, the facts were evident. I was the one in our friendship and socialising who followed illusion, whilst Kevin represented reality. I have to confess that my jousting at windmills and following illusive dreams has been a pattern for me over a lifetime. It has usually resulted in some success and elements of failure, monetary reward followed by financial loss, loves gained and hearts broken, then adventures far and wide, which on the face if it returned me back to the bottom of the rung of life to start all over again. So I have a great deal in common with the said Don Miguel de Cervantes Saavedra.

Whilst I understand the goodly Don and find some solace in his assumed title, I have no desire to find out the history behind his surname 'Cervantes Saavedra,' although in Spanish the meaning of Cervantes is "ladies man" and a Gaelic word for Saavedra is "Room or Hall', first appeared in medieval times in the township in Castile, Spain. It matters not really, for he will always be to me the Don Quixote of wild erratic fancy, of adventure after romance, rescuing damsels in distress and fighting windmills for the honour of it all. Or indeed staying within the aptly named 'room,' as he stayed indoors, as the wind blew outside his Castle walls.

As a rather outspoken and athletic young man, Cervantes took service with another Don; that of John of Austria; the very same great soldier of fortune who set forth to destroy the power of the heathen Turks in the old Mediterranean half of the east of the Ottoman Empire, way back in 1571. While the army of John won the battle, our young hero Cervantes was badly wounded in various parts of his body including the permanent loss of the use of hist left hand. Being the true optimist he merely stated that he had lost the use of his left hand for the greater use of his right one and proceeded to fight on for the greater good of his King Phillip. He also had a practical mind and considered that, as he had fought for God and his King, he might well be rewarded with a promotion to a higher rank and indeed received the entitlement of a pay increase. Fate was to play its part, for once being provide with a letter of recommendation from his noble Don John, Cervantes set sail for Algiers and both crew and passengers were sold into slavery. The heathen capturer of slaves, on sighting the glowing letter of introduction of Cervantes from his Commander in Chief considered him a man of some importance, so when it come to discussing ransom for his fat prize, he doubled it. Cervantes found it not to his liking at all and hatched a plan of escape with an easily persuaded guard of the prisoners. At the last moment the infidel for fear of the consequences of being caught deserted his slave companion when they were but halfway out to sea. Don Miguel was easily recaptured and thrown into the darkest of dungeons on order to stay put until his ransom was paid. So it was that the appointed time came when his parents, having scraped together all their worldly worth, arrived with a three hundred crowns to pay the ransom. The Algerian financial treasurers were insulted with this offering, considering their mistaken belief that their Spanish prisoner was a distinguished Nobleman with his letter of recommendation. They excepted the monies for the release of the Don's brother but he had to remain a prisoner until a few thousand more crowns could be raised and paid over the counter.

In the knowledge that his parents could do no more Cervantes escaped once more, but once more he was captured and condemned with two thousand strokes of the cat- o' - nine tails. It was not unusual for twenty strokes of this deadly whip to kill a man. Fortunately for the glib tongued Don, his sentence was never carried out. He was proven a man of great wit, a most likeable fellow and honourable courageous soldier. So the Pasha, the Algerian Viceroy took him under his protection. He lived in hope for his parents to find enough monies to negotiate his release and plucked up courage to live with dignity above that of his captors, despite the fact that he was in rags and loaded down in chains. Years of negotiation between his parents and some Monks who travelled between Algiers and Valencia proved hopeless over time. So in another attempt to escape he induced several of his fellow inmates to join him in an effort to steal a frigate and make a bold run for freedom and liberty. The plan might have worked if it had not been for one monk, a Dominican who had been entrusted with the task of buying his freedom from his captors. This being a third attempt to escape meant punishment by death. Once more Pasha, the Vice Royal , who came to love his proud Don, came to the rescue and he was forgiven. Finally his ransom agreement was met and just before he was to be sold off in a slave market, he was set free.

It was nine years since he had set foot on Spanish soil and one would think for such an adventure that he had experienced that he would have abandoned any notion of further adventure. But not our Don Miguel de Cervantes Saavedra! For he now ventured forth upon an even more perilous adventure than that of a soldier of ill-fortune. He became a hack writer of Spain in the later days of the sixteenth century.

So not unlike our intrepid hero, I like Cervantes, alas to my dismay, changed my life's way merely swapping one kind of slavery for another. In my days of former slavery, before I experienced my well worn calamity that led me to where I am now. The weather had at least been pleasant in my former hell, as it had been for Don Miguel in his Algiers, but now he was in this head of mine, and was back in Madrid. It was a dreary, hot as hell, wind-swept jump off of a place, only once he had left there, there was no where else to jump off too. He wrote a pastoral note of sorts called 'Galatea.' It had some moderate success, and he was paid a few hundred ducats for it. (Oh! how like me with so many of my Camino stories that I burnt the midnight oil for.) For he did like me, when future success seemed so imminent now, and got married. He soon found out that little truth lay in the old saying that two can live as cheaply as one. In addition, he now took into his household his widowed sister Andrea and her eight year old daughter, which men ceaseless toil. (again I knew this burden as mine was a brood of four unruly children that I slaved to educate, with little to be grateful for than the duty of which a father must do for his own.)
So, Cervantes, our writer of little renown, now burdened with endless drudgery for his wife, settled for misery and ceaseless toil. (Dam, what a coincidence was my own burden's lot). He had but one small orchard, five vines, four bee-hives, forty five chickens, one rooster, and one tankard for kitchen use, but little of nothing to support a family. Forty five plus one chicken meant that at least they had forty six days they could eat. The rooster being the last meal of some nourishment as a soup! He felt trapped as I, and at his wit's end and began his desperate efforts to make a livelihood which, it seemed at the time anyway, to be doomed to do for the rest of his days on this dreary earth. Then came a moment of a brilliant idea. He would find an appointment as a public servant to the King. For wasn't it that in his former service he he had been a soldier who help save the country at Lepanto and lost his left hand while defending his God, King and country? He knew his chances of an appointment were thin, but if he was to make his approach, he may well be appointed one of the four vacancies in the New World. Why not the the governorship of Guatemala, or the auditor position in Cartagena, a treasurer's job in New Granada or something else of a similar importance on La Paz? To his dismay, he was appointed to something not so far from home, the collector of wheat provisions for the fleet equipped to take on the might of England and its low countries.

All seemed fine and dandy but for the fact that he was excommunicated from the church for plundering the peasants while the public accountant found his books in a hopeless state of confusion and he was dismissed. So now in dire straits and poverty, he borrowed money to obtain some new britches and set his mind towards literature in the hope of a possible means of support. He thus sold himself to a publisher who agreed to pay him fifty ducats each for six plays, provided of course that the publisher liked them. This was no small order in a sixteenth century Spain where the majority of the populous of hack writers had written at least a dozen not so successful plays. All Cervantes gained from this adventure into the writer's world was a first prize for literature in a contest in Saragossa. Three silver spoons was the prize. They were of little use unless one had some food to stir in the pot for his family's consumption. It seemed to him that he was either stupid or an unlucky person, who could not escape tor dodge the bullet of disaster.

 For while he was once more forgiven by the authorities, he gained clerical service in the Royal Navy, collected his payment of several thousand reals he owed the government and entrusted a merchant heading for Madrid to deliver the monies to the royal treasury as soon as he arrived. The merchant (as merchant do) disappeared with the money and thus our unsung hero was forced to borrow even more monies to pay the government or go to gaol as a consequence.

Through all of this administrative and money experience Cervantes did not have the makings of a good book keeper but he once again tried his hand in business and of course failed dismally, landing him in debtors prison. So for such a long time he seem to have vanished the earth until his name is mentioned as the author of an imaginary Spanish knight known as Don Quixote de la Mancha.The first notice of this Opus were not exactly flattering but he was informed by a friend that his play had been read by the publishers and it was considered the worse piece of writing that had ever been noticed. As we all know, there has never been a monument erected to a critic and that turned out once his work did get released, the Spanish public loved it. Within two weeks of release three publishers in Lisbon had stolen it and kept the presses running hot with their pirated editions. This was very flattering for the author but not exactly so from a financial point of view. Cervantes therefore went to the law for an injunction against Lisbon publishers and returned to writing his now beloved Don Quixote with renewed zest.

It may well surprise us of this 21st Century who derive our pleasure from so many fine and famous authors of old, that they would consider the character of this 16th Century Spaniard to be so famously wonderful now, but Cervantes' contemporaries do not seem to have looked at our noble Don in that light. They accepted his true representative virtues as truely Spanish and showed admiration for his unselfish devotion to his ideal chivalry to which had in fact long disappeared from the reality of that time in Spanish life. They eagerly awaited new chapters in the adventures of Don Quixote.

Cervantes should have been a rich man for his famous novel and the associated series that followed, but it was not to be. The final scene of this tragic writer's life came in the form of a plagiarist of unusual skill who undertook to compose a rival series of the adventures of Don Quixote following so carefully in the footsteps of the original hero that it became difficult to distinguish the real Don Quixote from the false one. For this cunning forger wrote under a nom de plume identity. At some time or other every Spanish writer of renown has been suspected of having a hand in it. The shame of it all is that it deprived the real author of his just reward and robbed him of his well deserved fame. Cervantes, annoyed beyond words at this unfair competition and in fear of losing control of the end of his series , set out to prove himself as the original author of Don Quixote by paying attention to his unusual style of writing more than he had done before, but it was too late. A lifetime of toil and strife, the years of his Algerian captivity, together with his endless struggle against poverty were beginning to take their toll. He was sixty nine years old and everything he had ever tried to do had failed him. Early in April of 1616 he took to his bed. He did not have a cent to his name and lived in one of the poorest quarters in of the town, but until his very end he remained a soldier and, above all things, a Spanish gentleman and to the end he continued to write of his craft and character. Cervantes was buried in a simple ceremony at the Tertiary Order of the Franciscans and his bones we laid to rest in one of the many Madrid churches, one attached to the convent of the Trinity nuns. His grave has never been found, and his only surviving child, an illegitimate daughter died in 1652, so nothing remains of Don Miguel de Cervantes Saavedra except a dozen immortal characters in a book.

"So my dear friend David, now you may see the character of a man that was himself noble and somewhat mentally disturbed in true light. But do understand from our research that he has a glib tongue, so we shall see if he has mellowed from the experience of his difficult life on earth and trust his recognisable light of truth of his success within the Kingdom of Heaven with his fellow writers of renown in their rightful place."

The manner of the brief on our famous Spaniard took a different slant from that of my former briefs of introduction on past Masters at my table dear reader. For the other two men who were to come to the next Saturday dinner were so well known public figures that it I deemed it unnecessary to go into too many details about their lives. I then elected to do the brief by myself, allowing David the release from this burden to look more closely into the coming menu for the dinner.e was to consider choice of appropriate wine and soft cheese and in his thoughtfulness consider again the remaining condition of our guests not so healthy teeth structures. So it was that I turned to the next of the master writers and began to write his brief… Shakespeare, William.

Shakespeare exact date of birth is unknown but his baptism in Stratford Avon, in Warwickshire on 26th April 1546 confirms he was born somewhere in that vicinity at that time. William's father, a man of some standing in the community, was sometimes glove-maker, butcher and wool dealer. He was an upstanding citizen of Stratford, and held in sufficiently high esteem to be elected to the municipal office of this new small community. While he was once fined for maintaining a dung heap on the street where he lived with his family, the public records show that he paid the fine which indicates that he may as well been a farmer.

In contrast to his father, we know little of young William's early life, except that he was apparently the third of his parent's children, probably went to a local grammar school and probably would have gone much further than that if it had not been for the unfortunate circumstance that his father fared not to well and gradually lost his property and was then disqualified from holding any official position. So it was that young William was obliged to be as assistant to his father after the latter had returned to his trade of a butcher. It was whilst busily cutting the throats of his father's hogs that he indulged in the delight of entertaining customers, declaiming poetry and making high spirited speeches in lieu of actually doing much work. So, Alas, as he was 'gainfully' employed he, like his soon to be fellow guest as a Master at my table, Don Miguel the Spaniard, went and took himself a wife. Reportedly William was but eighteen years at the time and his life experienced and then pregnant Anne, of some twenty six years of age, took her Will in holy matrimony in the autumn of 1582.

It did arouse a bit of small talk around the neighbourhood, but such gossip troubled our young Bard not in the least. However, when the baby was born 'before its due date' as proof is in the pudding, so to speak, a nice little scandal was concocted by the good Christian people of Stratford. This was a latter day slap in the face by his community and a slur on his good name and that of his wife as far as he was concerned. So he packed his little family off to the city where familiarity did not breed contempt. The widely spread reputation of our lively young man, W. Shakespeare was considered by all and sundry as a man of education but out of his rural class and a 'rebel' by the local establishment. A move to the city was his decision to escape the bondage and small mindedness of his native home. He seemed to disappear from view for a time for the next eight years , occasionally appearing as an apothecary, a dyer, a soldier of fortune, public scribe and some time printer, only to disappear and reappear again in a different guise. After a time his name began to pop up with more regularity as one of those who worked for the stage. This was in a time when authors were considered as persons of some importance. By this I am not alluding to the fact that he had any instance success, far from it. In a small way he was initially a bit of a hack writer, but in more acceptable time and a marketing opportunity to sell works, he would possibly be claimed today, even more heroically as one of the one percent playwrights, poets and film script writers who actually make a living from their art form. Shakespeare lived long before an author's comings and goings were worthy of constant observation by the public at large. Despite years of research and studies by scholars of renown to this present day, we are still much in the dark on the data of his professional career.

Shakespeare's contemporaries were aware of his existence, but did not regard him with the respect that he truly deserved. In their eyes he was just another actor- manager- playwright and in those times they were a dime a dozen. Indeed, were we to invite all the great ladies and gentleman of greater London in 1599 when he acquired partnership in the Globe theatre and were we to ask who among their contemporaries had the best chance of survival during the next three hundred or so years, William Shakespeare would have been among the last to be suggested. He was however deemed worthy to be among the "King's men"- in the compass of actors enjoying the direct and immediate patronage of his Royal Majesty. So, in the blinking of an eye Londoners became aware of this myriad-minded little man from the provinces.

There were a whole thirty seven plays of what no on else before or since has been able to do. For he dumped the whole of humanity at our feet and said: "There you are my friends! Check it all out. I know it's a bit of a terrible mess, but don't get angry or annoyed with me because you don't like it. Mankind was not created according to my own specifications. All I do is show you what it really looks like. Beyond that my responsibility comes to an end." It pleased me to hear this, for it appears I am in the top percentile for work output in print and use of unique words, but when it comes to punctuation and spelling errors I err on the lower side of the statistic. (see Note below *)

The immortal William, having been the subject of several hundred years of the most minute form of scholastic criticism has, as a matter of course, been compared with the moon, stars and skies and every Tom, Dick and Harry of a playwright under the sun. The William of my telling compared with the appearance of a well worn dirty tradesman or indeed a hippie of the latter days of my youth; hiding so well the difficulties of the restless mind that those of us with such an affliction sometimes find unbearable, leading to a retreat into some seedy back room, smoking an endless chain of cheap cigarettes and drinking booze and to much coffee, All in order to write even more stories in the hope of tapping the muses for inspiration, to entertain the madding crowd, and to find paying customers who seem to be looking for some thing in the stories to give them some reason for living and hoping. Such a comparison of a character of this type draws a close analogy to the immortal real William. Observe him just after he he has made a hard earned haul from the depth of his spiritual connections, fished out of the muddy waters of the unconscious and dumped upon the street, quay or wherever the master happens to practise his trade at any particular moment in time, for there it lay, whatever it's worth may be. He was a little uncertain concerning the moral vale of his material and sometimes felt he had dug it all up from a grave of long forgotten divinity or from the seclusion of a forgotten garden some six or seven hundred years before his time of writing. There were skulls that come rolling out, notorious gargoyles of man-birds of prey hanged for a trifle murder and thrown in the river of no return at the time, only to be uncovered from the depths among the fishes, by the mind of a Master who wrote it all down for us to evaluate, rehash and close the pages on from time to time with a noise, a shake and a shudder.

If you but pay some some serious attention for a moment to the material Shakespeare dug up during his career a playwright, you will know what I mean. For Lord of great mercy upon us all! Oh, what a strange assortment of human beings came-a rolling out of his literary ladle! Saints and sinners, noble heroes and the most contemptible of scoundrel's, devoted wives and heartless wanton whores; people of capable acts so profoundly self-denunciated as others are delighted to commit eventually the most serious crime imaginable, as do wise men and fools, pedantic pundits and easy going scribes, hopeless vagabonds and priggish Courtiers. God and the devil fighting for their soul of a Hamlet or a King Richard- and drawing truce sometimes. Other playwrights have tried to do what he did, this stance of a little butcher boy from Stratford-on -Avon. They, all sinners or God bother-res later got stuck in their own doubts and meditations. They like all of mankind began to moralise and were (are) forever lost.

Shakespeare on the other hand never preached, nor did he ever draw any definitive lessons to be learned from the deeds of his characters. Not even the least intelligent of his spectators is ever left in doubt as to which way lies vice and which of course will lead to everlasting life. All true men of greatness, ever since the beginning of time, have been condemned in their own way to a boredom of profound loneliness. That is the price we pay for being set apart from the masses of our fellowman. Most of humanity throughout the eons of history are able to discern that this is a fair enough arrangement and accept it without complaint or regret. Shakespeare was no exception. He happened at a time when the centre of a stage in politics was so fully occupied by men and women of extraordinary vigour and violence that most extraordinary acts of mere creatures of the imagination were apt to pale by comparison. England had its fair amount of invasions and annihilations in his time, so a hapless public could not be expected shed too many tears over Hamlet's sad glee of listening to the woes of a luckless father. Nor could it tell a doubtful dodger in a smoke-ridden pub the meaning and importance of the Tempest play, while the Spanish Amerada fleet were near and ready at that very hour to invade. Indeed, who could tell old gentlemen and tarts in public bars, wailing over their pots of pale ale, telling their twenty odd years of Shakespeare's yarns of murder and mischief that these stories were of greater significance than the reality of the innocent victims of their King Henry's displeasure? Shakespeare wrote for a generation far too much occupied by the actual business of living madly, wickedly and sometimes glamorous gusto, to have much time to waste contemplating the reflections of their reality. To wit though, he was not entirely without fame in his own time. It was not those of his day whose children, nor indeed his children's children who would willingly acknowledge his uncanny and clever plays while dwelling upon the revenues accumulation by their roving plundering ancestors. No, they were not given to appreciate his true merit. It took nine generations of painstaking industrious scribes, well read teachers and commentators to turn him into a sort of textbook of Elizabethan literature. He has to the seeing eye most triumphantly survived as the most brilliant versatile entities of all those who ever held up a mirror of the imagination to reveal unto us the magical wonderful reality of their dreams.

After some eighteen years of being in the London theatre, on what later became London's 'Broadway', William once more felt the desire to take up roots from the digs of the city and live that life of great respectability. He was not exactly a rich man but both he and his goodly wife Anne had saved their pennies and now hoped to spend the rest of their days associated with the ladies and gentleman rather than be in constant companionship with tipsy harlequins and money grabbing businessmen and bankers. Instead they returned to their native city of Stratford. Anne tending her garden and her beloved mulberry tree and indulging in a new hobby of raising silkworms. Will for his part wrote on occasionally for his London friends until 1613, at which time the old Globe theatre was burned down during a performance off the hapless Henry- an occurrence to which many a pious peoples would hasten to observe an act of divine retribution. Shortly after that Will Shakespeare spoke his final lines and quietly bowed himself off the stage of life. About the final year of his life we know very little and do we really need to? For We without recovering his abilities as fallen heirs to his fortunate imagination do not need to be so granted this gift, we only need to venture into a library and read any of his plays that have carried down through the ages to be privy to that. So it was then that I completed this brief of our soon expected Master guest and return to the kitchen. David enquired: "So you've finish the brief on Shakespeare?" I answered in the affirmed and he followed: "Then are you still intent on inviting a third guest or are you going to stick with your usual habit? I replied: "Yes I am considering Charles Dickens, but to invite three may be a bit too much?"

In truth I had not given myself enough time to dally on my intended third guests but after being prompted by David, returned to my office desk and began to write in meditative contemplation Charles Dickens's brief. He was born February 7, 1812 in Portsmouth, England ,the son of John Dickens, a Navy pay-clerk, and wife Elizabeth, nee Burrow. He was a lonely little boy of indigent care from both parents who were once obliged to take up residence in Marshal's prison for debt and cared little but for themselves. Charles was first apprenticed to law when he began writing unpaid pieces for popular journals. His two volumes of 1836 Pickwick Club works were published under a pseudonym entitled "*The Posthumous Papers the Pickwick Club.*" The effect was a world wide furore of Dickens imitators. Pickwick parties, we're held as far away as Canada and Kangaroo Island and the first printed addition contained prints of Tasmania of all places.

Fame was assured for Dickens' *Oliver Twist* in 1838 and *Nickolas Nickleby* in 1839.As a novelist, realist, public speaker and critic, his popularity was universal and the words of his novels changed   contemporary attitudes. At first aware of Australia only as a place of penal servitude, Dickens in his Pickwick stories invades our colony in the transportation of convicts rehabilitated to the country and expanded in to his fascinating stories of crime on Norfolk island. He never forgot Australia's prison origins writing from his first encounters in *Nicholas Nickleby* and *Our Mutual Friend* (1865) his last complete novel. Even in *David Copperfield* (1849) he speaks of his characters   being dispatched to Australian to complete their sentence. Even when he was writing the kidnapping of *David Copperfield* (1849), in the last chapter he embodies material from *Sydney's Australian Hand-Book* (1848). Then in his Household Words Journal of 1850, in the first article Mrs Caroline Chisholm's Family Colonisation Loan Society appears. The discovery of gold in Australia lent much feasibility to his success here 'Down Under' as he had noted, even more on the countries reputation as a gaol. In his *Great Expectations* (1861)he tells of a convict who amasses great wealth in New South Wales and so evolves into an English gentleman. Dickens had intended to do a lecture tour in 1862 with the intent to write a travel book " The Uncommercial Traveller Upside Down'" but the tour was abandoned. In Australia as in England, his novels were adapted to stage plays as perennial favourites. The articles from 'Household Words' and 'all the Year Round' were widely published in "the Australian" and helped to impose Dickens's own view of Australia on Australian life and society. Dickens died on 9th June 1870 was survived by sons who lived worked and died here in Australia.They no doubt lived out the experience of their father's vision of our land and the legacy and imagination of his stories.

The clock struck six and I hurried, showered and dressed for the appearance of my guest.I had at least enough time to help David with the final meal preparations and table setting before their arrival. As the clock struck seven, as was their custom, Shakespeare and Cervantes were standing outside waiting to enter. Dickens was nowhere to be seen and I could only assume that the man of Great Expectations would appear in his own good time, having been given a late invitation by me anyway. They were being extremely courteous to one another, stepping back and forward, encouraging the other to first darken their way into my doorway. The Spaniard won, entering first and the two punctilious gentlemen we invited to partake of a small glass of sherry as an appetiser before my open fireplace. I had decided at the last minute to light it for the first time in a year as there was a chill in the air. It was the expectation of the wind of an approaching autumn and who should blow in a puff, none other than Charles Dickens. He hurriedly explained how he had been working at light speed with a group of keen angels, lecturing on early works of himself as dramatist when my note had arrived.

He began to detail, like a story from one of his plays, how he had returned to his heavenly office to read my invitation while I at that time was meditating on his brief history . He reminded me of my 2013 visit to the Thyssen - Bornemisza Museum in Madrid, where I had happened upon three distinct comical sketches of Don Quixote with his man servant, Sancho Panza, his horse Rocinante, a worn-out old sack of bones of a half starved thing, faithful like Sancho to his unruly master and in the foreground an inevitable windmill. It was to be the bane of his false flights into fantasy, fighting for the cause of his King and country or on an imagined adventure to rescue a damsel in distress, always jousting with a windmill in faithful service as a soldier of good fortune. At the precise moment of his departure to come to our dinner engagement Don Quixote leapt from the wall and turned to face another windmill and thus began his charge. Dickens explains: "I had the devil of a time getting him to settle back down and return to his appointed place on the wall. I saw the noble Don wildly waiving his lance and making ready to charge the windmill, and the next moment…"

Both Cervantes and Shakespeare look curiously at Dickens and volunteered that nothing like that had happened in their neck of the woods on the other side , but Shakespeare made a mental note to follow up on his return to the heavenly realm to see if there was any such happening somewhere else in the universe. He perhaps wisely figured that another play may be forthcoming and a grand vision to write a story engulfed him. Dickens was disrupted from when the sound of Cervante's drink slipped through his fingers and smashed on the tiled floor. He cried out in despair. "Mother of God!"and then shouted. "What is that crazy fool doing this time? Can't he just leave me alone for a single moment? What will he do next?" It may well have been a purely academic question, but he had an answer right away. Somewhere in the bowels of Spanish hell from the other side a voice rang out so loud and clear followed by a lot of shouting "Hang the dirty thief."

Cervantes ran out on my balcony to see what all the commotion was about, followed by Dickens and Shakespeare, with David and I following in hot pursuit. From the vantage point overlooking the street below, leading to the market square and ultimately the highway north was a large band of children shrieking loudly at a man on horseback. That man we need not have to be told was the familiar silhouette of our noble Don Quixote himself, followed by his faithful servant Sancho Panza. One glimpse in summing up the situation, it was clear that he had arrived to prevent a scandal. The children from the north side of the street with sticks, bows and arrows and a sugar bag full of rocks were about to do battle with a group of children from the south side of the street equally armed with weapons of mass destruction. The 'Lord of the Flies' gang of brats were the closest to us and I headed to break them up while David headed for the 'Kings of the North' gang being on the other side. Meanwhile our three guests stood by the rail on the verandah to watch the proceedings, like theatre goers enjoying the delight of the play at hand. I did a typical High school bully act and grabbed the ring leaders, pushing them aside then gave their heads a good crack together. It sounded like the crack of a whip followed by ringing rock bells. "Here you rascals!" said I: " This won't do, have you gone half crazy." The market place was busy and the vendors did their best to sell their food stuffs in the midst of this children's riot. " No Mister" cried a voice of an old Italian women wanting to sell her chickens and eggs to a customer who was doing his level best not to be penetrated by an arrow or end with a lump on his head from a flying rock. She continued: "I came here to try and sell a few chickens and now would you please looks at that crazy galoot on the skinny horse, all dressed up like a kitchen stove. Kindly see what he has got on the end of his stick? "

We all looked and burst into laughter; for on the end of the Don's lance was a chicken, neatly speared and floating above the crowd. He had obvious lost his way and when he found not a windmill, he thus set upon the chicken. He seemed satisfied with himself, having no desire to placate the outraged chicken women. God only knows what would have happened if Cervantes had not come to the rescue hastily and spoken to him sharply in his native tongue. The Don bowed low to his creator, climbed down from his horse, took the chicken off his lance, returned it to the now bemused chicken lady with a noble flourish and attempted to kiss her hand; a courtesy she so skilfully avoided with a sharp smack across his cheek. "hold on, now my noble Knight.That's gone far enough" Cervantes commanded. "get back on your creature of the imagination. It is their curse, but it is also their reward and I am sure they would not want it otherwise." The fellow Master writers, David and myself were not really sure of Cervantes intentions in his commanding statement. He may have meant it for the Don himself, the audience of the marketplace or perhaps in the vanity of the moment, his own glory of the baffling character of his creation or indeed to impress his fellow wordsmith peers in observation on the verandah. Like his creation, he bowed to the crowd, to the children now fascinated, who had long since stopped fighting, or standing in a daze with mouths wide open or indeed he may have meant it for the wordsmiths alone, as he gave them the last bow. The comedy of errors play ended on a bright note as he, ever so swiftly as he had bowed, took the chicken lady in his arms and passionately embraced her. She was so shocked to stop this unexpected show of affection, she turned scarlet and dropped the dead chicken of our noble knight at the hoof of Rochinante, the half starved horse, who accidentally stepped on it and with a final squark, as the air left its lungs expired, the curtain closed and the fun was over for all, and sundry.

After the happy hour of entertainment we all adjourned to my table, ate dinner and returned to the serious business of talking. As Cervantes had provided the entertainment as if by accidental with his witty his characters, Shakespeare, not to be outdone, in the exchange of urbanities paid a most eloquent tribute to the merits of his esteemed colleague and proposed a toast to the Spaniard. Whereupon Cervantes compared both his fellow playwrights with the noblest figure of all time, to the immortal Don King John, under whom he had fought at Lepanto and, in a sort of a sing-song voice, improvised a hymn of praise to all famous writers of the world of the heavens and cried out after filling everyone's wine glass and paying special attention to fill mine only with the lemon water in the jug nearby: "A toast to the muses, those noble Gods who influence our imaginations to do great deeds with their words." Then in the end he was completely overcome with emotion, broke down and wept into his second plate full of the desert. I asked David to bring him another clean plate but he begged him not to bother.

 Indeed this night we learnt more about the world in which they had spent their days and the world of their now heavenly realm than we could have done reading a host of library books. But if we had expected to hear some intimate or exciting secrets about the reign of Queen Elizabeth I or King Henry V111, European kingdoms or indeed the second and third Philips of Spain , we were to be sadly disappointed. As far as our guests were concerned , these might have only existed in so far as they related to the arts. Politics, so they hinted very briskly never interested them. They, of such fine intellects considered it a game for adolescents and, though they were conscious of their own shortcomings, they at least claimed to behave as grown ups. So I sat in complete silence and listened to their conversation which was a little out of character for me, for I have as one of my many faults, the inability to listen for lengthy periods without comment.(I am still in the learning curve there I am afraid.) Well what do artists talk about when they meet? They do what Engineers, Polo explorers and Lion -tamers do or any other other group of men or women do. They talk about their work. They talk shop! These three discussed different kind of plots. They quarrelled and howled about how a play or book should be. They compared the honesty of their respective publishers, the generosity of their patrons and the theatre, and what they would have to say if a group of modern composers or playwrights had been questioning them over drinks in some back room London pub, or indeed drinking in some American Speak-easy or Russian tavern in Moscow. At the end they even went into detail about the type of paper and binding used for on their published works. In short they thoroughly enjoyed themselves and we, David and I as mere innocent bystanders, were so fascinated by their conversations that neither of us to watch the clock. Midnight therefore took us all by surprise. I in ordinary circumstances might have caused panic but our guests were not of this world. They thanked us profusely for a most pleasant evening and slipped back into the twilight in.. David and I were left alone with our memories. "Two bottles of wine," he said. " and nine bottles of beer " said I. We thought that was the last of it, but for a brief moment in time, Shakespeare returned looked up at the clock with a half drunk expression and said: " At midnight noon is born." He left just as quickly through the opened window as he had arrived.

No sooner had this occurred than there was a knock at the door and Dickens also in his cups announced like he was mouthing Carl Jung: " We aught not live the afternoon of our life as we lived the morning of our life." He then also disappeared and we thought again that that was the end of it until we heard the clomping of a horse's hooves below the balcony. I stepped out o to see the good Don Miguel astride his horse. He looked up and he asked: "Is my Master still here, I fear he may not make it to his place in the ninth heaven tonight unless I give him a ride on my faithful horse." I did not wish to correct him, that he was talking of the seventh heaven and not the ninetieth, but thought the better of it and responded : "Do not worry Don Miguel, he has already returned there." The Don seemed a tad disappointed, mumbled something in his native tongue that I didn't catch, waved his spear in my direction, bowed his head as a mark of respect and began to leave. His faithful Sancho retainer was already asleep with his head leaning against the back of his Master as he sat astride behind him.

I wondered, as the image of Don Quixote vanished in the mist, how could he have possibly thought he could have such a burden of weary bones on his half starve horse, riding three a breast, even-though not real characters. I returned to the table with the bill for the wine detailed nearby. David's final remark made me smile. "You should keep that piece of paper Doug, as some young man may get his Ph.D now, writing dissertations on the subject of our guests attitude towards alcohol."

CHAPTER 13.

PLATO & CONFUCIUS-THE RIGHT ONES

It had been my habit to write the Christian names of my guests when I introduced them in a brief. But in the case of my next two guests I was at a loss. Even a diligent examination of a great many books or a Google examination revealed naught. They just didn't seem to have one. How would they be addressed by their families, teachers, friends and even their students? I had no answer, then it hit me- maybe their names are not their real names but a nom de plume. I would never really know but it was not a problem really, as throughout history there seemed to be only one Plato and one Confucius, for I had decided they were the right people to be my next dinner guests as the Masters at my table. For I , as the writer of this fair tale being now more than three quarters away from the final curtain of a book considered it a perfect time to introduce these two characters of history. Waking up from a deep sleep, even before the rising and entry of the first ray of light of the morning sun they came to visit, just for a quick look at me in my world, then quietly vanished again. This morning their ghostly appearance was the omen I needed to make up my mind to meditate on them and to bring them in for dinner this very evening.

I had decided then and there that I would be their only host on this occasion for I needed from some spiritual urge within me to meet them in quiet conversation pick their brain a little for my own benefit and that of those who, by the grace of Almighty God will read this little book. I had no idea what to prepare as a meal and mused at the fact that I would be pretty useless as a cook in heaven should I be called upon to do so as my heavenly duty. A hermit living in a cave or a penthouse dweller would have a better idea of cooking up a storm in their respective worlds than I. For most of the meals I went to the trouble of diligently preparing, I burnt the bum out. It was not that I didn't now how to, but more related to the fact that I would leave it on the stove for far to long, distracted by an unrelated event or just drift into a dream and forget about it until either the fire alarm went off or I could not sniff my way around for the smell of burning vegetable or chicken overcooking in a pot. Thank God I had Mirjana as a backstop and Charley's chicken with vegetables already cooked for me. So I would just settle for meat or fish on the BBQ and steamed vegetables usually or a salad, that way I could not get into trouble.

So it was that I decided in the case of my guest Confucius to have a Chinese meal delivered at the appointed hour by a local Chinese Cafe. As for Plato, of Greek origin, a Pilau rice cooked in a kind of Turkish style with lots of varied ingredient was the ticket. It also I could purchase from a local Greek cafe. I decided to get some Portuguese chicken wings and vegetable spring rolls as an entree for the main dish, as I figured this would appeal to both tastes as it did to mine. As for the drinks, I had no idea, but finally decided there was an adequate and varied supply of leftovers from former guests, so I figured I would just put the lot out on the table with a couple of wine glasses and they could help themselves. I, being a recovering alcoholic, would settle for my usual bubbling mineral water. As for deserts, well I knew that both races had a sweet tooth like me. So I settled for Turkish delight, Algerian style sweets and Belgian chocolate to satisfy and complete my 'menu.'

Next, I considered music. It could not be country, rock or blues and certainly not something too classical to suit both tastes. It came to me in one, flute music Brandenburg style. It was not that I was a great consumer of such music, but I had for a number of years attended the annual Brandenburg chamber music Christmas Concert in Angel Place in the city, as a matter of course. My then partner was a chamber music nut, but I grew to like that annual treat. I uploaded on my iPhone the " Brandenburg" Concerto
No 5 in D major which had a very high pitch flute, now usually replaced by a trumpet, coming and going like a kid playing hide and seek with the melody. a perfect fit for me in the future to strike off any fit of future melancholic behaviour.

It should be remembered that Plato was much more appreciated during the middle ages and the Renaissance than during the centuries that followed immediately after his death. Greece at the time had ceased an independent nation. The Greek people had deliberately committed suicide by their everlasting quarrelling amongst themselves and by their attempts working democracy in a society that was mostly a population of slaves. Plato was not in the habit of spinning yarns and ideals to students with one eye on the left of 'Nazi like' politic and the other on the next stagecoach out of town to Lisbon or the Americas. Plato wrote his guide book to applied politics at the very moment when it could no longer be of practical use to anyone. Shortly after his death the heathen tyrant of the North swallowed up the whole of eastern civilisation and Greece was reduced to a seventh grade province, and an insignificant part of the vast then Macedonian Empire, which within a few years reached as far away as the Danube and the Indies. Nothing much has changed in Greece it seems now in the age of the EU. But I digress.

Plato had worked in a void. The glory of the age of Greece, when Athens dominated the ancient world is still vividly remembered, but so was the shame of the years immediately thereafter, when the barbarians from Sparta believed in converting everything into butter by the spearpoint and deliberately destroyed what the Athenians had so painfully built up. They left the city a mere ruin, its walls gone, its public buildings destroyed and its population decimated by a plague. A word of warning perhaps for our times with the current Covid-19 pandemic spreading worldwide, and the leading light of the world dimming with it America's White House still stands but maybe one day in a not so distant future tourists will visit it in decay as they have the historic ruin of the Parthenon in the past. Perish this thought too, for I am getting ahead of myself here.

But while it has been possible to destroy the physical part of the city of Athens, which for four long centuries had been the centre of the ancient world, it proved much more difficult to destroy the beacon of "enlightenment thought of actual observation" which the Athenian scientists and philosophers had erected on the shores of the Aegean Sea.

While Athens had been destroyed as an independent political unit, it continued to be the most important influence as a centre of education of the Old World. For centuries Athens ceased to function as an international political powered commercial metropolis. However the dud eager students roamed Europe, Asia, and Africa travelled to the land by sea, herewith from the many academics thereon who they might prepare themselves for the difficult business of living. Universities as we understand them did not develop until centuries later. Teaching was still very much a matter of sitting on one side of a log while the axeman cut another to demonstrate how it was done and of course the difference that emerged is that serious young men of Plato's time knew exactly what they wanted and came to Athens not merely to get a degree. They went to Athens in search of the best product then available in the educational marketplace. After they reached their destination they paid a considerable sum of money for the privilege of following some Master who presided over the establishment of their choice and then they sat at his feet to listen to ask questions and to debate with him. No attempt was made by a strict Athenian teacher to put together what God had put asunder and if a student lacked natural talent which was believed to be a prerequisite for successful work within the realm of arts and science, he was not tolerated for very long. He may be told to go get a reliable job as carpenter or stone-mason, but if he lacked the grey matter for a PhD his studies then it would prove worthless.

So let me now give you a few dates to fix Plato's activity more definitely on your mind dear reader. Plato was born about the year 427 B.C. two years after the death of Pericles. Remember he was the most prominent and influential Greek Statesman, orator and general of Athens in the golden age, specifically between the Persian and the Peloponnesian Wars. (I digress, but it must be said to put you in mind of a picture of Plato and his time and purpose herein). In 404 Athens after a war of almost thirty years with Sparta surrendered and lost its walls, its navy and its leading position amongst the small nations that went to make up ancient Hellas. A decade or two after 400, Xenophon wrote the dullish book which all little boys who have ever studied Greek in these twenty three hundred years since have had to read .I mention this to the point of how far over the centuries the Greeks have fallen from their former estate. To get the picture even more clearly, ten thousand Greeks were obliged to hire out Persians mercanaries, whereas one hundred years before they would have been hiring out Greek people. Athens, when Plato happened to come on the scene, was passing rapidly through all sorts and kinds of government, from a not so happy and exciting experiment with short-lived despotic powers and even more disastrous intervals of pure crazy democracy, when the fair name of Athens was forever disgraced by the judicial murder of Socrates. That happened in the year 399 and Socrates was of course the teacher of Plato. 399 is the year on which to hang a peg of the whole development of Plato.

Plato made some three trips to Syracuse in which he was called upon as a consultant on political matters by the tyrant who then was head of the Government of this old Corinthian settlement. At the time Plato seemed to have been living under the delusion that sometime, someway, some great leader would send for him in a letter a content of instructions that may read something like:
"Dear Professor, you supposed to know more about government than any other living human being. I have everything under control here. I run the show and everyone knows I am the boss. No bureaucrat nor government subordinate can put an army and a navy together without my say for we have my army or navy , but if any officer is seen to be talking to a former politician I'll hang him right away. As for women, they enjoy the same rights as men. The bright ones are not held back merely because they happen to be women. We recognise the fact that we have to populate , for we take motherhood for granted as a part of nature, like rain or sunshine. It's the duty of every male citizen to be clean shaven. As for children you will of course be devoted to their education and study. Ever child must be given its chance. We do not want the dullest of children to be given the opportunity over the smartest just because they can pay their way, even thou I believe in equal opportunity. The trouble is they never stay equal for more than a few hours or days. After that, as far as I am concerned each must choose his own destiny, I do not want for them to be brighter than the Gods, those who have been sent to be predestined for the poorest and least favoured infants, to reach to unexpected heights, while others, who come into the world with ever possible advantage, remain numskulls all their life long days and die in the gallows or the poorhouse. I therefore expect you to arrange the school system upon such a basis that every one of my subjects will be given a fair chance to function to the best of his abilities and may derive great possibilities and an amount of satisfaction from being a resident of this earth and will be able to do more than clutter up the roads of progress by futile efforts to do more than he or she can do, merely because such a course of action satisfies his own vanity.

There are other problems which I need to discuss with you on your next visit to Syracuse. I shall, however, mention a few- public health issues, some kind of system that will prevent the mentally and physical unfit from breeding like rabbits and filling our lunatic asylums and poor houses with a cargo of humanity which the ship of state is by no means able to carry. But of these things- as I just said-I will speak to you after arrival, an in the meantime I remain your well disposed, Dionysius, Saint & Tyrant.

Some such letter of instruction may well have been written for Plato, as for I have hitherto told you, he had paid three visits to Syracuse were the tyrant was stationed. But he had to suffer for   the same disappointments as Confucius when, two centuries before that good and wise man had gone forth on a quest for his own 'intelligent prince.'

 On paper the scheme of both philosophers looked entirely plausible. But when it came to practical realisation of their plans, the human race obstinately refused to live up to such parchment theories. It was in its own sweet way not practical for its timing despite the logic of the philosophy. Plato was forever haunted by the fate of his own beloved and brightest of them all teachers, Socrates. The one who had been so ruthlessly destroyed by the then lowest of elements of Athenian society. It destroyed Plato's not so heroic beliefs in the common man, and student and thereby led him to devote himself for his entire almost eighty years training to a few chosen disciples in science and statesmanship. He was head of a private school for the majority his life and never got mixed up in politics. Outside his academic labours, Plato found time to write thirteen epistles and thirty - five dialogues in which he discussed every possible problem of life (and therefore of politic and statesmanship) which for one reason or another struck him as a fit subject for debate with his students.

 The esteem in which these ' conversations' were held is perhaps better demonstrated by the fact that practically all of them have survived, whereas the great part of ancient literature has been irredeemably lost, including some of the holy works of Christendom. But somehow the works of Plato were always most carefully preserved. Even during the most chaotic centuries since his departure from this planet ; from the fall of the Roman Empire to the present day, some of the most Platonic scholars have always been the most faithful to hide at least enough copies of these priceless treasures to save them for prosperity. So as a result we are throughly familiar with the ideas of this greatest of writers of antiquity. For there has never been a moment during the twenty three centuries which separated us from Plato when he failed to influence at least a few of the brightest Spirts of our races. We find his influence in the founding fathers of the churches, and the medieval scholars despite the influence and devotion to Aristotle. The eighteenth century, by way of example, known as the age of enlightenment, was endlessly and thoroughly Platonic, in-spite of its' endless repeated love for the common average man. Today, among the fury of conflicts let loose by the antithesis of Plato's ideal of a true leader. (No names no pack drill, as I am sure you know of whom I speak), the name of the great Athenian has been somewhat eclipsed by the prophets of violence and cruelty who now seem to be in full command. But mark my words! The moment some semblance of reason returns to our unfortunate planet, Plato will again come into his own. Homer of course was before his time, but very few writers of common sense, or philosophy of life are more often than not hopelessly outdated before the passing of a single generation. Whereas Plato, when he really lets go is able to forget for a few moments that his teacher Socrates was put to death for much less than telling his pupils simple truths. So it was that my distinguished Master was on his way to my table via my thought processes at this time. I had been thinking about his Republic Utopian form of political criticism. He having just lived through the terrible experience of seeing his beloved Athens go to ruins entirely through its own fault (* The USA and the West come to mind now).

He has Socrates, who is his hero of so many of his dialogues, discuss the vicious circle which is apparently impossible for mankind to escape from the bondage of its own political follies. Plato turned up at my table an hour before his planned arrival and that of Confucius, so it gave me ample opportunity to discuss his thoughts on democracy over tyranny.

I, after providing him with some pre dinner snacks of olives, cheese and biscuits and a peppermint tea I began to pick his brains:. "it goes like this." he said: " In the first flush of victory they, the victors of Democracy over Tyranny, kill many of their opponents, send a few more into exile, and then settle down to show the survivors how the world should be governed. But soon the democrats turn out to be as the plutocrats and the tyrants before them. They use the powers of their numbers to get the majority at every election and then they do as they please because whatever they decree is based on a 'legal majority.' Therefore they are entirely within the law when they divide all offices among themselves and when they need to keep the people happy, they constantly increase the numbers of dole moneys to keep their constituents pacified so they will continue to gain their votes. Of course, in order to retain the good will of the masses, they need to do something that the tyrants and the Elite of the distinguished nobility, wealth, education corporate, religious or political or indeed military dispense with. They just flatter the masses of men of quiet desperation and increase their stance of vulgarity. Manners are course and discouraging words be their cause because no one to show them better. The mad pursuit of wealth for wealth sake or what usually goes with it and is power for the sake of power, must eventually destroy democracy to be followed by another period of decline. For in such a state, anarchy gains until it presently finds its way into the private homes and even gets into the head of the animals. Fathers get accustomed to stoop the level of their sons and the sons behave with insolence towards their fathers, for they no longer have any fear of retribution. The teacher begins to stand in awe of his pupils, and as a result the pupils despise teachers. From that moment on young and old are equal, and the young are ready to compete with the old in word and deed, while the old feebly imitate the young.

So I asked: "What is the result of all that?" Plato responded with: "The excessiveness we increase of this so called liberty causes reactions in the opposite direction, for an excess of liberty, whether a nation or individuals, seems to pass into slavery, and the most aggravated form of tyranny arises invariably out of the most extreme form of liberty, for the moment liberty becomes license, dictatorship is near." I want to take this a step further: " Plato, how does this evolve?" He answered with some conviction: "The rich became afraid that the prevailing democracy will rob them of their very last dollar, so they begin to think of ways to overthrow their enemies, and at that precise moment some enterprising reader is apt to seize power. He surrounds himself with an army, kills firstly his opponents and next befriends those who might be dangerous, having purged the state , he establishes himself as tyrant and sole ruler."And " says Plato, "there is no longer room for philosophers who preach moderation and mutual understanding. The poor philosopher is now a man fallen like a wild beast and, if he is wise, so he will retire while he still has time, and take shelter under a wall while the storm passes," Well in that argument you have the motives of Plato's whole career. While the storm is raging, there is nothing the man of contemplative turn of mind can do. Let him rather take shelter and the "Perhaps" for like Confucius he is not so certain whether that day will come. It is true to take such an approach to even current day political climate in that regard. As any well trained Gladiator will tell you some half-witted barbarian strong arm with careful trained army will do infinitely better at business ideas rather than with with the bomb. It is not cowardice that makes a philosopher take this step, it is in the sense of the fitness of things that he realises that, he is being a doctor of the soul and is not unlike the doctor of the body, who is found behind the lines and not in he front rank line of fire.

I was milling this over in my mind as we sat there in conversation. Having settled the matter to his own satisfaction and finding his ideas worked at least on paper, Plato concentrated all his efforts upon trying to discover how the human race could be made to behave according to the laws of reason, by whatever method and elements which might endanger development, it could then be eradicated. He then could perfect a state of an establishment in very much the same way as a better breed of horses or cows, pigs, sheep or inferior grain could be developed out of inferior varieties. A most noble and praiseworthy idea of which the greatest minds of all times have occupied themselves   at some period in their lives. Some of them approached it from the solemn and dignified angle, which is so characteristic of Plato. Others, like the carpenter from Nazareth tried to solve the difficulty by placing himself the human race under the direct superintendence of God. Still others like Voltaire, and Dean Swift used satire, Thomas More thought he could do it by putting a china egg into mankind's nest and called it a 'Utopia.' Descartes endeavoured to give us a solution by mathematics. Spinoza gave it an ethical twist. Karl Marx took economics as his particular bent of research. Rabelais clowned everything into a world of his own making, In effect there have been all sorts of philosophers, sages, and master minds, some genuine some not so, who starved in garrets and died in cellars, that they might bestow upon their fellowman a blueprint of salvation, searching the heavens and hell for an answer to that all important question.' How can we possibly save mankind from itself?" In the end it was Omar the tent maker who summed it all up in his own life long investigation in this simple stanza:

"Myself when young did eagerly frequent
  Doctors and Saints, and heard great argument,
  About it and about: but evermore
  Came out the same Door as in I went."

Saturday evening, the bewitching hour and the time for me to give the mind of Plato a rest for the entry of Confucius was at hand. As sure as clockwork came a knock at my door as the clock struck seven bells. I opened the door slowly and there stood the old Chinaman Confucius. It was so easy for me to recognise him for he looked exactly like his pictures. He did not offer to shake my hand but we both stood repeatedly bowing three times to each other until I took my guest through the entry door . He gave me one more quick bow before entering and made his way to the fireplace, where he surprisingly shook Plato's hand. Then I noticed he was followed by a young Chinese citizen dressed in ordinary civilian clothing. He also bowed three times and explained: " I am a descendant of Confucius, I am the grandson in the forty- second degree, but", and with a sly smile, "Well may, of course, have lost count, for it has been a very long time. I was a student in what was then Cornell, in the agricultural department, when the Japanese invaded our country. On my way back home I was shot through the heart. It was a painless death." He added: "Excuse my intrusion, my honoured ancestor here suggested I accompany him as his interpreter, as he is a little difficult to talk with considering he has lived a few hundred years ago. But we are of the the same blood and we get along very nicely. So have no fear I will make it easy for you and your honoured guest." I noted that a change had come over us all. Quietly unconsciously or soberminded and exceedingly unceremoniously Plato dropped a rather free and easy manner of proceeding with an open ear to what was being said and done. We adjourned to the dinner table were I had placed out the take away meals as if they had been cooked by a professional chef. My guests began to eat and I encouraged them to feel free to pour themselves a wine or mineral water as they saw fit to do. Confucius's young descendent of a fortune age was first to reach for the bottle of red wine, but he did not pour it for himself but rather a very small glass for his grandfather. Confucius was the first to raise his glass with a slight head bow of 'thanks you and good cheer,' Plato followed with a small red wine too and the young interpreter and myself settled for a mineral water. We all tucked into the food and took a break before we renewed our conversation. I then set my iPhone to the app for the former flute but now trumpet soft notes of my Brandenburg selection. Both Plato and Confucius closed their eyes while listening to the music, like they were in some deep form of meditation.

The meal, I am pleased to say seemed to be entirely satisfactory to my guests and Plato found special pleasure in the size of the olives, which he told me were almost twice a large as they use to be in his younger days." "When" he adds, " The gods provided us with our meals, for whenever one of my students got hungry, we plucked him a few fruits from underneath the trees whereI used to teach and we were not forced then to interrupt our discussions." I told him that is hardly the way teaching is done nowadays. " Why not? "asks Plato: " are not your students interested?" I answered " Yes, but in a different way?" Plato continued his enquiry " Is there a different way?" but I distracted the young interrupter asking him if he would like desert, as I preferred to change the conversation. I figured it may lead us to painful confessions about the attitude of our modern student towards all problems learning not immediately connected with the practical purpose of making a living. Fortunately, the young man asked for tea and my fellow guests did likewise. I had in my haste to make the tea using the old tea pot which was my mothers Delft one. Confucius examined it carefully and through his interpreter told us it compared very favourably with one he used when living with the Marquis of Ts. Then he added an afterthought, again via his interrupter grandson : "that was in the days when I was still full of hope that I might find one ruler willing to give me a chance to put my ideas into actual practice, my ideas about government based directly upon the principles of righteousness and virtue. But the invitation never came. Circumstances were too strong for me. I had only one chance, but the prince grew tired, and I was obliged to withdraw."

For a moment he withdrew back to that time with a rather sad look on his face. However, he quickly returned to his former photographic image facial expression. The night was turning cool so we withdrew to the lounge around the fireplace. Plato sat in my favourite chair and next to him sat Confucius, and I sat in the midst, back a little from the fire and in a perfect position to take the best seat for my purpose. Once we all settled, the grandson as a mark of respect moved his chair and sat directly behind the old gentleman and as we continued our conversation the young man translated Confucius's words so rapidly that to us it wasps if I could hear every word in his native tongue. This unknown tongue seemed to flow like honey into its English linguistic equivalent, so it was through this language it had become for me a 'true meeting of our souls.' and we were tuned into the same intellectual wave-length. We kept the kettle on the fire and on the boil, refilling our cups from time to time with tea from the topped up pot the next three hours of conversation. There was one subject that seems to be uppermost in the mind of my guests. Each of the two masters had given the subject of Government as much attention as any human being who has ever lived. It was the question of how to put government in the handle of those best equiped to hand the difficult tasks of power.

They were of course familiar with every scheme that has ever been devised to safeguard a nation against tyranny. Tyranny either above or below. Democracy, totalitarianism, authoritarianism, dictatorship, experiments with socialism-all proved to be a problem not merely for our own day and age but as old as the human race itself. Confucius would give us examples that went back more than twenty five thousand centuries. Plato would answer of his experience before the beginning of Christianity. The young interpreter who seemed to know his global history offered his opinion of the difficulties Emperor Charles had encountered four hundred years before. I offered my opinion of the various Government problems of our time but to tell you the truth we got nowhere at all in this conversation. So we returned to one question: with a double edged sword: " How can we possibly prevent a single man or a minority forcing its will upon the majority?" and "how can we be sure that those best fitted to rule will do the actual ruling?"

Finally before the end of the evening, we seemed to be reaching a conclusion. Both Confucius and Plato agreed that beyond a reasonable doubt, a government, equally satisfactory to all people would never be possible until, firstly, the whole of mankind could be taught to accept a 'moral basis' for behaviour, not merely as private citizens, but also as members of the community.and we all posed a follow up question:

"How could this be brought about?" We all agreed that it could only be done by substituting love for good of the community at large, for the old attitude that man is a predatory creature, forever in search of his ongoing and ready to trample down whosoever came in his way while he was in search for food, clothing and shelter and a little luxury for his family. We had no disagreement on this subject., but the moment we reached for conclusion, then we were once more face to face with that perplexing question: "Was there moral a basis, and if there was, how could a sufficient number of people be persuaded to accept it and fight for its maintenance with their lives?" Religion? It had tried and found wanting, Education? We had educated and educated and continued to educate and how much good had it done over the course of history? It had disseminated a lot of diverse characters and content and quite useless information but it had not noticeably added to the wisdom of the populace. And so we continued until the hour of departure came.

 But this was no sudden lowering of the light, no sudden darkness, no sudden disappearance of my Guests. Confucius seemed to anticipate that soon the moment would come for us to bid each other a goodbye. Some ten minutes before the clock struck the hour of midnight he got up and this grandson, who had proved to be a most delightful participant of the evening, assured me that he and his grandfather had the best evening of enjoyment in centuries. Plato did likewise although not in such flowery language. Somewhere in the heavens I heard Desiderus Erasmus, The Dutch humorous and scholar call out that he too had listened and enjoyed the evening's conversation as much as the night he had spent at the home of his beloved Thomas More.

 Then there was a ceremonious bow between us all as the clock struck midnight, the candles went out and the embers of the fires slowly turned to darkness, leaving me with some delightful memories: What must I do, I asked myself? I heard deep within subconscious: "work, for until we find a wayout… otherwise…" Otherwise what?" , Then an inner voice: "Otherwise there won't be any human race left to worry about.…"

 I was thinking back now of my 2015 Portuguese Camino, looking for an answer to my life's dilemma back then. Questioning my 'moral basis' as it were, and finding none penned a poem which summed up my state of mind at the time and I was even more conscious of the proof in the pudding in eating of the first opening line of the poem. I had just penned - "Pilgrim, there is no answer, there is no Way." I was the Pilgrimage of The Way of St. James for the second time on my Journey. This one was in search of a new lover, considering (perhaps) that a women was the answer. Adam's life giving rib had not formerly proved to be, but maybe this time it would be different. I had once more turned to a women instead of turning to God.

The first journey had been to let go the tragedies of my life that had beset me, left me a screaming wreck of a man and the outcome was, well it led me to The " French" Camino along the Napoleon route. The Way of St James whose remains reportedly lay under the altar in the Cathedral at Santiago some 800 km away. I walked 'The Way,' to let go a lot and I did, but I wasn't living the message of the goodly Saint who had preached the simple spiritual message :"Actions speak louder than words." I missed the point of it all, thinking then that I was still a part of the old way of life and needed to get back to it on my return to Australia.

I arrived feeling I was renewed so to speak, so I threw myself into all kinds of projects, from writing books to recording my songs to property renovations, daily trading the stock market while still attempting to do contact work in business development. I crashed, ended up in a rehab hospital in deep depression again. On a recovery of sorts I returned to The Camino searching for that elusive lover, thinking that a women was that answer instead of God. For I was searching for a way out of my spiritual hole, of what seemed an incurable malady. I reminded myself back then that my ego was equivalent to being a grain of sand on the beach, but in reality it wanted to be the beach and for a while longer I lived my life as if I was the beach, as I was in my not so humble opinion top dog again and as a lover..well I found the folly once more of lust over love and I landed back in a rehab hospital a little more worse for wear than before.
I lost a year of my life, returned to exercise and once strung out enough, set about once more for my third Camino. This time on the French route again I walked though sunshine and sorrow, sleet rain and almost snow. I was sick in body and mind now to a greater degree than before, but to walk The Way once again, then walk the Wicklow Mountains in Ireland and the Aran Isles where I walked upon one side and peddled a push bike down the other. Finally on the Barrow way I cracked again, not mentally mind you, but spiritually. I was now heading for a kind of acceptance of who I was and what it is all about for me. Three novels, two albums and two poetry books later I came to a kind of acceptance that has led me to writing this book…and so it continues.

Pilgrim, there is no other
there is no way
only wake trails on the waters
wake trails to the shore.

Cast a stone to water
watch the wake trails fade
life is like that
a fading thing.

Cast my burden like a stone
into the river of life
watch the ripples flow to shore
they just fade away and die.

And the river just flows
and the lake stays still
and there is nothing but ripples
every now and again.

Feel the wind ripple the waters
like loves and dreams of the past
the wake trails from water to the shore
they just fade and die.

Put down the book and the pencil
hang up that bold guitar
let the songs and the memories fade
like wake trails to the shore.

Just fading memories of the past
they do not last for long
like wake trails to the water
like wake trails to the shore.

Wanderer on the Camino
your footprints there no more
markers of your journey's end
it too will fade away..

Like a stone cast to water
watching the wake trails fade
looking back on the path you may,
the footprints made are gone.

Pilgrim,
there is no other
there is no way
only wake trails to the shore.

CHAPTER 14.

OMENS FOR A NEW AGE

It   has been my habit over the first two decades of this century to catchup with an old friend our mutual working days for the same International Corporation well before our respective retirements. We usually meet on monthly frequency since we both have the retired time for longer chats. Our chewing the fat, so to speak, over a range of topics as diverse as the state of the national and the current world economic situation, usually expands into how the investment market is weathering the current storm of ever changing growth or the diminishing returns for our respective retirement savings; the influence of monetary policy and our own financial survival under mitigating circumstance, like the world wide pandemic of Covid-19 by way of example. The subject then slowly but surely leads to the goings on with our offspring and the joy of having grand kids in our lives. Once we reach for a second cup coffee, it's usually an in-depth conversation on our mutual love of Rugby Union football and the pros and cons of changing the rules, global and local management of the game and the commitment of players to their chosen sport for which they seem to be to be over paid. Ultimately though, we always reach a point where we talk about our belief and the benefits of having a Faith or not. The latest get together was no acceptation and Ron, my friend of whom I can rely upon for logical and no holds bared forthright straight shooter answer on most things, enquired: " So what is it that you have your teeth into now Doug?" I spoke briefly how my AA programme was helping me stay sober a day at a time but more importantly that I had hung my hat on a 'spiritual' path both for now and in the future. Ron in his forthright way remarked: "Well, what's so different to what you believe in now than your once strong belief in your Catholic faith?" It is I find difficult to express in a simple logical way the meaning of 'spiritually' as to the traditional belief of any Christian religion, which also applies to non-Christian faiths too I might add. I did my best to explain it as "Spirituality, in a Christian sense, in comparing apples with apples, is a faith of handing over to ones own conception of a Higher Power or a God of ones' own Understanding." Ron enquiringly responded : "I can't see any difference in that, it's not so complicated in my opinion, I believe in God, and that's that."

Of course Ron, my friend, knowing me over all the years like he does, sees the Don Quixote chasing windmills in me and was not going to take the punches I was throwing on the subject lying down. So I felt it my duty to explain a little further my new found philosophy of recent days. "I too believe in God mate, I always have, be that with some doubts as to the reality of it all in the past crisis." My view is different now i's not just believing but living it as a handing over and being lead by the Higher Power. A total surrender to the will of God, if you will." Ron's quizzed his response: "But you can't just not ignore the reality we live in and expect God to take charge, you have freewill to do as you please, good, bad or indifferent." I replied : "Yes, that is true too mate, but I see it as living in this world but not of it, I guess much like the St. Anthony of the Desert and St. Francis of Assisi for example." Ron gave me a sceptical eye: " It's just not practical this way of thinking in today's world." Ron, for all his logic had the strongest of faith and does more charitable works for others than I have in my little finger. So, I managed to change the conversation back to our greatest mutual love, Rugby Union.

I did not want to get into a debate with Ron over religious belief. Frankly, being still on an early learning curve with the subject matter in action .i.e. to allow the God of my own understanding to always lead me in my decision making and actions is a tall order for anyone. Well it is to the world at large and that is reality. My motto is that I will accept God's will and live with it as he sees fit and not as I see fit. It is fine to boast of a philosophy of belief when one has an unlimited supply of food, clothing and shelter, and money in the bank for a rainy day. Easy to state that one has lost the fear of financial insecurity when you are one of the five percent of the world population that is far better off personally than the rest of humanity. But I wonder if the bottom fell out of my financial world, would what I perceive as real "Spirituality" now be so for much longer. So, will I still be sprouting my belief in a Higher Power when I hand over to completely and do his will, as he thinks fit? Ron is right in the practical belief in God, which is the belief of most of God bothering mankind. At least in our western world we have a duty to get on with the business of living, providing for our love ones amid all the material consequences that go hand in hand with it. My idea is to live according to the Spirit and hand over as best as I can, but is that the practicality of it? Well this little black ducks is no saint and I still often follow my own head instead of the instinct of the heart of love, which is the ultimate of what I am attempting to understand and act upon. I struggle with it all, the consequences of my actions; for I so much want to believe this so called "Spiritual" path is at the way of the future. But the cause to consider the 'Omens' of chance and opportunity as being far more fulfilling in a Spiritual action in my awakening is yet to materialise too 'Behold.' I am given to understand it comes only with daily practice. This Spiritual life of handing over and acting without fear comes with continual practice on a road less travelled for the future.

I know writing here in this righteous way seems to be a no-brainer. However, the way of life of the logical linear brain has its place in the decision making of our world but it is more like the action of the one-eyed giant of Greek mythology approach to life when it comes to the God part of belief. Whereas the feelings of the heart over the head and the Spiritual ethic in the everyday is, to my way of thinking, the one approach of Faith that is central to what is the new way of life and action for the common man in the 21st century. The old way of the logical linear reality was the way of the past, but I fear it cannot be so for the future of our fast changing digital and scientifically challenging AI world of tomorrow. We of the "baby boomer" age have a duty to give our children, and even more so, our grandchildren, good reason for living and hoping. They are already on a different plain to us in an Avatar like way. It is my belief here and now that mankind will ultimately have no choice but to connect with the Spiritual over logical in the God matter to make it alright in the end. Meanwhile, it has given me food for thought to investigate this philosophy more introspectively.

There is but one great and universal desire man expresses in all religious, art and philosophic meaning of humanity, the wish to pass beyond himself in the now. This search we have had since the beginning of humanity expressed in an infinite number of fields of endeavour, of religion, philosophy, psychology, art, literature, and those other field of endeavour which concern themselves with dynamic life processes. At its core has been the consciousness that   man could and wanted to live life with an orientation towards all persons and events such as would give his life a sense of meaning, purpose of reality and eternity. The desire is the underlying motif for the search, the finding and the actuation of the religious way of life defined herein the following pages and so I turned to the great minds in my search for meaning, in my quest towards my God…. in my search for Spirituality:
" Blowing through the heavens and the earth and inner heart of heart is a gigantic breath- which we call God.   Plant life wishing to remain undisturbed in stagnant waters, leaps up from within its roots shaken and disturbed; "Away, let go of the earth, walk." Had the tree been able to think and judge, it would have cried: " I don't want to, what are you trying to make me do ! You are demanding the impossible !" But the Cry without pity, kept shaking its roots and shouting: "Away, let go the earth and walk!" it shouted, life escaped the motionless, the tree was liberated. Animals appeared-the worms making their home in mud: "we're not budging." but the terrible Cry hammered itself pitilessly into their loins: "Leave the mud, stand up, give birth to your betters."
" We don't want to. We can't."
" You can't, but I can,. Stand up !"

Man is a creature with head, arms and torso of a human and the waist of body and legs of a horse. But the body from waist to the head is tormented by the merciless Cry: And Lo ! after thousands of eons man emerged, trembling on his unstable legs. He too had been worked on by the terrible Cry for eons, to draw himself out, like a sword from its animalistic scabbard. He also is fighting the new struggle - to draw himself out of his human scabbard , he calls out in despair: "Were can I go, I have reached the pinnacle, beyond the abyss." and The Cry answers: " I am the beyond. Stand up!" all things are centaurs. If it were not so, the world would rot into inertness and sterility." (Nikos Kazantzakis, 1885-1957, Greek writer.).

"We all know there are regions of the human spirit not deprived of action or expression by the world of physics. In the mystic sense of the creation around us, in the expression of art, in the yearning towards God, the soul grows upward and finds fulfilment in something implanted within nature. The sanction for the development is within us, a striving is born from a greater power than ours. Science can scarcely question this sanction, for the pursuit of science springs from a striving which the mind is impelled to follow, questioning that will not be suppressed. Whether in the   intellectual pursuits of science or in the mystical pursuits of the spirit, the light beckons ahead and the purpose surging in our nature responds". (Sir Arthur Eddington, 1882-1944, English physicist, astronomer.)

"Know that, by nature, every creature seeks to become like God. Nature's intent is neither food nor drink nor clothing nor comfort, nor anything else in which God is left out. Whether you like it or not, whether you know it or not, secretly nature seeks, hunts, tries to ferret out the track on which God may be found " (Mustier Johannes Eckhart, 1260-1327, German scholar, mystic.)

" We do not understand, but somehow we are part of a creative destiny, reaching backward and forward infinity-a destiny that reveals itself, though dimly, in our striving, in our love, our thought, our appreciation. We are the fruition of a process that stretches back to star-dust. We are material in the hands of the genius of the universe for a still larger destiny that we cannot see in the everlasting rhythm of worlds. Nothing happens but what somehow counts in the creative architecture of things. We fail and fall by the way, yet redeeming grace fashions as anew and eliminates our failures in the larger pattern. The pangs of pain, of failure, in the mortal lot, are the birth-throes of transition to better things. We are separated for a time by indifference of space and by our blindness which spells out and isolates us, but in us is longings for unity. We are impelled by a hidden instinct to reunion with the part of the larger heart of the universe."
- John Elof Boodin, 1869- 1950, American Philosopher.

Life does not need comfort, when it can afford meaning, not pleasure, when it can be shown purpose. Reveal what is the purpose of existence and how it may attain it-the steps he must take- and man will go forward again hardily, happily, knowing that an effort, which takes all his energy because it is worth his full and constant concentration, is the only life deserving the devotion, satisfying the nature and developing the potentialities of a self conscious being. If I could be perfectly honest and transparent, what would be the deepest and most central need to my human self? The answer would be my lifeblood to exist.

But then my ideas and emotions split into two different directions- on the one hand self preservation and that means change, commitment, giving up oneself or at the very least discovering or at least could discover, if I have the then ability to see reality as it is-that persistence without change is death, is nothing, is just what I am afraid of. But the second desire, inspire of myself is to renounce self preservation. Not try to be the Superstar God above time but in time, above change in everlasting youth and emptiness. The deepest of my desire tells me to face reality, to be as human as I can possibly be, and that means going through change, through the death of the old Doug, keeping nothing, not even my old life, in fact my present one. To be poor in spirit, being one with the universe, being willing to face the darkest enemy of my soul, that means facing God. This is what I wish for most of all in all my being, even if I know it now or not.

But in looking over my past life experience, I cannot reach the conviction that it has not been my seeking and searching that has been important, but rather the awareness of being sought and found by another. The Bible of my youth expressed, particularly in the Old Testament, the view that the living God who through chaos and confusion of life gives it strength and vitality and hope, and therefore fashions and creates and finds and thus gives existence. It is he who speaks, as he did through the Prophets, and reveals his will and sets life before it seals its imperative. The sense of moral obligation, his commanding and my response, is the will to obey or disobey. The Prophets had their Devine impulses, their crisis in a cave or dilemma in a national one. And then there is that sense of mission, then along comes Jesus's vision as he comes out of the baptismal waters.They all had (have) an authenticity about them which seems not nearly a personal conviction but almost a universal responsibility. I suppose my child like sense of script in my youth embedded in my heart my many attitudes and forms in which my past experience of life has been clothed, he that I, as a free wheeling young man chose to ignore, yet still find it is a kind of scaffolding to my inner temple of seeking this "Spirituality," that I now profess to be moving towards. Of course it was not just the Bible, particularly the New testament, that I have come to appreciate with some understanding, but the history of the East, the West , the North and the South, and the history that is unfolding in the now.

It has been the psychological forces that have been at play, for the past me that was religion was simple necessity. In fact, the only real possibility, as other ways seemed back then to be a dead end. In the only kind of world that I have ever known and the ones that I have been educated to accept - Old and New Testament, and the history books of my former education; the related loyalties to such teachings now are not enough. Those 'teachings' placed life in a context that provide a goal in the fullness and richness of a conception of the Sovereign rule of God. Perhaps the Spiritual change that I am grasping for now, what I am alluding too here is best expressed by Lao-tau, the 6th century philosopher: "As rivers have their source in some far off fountain, so the human spirit has its source. To find his fountain of spirit is to learn the secret of heaven and earth."

The Paradoxical Statements of a new spiritual way may best be stated in poetic form by a Master greater than I, Jesus of Nazareth "Whosoever shall seek to save his life shall lose it, and whosoever shall lose his life shall find it." and this statement: "He who humbles himself shall be saved; he who bends shall be made straight: He who empties himself shall be filled." Lao tzu, 6th century B.C.philosopher.

 "The Way" rest on the assumption that there are two centre inner personal structure, the central consciousness know as the "Ego,",the conscious willing factor, frequently referred to as " Self' or ' Seeming Self." the second is the point of total personality, both conscious and unconscious, often designated as 'The Self," the " Christ within," the "Real Self" or the "Creative Centre. "Whenever the Ego self becomes inflated and thus egocentric, it mistakes itself in totality, it become the "foe" of the" Real Self"-that central being that is sacred in its spirituality. I like to express this 'ego self' as the part of me that is but a grain of sand on the beach that thinks it is the beach. It is my greatest impediment to my spiritual journey. "The seed that is to grow must lose itself as seed, And they that creep may graduate through chrysalis to wings. wilt thou then, O Mortal, cling to husks which falsely am to you the self? (Wu Ming Fu, poet, philosopher.)

 The search and the finding: "Neither in the world of nations, nor in the world of the nation, will individuals sacrifice their interests. They cannot do it, it is impossible. They have not reached that stage of ethics development. But there is a handful of individuals, perhaps hundreds, even thousands who have reached it. They have learnt that the moment has come where they must sacrifice all. At first they do it slowly and then with increasing intensity, and then particularly in the last-one hundred years with a truly sickening acceleration, first with nation, then the world of nations has become one body. There is an unconscious growth below but the sacrifice mending above is fixed. His pangs of birth are at hand. He dreams of better things, but how to achieve them he does not know.The World Man now longs as the individual man has long-time after time, for newness of life. And the same answer to the World Man is the same answer that was given two thousand years ago to the individual man: "He that is able to detach his life, the same shall find it." (John Middleton Murray).

The World man of the 20th century who got the Spiritual essence to the individual man's Spiritual path was Martin Luther King. His "I have a dream" speech was one of a kind in the fight for freedom of the oppressed, but his final personal, poignant and eerily prophetic speech was the one he made the night before he was assassinated; expressed in his willingness in the letting go to the Spiritual essence of himself. It is a timely reminder for me:"I am happy tonight, I am not worried about anything. I'm not fearing any man. For I have been to the top of the mountain and I've seen the other side. Mine eyes have seen the glory of the coming of The Lord."

There is no way of making a person true unless he gives up his own will. In fact, apart from complete surrender of the will, there is no traffic with God. But if it did happen that we gave up completely and dared to put off everything, physical and spiritual, for God's sake- then we should have done all and not before. Such people are rare. Aware of it or not, people want to have the "great" experiences; they want it in the form, or they would be satisfied with whatever he does with his own.

I have come to believe in a Power greater than self though the healing essence of the AA fellowship. It was through the calamity of so much tragedy in my life that I came to the drop off point of having no way out of my dilemma of drinking to kill pain, of crying out to God of my religion and educational understanding and being left wanting. Of being in depth of depression, anxiety and the lack of will to live. I was so broken, my head said death was the only answer but my heart said live, really live. But how to do that, for the more I stepped out the less there seemed to be any answer. So I just had to let go, cry out for medical help, for the help of God, for the help of AA to learn tp pray in a different way all over again. Pray in a way by handing over as outlined in the AA steps to recovery.

Characteristic of the so called typical alcoholic is a narcissistic egocentric core, dominated by feelings of omnipotence, intent on maintaining at all cost its inner integrity.....Inwardly the alcoholic, is and must be the master of his destiny, he will fight to the end to preserve that position. So it seems for a while that I had this " Spirituality" thing licked, but had I just swapped one religious set of principles for another? Was it that omnipotent self defiant ego spirit that I was trusting in? Is it really spirituality when I profess to hand over? Well it came to pass that by inhaling the essence of God through the AA programmes 12 steps, by handing over with inner peace, my understanding of a Power Greater than self, to help the still suffering alcoholic, then I am living a spiritual life. That is to say too, that I remain sober a day at a time to help another remain sober a day at a time.

An answer came with Bill Wilson, the AA founder summing up this living spiritual God path best, at least for the alcoholic like me anyway, when he stated: "Those of us who have spent much time in the world of spiritual make believe have eventually seen the childishness of it. This dream world has been replaced by a great sense of purpose, accompanied by a growing consciousness of the power of God. We have come to believe He would like us to keep our heads in the clouds with him, but have our feet firmly planted on earth. That is where our fellow travellers are, and that is where our work must be done. These are the realities for us. We have found nothing incompatible between a powerful spiritual experience and a life of sane and happy usefulness."

I think the poet who best expressed the search and findings of the spiritual was none other than T.S. Eliot, English poet in this extract from " East Coker"IV and the "Little Gidding" V in Four Quartetes:

I said to my soul, be still, and let the dark come upon you
Which shall be the darkness of God...
I said to my soul, be still, and wait without hope
for hope would be hoping for the wrong thing;
wait without love.

For love would be love of then wrong thing;
there is yet faith;
But the faith and the love and the hope are all still in the waiting
within without thought, for you are not ready for thought;
So the darkness shall be the light, and the stillness the dancing.

....

We shall not cease from exploration
And at the end of our exploring
Will be to arrival at where we started
And know the place for the first time.

It is all in the Technique I could hear myself say: It seems now that the meditative way therein is the essence of tapping into the Power of God, of the Spiritual. It seemed now the progressive realisation of a worthwhile Spiritual way out is a way in a life with a God of my own understanding in meditative prayer. I have to admit that I don't do it very often but when I do miracles seem to happen for my betterment. Prayer is the act in which man opens himself to the total values for wholeness to each situational moment of life. It is an affirmation of a fundamental mental dedication to each moment's emergent highest Value. It assumes the Other, the eternal Thou as a given. It assumes the presence of a mystery, and of the possibility of grace (that hidden abundance of God- a supernatural gift of spirituality embedded by God for our salvation). Its in the words of that first commandment that Moses reportedly receive up there on that mountain in conference with God and carved in stone, the act of loving God with our whole heart, soul, strength of body and mind as can be brought possible into consciousness.

In contrast to various forms of meditation, prayer is a relationship between the **I**, of the situation, which is the **I** that is functioning, and the Meaning transcending both the **I** and the situation but manifesting itself within both. It is a continual yes-saying to the fact that there is a purpose larger than mine, for which I can work. For that **I is the God** in the manifest. In this way it is the means to open to the alternatives to open to possibilities, its a marvellous preventer of egocentricity. And it therein is that state of reality, in that meditative prayer state that this decision says 'Yes' to whatever alternatives seem to belong to Purpose and must be taken in advance before any specific moments are or can be known.

"If worship is the highest activity of man's spirit we shall expect to find it difficult, but we shall also expect to find that there are avenues leading to worship for all sorts and conditions of men." (Author unknown).

"Meditation and Freedom- Give freedom to the ones who dwell close to your heart, not by separating yourself from them, try to draw apart, for that often holds them in closed bonds. Give freedom in every thought, give love, overflowing love- with no restriction in your mind, no question of any kind. As you fully let go, each one will swing into his own acceptance place. Nothing relinquished is lost; everything find s its true balance, in equilibrium, in God. It leaves each soul loose and free in the mind to swing into Universal Life- a creative being in God, alone, at one with God. Be not held by false illusion of your worth pride and self condemnation for they walk side by side. Rid yourself of condemnation, and give freedom to the ones you felt called upon to please. Rejoice over the falling leaves of self- you will be light and free indeed when all sense of ownership is gone forever. Realise that each soul is related to you. When you recognise that every one is part of you, you will find you cannot withdraw from another. Open your soul to the sun; you know how to loosen every knot, release every cord and leave everyone free. No one comes to you by chance, give of your bread to all who would approve each- one give them space, quietude, love.

 Love gives; love withdraws. Love warms and frees the will for most man, so he may receive his own inheritance and make his own decisions."
 - Elise Organ, 1876-1954, American Writer, mystic.
The Technique of being your own Psychotherapist.

Keep a journal. There are ways you can work alone. One method is to keep a notebook in which to write down, during times you keep for yourself, answers to, or at least struggle with, such questions as: what are the excuses I give myself, or hear from others, for not working at this journey? Like "I can't do it now, there isn't enough time?" or " I have a headache." Each of us all have our own excuses. For every excuse try to see what happens if you face it and try to work through it.

"What kind of people bother me the most-keep me from concentrating? (eg. whining people, augmentative people, noisy people, "look at me" people, and so on). Try to discover whether the negative qualities they have may also be in yourself. If so, they must be acknowledged before being harnessed creativity. They may have come from childhood experiences with parents or siblings, experiences that have never been resolved.

 When I am scattered into depression because of the shattering of my ego image what is my first response? Ask yourself this question; Is life one series of events, lucky or unlucky, meaningful and meaningless, strung together from birth to death? Perhaps ones life is something different, something in which I have full participation as I move in the direction of my goal not always known, but 'there' all the same. What if the unwound self asks the question the Lord asked Adam-" Where are you?" To write the answer to this question, from time to time, as a kind of personal history can bring unexpected healing.

Another method in technique to self analysis is to write a graphic account of the kind of person my parents wanted me to be? And what kind of person I believe I am now? What kind of person could be the opposite to both those images? Such comparisons give vital clues to self image and often hold them to patterns of resistance to change and regression because it describes what threatens. By facing behaviour triggers of life that effect us or block in our patterns of behaviour we begin to honour and utilise in a positive way those feelings. Try to list which of the following you use to " escape from freedom: altruism, pseudo generosity, doing good for others, but with hidden motives , hospitality and self pity, busy-ness, pressure from without and a calamity from within, a sense of self worthlessness, 'the little old me' syndrome, independence that is arrogant, attachment to physical symbolism.If you are writing to locate some of these escape devices, acknowledge them, you have taken one more step on the pathway of your spiritual journey.

Writing like life itself, is a voyage of discovery. The adventure is a metaphysical one: It is a way of approaching life directly, of acquiring a complete rather than a partial view of the universe. The writer lives between the upper and lower worlds. He takes the path in order to become the path himself. I initially wrote to overcome deep pain and anxiety, in overcoming tragedy I journaled every day and wrote a lot of dark poetry too. It led me to writing stories but always seem to include something of a spiritual nature within theme. I did begin in a swamp of chaos and darkness, but my creative imagination overruled the pain of it all. This has resulted is a number of books that are read by those interested enough to hear the news from the great beyond.

However, I don't consider myself a typical writer, but more a doer of the knowledge of a subject matter in a practical way, doing it out of the closet so to speak for the completion of knowing, for my ultimate spiritual benefit and in doing so keep me on the right track to serve you as the reader. For in that I am serving God, and in that I am on the right journey for spiritual fulfilment. At least that is what I tell myself. Is it just egocentric behaviour or is it spiritual consciousness that is the pattern here? Well time will tell and you and I will see.

Knowledge is the beginning of practice; doing the completion of knowing. We of this present-day world make knowledge and action to different things and go not forth to practice, because we hold that which as we have to have the knowledge first before we are able to practice. Each one says: "I proceed to investigate and discuss knowledge; I wait until knowledge is perfect and then go forth and put it into practice." Those who to the end of life fail to practice also fail to understand. This is not a small error; no one came to it in a day. By saying that knowledge and practice are a unit, I am herewith offering remedy for the disease." Wang- yang-Ming, 1472-1529, Philosopher.

We ought to learn how to keep a free mind in all we do, but it is rare "…..The more we become conscious of ourselves through self knowledge and act accordingly, the more the layer of personal uncon-scious that is superimposed in the collective unconscious will be di-minished. In this way there arises a consciousness which is no longer imprisoned in the petty, over-sensitive, personal world of the ego, but participates freely in the wide world of objective interests.   This widened consciousness is no longer that touchy, egotistical bundle of personal wishes, fears, hopes, dreams and ambitions which has to al-ways compete, compensate or correct by unconscious counter ten-dencies; instead, it is a function of relationship to the world of objects, bringing the individual into absolute, binding and indissoluble commu-nion with the world at large, The complications arising at this stage are no longer egotistic wish-conflicts, but difficulties that concern others as much as oneself. (Carl Jung, M.D.1875-1961 , Swiss psychiatrist.)

Its time now to lean toward a directive in a new way community- We need to start a new (spiritual) community, which shall be a new life rich in the interconnection of character. We each will fill our own nature and deep desires to the utmost satisfaction and joy in the completeness of all as one. Let us be good collectively instead of just alone in our own spiritual home. Let us be self assured that our intrinsic part of us is the part, the believing part, the passionate, the generous part. If we make mistakes, what does it matter? If we have to start again, what does it matter? It is progress not perfection that we are about. We may laugh at each other, may like or dislike each other, but the important thing is the good that remains, and we know it. And this community shall be established on the foundation of the known, the eternal good part of us. The present way of community consists of a myriad of contrivances which prevent us from being let down by meanness in ourselves and in our neighbours. It is like a car that is fitted with non skid, non punc-tured, non burst tyres and none of this and that contrivances, that it simply can't go anymore. I hold this to be our most sacred duty that the gathering of a number of people who shall so agree to live by the best that they know, that they shall be free to live to the best they know. This ideal, this religion, must now be lived and practiced.

It is in our new hope that we shall be a life wherein the struggle shall not be for money, for power, but for individual freedom of common effort towards good. So that the new riches, the new power is in our efforts both individual and collective towards goodness. Every strong soul must put off the old and embrace the new, put off the vanity and fears and be venerably naked like with our fellows: weaponless, armour-less, fearless, without sword or shield or spear but with our naked hands and open eyes. Not the self sacrifice of old, but the fulfilment, of the spirit and the flesh in league together. Each man shall know his part of the greater body, each man shall submit his own soul, and will not be supreme even to himself. " To be or no to be" that is no longer the question. The question now is how shall we fulfil our declaration that God is and he leads. It seems to be that we live in a material world that God is not there unless it suits the occasion that he be. A community dream, a factual functioning reality, individually and collective with common purpose, God centred, spiritually centred and thus community and individually centred for the common good; that is all I am proposing.

A genuine faith recognises the fact that it is through a glass darkly that we see; by faith we penetrate sufficiently the heart of the mystery of God. A genuine faith that we are not overwhelmed by, a genuine faith that resolves the mystery, recognises the aspects of life or the aspects that explains its existence even after all known causes and consequences have been traced. To recognise what points beyond itself to God is to assert the mystery of life and does not dissolve life into meaninglessness. Faith in some ultimate unity of life or some comprehensible purpose which holds all the various and frequently contradictory realms of coherence and meaning together, that does not mark his mysterious source as merely as " X is the unknown quantity." The Christian faith, at least is a faith of revelation. It believes that God made himself known. it believes He has spoken through the prophet and finally in His Son. It accepts the revelation of Christ as the ultimate clue the mystery of God's nature and purpose in the world, particularly the mystery of the relationship of justice to His mercy. Whilst these clues to the mystery do not eliminate the outer limits of objectivity- that the mystery of Faith, of God, of Spirituality is still illusive. God is hidden. He is most apparently absent from those who seek him, although we who believe in him and have been blessed from time to time by what one might call 'miracles of grace,'we have no more logical proof of his existence than a true sceptic has of proving he doesn't exist. It seems God bothers are the ones who are truely troubled by this, whereas non believers care little to nothing about the subject matter unless they are challenged by it. I myself see the mystery of God explained in nature and the universe. I can use logical arguments to that effect through vivid examples of the whole of the earth and the universe or simply in the cycle of a tree, the seed that it shoots to grow from, the chemical composition of the soil it feeds its roots, to its cycle of life. It just happens to be my belief in nature as a way of explaining the mystery of God. It is my way of expressing an article of Faith that God exists. When I read Shirley MacLeans " Camino" journey, I liked in particular her way of explaining the mystery of her brand of belief: "The absence of evidence should not be confused with the evidence of absence." This was a wild shot over the bow of the sceptics who had taken shot at here about proof of life. I hasten to add that I have known over many years God has granted me many graceful rewards every time I hand over to him and let him direct my life. The trouble is for, me at least sometimes I forget, I just don't know if he is about and I lose faith again and the old sceptic moves into my temple of the spiritual belief and I am lost for a time.i.e. until I turn back to him, for he is love. This is my article of Faith. "God I believe, help my unbelief."

CHAPTER 15.

THE VOYAGE TO A NEW LIFE

The alarm sounded in my head at 6.am. on the dot, as it had done every day over the preceding six months of my cave dwelling. My immediate thoughtless action was to immediately jump to my feet, throw on a T shirt, a pair of shorts, socks and joggers, then after the usual morning relieving of overnight ablutions, I hotfooted it on a pathway though the little village centre, along a footbridge that ran alongside the river, to where it met the ocean. I would then dispense with my joggers and make my way along the beach, a distance of some three kilometres. Alone on my journey it was regular occurrence for the same big black crow to come to visit. I would repeatedly cry out to it: "Go away with your dark negative energy, go back to where you come from I beg you, I order you." Invariably the black sign of my darkness would hang about waiting for my depressive state of mind to invade again even more deeply. It always did during those dark days of depression.

My journey along the beach each day had a healing side to it though. I was not so mindful of the time as every day my depression and deep despair seemed to worsen for a long time. In was a kind of "ground hog ' day if you get my analogy for my state of being. The groundhog it is said comes out of its hole at the end of hibernation and if it sees its shadow even if the weather is sunny, it goes back into its hole on the pretext that it is still winter and does not emerge again until it figures it is summer again.

Firstly it was the crow, then a group of old NRL fanatics talking up their once youthful football skills. Seated there by the river-head and beachhead pontificating how they in their prime played the game and, as they told their 'story' repeatedly, it always it appeared to me that the more they fed their former football prowess the the better they were. Only once out of loneliness did I dare stop to give an opinion, having played the game in my youth. I was told to shut up, mind my own business and anyway what would I know. I was thinking as I walked away: "Well I did Captain a team that won the North Coast competition in reality. However, when I evaluated anything in my then state of mind, it was true it seemed, I didn't know much. I sometimes wondered what those football heroes of old did with the rest of their day after their football church was over. In such a small village there was not much else to do but go fishing or play golf and talk about your neighbour. Well if you didn't have that, what else was there.

Further along the beach I got a 'early every morning' wave from a middle age couple sitting up on a sandhill to watch the sunrise over the ocean. Like 'birds of a feather' chatting while drinking a morning coffee from a thermos flask. In a small village community tongues wagged and it was rumoured they were having an affair behind the back of her husband who was wheel-chair bound. Such gossip I ignored and had no opinion on, I was much too far gone to want to know the goings on of the masses of mankind in their own quiet desperation. Another kilometre along the beach I encountered a man with his two terrier dogs. Jock and Jess, I did my daily pat on my daily loneliness excursion and always got rewarded with a kindly lick in return. Their owner John drove a local taxi service n his private car. In the main he transported patients of age too and from their regular medical treatments in another nearby town, waiting for them, for the return journey then took them for a bite to eat and got his just reward. It was a government contract so his income was guaranteed. He was for a time the only other person I spoke to most days.

Sometimes on my return journey homeward bound, I would sight a pod of dolphins rounding up a school fish, forcing them toward the shoreline to take easy picking for their main meal of the day. On another occasion a large whale breached not more than 50 meters from the shore. The barnacles on its torso clearly visible to the naked eye as it rose itself, inhaling air and spraying out a shower of water from it sprout. Such marvels were repeated with birds and animals on regular occasions as I ventured further into the bushland in my effort to recover from the depth of despair.

Another daily action, each time I walked the beach I would stop and select a small smooth usually black stone to run between my fingers on the way home. As I walked in to the dining area I placed the stone in a large dish and left it as it grew into a pile and it was a near artwork in progress. Then I would take to meditating as best I could for as long as I could stand it without going crazy, prepare and eat my everyday plate of muesli or porridge, yogurt, tea and toast. The next action was to take a backpack, throw in an apple, includes a tin of bake beans with a spoon to eat with, toss in some nuts also and an apple then head out all day hiking. Usually I was in the depths of despair and on two occasions in the midst of the bush went to the edge of suicide.

Given time things improved somewhat, but I was still depressed, on heavy sedatives and could not sleep without medicating. I managed to write a book of poems; mostly dark deep and meaningful grasps for a way out of my mental dilemma. I also joined a local bush walking club and met once a week with them for either day walks or weekend camp outs. Sometimes also, I would go fishing with a fellow walker. I was no fisherman and didn't catch a thing but I appreciated the company. Indeed back then I was not true to my natural self, I didn't talk much. In time I got a once a week gig serving teas to old people in nursing home where my Mum was a resident. It was an eye opener to be with those old suffering souls and while it seemed to me that I was of little use, the oldies loved the attention I was giving them. Also I joined a meditation and rehabilitation discussion group for a time and began to come out of my shell. I tried every type of meditation exercise class that seemed to be in existence at that time and soon I was attending a regular pottery class to help me with a creative outlet. In time I felt I was ready enough to return to the city to find a job. As all my funds were running low, for I was living on capital saved and with nothing coming in it was time to return to some semblance of reality. My first act was one morning when I got the urge to change my way of life again, I began to return a stone at a time in a ritual reflective manner back to the beach were they came from. When I got half way through my daily ritual one morning I just picked up the remaining stones and tossed the lot outside my front door. It was before mid-morning I loaded up my van and was winging my way back to the big smoke for the next faze of my recovery.

 The road to recovery became much rockier than I had bargained for back in Sydney.I found myself a place to rest my head, in a dungeon like unit with one side being open to the afternoon sun overlooking a garden and a tree filled bushland near by. However, the main bedroom was partly below ground level and the spurs from the moss on the walls ultimately effected my lungs, so it meant I had to move on. It was for the best in more reasons than one. While I had invited an alcoholic mate to come and take up residence with me to help share the cost of rent and grocery needs, I had not as yet found a job to offset the cost of living, so initially a flatmate had seemed a good idea at the time. However I deplored his habit of smoking inside the place and finally encouraged him to smoke outside. More than that thou, it was his drinking to excess and the the fact that I had to often vent my spleen at him for being behind on his rent. I was the better part of a year since I had ceased drinking alcohol of any kind. It had been in an alcoholic fit that I had first hit rock bottom and sent me i in a reeling mess down the hole of depression in the first place. I had not realised it then that iI was an alcoholic and had stopped only through the fear of perhaps doing myself in under he influence. The tell tail sign came when I started to feel better and join my flat mate in a drinking spree. The old me emerged in an even deeper state of depression and anxiety and five weeks in a rehabilitation clinic was the outcome of that little episode. I quit for good after that as I feared I would take the same route as my father with alcoholism, but at that point I still didn't believe I was alcoholic.

On recovery I found contract work as a business developer consultant, moved out of the flat and got myself a mortgage and my own property and began again into a work a day world to climb the ladder of reality. It was in another rehabilitation clinic and a cocktail of antidepressant medications and shock treatment that my state of mind finally lifted and I began to see daylight again. A miracle of sorts happened whilst in rehabilitation for the second time that changed the course of my life thereafter. I happened upon a retired old psychotherapist in my hospitalisation, as he was undergoing depression medical treatment for alcoholism at the same as me. We became friends then and there. This new found friend of the programme could tell that I was just like him only I could not see it then. I had previously attended the Black Dog programme for depression under the guidance of Professor Gordon Parker, who at the time, in his wisdom had administered only a heavy sleeping sedative to help me through the days and night of mental torment to overcome what seemed an impossible debilitating illness. It did the job of helping me catch up on sleep, particularly when I did my time in a sort of spiritual hiatus walking the beaches and doing nothing but meditative walking and writing dark poetry. God saw to it that I needed more time to recover. As one of resident psychiatrists had said to me in my first rehab when I had approached him for advise once: "Trust in the slow work of God." I had felt like choking him to death on the spot at the time, but he proved right. I must have been a tough nut for God to crack back then. For it took, all in, a one year cycle - a marriage breakdown, the divorce proceedings in court over material possessions, the suicide of a friend, the heart attack death of another, the loss of home, business and family to a greater degree all coming to a head with the suicide of my second eldest son before I found my way out and for the first time in my life, leaned my ladder to the future up against the right wall for a change.

Bill Wilson, the co founder of AA had stated " We perceive that only after utter defeat are we able to take our first steps towards liberation and strength. Our admissions of powerlessness finally turn out to be firm bedrock upon which happy and purposeful lives may be built.*" William James years of study on world religious experiences was a gift of religious conversion for him. The title "The varieties of Religious Experiences" which I have referred to earlier in my work, was not an easy read for Bill. James then father of modern psychology, as mathematician, engineer and chemist and M.D. applied the same methodology in writing the large masterpiece as he had done on his varied of academic subject matter. However, Bill's natural ability to decipher share values, having investigated the assets and liabilities of a company, its management, its product and the possibilities of it future success proved him to be the best catalyst to explain James work and to break it all down into three common denominators. This Harvard Professor, long in his grave, without even knowing it, became a corner stone of AA for Bill Wilson and his founding principles. His work seceded and written into the AA programme, as equally as Dr Karl Jung's works on spiritual consciousness, as equally as Dr Silkworm and the Oxford Groups principles The book consisted of very large numbers of religious conversion experiences, and underneath the professor had written studious analysis. James' book was intellectually a tough one, but Bill use of certain common denominators seem to cover all basis of the work irrespective of which way James presented them.

The first common denominator was calamity. Nearly every recipient in the study described how they had met utter defeat in some controlling area of their life. Every resource of courage, understanding, and will had failed. Each had been beaten into despair upon a wall and had seen no way over, under, or around. This was an essential condition of the experience to follow. The next condition was collapse- an admission that from the very depths of being that defeat was utter and absolute. Each individual had to concede that he simply couldn't go on living upon his own stream. The third condition was the cry- an appeal to a higher power for help. This appeal could take innumerable forms. It might be accompanied by a faith in God or it might not, but an appeal it had to be. The cry for help could course through religious channels, or a despairing agnostic could look at a growing and reflecting tree, could respond to the law of its nature and he, the human, might then raise his voice to the God of nature. Then the transforming experience could set in, sometimes like a thunderbolt, as with St.Paul on the road to Damascus; or very gradually, followed by repeated appeals, the individual would slowly grow into a new state of consciousness and release. Utter defeat, the complete admission of helplessness, and appeal. These were the essential things. Likewise I made my appeal and the result was forthcoming, but it took more defeat and further trips to rehab before the penny dropped completely. Countless other Alcoholics before me received the gift of recovery had known utter hopelessness and had learnt from medical men, yet they had not received the gift of sobriety. I understood it more now than ever through the AA way, the appeal to a higher power was the key, the admission of hopelessness felt deeply enough for me to begin to receive faith and then the release by the hand over. Acceptance and action was the way, but not just handing over to a God of my own understanding but actually allowing that guiding power to influence my every action. To take charge, a tall order but one I continue to work on. The chain reaction in meetings of telling what happened to me, what changed and what is like now, giving every listening Alcoholic in the fellowship a chance to gain something beneficial towards continuing to remain sober a day at a time. Likewise the sharing of their story helps me in my recovery too. It is the overriding step 3 of the programme that is the guiding light to helping remain sober a day at a time by handing over to my higher power. It was not just the AA programme though, for I continued to suffer episodes of depression despite my best efforts to beat it, despite medication and counselling sessions.   It was my three pilgrimages through Northern Spain on the Camino de Santiago, the walk on the wild mountains of Ireland, the Aran islands, New Zealand 's hills and valleys and here back home, walking the beaches and bush of Australia that has been a large catalyst to recovery also. Those ' Spiritual like ' Camino's have been the a key to my journalling, daily wandering, writing poetry and recording many of my songs and the writing of a plethora of books on the matter at hand has helped me on my quest along my now spiritual route back to God.

For how can I describe this my manifestation of my Higher Power. The God who was once a religious condition and a conviction of Faith through my analytical logical, conscious mind that has now been transformed into a manifestation of my imagination. I dare not define him, but if I was given cause to do, then he could perhaps be summed up in the words of Rufus M. Jones, the late 19th Century and early 20th century American philosophers summary: " The God whom we learn to know in Christ- the God historically revealed - is no vague cause, no abstract reality, no all negating absolute. He is a concrete person, whose trails of character are intensely moral and spiritual. His will is no fateful swing of mechanical law; it is a morally good will which works patiently and forever toward a harmonised world., a Kingdom of God. The central trade of His character is love. He does not become Father. He is not reconciled to us by persuasive offerings and sacrifices. He is inherently and by essence disposition Father and the God of grace. He is not remote and absentee-making a world " in the beginning, "and leaving it to run by law only occasionally interrupting in normal process. He is imminent spirit, working always, the God of beauty and organised purpose. He is Life and Light and Truth, and Immanuel God who can and does show Himself in a personal Incarnation, and so exhibits the course and goal of the race."

He is the Way.
Follow him through the Land of Unlikeness;
You will see rear beasts, and have unique adventurers.

He is the Truth.
seek him in the kingdom of Anxiety;
You will come to a great city that has expected your return for years.

He is the Life.
Love Him in the World of the Flesh;
And at your marriage all its occasions shall dance for joy.

Note see * Twelve Steps and Twelve Traditions .p21

I think it's entirely appropriate to end this chapter focusing on the mystery of a modern Mystic who wrote a letter to a young Poet which sums up the sense of this chapter of a voyage to a new life. It may well have been entitled a voyage of the inner self. The author of the letter was a German poet who was born in the late 19th century and died in 1926. " Think of the world you carry within you, and call this thinking what you will; whether it be remembering your own childhood or yearning towards your own future-only be attentive to that which rises up within you and set it above everything that you observe about you. What happens in your innermost being is worthy of your whole love; you must somehow keep working at it and not lose too much time and too much course in explaining your position to people....

And if it worries you' or makes you afraid to think of your childhood and of the simplicity and quiet that goes within, because you cannot believe any more in God, then ask yourself whether you really ever lost God? I think not rather, that you have never have really known him? For when should that have been? Do you believe that a child can hold him, whom men bear only with effort and whose weight crushes the old? Do you believe that anyone who really had him could lose him like a little stone, or do you think rather that whoever had him could only be lost by him?....."

 Why do you think of him as a second coming from eternity, the Jesus of yes-terday as a future one, the final fruit of a tree whose leaves we are? What keeps you from projecting his birth into coming ages and living your life like a painful and beautiful great rebirth? How is it that you do not see that every-thing that happens is always a cycle of-natural order, that a beginning in itself is always beautiful? If he is the perfection, must we not be the lesser before him, and what sense would we have of it all if he, whom we long for, had al-ready been?

 As the bee brings in the honey, so do we fetch the sweetest out of everything. Even in our insignificant, even if what we do is trivial, if it but happens out of love, then we begin, with work, with silence or with a lonely joy, with every-thing that we do support and participate in, we begin to know him as our fore-bears could not live to know. And yet they, who are long gone, are in us, as predisposition, as a charge upon our destiny, as blood that stirs, and as gesture that rises spout of the depth of time. Is there anything that can take from you and me that hope of one day being in him, the furtherest, the ultimate?

Celebrate Christmas in this devout feeling, (celebrate Easter equally so) for perhaps he needs this fear of living from you in order to begin; these very days of your transition are perhaps the time when everything in you is working for him. Be patient and without unwillingness and think that the least we can do is make his becoming harder than the earth makes it for the spring when it wants to comes...."

Pope Francis, the Vicar of Christ on Earth, the Holy Father of the Catholic Faith, meaning Universal, Church has had a continual struggle with his own belief in God. It should be said that the aforementioned 'Title' was reportedly given to St.Peter by Christ when he said: " Thou art Peter, and upon this rock I will build my Church." Of course Orthodox Catholics, who have their own Pope, would fervently disagree, as would all those other Christian religions who for one reason and another broke away from the teaching of the Holy Roman Catholic Church over the past two thousand years and have their own priestly hierarchy of lineage and' corporate' administration. These various religions, to my way of thinking preach a surface belief and not so much a spiritual one. Perhaps the Eastern religious philosophies have the game sown up as they seem to be more in tune with the reality of life in their daily meditative practices of being in the now, and don't see necessity or need for defined God. One might argue that Christ instruction to Peter has naught to do with a Club of Rome Christian Pope any more than it has to do with the Archbishop of Canterbury, nor the Pope of Constantinople on Mt. Athos who gives instruction to Vladimir Putin on matters of faith and morals. In fact, one may come to believe that Christ meant something all together different; that of a teacher instructing his chosen leader to administer God's spiritual intent. "Thou art Peter (Meaning Rock), I will build my Church (build my house of spiritual worship, for my followers).

Winding back to the Holy Father, Pope Francis and his own crisis of belief. The young charitable man about town, right up to the time of his ordination to the priesthood struggled with the God particles and the Church of Rome. Jorge Mario Bergoglio, the Pope's birth name before he adopted the name Francis as Pope, possibly from the spirit of the goodly Francis of Assisi. Bergoglio was no doubt influenced by the poor, the death and destruction during the era of the Dirty War in his country or possibly it was as a rebellious Jesuit when he stood always a little aloof of his brethren brothers of the Senate of Roman. He didn't take the path of the tradition Roman leader priesthood , but more one of the people, an ecumenical one. He was no doubt influenced by the founder of the Jesuit order, Ignatius Loyola, the venerated Barque Catholic priest who together with Peter Faber and Francis Xavier founded the religious order- the Society of Jesus and became its first Superior General in Paris in 1541.

I want to digress a little more to this Jesuit founder before returning to the present Vicar of Christ , Pope Francis, and the significance of my findings on this Pope's 'spirituality.' It is in order to determine some facts relating to my own faith, crisis of conscious and path and hope of spiritual liberty for myself and maybe you dear reader.

The long spiritual training of eleven years of theological education, formative study and disciplined prayer of Jesuits was the Ignatius way for the Society of Jesus, to discover God's will. This means the best route to determine God's will is not to go out into the world and search but to burrow deep inside yourself and listen for God there.   Mark Thibodeaux called it " God's voice within."and hearing it requires a lot of patience. In his book of the same name he writes : "Ignatius was a keen student of human nature, a beloved spiritual master, both in his daily life and prayers, he came to understand an important truth: God desires for us to make good decisions and will help us do so. All we need to do, besides having good intent, is not only to rely on our (literally) God given reason but also to pay attention to the movements of our heart, which is all given (?) us by God."

The now Pope Francis has had in his life-time three mentors; the first was his grand mother Rosa who shaped a profoundly ambitious and disciplined young man with humility, faith and love. The second was the influence of his atheist mentor Esther Ballestino, an avowed Marxist and atheist who educated him in the world of science and under her tutelage he complete a university science degree.They engage in regular political discussion and debate. Whilst her laboratory was devoted to the scientific method, she seemed to live her life according to the Socratic method of questioning and debating with her employee and colleagues regardless of their religious creed or political belief. Francis credits her teaching and values of disciplined hard work to help shape him. They had many a serious discussion and argument and with further study he went on to complete other degrees. The third and final mentor of his trinity was of course that of the Jesuit Ignatius Loyola, whom he would follow in disciplined pray and spiritual exercise from the days of his noviciate, ordination to the priesthood, teaching of students in all areas of Jesuit education to the priesthood and finally to his now role be the Pope of the Universal Church based in Rome.

In a document Bergoglio wrote just prior to his ordination, which he called his creed, we see the influence of all three of his mentors: "I **want to believe** in God , who loves me like a son, and in Jesus, The Lord, who infused me with His Spirit, to make me smile and, in so doing, led me to the Eternal Kingdom of Life.

I believe in the Church.

I believe in the history that was pierced by the gaze of love of God, who on the spring day of September 21, came out to meet me and invited me to follow Him.

I believe in my pain, made fruitless in selfishness, in which I seek refuge.

I believe in the stinginess of my soul that seeks to take without giving.

I believe that others are good and that I must love them without fear and without ever betraying them, never seeking my own security.

I believe in religious life.

I believe I want to love a lot.

I believe in the daily burning death from which I flee, but which smiles at me and invites me to accept her.

I believe in God's patience, welcoming, good, like a summers's evening.

I believe that my father is in Heaven, next to the Lord.

This Pope who at his foundation and way of leading the Church is in his holy faith a characteristically modern day version of Cervantes's Don Quixote. He is in his most radical part of uprooting homosexual in some of his priests like the immortal Don jousting with windmills; he has also purged the Church of many of its Bishops and priest who are pedophiles. The first time this was attempted was in the 12th Century change of rule during the Spanish Inquisition. Priests who interfered with young boys in their initial confession before receiving the Holy Communion at that time could not be disciplined. The Pope then could not purge the outrage issued a decree to change the law, so that a child's age of reason was no longer age eleven but became age seven. This then gave some justification that the child could reason right from wrong and the blame then held the child responsible for tempting the priest into an occasional sin. Pope Francis being a man of the Church is also an ecumenical man of the people, a stickler for disclipine of his priest, his flock, carting the message of spiritual hope for the world at large by being a true leader who know when to cut, divide and conquer, as equally as unite and guide for Christ, for God. It is his spirituality I seek to emulate despite the fact I do not practice the faith of his church now.

Notes to myself on the way down into the dragons mouth which become a lotus flower of creative ideas whilst recovering in rehabilitation.

Considerations for meditation:

"Acceptance of the inner core of being a loner and and outsider, as it is here (in heaven) from the inside out. Numerically I belong to the 2-3% of the population, that three out of every hundred who fit into the cube, while others are square pegs trying to fit into the round holes. This is an enormous discovery when in the passage of time we truly accept we are born outsiders ."

"Be gentle with myself, use no force, the energy will flow with me in time.
Go with the grain in the wood , otherwise you will get blisters.....
Go with the inner river of life. "

"Go with the inner river of life, go with the flow...
Put your boat of personality into the inner river of life and go with the current

into open waters. Once I get the drift of this, it's just a gentle movement of the rudder to keep on course. let it soaking the marrow of your bones."

"Surrender the ego i.e. I is a little I, name and mine."

" gradually be surrendering the ego- taking risk to let go and keep on letting go. I will come to a vacuum into free fall into the dragon's mouth, into the bottomless pit where the dragon lives- it will become a lotus flower of creative ideas."

"Be gentle with your self- use no force- go with the grain of the wood- otherwise splinters. "

"We may take a parachute , a crutch to lessen the fall, but be aware of the residual nervous tension remaining."

" I will know what the inner residual tensions are by the coil tensions of remaining fear, anxiety obsessions and compulsions."

" We surrender to win,
we give way to keep,
we suffer to get well,'we die to live-
it is the opposite of what the world has to offer."

"The way is the middle road, it can't be achieved by linear, rational, sequential, logic means. Those ways are half brained. The way of the spirit and the imagination are the third way tempered by your boat of personality floating on the river of life. Remember to adjust the rudder of existence from within my spiritual core. For we are seekers of the inner truth which becomes the universal truth."

"Surrender moment to moment to moment until I rest in thee."

"Our hearts are restless until we rest in thee."

CHAPTER 16.

A METHOD TO MASTER

David and I met at our usual Sunday day morning cafe location for our so called 'Spiritual discussion," in the vain hope that we might gain a measure of directives on our daily journey of being in the world but not of it so to speak. We had been discussing mindfulness and the benefits of the practice. I was reminding him of the theme of my book herein and the nature of my meditation practice to call on Masters from the past to be guests at my table. I had come to some ultimate conclusions from those Masters about which I felt I could gain the most benefit for my own spiritual well-being and perhaps others who read this little work. It was therefore a natural progression to ask my friend of psychotherapeutic emotional wellbeing of older people about his recent podcast written summary of mindfulness practise for those under his cared. He most happily obliged and gave me permission to reproduce this here. I feel it a fitting guide into meditation of a varied and deep spiritual kind. So without any further ado, here it is:

"The essence of mindfulness and meditation is living in the present moment.We become aware by stepping back and observing our thinking, feelings and experience. Mindfulness is essentially a personal practise which is customised through trial and error to best meet the individual's needs. Some suggestion that may help you when starting out are as follows.

1.Find a quiet place where you feel relaxed and won't be disturbed. Often getting into a routine seems to help and this includes having a particular time to practice.

2. Begin with small steps, say for five minutes at a time, and increase this as you become comfortable.

As you go on in mindfulness it can eventually become a moment by moment exercise being used throughout the day. For all who have tried and continue in mindfulness and meditation the results are matters of fact and experience. Some of these include peace of mind in the face of difficult circumstances, wisdom outside one's usual capability and handling painful thoughts and feelings far more effectively. As we practice mindfulness, we become more and more conscious. Those things that used to draw us down tend not to hold sway any longer. Different states of fear, such as anxiety, dread, and worry occur because we negatively project into the future. Guilt, regret and resentment are produced when we focus too much on the past. In mindfulness, we begin to let go of our relationship to the past and the future and have to emphasise in present moment awareness. Most worry is repetitive, fruitless, uncreative and unproductive. Through mindfulness we can identify thoughts that are useful and set them aside. This new state of awareness then allows room for solutions to enter our lives and deal with things in a far more effective and creative way. Through mindfulness   we become aware and observe our thoughts and feelings non judgementally and remain in its present moment. In this state we are liberated from tyranny of the past and the future. We are at peace right now. It allows our thoughts and feelings to be as they ought to be, so we do not resist what we are experiencing. It's not about suppression or denial it is about acceptance of what is. Some of the techniques you can use to practice mindfulness are; the use of illustration, conscious breathing and sense perceptions. lets talk through these in a little more detail:

No 1. Use of illustrations: Imagine you are on a bridge looking down and visualise objects floating pass in the water. They may be branches, leaves and other debris. These represent thoughts and feelings. Instead of being caught up with them, we can stand back, watch and let them go by or deal with them as we choose. We are now in a much better state to deal with and resolve challenging thoughts and feelings.

No 2. Conscious Breathing : This is the way to anchor yourself to the present moment. There are many therapeutic breathing exercise you can do. One easy exercise is to slowly breath in and through your nostrils into the lower abdomen being aware expanding. Then breath out through the mouth being aware of the abdomen as it contracts. It will take a few breaths before a sense of peace is experienced and a centring back in the present moment occurs.

No 3.Sense perception: This technique also enhances present moment awareness. Often going into nature can help. Become aware of what you are hearing, seeing, smelling and touching. Be fully where you are, Enjoy! And let go of interpreting everything. Just be! If feelings are particularly troubled, you can start with observation of thoughts and feelings and then if needed, use journaling as a means of working through some of these. Sometimes it may be wise to seek counselling with a trusted confidant or counsellor who will actively listen, understand and draw out those thought and feelings. The ancients have alway known the benefits of mindfulness and meditation. Science and research are increasingly confirming this ancient truths exemplified beautifully in the following text ; " Be still and know that I am God. "

I left David in deep thought as to my own former meditations that I had in fact given up some time ago, except for the recent calling of the Masters at my table, to develop from their ability and influence, a better judgement for living a spiritual day at a time progressively towards a common goal. It had sparked in me a desire to return to the practice. My former practice of meditation commenced with India chakra techniques, eastern chants, visual meditations and active slow-motion methods within the bounds of nature. These reached a crescendo in the John Main breath "Mar- ra- nar- tha" meditation and finally the breath alone itself. However, when I considered I had recovered mentally enough I dispensed with the mindfulness practice of meditation. So both the writing of this book and listening to David's podcast has now set my mind to making it an every day practice again Using one or more of my previous meditative practice. If nothing else, it will put me in the right place to call on the God of my own understanding for guidance and prayer, and help prepare a guiding job breakdown to work upon my spiritual path back to God. For I am given to believe that the Pope himself as a once spiritual director had to first learn and then teach new groups of novice Jesuits the daily routine of a new way of spiritual life based on centuries' old traditions. He had to show and tell, to learn the structure, the daily routine, and how to live in a brotherhood. Yet, it is the adaptation that is the key to a Jesuits life. Trying to follow God's lead, the spiritual director knows when to stick to the rules and when to allow some flexibility, especially when his group of novices come from very different backgrounds and ages. He has to have good intuition and judgement, or in Jesuit language, he has to be very discerning in approach.

It was the 1959 appearance of Pedro Arrupe , who became Superior General of the Jesuit Order globally, that put a flame in the belly of the young Bergoglio, Pope to be. His star of spirituality was like a flame to the whole order globally. Arrupe had lived and worked in Japan prior to the Pearl Harbour attack; he had been arrested shortly thereafter, imprisoned , and kept in solitary confinement forty three days. On August 6, 1945, he was in Nagasaki, where he was novice master, when the atomic bomb was dropped. He turned the noviciate into a temporary hospital, caring for more than one hundred and fifty victims.

In 1958, the Jesuits made a province in Japan and named it Arrupe as their first provincial. It was his missionary courage and devotion which inspired millions and would make him one of the most famous Jesuits in history. He embodied the Jesuit- like idea of the priest as frontiersman. Pedro Arrupe, who almost completed medical studies before entering the Jesuits, embodied Ignatius's ideal Jesuit: "a contemplative in action." He was charismatic, loyal to his Barque origins but global in his spiritual and political conviction; a real go-to leader who inspired priest and pastor alike. A prayer of Arrrupe which was not unfamiliar to the young pending Pope devoured them all with head, heart and soul:"Nothing is more practical than finding God, that is falling in love in a quiet absolute, final way. What you are in love with, what seizes your imagination, will effect everything. It will decide what will get you out of bed in the morning, what you will do with your evenings, how you will spend your weekends, what to read, who you know, what breaks your heart, and what amazes you with joy and gratitude. Fall in love, stay in love, and it will decide everything." Who would not be impressed by that prayer of belief in action. It reportedly was this man's actions that impressed the already committed young Jesuit Priest who was destined for Rome as the next Pope. I did not see myself in that priestly way, but I have to admit that my Camino journeys had set my feet upon the pathway that is a basis of that prayer for my living, breathing, working and being committed to creative pursuit, that has fired my imagination and ruled my every waking hour ever since. It is a kind of shadow of self that's slowly but surely approaching daylight and I believe has me treading a "spiritual path' that is now evolving. Oh! but ever so slowly!

It was on that first Camino de Santiago that I discovered a creative side that set me on the path to writing poetry, fictional and real works in books and inspired me to write lyrics and record my songs. But possibly what was more apparent was the journey inward that was helping me in my recovery of letting go to that inner spirit. It happened in moments on the way of inner aloneness, with nature and the spirit. Alone with my thoughts and my feet pounding a beat to the rhythm of my heart. The practice of six-in-six-out breathing pattern. A meditation practice I had learnt through attending a variety of mediation practices. The six by six pattern of breath through the nose in getting the mind into a "theta" place of mindfulness. The " beta, alpha, theta"state of practice I had learnt from attending many a mediation sessions of Sandy MacGregor's live in meditation sessions.(www.calm.com.au), helped quiet the mind and the heart and carried one to the place of the soul.

 Put briefly, the 'beta" represents the walking experience of the mind in full flight; the "alpha" is more like that state of mind whilst meditating in a relaxed position, and the 'theta" is the ultimate- the not-thinking; or what one might call mindfulness. The best analogy that comes to mind is "beta" being like the TV in picture mode, the "alpha "is like when the TV is in a test pattern of still picture or little movement and "theta" -"when there is no picture at all, just a blank screen. In point of fact these are classic name of three of the five EEG band waves which are delta, theta, alpha, beta and gamma. They are measured in cycles per second or hertz (Hz). Some are fast and some are slow. Beta brainwaves (13-38Hz) are small, faster brainwaves associated with a state of mental intellectual activity and outward focused concentration. Binaural beats in alpha frequencies (8-13Hz) are thought to encourage relaxation, promote positivity, and decrease anxiety. The next state is theta brainwaves and are of even greater amplitude and slower frequency. This range is normally between 5 and 8 cycles per second((4-8 Hz) and is associated with the behaviour of alertness, orientation and working memory including enhancement of cognitive and perpetual performance. When we take time out and begin to get into a meditative state, we are in theta. Delta is the next stage which is when we are asleep and the brain wave are the slowest highest amplitude vibrations (1-3 HZ). At the other end of the spectrum are the Delta brainwave frequencies. The rhythm is a relatively high frequency (30-80HZ) component of these fluctuations. Gamma is modulated by sensory input and internal processes such as working memory and attention. It is responsible for learning memory and information processing. In optimal condition Gamma waves help with attention, focus, binding of the sense of smell, sight and hearing, consciousness, mental processing and perception.

 Our purpose is to reach a mindfulness state that opens us up to a state of mind which puts us in amplified tune for the direction and message of our Higher Power. In a sense, it is when we hand over to our Higher Power that we are attuned to the God frequency. This is a normal state of wakefulness in which a person is self awake and aware, but guided by whatever or wherever our concept of God of our own understanding is. This state of consciousness is best achieved as a relaxed state of mind. We let go of the worries of the world, don't try to influence outcomes, or direction, allow the unfolding of what happens to be dictated by the universal guidance of the God of our own understanding. Easier said than done, to let go completely; for it is the ultimate goal, the one that we pray in the third step of AA, " God, I offer myself to Thee- to build with me and do with me as Thou will. Relieve me of the bondage of self, that I may better do Thy will. Take away my difficulties, that victory over them may bear witness to those I would help of Thy Power, Thy Love and Thy Way of Life." The promise here is that being all powerful, God provides what we need., if we kept close to Him and performed His work well. Established on such a footing we become less and less interested in ourselves, our plans and designs and more and more become interested in seeing what we could contribute to life.

I harkened back for a moment to an experience of meditative state I had entered into in my first novel 'The Sword of Discernment' (Pg 194), where I had chosen, as I walked on instinct, to turn off my LED head lamp and in the darkness of the night, felt my way along at a steady pace , like a blind man without a cane. My instinct sharpened with every step and I actually closed my eyes from time to time as I gained more confidence with my experiment. I was mindful of the swing of my legs, the sound of the earth benefit my feet as my boots hit the surface, as it changed from tar to rough stone, gravel and back to dirt, I repeated in my head: " Cobble-stone, gravel, rough rock, pebble stone." It was an enlightening experience and I only knew that I could move by instinct, handing over my thoughts to instinct... so many miracles happened to me on that first Camino, I had almost forgotten about this experience and the practice of meditation in action.

The trance like state of poetry in motion occurred involuntarily and unbidden. It was like a hypnotic, meditative magic flow of action prayer, an altered state of consciousness. Such a stay of trance has been defined as a place of dissociated plane where at least some cognitive functions are disabled; which may be expressed as a 'hypnotic trance.' The term trance is also associated with meditation, magic, prayer and altered states of consciousness. Stories of the giants in the Middle Ages, myths, parables, fairy tales, old lore and storytelling from different cultures are themselves potentially inducers of trance. Often literary devices such as repetition are employed as a means of trance induction and such methodology's use in meditation in a repeating of a mantra to reach a induced state of consciousness with the outcome of altering the mind to whatever the vision or mantra brings to the participant in practice The military historically have used march music to induce soldiers to march in unison into a trance like state, where they bond as one in the riggers of training, comradeship and chain of command. Long distance marching to a beat of the drum has been employed throughout the ages, beating to a monotonous wilful beat at the pace of the march or heartbeat. High pitched fifes, flutes and bagpipes were used for their 'piercing' effect to play the melody, this would assist the morale and solidarity of soldiers as they marched to do battle.

Mystics on the other hand generally entailed direct connection, communication and communion with a Deity-Godhead in trance- a cognate experience of mindfulness at a much deeper level. Saints, Christian mystics and hypnotherapists are credited with the promotion of a tranced like state and cursive powers that may be an outcome. Trance conditions occur in different states of mind, emotions, moods and even daydreams. All activities which involve the filtering of information coming into sense modalities influence the brain functions and consciousness. Trance may be understood as a way for the brain to change the way it filters information in order to provide more efficient use of the mind's resources.

In ancient times pilgrims visited the Temple of Epidaurus for healing sleep therapy. The healing temple was named after Asclepius, the son of Apollo. At the temple various priests and physicians would assist those who sought a session of healing by the influence of the son of the God Apollo, by assisting them into an induced sleep state of meditative practice. It was supposed that Asclepius effected cures of sickness in dreams. The practice of sleep meditation in the temple became a common pilgrim practice. The Greek treatment was to incubate and focus on prayer to Asclepios or healing. The Oracle of Delphi was also famous for trances in the ancient Greek world; priestesses there would make predictions about the future in exchange for gold. Trance in its modern meaning comes from an earlier meaning of a dazed, half conscious or insensible condition, sometimes called a state of fear of evil or as in the Latin, to transpire 'to cross' or 'pass over.'

In the now, having considered the various conditions I had reached in 'crossing over,' so to speak, in my meditative practice of bring Masters to my Table, I felt it time then to revisit those experiences to glean from those meetings the lessons to be learnt that may well be used in my spiritual practice in every day life. Mindful of the fact that through meditation and autosuggestion my will may well convince the subconscious mind in faith to follow a definite plan of procedure for which I desire. Faith in that development of will to master the principle that this meditative state of mind voluntarily applies in daily practice. Such repetition being tuned into by lessons from the Masters seemed to be the only way to voluntary development of my spirituality in an emotion of faith. I reminded myself that by faith in myself, faith in the Infinite, I would thus gain the eternal elixir to power, and action to the impulse of my thoughts. Those Masters had by their presence at my table, given me some leading internal lessons from their life and experiences to set into motion a template for living more in the Spiritual vain.To utilise my time in my dotage, to move from my former life to one of living in the world but not of it. Of transforming my spirit dreams into reality for our own betterment and for the benefit of all concerned.

The ideas I gathered from my time with the Masters I now needed to review, to give the orders to my subconscious mind, to present those ideas as a means of meditative practice, in faith to hand over the lessons learnt and believed in to my Higher Power, in which I now believed was my ultimate guide to live a worthwhile life of spirituality. I had learnt by trail and error, experience and education to gain success in the material world but things are now different. It was by failure, misfortune and suffering that I had arrive at this spot I now needed to know that I could put into practice though an alliance with those Masters a new form of spiritual cooperation with them- I needed to apply the lessons they had shared with me and undertake to apply them in daily mediative practice. Such knowledge has no value except that which can be gained from its application towards a worthwhile end. I now had the reliable source of each Master's particular talent that I could tap into at will for any undertaking in the future. The specialised knowledge of the Masters, my own God given talents and the use of my imagination were being the only ingredients I needed. The knowledge and the template needed to begin my successful transformation into living from within and without in a way of life more spiritually real than my former lifestyle.

In the process of recalling qualities of leadership, two of my former bosses in my younger corporate days came to mind. Both men during their lifetime epitomised the lessons from the Masters, particularly those of leadership and courage. The first of these was Don Richie. Don lived near the Gap at Watsons Bay; a popular visitors destination which has gained infamy as a suicide spot over the years.

Don was known as "The Angel of The Gap," for he officially saved over 160 people from suicide there. Don learnt the qualities of leadership during his Navy days in WW11. I knew him for his kindness, his leadership as my boss when he was the National Salesman of an Insurance Company where I had a middle management role. Don was both forthright in his duties, warm hearted and kind to the core. His management style was more as a caring leader when a subordinate Manager was sometimes required to go against natural instinct in a dogmatic dispassionate approach to the role. To a great degree it was necessary with a team of unruly salesman. Don knew how to apply all forms of management styles but always with an amiable way of getting the best outcome. He was a team builder more so than an individualist leader. Don was awarded the medal of the Order of Australia for 'service to the community though the programs to prevent suicide.' His family reckoned he had saved 400 plus,It didn't really matter, he just saved lives and I wish he had been around when my own son Peter took his own life. A monument to "The Angel of the Gap" stands in his honour at Watson's Bay Gap as well as a walk known as " The Don Richie Grove walk."

Sometimes we humans have not got it all together and Don's methodology shows how simple natural action can be the best way to lead with the courage of ones convictions. Don kept an eagle eye on the Gap from his home across the road and as individuals walked to the cliff edge, looking at the crashing waves below, wondering whether to jump, Don would approach them with a smile asking," why don't you come and have a cup of tea?" He would bring them to his home offering tea, coffee or a beer. There was no counselling, no advising, no prying, just one caring human being lending a listening ear to another. Some of these people had mental problems, some medical difficulties, and some were just having a rough patch in life's journey. For many, a listening ear was apparently in what they needed as they changed their minds about jumping after the chat and turned back home. In his own words his simple approach of " What are you doing here? Please come and talk to me. or something like that was enough to get their mind away from going over the cliff. Then this was followed after a cuppa or beer with "Tell me why, what are you worried about?" For fifty years Don extended a helping hand. Sometimes in our busy lives we can forget about people; those who need help, who are just trying to do their best to get by, who are facing this own stress and worries. There are people these days who are more behind the computer screens than ever since Covid-19 took effect. Irrespective of their role in life , they are people none the less, not objects at the other end of the phone, the screen or the email message. Don's message is a timely reminder of leadership in action, a simple message of starting a conversation, give a smile, give a hug, give a genuine compliment, give someone a call just to see if they are ok. My own life, with all its heartaches, and broken dreams now lives the lesson that Don was teaching all those years ago. It is not about me its about what I do with me for the benefit of others that is the key to successful leadership, love and life.

John Healy was my next Boss after Don Richie, with another competing International Instance and Investment company. John was also the fitness coach to he Parramatta Eels Rugby League and during his five year stint there, due in no small part to his fitness programme, they had won all premierships when the Healy Fitness programme was in play. For the next thirty years John was directly associated with my old school and that of my sons, St. Josephs's College. Joeys's ultimately built a Gymnasium to his specifications. John's association with the schools 1st and 2nd Rugby XVs Rugby teams saw them as leaders of all the GPs competitions. The first Rugby XVs teams won 19 times due to a great degree to his fitness programme which he proved effective for himself too; for he lead everything by his own actions in doing no less than best athletes did. in training. Of the 19 premiership the teams won 12 as Champions. .i.e. they won every game they played against the other GPs schools of which there are eight in all in the Sydney competition.. In addition the 2nd XV teams won 20 times.These statistics alone indicate the great value John brought to the College's training on his terms of strength, fitness and commitment. Apart from his management duties In the insurance industry through which he excelled, he was committed to City Tattersall' s Club as both fitness coach to businessmen and Club chairman for a time. John also did regular charitable works to those less fortunate including the Matthew Talbot hostel for people down on their luck. In 1998 John received the Medal of the Order of Australia "for services to the community through charitable organisations and for his work with young men in their sport and personal development." John was quoted with: "Success is the peace of mind that follows as a result of knowing that you have done the best that you are capable of doing.'And he often added " God has given you the talent- but mental toughness is up to you."

So it was that considering all this I turned to those of my Master that I had occasion to chat with and to determine from my findings anything that I could find of benefit to improve my spiritual well-being for myself and anyone who may read this book. Noting also that I may well be overlooking 'something or other' that may apply to you dear reader that is unique to you, that you find in your own humble way to use for your better self and others you know.

Now, from the Masters at my table I first turned to Napoleon, the first of my Masters with whom I had dined and noted that he had all the right attributes of leadership in a positive way, despite that fact that his moral code was ruthless and self-seeking and his egotistical way in the end contributed to his downfall. To recap, Napoleon was an intense flame that burned with desire and he had unwavering faith in 'his' cause to burn so brightly and to ultimately burnt out like all such leaders. Napoleon, like Hitler, Mussolini and Stalin after him, was a leader by force. He fell ultimately to his own egocentricity as do all dictators.. If there is a lesson to be learnt on the positive side of Napoleons leadership; what he had is unwavering courage, self determination in leading by example, a keen sense of justice that was respected by his followers, but from which he ultimately waived.A definiteness in decision making and planning, participating in the action more than was expected of him; a forthright personality that while not admired so much was respected. He defined leadership for himself and to his followers so that there was no misunderstanding by his troops who followed and those who paid the bill for his war efforts. To his credit he mastered all the details of his glands, accepted full responsibly for all his actions and was cooperative but only when it suited his cause. In summary, his greatest attributes were his burning desire in following his ambitions that he attempted in his unwavering faith in eventually making it happen to his liking. His great weakness was his ego which was his Waterloo. As for the other Master guest who shared the table with Napoleon, I found him of much more value than Napoleon in the area of his spirituality.

Beethoven was deaf and yet he managed to leave so much music to sooth the savage beast within us, that we are bound to be God-like. It was his affinity with nature that was the catalyst for his genius of turning the seasons of wild oceans, lightening storm skies and deep forest movement into vibrations of prayer to touch our very souls. He often called God his 'great tone Master,' of whom he believed in deeply and therein lay the lesson for me and you dear reader. We hone our skills, our creative talent and with all our might, offer it all too God to do with as he pleases. Beethoven lives with us still in his music and we play out the themes of his greatness every time we walk a beach and hear the ocean roar, the sky fill with rumbles and lightening strike and every time we wander deep into the bush. What had I learnt from my next dinner guest that resonated with my soul? What could I benefit spiritually from the nature of a simple man. Much like Beethoven, the man who perhaps was the most influential to us all in these troubled times is St. Francis of Assisi, for he too was akin to nature. He gave up a life of wealth to live a life of poverty. While he grew up with a privileged life, he gave up a life of wealth to live a life of poverty. Francis saw through it all and in a sense saw the world upside down. This founder of the Franciscan order of friars, was (is) renowned for his love, simplicity and practice of poverty. His mission, followed by his brothers and sisters in Christ, imposed a vow of poverty which he had undertaken himself; actively and passionately preaching a message to succour the poor, hungry and sick. He is best remembered for his generosity and love of animals, once stating: "The animals of God's creation inhabit the skies, the earth and the sea and have a part in our human life. We therefore invoke God's blessing on these animals over all creatures of this earth." He was known to have communicated with birds and animals as he did with people. Those who tap into the energy and spirit of their maker seem to have skill above others to the point of being miraculous. It seems with this skill comes a great deal of suffering. Francis was no exception having been inflicted with the first of stigmata's since the death of Christ.   Whilst praying at la Verna in 1224 Francis, had a vision and was miraculous marked with the stigmata wounds of Christ; the nail wounds on his wrists, his feet and the lance wound on his side emanating a seraph in the form of a cross. The miracles accredited to St Francis include returning people from the dead much like Jesus reportedly did. Many a sailors has reported they were saved from shipwreck by invoking a St Francis prayer. Others in prison were released to freedom, women claimed they were freed from reproductive problems while the blind regained their sight. So what is it that we can learn from this man apart from being charitable to all men and beast? Well, like other Masters who later dined at my table, he is a Saint for our times, for he stood for social justice. So the lessons learnt are: We should walk as we preach, not to apply knowledge learnt is meaningless, we have been called to heal wounds, and patience and humility banishes worry and anger. We should keep a clear eye towards life's end and not just pray but become prayer. As for the other guest with St. Francis that evening, Ralph Waldo Emerson, the lessons to be learnt from that humble human who directed and preached his brand of direct contact with God, relates more to us now than anything else. His daily diary jottings endorsed this. "To live in daylight compartments, not to be thinking to the past nor the future, but in the present moment. Sufficient for the day is the trouble in it." In summary though, we do not have bad days just bad moments.

Bill Wilson and Bob Smith, my next dinner guests for those of us who are alcoholic, had a special message that may well be beneficial to any person who seeks to live a life of spirituality and who is not necessarily alcoholic. Bill summed it all up in his writing of the seventh step of AA:" Humbly ask him to remove our shortcomings." We of the fellowship AA s do not enter into debate with the many who still so passionately cling to the belief that to satisfy our basic natural desires is the main object of life.

For thousands of years we have been demanding more than our share of security, prestige, and romance. When we seemed to be succeeding, we drank to dream even greater dreams. When we were frustrated, even in part, we drank for oblivion. Never was there enough of what we thought we wanted. In all these strivings, so many of them well-intentioned, our crippling handicap has been our lack of humility. We had lacked the perspective to see that character building and spiritual values had come first, and that material satisfaction was not the purpose of living. Quite characteristically, we had gone all out in confusing the ends with the means. Instead of regarding the satisfaction of our material desires as the means by which we could live and function as human beings, we had taken these satisfactions to be the final end of life. Seldom did we look at character building as something desirable in itself, something we would like to   strive for whether our instinctual needs were met or not. We never thought of making honesty, tolerance , and true love of man and God the daily basis of living. Bill pointed out that the basic ingredient of humility is desire to seek and do God's will. Dr Bob, for his part lived it with his basic philosophic simplicity of "Trust in God", clean house (.i.e. make amends) and help somebody. He had the expectation to 'burn the idea into the consciousness' that he could get well regardless of anyone with but one condition- he trust in God and cleared house with those he had injured by his past alcoholic actions. He was a work in progress without perfection and he carried that through to every alcoholic patient he dealt with. The proof being in the fact that as an MD and sober humble man he saved over 5000 alcoholics from a fate worst than death by his example, he help others to learn to do the same.

Being conditioned from childhood to the Christian central message of Christ death on the cross, followed by his resurrection and ascension into heaven, it naturally followed that my brothers mentors taught this as good news. It mean that Jesus Christ was the Incarnate Word and Son of God, Saviour and Lord, and that through his life death and resurrection we have forgiveness and redemption from our 'sin'- mistakes, defects of character, or as you may will wrong doing. The 'Good News' is that we have new life from the power of the indwelling Spirit of Christ by his sacrificial act and we are thus reconciled with God. In this way there is no gospel message without the cross, for it is through Jesus' atoning death on behalf of sinful humans that justification and reconciliation with God is possible. This Christ central message to me from a Master at my table, seemed to put it more simply in a spiritual sense " Unless you eat the flesh of the son of man and drink his blood you shall not have life in you. He who eats my flesh and drinks my blood has life everlasting and I will raise him up on the last day." The dinner with Jesus and Mohammad reminded me that he reportedly made this statement at his last supper with his Apostles, as he broke the bread and drank the wine encouraged them to do likewise. In my now adult life as a non practicing Catholic, I am more inclined to draw a conclusion that Christ's words here and actions at the final meal were a spiritual example to us. That we must take on his flesh 'spiritually' by our actions in our daily life with others, and that for our own spiritual well being we must; drink of the blood of that 'spiritual connection with God, our Father' by daily practice in prayer and doing good works to avoid living by wrong doing (sin, if you will). The Christian act of a priest serving his congregation the communion host is but a reenactment of the last supper and our lesson to learn to go forth and practice in our daily life. Catholics seem to take this one step further, literally believing that they are eating the body and blood, flesh and divinity of Jesus Christ every time they take communion. So it was everyday prayer, belief in his message and sacrifice acts, spiritually or in reality that we gleaned from Christ's message at our dinner table together.

It may come as no surprise that Muslims deny Jesus died on the cross. In their belief, the Surah Chapter in the Koran (4:155-159), is taken by many as claiming that although the Jewish leaders tried to kill Jesus they "did not kill him, nor did they crucify him, but they thought they did." For Muslims it's unthinkable that God would allow Jesus,

God's appointed prophet, to be crucified. That event which is the font and heart of Christianity is held by Muslims to be unhistoric and incredible. Mohammed had taught that there is no need for something like Christ's atoning death, for each person is to be responsible for their own actions. Sin by this way isn't a matter of the tools of depravity of human nature but more a weakness, defect or flaw in human character. Christian's believe in the Deity; the divine nature of Christ as being the Son of God. They also believe that God is a Trinity of Father, Son and Holy Spirit. A vehicle by which we may enter into union with 'The Trinity,' as it was given by Christ death and resurrection. We have been granted the Spirit to embrace our own salvation. Mohammed did not see Christ as Divine but rather a prophet like himself , a holy man who preached the word of God but was not God's son. The Bible tells us that Jesus is the word of God, the Koran teaches that he is only "a Word." The Bible says he is the Creator, the Quran describes him as one of the created. The Bible teaches that Christ is superior to the Prophet, but the Koran makes no distinction between any of them. The Bible tells that Jesus is God's son, the Koran tell us that Jesus is not the son of Allah. Mohammed made a big mistaken in his teaching on Christ. He said Jesus is a prophet. Muslims know and believe that prophets don't lie and it never says in the Koran that Jesus ever lied. If Jesus told the truth, then we must listen to what He says " He is the Son of God." He also taught " I am the Way, the Truth and the Light, no one comes to the Father except through me." Both Jesus and Mohammed had the one thing in common, the power of prayer, even if the diversity of their religious followers are not quite on the same pathway of getting to heaven. Mohammed, as do his followers, also believe that Christ will return to earth. For my part, I am given to believe that irrespective of Christ being crucifying or not, his time and the method of his death, he is to me in a heavenly realm and I content myself in believing in a Manifested Jesus, or a Higher Power greater than any logical linear workings of my mind. God, Jesus, the Holy Spirit and Muhammed's " God is One and Mohammad is his Prophet' is all wrapped up in one's 'spiritual manifestation ' of living accords to his word. In my case it's in the 3rd step of AA; "handing over to a Higher Power." and the 12th " having had a spiritual awakening ...... we help other Alcoholics to do the same. "

 I harkened back for a moment to the words of Napoleon Hill in his "Think and Grow Rich' rules of engagement for getting what you want; " In your search for the secret method , do not look for miracles, because you will not find them.You will only find the enter into the laws of nature. These laws are available to every person who has faith and courage to use them. They may be used to bring freedom to a nation or to accumulate riches (material or spiritual).... leader's in every walk of life decide quickly and firmly. This is the major reason why they are leaders. The world has the habit of making room for the men or women whose words and actions show that they know where they are going."   Mahatma Gandhi harnessed the forces of God and nature when he needed to get his point across. He came to power by inducing over two hundred million people to cooperate in a spirit of harmony. By tapping into the Infinite Intelligence (God source) and channel by way of his own example a spirit of definite harmony. Gandhi's walking to the ocean in defiance of British law to make salt is probably the best example that comes to mind of utilising the forces of God and nature. My dinner guest with Gandhi that evening was Rasputin, who using his own belief and admission in the power of God and his own mental toughness achieved what may have seemed miraculous. It was not so, just the working of someones mind who understood nature's cures, the power of prayer and a touch of placebo! The guest that followed had their own causes that emulated success and the faith in their ability to lead with the courage of their convictions. Medgar Evers, Martin Luther King and their dogged persistence in the face of authority caused millions to march for civil rights for the black communities of their time.Their effort resulted in Civil Rights laws for Negroes in America to changed the system for the better. They were willing to die for their cause and they did, but their legacy lives on, although the world sometimes slips back into old habits, as the current "Black lives Matter" cry endorse. It reminds me to stay vigilant for the cause of 'spirituality,' for now more than ever in these troubled times we need to turn to our maker.

The two Master inventors who came to my table had one thing in common, apart from their brilliant genius in tapping into the laws of nature, they both had faith in their abilities to uncover many of nature secrets, the spirit of unremitting toil with which they so often wrestled victory from defeat. Edison built up a material fortune by his inventions and the taking of others' ideas and using and sometimes patterning them as his own. Edison received his own just reward but can't have been content with taking advantage of the inventions of one who tapped into the universal power as well as the earthly ones, to achieve greater over all benefit to mankind. For Nicola Tesla tapped the very source of God's energy and harnessed power beyond our wildest dreams. Nicola's hidden legacy is still unfolding, even though he died a poor man, he was rich in spirit and had a touch of St. Francis of Assisi about him. I hasten to add that his diet and daily exercise programme, along with Gandhi's ideas on diet and fasting I have taken on board and include in my daily routine sometimes.

As to the next guests, suffice to say that the study of the mind of Swedenborg and Carl Jung gave me great pleasure and cause to understand mystical connections to nature in the material world, as well as the everyday ethical standards of consciousness and belief in a God of my own understanding. There was a kind of analysis and paralysis in understanding these two geniuses, but I now believe I have come out the other side of it, for to keep ' Spirituality ' simple is the best way for this simple mind to practice these principles in all my affairs anyway. Then to the writers that followed. Well it may be summed up in equal parts for all is told in the words of their writings. For in a Don Miguel de Cervantes "Don Quixote" quote is a summary of my spiritual destiny: "Destiny guides our fortunes more favourably than we could have expected. Look there, Sancho Panza, my friend, and see those thirty or so giants, with whom I intend to do battle and kill each one and all of them, so with their stolen booty we can begin to enrich ourselves. This is noble. righteous warfare, for it is wonderfully useful too God to have such an evil race wiped from the face of the earth." "What giants?" asked Sancho Panza. "The ones you can see over there," answers his master," " The ones with the huge arms some of which are very nearly two leagues long." " Now look your grace" said Sancho, "what you see over there aren't giants, but windmills, and what seems to be arms are just sails that go around in the wind and turn the millstone." "Obviously" replied Don Quixote,"you don't know much about adventures." Then a line or two from the Bard's pen which was spoken by Polonius, a pep talk of sorts, in Hamlet, Act 1, Scene111: "This above all, to thine own self be true, and it must follow, as night follows day, Thou cannot then be false to any man." And in a radiance of illumination for me, as it may be for you, is from my final guest, the pen of Charles Dickens: The sun- the bright sun, that brings back, not light alone, but new me, and hope, and freshness to man- burst upon crowded city in clear and radiant glory. Through costly-coloured glass and pa- per- mended window, through Cathedral dome and rotten crevice, it sheds its equal ray."

 As to the workings of the minds of Plato and Confucius, the last two Masters at my table to and end the lesson of my spiritual progress and trust, if I may be so bold to say, yours too dear reader. It befits firstly to let Plato fulfil the task with his famous line "Opinion is the medium between knowledge and ignorance." "If a man neglects education, he walks lame to the end of his life.". "All men are by nature made of the same earth by one workman." and this line perhaps gives a hint to my purpose in writing: "Books give soul to the universe, wings to the mind, flight to the imagination, and life to everything." As to the man of some thousands of years, Confucius. I'll end on his most fa- mous quotes that are akin to finding ones' spiritual whole: "The man who says he can and the man who says he can-not are both usually right." and another; "Your life is what your thoughts make it." And as for knowledge being the ex- tent of ones ignorance, well, in my case, like many a man who is digging deep- er, we tend to make a lot of mistakes. So I like this Confucius quote to end with and to apply to in understanding it my spiritual path in life: " The man who asks a question is a fool for a minute, the man who does not ask is a fool for life."

 I had been thinking about a daily spiritual routine that I could put into practice from what I had learnt from The Masters at my table. Pope Francis first came to mind in his being taught the Jesuit way to the priesthood when he was a novice . Add to his regimen meetings with novice masters to discuss his spiri- tual life and discernment, manual labour and forays with his in-house commu- nity to perform included work in the wider every day community life outside the seminary. It included work performed in hospitals, schools and homes too. It was not so much these activities but the day by day routine of Pope Francis' early life that help me format what I waa endeavouring to achieve. He at6.am started rising to the sound of a bell and on his knees by his bed for immediate prayer of the Te Deum, the traditional Catholic hymn of praise, in Latin; then it was to wash and dress. By 7.am he rushed to chapel for silent or communal prayer followed by daily Mass. At 8.am. breakfast it was in silence with one hour of manual labour - cleaning toilets, washing dishes or accepting duties listed on a chalk board. 9.am. classes in Latin, Greek and public speaking, with a break at 12 p.m. More prayers of discernment, 1.pm. was lunch in silence while one of his peers would read a lesson or prayers from Jesuit history. 2.pm. a brief prayer session in chapel, followed by fifteen minutes of recreation in the courtyard with his fellow novices. 2.30p.m. was a thirty minute nap followed by classes for two hours until 5.30 pm. It was time then for sport- usually soccer or basketball which was always followed by a cold shower, then more prayer, and fifteen minutes of private meetings with novices, and masters. 8.pm. Dinner, which always included a soup that the novices help to serve. Then they would always practice rhetorical skill in front of a group while others ate in silence. Dinner was followed by another short recreational break during which the novices could have a general chat. 9.30.pm. more prayer and one last visit to the chapel for a final prayer. 10.pm. it was bed and sleep. The next day the same process was continued all over again.

In my boarding school days my own routine was not much different except in the summer time it was not Like Francis 6.a.m. out of bed start, but 5.am for me, as I had to be on the water with the rowers at 5.30 a.m. before returning for a cold shower and Mass at 7.a.m. In winter I got to sleep in until 6.a..m when the same routine with some minor exception to the Pope's training were administered. Our breakfast at 8.a.m. didn't include silence, except that we did have a week of silence in our annual retreat. We were not allowed to speak to each other all day during that retreat and at meals a spiritual reading would be read by the participating Marist who happened to be on duty at the time. We had limited manual labour to do but it did involve tending to the school's sheep during crutching time or when they need to be shorn. There was no break for a sleep during the day and we in senior years at least, returned to night study from 8.30.p.m. until 9.30.p.m before bed by 10.p.m. Otherwise the routine was not unlike that of the Pope. It was excellent discipline for my corporate and later entrepreneurial business career.

That too all went asunder along with my family, business and mental breakdown. Although in no small part the suicide of my son Peter had shattered me, I had long before that come to accept as normal a new career - that of a drinking one and it was inevitable I would crash and burn eventually irrespective of circumstance. The crunch that followed had me in deep depression for a time, as I have previously eluded too. I had a routine at that time that kept me out of my head as much as was practicable in the then process of recovery. So it was now that I needed a new routine practice to set myself based on the findings I had gleaned form the Master at my table. Firstly though I needed to reconsider the main points to apply from those of the Masters; things to remember before writing a template of daily activities to work on. One of prayer and meditative practice, one of diet and exercise, of fasting and favour, of journalling and writing for my spiritual betterment, of being there for my friends in times of crisis and as a shoulder to cry on so to speak, of acceptance of ageing, of taking into my stride the simple things as being the best things, of relaxation and adequate sleep, of being in touch with nature to recharge my body and mental battery. Of a routine of regularity in all I do in a day. To live in the day only; not to worry about outcomes and to take everything in my stride as a learning curve for my betterment.

To leave the gate open for spiritual knowledge to flow in. To always be willing to hand over to my Higher Power to rule and guide my remaining life for his will not mine. Thus I had a method and I had written a daily plan of action which must take some adjusting. So to where am I to take this journey from here?? "The spiritual life cannot be made suburban." said Howard Macey. "It is always frontier and we who live in it, accept and even rejoice that it remain untamed." So a plan to work from is okay provided that it is not the path but just a template to work from. The greatest obstacle to our dream is the false self-hatred of mystery. The most important aspect of a man's world is his relationship with God and with the people in his life, his calling, the spiritual battle he faces and wrought with danger and mystery. That is not a bad thing, it is joyful, rich and in part to an essential of our soul search to adventure.

There is a line I read flicking through a book on prayer that was a rare insight into my further adventures into the unknown. As I drew near the close of these writings thinking the world needed another book, and this one being a spiritual template , I figured I had created one. It is a worthy read. But the insight in the sentence that   follows set me back to thinking of my purpose in a different light. For up to now I had dictated the plot, the brief of each Master at my table and come up with tried and true methodology to a spiritual path, or so it seemed. These are the words on the page that jumped out at me: "Don't ask yourself what the world needs. Ask yourself what make you come alive, and go do that, because what the world needs is people who have come alive."

 I was reminded of a line I had quoted to a young lady on the Camino who was having some difficulty with a relationship and was walking the Camino to let go, as you do. The quote was from from Robert Frost's poem which I had heard so many times before: "Two roads diverged in the wood and I, I took the one less traveled by, and that has made all the difference." Like most of my long spent life and like the masses of mankind, I had spent the major part of it trying to eliminate risk, to squeeze it down into more manageable parts. It doesn't work, it cursed God's plan. It succeeds in a closet of self protection and then we wonder why we are suffocating. It always revolves around two themes, the seeming of a final competence and a rejection of anything that can't be controlled. A man is no more a man than when he embraces his adventure beyond his control or when he walks into a battle he is unsure of winning. Now of the many quotable quotes in the Indiana Jones films, the one that resonates for me here is in "Raiders of the Lost Ark,' when Indiana Jones is face with vital decision to follow the Ark which is in the hands of the Nazis or go get help. He quickly decides on the former turns to Salam his side kick and says: "You go find Marcus, go get some help. I am going to follow the Nazi Army and the Ark. Salam enquires "what are you going to do?' Indiana replies: "I don't know I am making this up as I go along." Here is the faith to adventure into the unknown and so it is with our spirituality. It is a new and possibly dangerous adventure that must be done. We must dig deep into our resolve and work at it irrespective of a plan of attack or an unknown stepping out in an unplanned quest into nothingness.

So where does prayer fit into all of this? Well, in our stepping out there, prayer is the innovation to activate an affinity with the object of worship. We seek guidance through prayer which gives us the courage to do whatever it is we decide to do by communication and hopefully the intercession of God. The practice of prayer is attested in written sources as early as 5000 years ago. Today, most religions involve pray in one way or another. Science regards prayer as mostly concentrated on health of the sick or injured with contradictory results. Various spiritual tradition offer a wide variety of playful devotional acts, like prayers of gratitude and thanks-giving before and after meals. Some bow their heads to pray, others like Native Americans dance as a form of prayer, Sufis whirl, Hindus chant a mantra, Jew's sway, Muslims bow, kneel and then postulate. Quaker's keep silent while others have standardised rituals and liturgies like the Catholic, some prefer prayer without preparation.

It seems that Prayer is one of the leading pastimes in self reflection and gratitude that helps us to grow. To have faith, to depend upon the God of own own understanding on our new spiritual adventure on a daily basis is a worthwhile quest. In summary then, prayer is the coming to understand of oneself, to promote virtuous ideas and personal character for growth. The benefits of prayer are to bring ones self as well as ones Higher Power into unison to reduce ego and promote humility. Prayer and meditation regulates the heartbeat, making it stronger and less active. It increases the life threatening effects of stress and disturbing environment and efficiently helps us age more smoothly.

Prayer teaches us to be humble. Meditation on the other hand helps us to tune into God. When we are going through a very emotional stage both prayer and meditation helps us in our belief that here is a a higher power who can help us solve our burdens. Reflecting on our problems through prayer and meditation helps relieve and initially lift the barrier of turmoil to gain further strength in our Higher Power belief and relief. To keep ones faith after a situation leaves us with an emotionally distraught recovery- the aftermath helps us keep our faith that everything will be all right in the long run. The expectation that God doesn't work as we expect, but leads us and we must learn to trust in his slow work. Thus we handle day by day issues with prayer and meditation which is the elixir for our on-going spiritual adventures. So with this in mind, I am listing here some prayers that I trust may be a further recipe in my recovery and maybe help you too.

For I am not recovered, I am but on a spiritual journey that is still in its infancy and without being smug, I feel you may find beneficial as I am still doing. So this book is in a sense finished but pray and meditation is in itself a daily act and with a continuous beginning will remain unfinished.

CHAPTER 17.

PRAYERS FOR THE FAITHFUL

Perhaps it is fitting that I begin this final chapter as an epilogue of the Desiderata. It was found in a church some two hundred year ago, left by an anonymous author, and that is fitting too, for you and I can both lay claim to it. So without any further ado, I bow out from this little work of 'spiritual messaging" and leave you to read, pray and hopefully meditate on the meaning of it all.

Desiderata.

Go placidly amid the noise and haste, and remember what peace there may be in silence. As far as possible without surrender be on good terms with all persons.

Speak your truth quietly and clearly, and listen to others, even to the dull and ignorant, for they too have their story. Avoid loud and aggressive persons, they are vexations to the spirit.

If you compare yourself to others, you may become vain and bitter; for always there will be greater and lesser persons than yourself.

Enjoy your achievements as well as your plans. Keep interested in your own career, however humble; it is a real possession in the changing fortunes of time. Exercise caution in your business affairs, for the world is full of trickery. But let this not blind you to what virtue there is, many persons strive for high ideals, and everywhere life is full of heroism.

Be yourself. Especially do not feign affection. Neither be cynical about love; for in the face of all aridity and disenchantment it is as perennial as the grass. Take kindly the counsel of the years, gracefully surrendering the things of youth.

Nurture strength of spirit to shield you in sudden misfortune,. But do not distress yourself with dark imaginings. Many fears are born of fatigue and loneliness. Beyond a wholesome discipline, be gentle with yourself. You are a child of the universe, no less than the trees or the stars, you have a right to be here. And whether or not it is clear to you, no doubt the world is unfolding as it should.

Therefore, be at peace with God, whatever you conceive him to be, and whatever your labor and aspirations in the noisy confusion of life, keep peace in your soul. With all its sham drudgery and broken dreams, it is still a beautiful world.

Be cheerful. Strive to be happy.

This is the seventh of my books that have been granted me in my recovery as if by a miracle. For they came to me out of the darkness of depression and despair into a new light of creativity- as if by my writing the mission of my purpose, my journey herein is unfolding. For it is apt that this book should end with parting words of prayer. If it were not for my wandering on the Camino, my out pouring in word and in deed may never have occurred. So more so the attendance at AA meetings and the practice of the steps of the fellowship am I enlightened to a new way of the Spirit. It is as if my books stand side by side as a testament to a journey inward. In the Big Book of AA (page 68), Bill Wilson stated: "Perhaps there is a better way- we think so. For we are on a different basis; the basis of trusting and relying on God. We trust infinite God rather than our finite selves. We are in the world to play the role He assigns. Just too extend that we do as we think He would have us, and humbly rely on Him, does He enable us to match calamity with serenity."

So we can trust God and clean up our own defects of character, asking each morning in meditation that our Creator show us the way of patience, tolerance, kindliness and love. In the the Big Book, 'Into Action'(page 83), Bill adds: "The spiritual life is not theory. We have to live it. Unless our love ones expresses a desire to live upon spiritual principles we think we ought not to urge them. We should not talk incessantly to them about spiritual matters. They will change in time, Our behaviour will convince them more than our words. We must remember that ten and twenty years of drunken (non spiritual) behaviour would make a skeptic out of anyone."

Here I sit gazing on the many thousands of words I have written in my journey towards the light. I find here that my spirituality is equally challenged by my defects of character but within them I embrace both as a two in one flesh approach to life on the inner self and the one of darkness that lay on the surface of my existence. I have to marry one against the other, held together like my books upon the shelf, with books ends at either end. For these book ends come in the form of prayer, one being the third step prayer and the other the seventh. Here in I relate them to you for your own spiritual well-being as to mine:

The 3rd Step Prayer: "God, I offer myself to Thee- to build with me and to do with me as Thou wilt. Relieve me of the bondage of self, that I may better do Thy will. Take away my difficulties, that victory over them may bear witness to those I would help of Thy Power, Thy Love, and Thy Way of life. May I do thy will always!"

7th Step Prayer: " My Creator, I am now willing that You should have all of me, good and bad. I pray that you now remove from me every defect of character which stands in the way of usefulness to you and my fellows. Grant me strength, as I go out from here, to do your bidding. Amen."

So, in moments of doubt and fear I turn to the prayer of the " Wisdom of St. Teresa Avila:"

God is all you need

Let nothing disturb you,

Nothing make you afraid.

All things pass,

God remains.

Be patient,

And you will attain your heart's desire.

With God your own,

You cannot lack,

God Suffices.

Amen.

And it is a fitting note that I should end this little work with the Prayer of St. Francis of Assisi.

The St. Francis prayer.

Lord, make me an instrument of your peace,

Where there is hatred, let me sow love,
Where there is injury, pardon.

Where there is discord, union.

Where there is error, let me bring truth.

Where there is doubt, faith.

Where there is despair, hope.

Where there is darkness, light.
Where there is sadness, joy.

O Devine Master,

let me not seek to be consoled,
but to console,

to be understood as to understand,

to be loved as to love,

for it is giving that we receive,

it is in pardoning that we are pardoned,

and it is in dying that we are born to eternal life.

Footnote: I draw an analogy that my ego is but a grain of sand upon the beach bu forever in danger of thinking it is the whole beach. Despite all my best 'spiritu intent herein, my self-less progress is slow. I best go and ruminate upon tha perhaps it's time to get myself off to another AA meeting.

Doug McPhillips, poet, singer, songwriter, author, commenced his journey of discovery over a decade ago after life changing experiences.

The many tracks he has traversed through the Northern Hemisphere and down under in Australia and New Zealand has resulted in the facts and fiction of this novel.

Doug had recorded and sings songs interrelated to this work with unique melody in true Australian style.

Doug has written three novels, an autobiography, two books of poetry, a travel guide and this book of inspirational guidance. He has also co-produced and recorded two albums of his songs.

www.caminoway.com.au

Doug divides his time between work and play with friends and those who may seek guidance in following their hearts desire. You can check out his qualifications and experience on file on the aforementioned website, Facebook and LinkedIn.

Ingram Spark Publishers
1 La Verge TN37086
Nashville Tennessee.

Printed in Australia
Lightning Source
76 Discovery Road South
Scoresby, Victoria 3179

"To copy the truth can be a good thing,
but to invent the truth is better, much better."

- Giuseppe Verdi.

5/07/21. DMcP.